A LADY'S DUKE

The Dark Dukes
Book 1

J.M. Diedrich

ARE YOU SIGNED UP FOR DRAGONBLADE'S BLOG?

You'll get the latest news and information on exclusive giveaways, exclusive excerpts, coming releases, sales, free books, cover reveals and more.

Check out our complete list of authors, too!

No spam, no junk. That's a promise!

Sign Up Here

www.dragonbladepublishing.com

Dearest Reader;

Thank you for your support of a small press. At Dragonblade Publishing, we strive to bring you the highest quality Historical Romance from some of the best authors in the business. Without your support, there is no 'us', so we sincerely hope you adore these stories and find some new favorite authors along the way.

Happy Reading!

CEO, Dragonblade Publishing

Dedication

*To Sarah and Tabitha; the sister that got me started,
and the sister who kept me going.*

Acknowledgments

In order:

To my sisters—you know what you did.

Romance author, Lauri Robinson; you gave me the confidence to put myself back in the querying trenches and attempt something new. New being two words: "twitter" and "pitch".

My second "twitter pitch" brought me to you: Gwyn Jordan, literary agent extraordinaire. Agent, partner, friend. You said, 'trust me'. I did. Here we are. (An HEA in my book.)

To my Dragonblade family: Kathryn Le Veque, Shawn Morrison, Mary Ellen Sexton, and so many others I know work behind the scenes to make magic happen.

Reviewers, readers, those of you brave enough to read a novel by a debut author:

To Every. Single. One. Of. You.

Thank you.

CHAPTER ONE

Dear Charlotte,

What luck you've finally arrived in London! No doubt that uptight brother of yours has you jumping through rings of fire to prepare for your first season: dress fittings, etiquette lessons—I shudder to imagine. But do not fret; as long as you keep your chin up and remind yourself—and any grasping debutantes— that you are the sister to a duke, you will be a success.

Speaking of people too rich and proper to drink their tea from the wrong side of their cup, the gossip mill has it that the Duke of Camine was recently seen parading through the streets after a night leaving a particular woman's home. But a flutter of lashes and one of the greatest ducal titles falls into the trench- es of seduction. Isn't that deliciously naughty? We all must strive for the same.

Forget whatever sad excuse of a life you had in the country because here you'll make up for it with the ever-scandalous escapades of the ton.

I expect your name to become linked to infamy, dearest friend, or I will be forced to needlepoint! And let's be realistic. Surely, someone as fierce and clever as you can outdo a simple duke!

Your friend,
Diana Yamsbee

Charlotte laughed into her hand. Diana Yamsbee had boldly penned a letter addressed to *The Lady Charlotte Louis* without introduction nine months ago. Since that time, they'd exchanged countless letters. Diana, regaling the Duke of Lux's sister with the antics of London, with no tidbit of gossip unreported, and Charlotte, detailing the less scintillating but always present comings and goings from the countryside. Her correspondent was a secret Charlotte kept all to herself—and now that she was in London, she hoped they'd at last meet face to face.

Despite the newness of her surroundings in London, her brother had taken great pains to redecorate her chambers here to an almost identical degree to her rooms at the country estate, down to the rose drapes and blush-pink carpets she'd hated since girlhood.

But while the room did lessen her longing for home, the noise from the busy street outside and the smell of beeswax and oil from the lamps in the hall made it impossible to forget she'd left everything she'd known behind to embark on her first adventure as a grown woman. And she couldn't contain her relief.

Diana was right; the growing anxiety since the carriage ride through the bustling thoroughfares and heavy smog were nothing now that Charlotte had finally escaped to the city. There'd be no more somber afternoons quietly reading on the estate. No more silent dinners eating alone while her brother finished business with his solicitor in town.

Here, she'd start over. Once the season officially began, she'd have no end of balls, theatre, and promenades through the gardens. Perhaps she'd even receive attention from a suitor or two, with a stolen kiss to bring to her dreams at night.

Polluted air or no, she'd seize this opportunity to break free from her past life and breathe in the beginning of freedom.

Infamy was only the start.

Picking up a piece of cardstock, the Louis family crest monogramed on the top, Charlotte put quill to paper, her smile wider than ever.

Dear Diana,

Your letter came right in time.

Since arriving not yet a week ago from our country seat, my brother has hired four chambermaids, two cooks, and a lady's maid—all for my use. As if I have a clue what to do with so many pairs of hands! My own work perfectly fine, and calling for a simple changing of sheets is ridiculous. Though apparently, this is one more mark against my education because doing personal chores has brought nothing but endless lectures from all parties. Not even Mama, God rest her soul, made the staff do such menial tasks when she and Papa were alive.

Unfortunately, the staff seems as frazzled as I on what to do with me because every morning, noon, and night, they stare at me, faces expectant. It's not like I'm an expert on a lady's manner of conduct. I've done nothing but stay in the country and read and collect bugs for the past twenty-odd years. None of which are considered appropriate pastimes for a lady in society. The current heir—a grandson of my grandfather's cousin we've never met—is a clergyman in Weymouth. My brother mentioned the man's mother, one Mrs. Norris, writing some letter in objection to me coming "out" to society, claiming my life in the country would embarrass the Louis name until I was properly acclimated to polite society. Renard promptly dismissed the insult and the woman's insistence to "turn me out" herself. Horrid woman, wishing to ingratiate herself to the family, no doubt vying to match me with her son. There's little hope of her son being the next duke, when Renard is young and healthy and sure to bear his own sons.

Now I've arrived in London, I do feel a modicum of regret for never putting those horrible lessons into practice. Let us be frank: Half the rules on social etiquette and formal address are forgettable, and remembering the other half is merely a problem of knowing the right answer but having no practical experience. For my own reference, perhaps I shall start a list: The Things a Lady Must Do Before Morning Tea. And now that you mention it, I'll start with the infernal reason why tea must be served and drunk on a particular side, for I certainly do not know and can't muster a plausible reason to care. I have no idea what prompted my brother to bring me to London when he's never cared a fig for my mixing with society. Aside from his new uncharacteristic interest in my lack of manners, it's been good catching up. We've been a part so long, perhaps I'll suffer through a few more parties if it means we can grow close once again.

And now that I have arrived, perhaps you and I may finally have a chance to meet face to face in person. Your letters have been a comfort like no other, but I'm beginning to feel as if you are a ghost of my own making.

A light tapping at her bedroom door preceded her brother's voice.

"Charlotte? Are you awake?"

Charlotte set down her quill and read the small clock above the mantel, noting it was still too early for anyone else to be up. Concern flooding her veins, she secured the dressing gown around her waist with a cinching of her sash, crossed the room, and opened the door.

Renard Louis, Duke of Lux, looked disheveled in the same cerulean, wool overcoat he'd worn to dinner last night with his fair hair standing up on one side—coming straight from whatever mischief a young man found in London on a Tuesday evening—but his sandy eyes were bright and one could only describe the smile on his face as *pleased*.

"Just come from a brothel, Ren?" she teased, with only a modicum of envy. Diana had made the ill-reputed establishments, with their painted women and colorful entertainments, sound like quite a remarkable sight.

His smile slipped to set her with a severe frown. "That's hardly the language of a lady."

Charlotte resisted rolling her eyes, forgetting her brother had lost his sense of humor along with his valet. She'd add *doesn't speak of anything remotely interesting* to her list of what a lady shouldn't do.

"Did you need something?"

Smile resurfacing, Renard inclined his head. "May I come in? This will but take a moment."

Opening the door wider, her brother crossed to the divan by the fire but didn't sit. In fact, the way he kept tapping his thigh with his right hand and following the same path along the fireplace was an outpouring of energy she hadn't observed in ages.

It was good to see him in high spirits. The past years she'd seen nothing but a figurative cloud above his head, not that he'd entertain a forthright discussion. They'd each dealt with their parents' deaths in their own way. He'd chosen distance and drink; she'd chosen hopes and dreams she was too embarrassed to mention out loud.

Praying the storm had at last passed, she shut the door and enjoyed a small smile of relief.

"If you continue to pace like that, my carpet will have permanent bootprints," she said.

He stopped and threw her a grin. "I have exciting news."

She laughed. "I gathered. Will you tell me or am I to guess?"

"You are to be married!"

Charlotte blinked, unable to find a correlation between her brother's smile and his words. "No, I'm not." Surely, she would have remembered someone asking. It was apparently what women like her lived for.

Renard clapped his hands together, his glee spilling over into his words. "I've been in contact with the Marquess of Slasbury. He has officially asked for my blessing to court you. He plans to visit by the end of the week after he returns from his travels east. With a little encouragement, he as much as confirmed he'd make a proper proposal by month's end."

Charlotte touched her temple, her neck—no fever or lesions. No, surely, it was Renard who'd experienced a blow to the head.

She couldn't be engaged. She'd met the marquess once, going on a year ago for heaven's sake, and the introduction had not gone well.

Surely, her brother was teasing. Her first outing two nights ago hadn't gone exactly to plan, either, but that didn't mean he needed to cart her off before the season even started.

Hoping a bit of contrition would placate his fears, she said, "If you're concerned over the fuss at Lady Dunberry's soiree the other night, the spilt lemonade wasn't my fault." Because, seriously, what woman held a luncheon outdoors during the mayfly molting season? "Anyone could've dumped the bowl on Miss Turner's dress to stop the swarm. I just happened to be the closest."

Her brother stopped his pacing to grasp both her hands in his. "This isn't a punishment, dear sister. This is a *gift*, to both of us. Now you'll not have to go through the rigors of walking through society. The marquess is a young man and understands you haven't been tried as a woman of a household. There is little worry over his patience as you begin your lives together."

Charlotte pulled her hands free, the reality of his earnestness finally registering like a lead ball to the chest. "Renard, I can't get married." She wasn't ready or willing, not that her brother would listen over the patting of his own back. A different approach, then. "Can't I have time to think about this?"

"What?" Renard glanced at her, his gaze still on his bright, unencumbered future. "Time, yes. You have the rest of the week to prepare your expression of surprise. Though I doubt the marquess will care how greatly you can feign your appreciation."

Charlotte gritted her teeth but forced her tone to be calm. "Renard, I don't think a week is adequate time to come to terms with marriage. Give me a month at least." *Until I can come up with a viable excuse to book a ticket to America.* "If the marquess is as keen as you suggest, surely, he wouldn't fault me for being . . ." She chewed on the word before she settled on an exaggerated, "Delicate?"

Renard scrunched his nose. "Why the delay? I brought you to London to find a husband, but now a husband has found you! This is marvelous news." He nudged her chin with brotherly affection. "You need not worry over a thing. I will take care of all the details." He ran a hand down his rumpled shirt, seeming to realize he was quite a sight for the household and turned for the door, calling over his shoulder, "After a quick bath and shave, I'm off to the solicitor's office to draw up the papers. Don't wait on me for dinner."

Charlotte lunged forward, needing to stop this madness before her brother signed her life away. "But—"

The door snitched shut, leaving her standing alone in her room, the silence carrying the same oppressive weight as always but with an added ringing of infinite change.

This couldn't be happening!

Her brother couldn't force her to marry some man she hardly knew.

Except as her guardian and the sole living male member of their family, he not only had every right, he didn't need her consent. *Is this why he brought me here?*

She stumbled her way to her desk and dropped into the chair, her legs unable to carry her weight any longer. Her gaze snagging on her friend's letter, the words 'debauchery' and 'infamy' stood out, their once-bold letters of hope now harsh taunts in ebony ink.

The vise-like grip in her stomach tightened. There went all her plans of escape. There'd be no adventure, no courting, no excitement. With her betrothal contract all but signed, she'd be thrown into the role of hostess and gentleman's wife without any advice or experience.

Picking up her unfinished letter to her friend, she stared at the scripted "Things a Lady Must Do," the title taking on new meaning.

Was *that* the great secret to being a proper lady—doing what one was told without complaint? Being pressed to decide between two impossible situations? She could either marry the marquess and give up any hopes of independence, or she could refuse and suffer the never-ending matchmaking of her brother. For there was no question of her brother—the stubborn Duke of Lux—giving up. Ever. And his next pick of husband may not be as kind a choice as a young marquess.

At this point, she'd do well to finish her list of a lady's proper conduct or risk the marquess throwing her out on her ear.

Charlotte stopped, her letter falling from her fingers. She watched it flutter to the desktop as her thoughts stumbled. If she were truly an unsuitable bride, surely, no titled man would agree to a marriage? With the trust her father set up to be distributed on her twenty-first birthday, there'd be no need for the security marriage would provide other ladies without means of their own, or the societal shackles.

It couldn't be that easy. A few crass words, slurping her soup at dinner, and this ridiculous offer would disappear? She frowned. Her dowry was substantial and her family's lineage impeccable; little indiscretions may not be enough. No, to be rid of all marriage offers permanently, she'd need to take more drastic measures.

She had little knowledge in the way a proper lady *shouldn't* behave any more than how a lady should.

Her gaze fell on her friend's letter and a resurgence of resolve stole through her, along with an idea that surpassed impropriety.

Her lack of the specifics of etiquette wouldn't stand in her way. She knew without a doubt if she decided to list all the things she *did* desire out of life, there'd be more than enough to keep a stuffed peacock like the Marquess of Slasbury from signing anything.

What she needed was a scandal. One big enough to tarnish her reputation so there was no hope of a future groom.

And Charlotte only knew of one surefire way a lady could avoid marriage. One that required nothing but the courage to face the scrutiny of society.

Well, she'd never been part of society; there was no use failing her way through it now. So only the one obstacle remained.

Her gaze landed one final time on her friend's letter, and a slow smile curved the corners of her mouth as she remembered the other bit of gossip Diana had included: the name of a particular gentleman who so happened to be a close friend of her brother.

A rake hellion who sounded more than up for the challenge of educating an innocent woman in the ways of adventure and scandal, no seduction required.

CHAPTER TWO

HAMISH HURSTFIELD, DUKE of Camine, stumbled into his townhouse flat after a rousing night of poker and drinking, his pockets full, his head swimming, and in great need of a bed, preferably a willing woman's.

Squinting at the bright hall lamp, Hamish wrestled with his overcoat. It took far more coordination than a gentleman wished to admit removing his hat and gloves and place them on the entry table, or coatrack . . . He squinted harder . . . A fichus with a table-like quality.

Percy hadn't been joking when he'd said that absinthe drink kicked like a Dales.

If the knocking in his head was any indication of the hangover to come, he'd be smart to drown out the pain until the buzz lessened. Mission now set, he stumbled his way towards the door to his study, praying he hadn't gone too far past his limits and started conjuring images of little, green fairies and leprechauns in ugly, velvet vests.

It took him two tries to turn the knob, and two more to push open the door with any adequate strength. He'd hoped to find a fire left by some insightful maid. What he *expected* to find was an unoccupied room several years behind redecorating.

What he found was both . . . and a woman.

Hamish looked around, confirming the darkness from the dozen-paned window behind his desk. Night was here, and, yet the woman was also.

It seemed he'd surpassed his impressive liquor threshold by astronomical proportions because the woman standing in the middle of his study—eyes huge behind wire spectacles and donning a far-too-innocent grey frock with little, bead buttons down the side—bore an impossible resemblance to his best friend's sister.

Hamish rubbed at his eyes, but the apparition didn't waver. God, he wasn't *that* desperate for a woman. A straitlaced, obedient dove would never do. He tilted his head, waiting for the willowy figure to fill out into a curved and kohl-eyed temptress.

The image did not change. Instead, at his attention, the lady met his stare boldly, a slight smile on her pink lips.

And Hamish imagined those dainty little lips doing wicked things. He grinned back, reconsidering the merits of a doe-eyed beauty.

He sighed, dismissing the notion regardless of how his cock swelled. No fantasy would supersede the knowledge of reality that she—while a figment of his imagination—was Renard's sister and, therefore, off limits, even to his subconscious.

Proper ladies didn't visit unmarried men. Proper ladies didn't stare boldly—

"Hello," she said.

—and proper ladies absolutely didn't greet men in such an informal, husky tone.

Hamish had to give it to his imagination; if there were a single chance in hell he'd be attracted to an innocent lady of the *ton*—even the forbidden fruit that was Renard Louis's sister— she'd have that voice.

What a shame the real Lady Charlotte Louis was safely tucked into bed—night rail laced all the way up to her chin, benign visions of white lace and husband-snaring filling her dreams—like every other proper, boring lady of her station.

"Aren't you going to say 'hello' as well?" she asked.

He shook his head. She even *sounded* real. No more of that

green liquor until he made solid plans for a tryst with Crim.

The very idea of Lady Charlotte Louis, daughter of a duke, now sister to a duke, to be here. Why, the lady would had to have sneaked out from under her overbearing brother's watch, traversed the dangerous London streets in the dark, and boldly knocked on an unmarried man's door.

Quite a feat and one Hamish would have no choice but to find refreshing if it were true. But even if all of those impossible things were to mysteriously come to fruition, no proper housekeeper of a gentleman—especially the inscrutable scoundrel Duke of Camine—would admit such a visitor at such an hour.

Hamish wouldn't dwell on the fact that his most recent addition to his household staff was neither proper, nor respectable herself. But even Camille wouldn't be so foolish as to . . .

He sobered instantly with a violent prediction and a vulgar curse.

"You're really here." He took in her modest dress and confused expression again, his mind playing an unpleasant game of hazard, coherency the dice.

"I am," she said. "As are you."

She was? She was what? Wait, what was with that gleam in her eye? "Why are you here?"

She blinked, her spectacles slipping just enough to reveal eyes the color of sea stone. "I have business with you."

Business?

He scrambled over to his desk, looking for a glass of water or brandy or something to make sense of all this. *Think, man!* For this unsoiled dove to be here, something drastic was afoot.

He stopped, reorganizing his thoughts. Clearly, the woman didn't mean "business" as in trade or negotiations.

What did that leave? A horrible sense of direction? An accident?

Hamish went cold. Renard had cried off their usual poker game tonight, claiming he'd had a previous engagement.

Which meant one of two possibilities: a race or a woman, the faster the better. It was far less likely a fight over a woman would constitute a midnight visit from his sister. The alternative was beyond thinking. If Renard had fallen in one of the narrow street races in Dockside, with the disease-laden Thames River on one side and possible trampling—

"My God!" He upturned the chair at his hip in his panic. "Has a physician been called? How badly is Renard injured?" He came around the desk, cataloguing how drunk he really was and assessing whether or not he could retrieve his ducal physician in his curricle.

Lady Charlotte watched him, puzzlement on her face, which then cleared with a small laugh. "Be at ease. My brother is unharmed at home."

Hamish stopped, her chesty laugh caressing him between the legs. "Your brother . . . is safe?"

She nodded.

He frowned. "At home?" Frustration over what he was clearly missing incited his normally reined-in temper. "Then why the bloody hell are you here?"

A frown formed between her brows. "As I said, business." Retrieving a folded stack of papers from her skirt pocket, she opened the sheaf and smoothed out the creases, her gaze expectant. "I have a list, you see—matters of which I wish to discuss with you."

His gaze once again slipped to the darkened window, sure *The London Gazette* would've reported if there were to be an eclipse today. "Right now? In the middle of the night?"

Her own gaze flicked to the window as if just realizing the hour. "I can come back if that is more convenient? Is six o'clock too early?"

Six o'clock. Good God, she couldn't mean . . . "In the morning?"

"Do you not rise early?"

"No one rises *that* early." No one who wasn't a field hand or a fishmonger.

"Then we may proceed?"

Hamish ran a hand over his face, now certain he wasn't drunk enough to continue this circus of a conversation. But the sooner the lady stated her "business," the sooner he could find that bed and wake up tomorrow with everything back as it should be.

Finding his seat behind his desk, he previewed the household account ledgers Camille must have left out for him without seeing any of the numbers.

"Very well." He waved her on. "What is on this list to which I must be privy? Names of modistes? Milliners?"

She raised her chin. "I've compiled a list of shortcomings I wish to rectify."

He frowned up at her. "That's all good and fine"—*and interesting and unexpected*—"but what has that to do with me?"

"You are an esteemed member of society. A worldly man with vast experience."

He wouldn't deny his influence or pedigree. But that all remained to be seen.

"Shall we begin, then?" she asked.

Begin what? The lady hadn't clarified anything. But because he had no civil way of knowing how to turn the lady away, he gave way to madness and said, "Go on."

Rustling the pages in her hand, she cleared her throat and said, "Number one: Learn society rules."

He covered his snort by turning a page in the account ledger in front of him. Lady Charlotte Louis may have been a scandal in the making, but at least she was aware of the fact. But that was plain idiocy. No woman raised as a duke's sister would be so reckless.

Hope filling his voice, he asked, "Does your brother know you're here?" Perhaps Renard was waiting outside and was too embarrassed to join the conversation. The man may be forgiven for his loss of decorum; having a sister did happen to throw a man off-balance. He had one especially maddening sibling himself.

Charlotte looked up from her papers, her spectacles slipping down her frowning face. "Of course not. My brother would never have let me come."

He ran a hand over his face, hope dissolving. "Do you know *why?*"

"He said men were not to be trusted." She waved a hand dismissively. "I assume it has less to do with your reputation and more to do with those pesky rules."

He turned another page in his ledger, having absorbed nothing of the previous figures. Renard Louis was his oldest friend, a force in society, and an honest man to the point of often being perceived as brutal, but clearly, he was a fool. His sister had arrived from the country less than a week ago, after a decade of isolation due to poor health, and she was already hem-deep in impropriety . . . and at such an ungodly hour.

He stood in one fluid motion and crossed the room, yanked the bell pull twice, in honor of said hour, doing what he should've done the moment he'd seen her in his study, and returned to his desk. "My reputation is the exact reason for 'those pesky rules,'" he said. "An unmarried lady in the home of a bachelor calls virtue into question."

Lady Charlotte cocked her head, reminding him of one of the owls in the Tower of London's menagerie, though the upswept coiffure of blonde curls complemented her face without the ridiculousness of feathers or adornments.

"Have no fear, Hamish," she said. "I promise, if anyone accuses you of losing your virtue because of me, I will set them straight." She went back to her pages. "Number two: Learn to ride a horse."

He stared. He didn't know what to react to first, the fact that the lady had used his given name without a trace of a blush, or the sheer lunacy of her believing she needed to protect *his* reputation.

A knock at the door saved the lady from overhearing his curse.

"Enter," he barked.

Mrs. Camille Forthright, his housekeeper, marched in, her dark hair and gray dress pristine, as if being called upon in the wee hours would not keep the young woman from looking anything but perfect. "You rang?"

Hamish gritted his teeth. Lady Charlotte wasn't the only one in need of a lesson in rules. He couldn't stop himself from muttering, "A proper housekeeper would have sent the young lady away."

Mrs. Forthright glanced at Lady Charlotte and grinned.

Hamish bent over a clean card and scribbled a quick note to keep himself from throttling the both of them. Sealing the card, he extended it to Mrs. Forthright. "See this reaches the Duke of Lux. His hands only."

"Of course." His housekeeper turned and bobbed her head instead of a curtsy, another unacceptable transgression. "Lady Charlotte."

Hamish waited for the lady to ridicule his servant's lack of manners, but Lady Charlotte smiled.

"Thank you for your help, Mrs. Forthright."

Hamish swore he saw his housekeeper wink.

"My pleasure," she said.

His eyes narrowed as the door latched shut. Women. "Nothing but trouble," he grumbled.

The beginning of a conspiracy was in the air. Hamish eyed the clock, contemplating if it was too early for tea.

"Number three," Lady Charlotte continued. "Learn the waltz."

Hamish went back to the ledger. "You can't waltz?"

"Even with my governess's best efforts to teach me, my brother specifically forbade me to exert myself. The staff was too frightened of him to disobey." She sniffed. "Rather insulting since I can keep a secret. He'd have never known."

That got a chuckle out of him. The Duke of Lux would have hired additional hands to make sure the regular staff had done precisely as he'd ordered. Bossy, overbearing, stubborn ass—no wonder he and Hamish got along so well.

"Think of a waltz like a polka with a bigger sweep," he said. "They're all similar."

"Hmm. You've uncovered a more critical concern."

He looked up through his lashes, seeing a charming wrinkle between the lady's brows. Knowing young ladies and their annoying habit of falling into hysterics when a man didn't differentiate the importance of proper pastimes, he waited, surprised when she tapped her chin and smiled.

"I shall learn to dance," she said. "Then I'll learn the waltz. May I borrow your quill?"

She approached his desk, her walk childlike and carefree and making it abundantly clear she wore no corset beneath her blouse.

Hamish felt a rush of heat as she leaned forward, her breasts pressing against the fabric indecently, her nipples dark patches against the white. He stared at her extended hand.

"The quill?" she asked.

He released his hold, gritting his teeth a second time when her slender fingers brushed his hand.

Damn Renard! Concern over his sister's health aside, Lady Charlotte was not a child. A woman of twenty needed a corset and gloves and a small army of chaperones.

She crossed out a line on her page with one confident stroke and wrote something in the margins too small and cramped for him to make out before she offered the quill back.

"Thank you."

Thank God for oak desks and reinforced trousers. He cursed.

"What was that?" she asked.

"Never mind," he said, not bothering to temper the growl in his throat. "For a lady shut away with little entertainment, didn't your governess teach you anything?" Like when a man was in physical pain!

"Nothing of use, aside from French." Her voice brightened. "Which is why I insisted on enrolling in Cambridge."

He choked on air. The quill snapped in his shock and sent ink splattering across the desk.

She wrinkled her nose. "Of course, there are more rules about a lady attending a man's educational establishment. Even if the school would have allowed such a concession to my gender, my brother forbade me from any such ventures. As incentive for me to remain in the country, my brother hired special tutors from across the empire. I speak five languages, play the pianoforte, draw well enough to pass as a master's apprentice, and have a firm knowledge of science and medical procedures."

Madness! If half of what the lady said was true, Renard had a lot to answer for, first and foremost the fall of polite society.

Hamish was delighted against his better wishes. Suddenly, a night of overindulgence with his boys wasn't the most interesting thing he'd done tonight. "No needlepoint?"

"There wasn't time."

She was so serious, Hamish had to work hard not to be charmed. He'd met the lady once before, years ago at the Lux country estate. She'd been quiet with her long hair plaited down her back and her face permanently hidden behind a book.

Now years later, Hamish saw what he had not then. Long limbs and the family nose, where her brother wore it as an arrogant slope to look down upon his peers, on Lady Charlotte, it was refined, pretty even. Bright eyes, green gold, stared at him full of curiosity and life.

A sudden image of her beneath him, those eyes wide with another sort of passion, made the room and his trousers feel unbearably small. He forced himself to look away, making a mental note to avoid the lady at all costs in the future.

Where the hell was Renard?!

"Those don't seem unreasonable," he said distractedly. Taking stock of the papers in her hand, he said, "What else?"

Papers pressed to her chest, she pursed her lips together. "I'm not sure I should share them with you until after."

"After?"

"You may not find them suitable for a lady."

Interest piqued, he crossed his legs and leaned back, ledger and ruined desk forgotten. The hell with it. The evening was a growing scandal. Why stop now? "I must know."

She searched his face and, seeming to find what she was looking for, nodded, and said, "Number four: Learn to use profane language."

It took sheer will to keep his face impassive. "Looking to shock the *ton* at the next ball?"

The lady tapped her chin. "I believe the expression is 'make a sailor blush.' I hear they're the gold standard for foul oaths."

Hamish's face ached from holding back a grin. By God, she was more interesting than she looked. "Why must you take it that far? Surely, a well-placed set-down is arsenal enough for a young woman."

Her brow quirked. "If you're going to do something, strive to be the best."

"Naturally." When was the last time he had enjoyed a conversation this much? Less than a week before the official start of the season and shallow ballroom conversations centered around dull society gossip and dandies hunting for suitable brides.

"Number five: Be less complicated."

Hamish quirked a brow. "A noble endeavor. If you accomplish such a task, you would be the first woman in history," he said, hoping to dissuade her from further discussion. "But I suspect your fourth goal will work in opposition to your fifth." And first.

Lady Charlotte shook her head. "If you don't like that one, I'm sure you won't enjoy the next."

"Which is?"

"Be *more* complicated. I was told a man likes a woman with a bit of mystery."

The lady was a walking contradiction.

Mystery? His head hurt thinking about what an innocent could possibly know about what "mystery" meant to a man.

"Who told you that?"

"Diana Yamsbee." She continued without explanation, head bent over the papers in her hand, back to squinting. "Number seven: Learn self-defense."

He jolted. Taking in her slender fingers and the delicate lace around her wrists, the idea was deplorable. "Out of the question."

Her head popped up. Her spectacles turned askew before she put them to rights. "One can never be too careful. Nothing strenuous. I am too slight to overcome a foe with real power. A bit of fencing would suffice."

She tapped her mouth with the papers' edges, bringing his immediate attention to the fullness of her lower lip.

"I wouldn't mind trying my hand with a pistol," she said.

"Your brother will never agree to such a risk." The way she kept fumbling with the papers in her hand, she would be more likely to set a firearm off on herself before any target.

She sniffed. "Which is why my brother will never find out. And it goes hand in hand with number eight."

He would not ask, couldn't ask, but her enthusiasm was catching. "What's number eight?"

"Punch someone."

"What?!" Hamish sat forward suddenly; his knee connected with the underside of his desk.

"Strike someone," she said, eyes bright. "In the face."

It was by far the most unladylike thing she had said since her scandalous arrival, and yet, he was smiling. He could tell by the strain of unused muscles in his face. "How primal."

"Oh, don't get me wrong. I do not condone violence. A good set-down *is* still preferable to bellicose tendencies. I mean simply if an individual comes into my sphere who is deserving of a battering, I hope I am available to administer the blow."

She could not be real. Talking with her was equal parts ridiculous and delightful. He had not heard anyone speak so candidly . . . ever. He was in real danger of enjoying himself.

"Number nine: Sing the anthem to our queen."

No matter how hard his jaw clenched, laughter worked its way out. "You can't be serious?"

She stared at him, seeming surprised by his amusement until she blinked and cleared her throat. "Serious." She rifled through the pages in her hand. "Yes. Be more serious. That's number thirty-seven."

"*Thirty-seven?*" Good God, she had at least three other pages. "How many are there?"

"One hundred and eight."

He stared.

She stared back, her gaze piercing.

Hamish decided the lady's eyes were more distracting than her gloveless hands and her lack of corset put together.

"I had but a small portion of the morning to write them down," she said, as if the amount of time she'd had to work with explained everything. "I'll have a more comprehensive list after I take some time."

He should have packed her up then and there. Forced her into one of his carriages and dealt with the Duke of Lux's fury at sending his sister away. The girl, while lovely as a dove, was clearly not in her right mind. To say such things with conviction . . . "What's number one hundred and eight?"

She glanced at the last page and then said, "Ride a horse unsaddled."

He took in her full skirts, imagining the lady with a broken neck, and his chest gave a mysterious squeeze. "Impossible."

"Miss Yamsbee assured me it is possible."

Hamish ran a hand over his face, praying Renard would show up in the next ten seconds before he expired on the spot. Clearly, this Miss Yamsbee was interested in manipulating Lady Charlotte into ruining her reputation to further her own agenda. She must have seen the glint in the lady's eye and come to the same conclusion he had in their brief exchange: Lady Charlotte would take the season by storm, scandalizing the *ton* until they were little better than ducks eating from her hands. The men at least.

Hamish's hands tightened into fists, the idea of other men going near her hands or her feet, or even looking in her general direction making his gut burn. Indigestion from the evening's dinner, no doubt.

"I see I've shocked you," she said. "If it sets your mind at ease, I will give you my full list before the date in question so you don't go into this unaware."

His attention snapped back to her. "A full list?"

She nodded emphatically. "I believe in total honesty."

Something else she and her brother shared.

His brows knit together. "What date?" Had there been an invitation he'd overlooked? Renard had never given a fig about parties. Perhaps with his sister in town, the poor bastard felt obligated to join the season.

Despite his disdain for the mind-numbing niceties of London society, especially during the season, Hamish wouldn't hesitate to use his name to open any door his friend needed.

Lady Charlotte straightened. "Didn't I mention why I was here?" She removed her spectacles, polishing the lenses with a handkerchief from her pocket before replacing them.

When her eyes found his, Hamish had the unmistakable feeling of a cage snapping shut.

There was nowhere to run from that direct gaze.

She smiled, as if she knew there was no escape. "The reason I'm here is to proposition you into ruining me."

CHAPTER THREE

CHARLOTTE DETERMINED OF all the expressions Lord Hamish Hurstfield had given since her arrival, his shock was her favorite: dark brows raised, his square jaw slacked to soften an otherwise unforgivingly handsome face. Unfortunately, he recovered remarkably fast.

"Lady Charlotte—"

"Call me 'Charlotte.'"

Another amusing expression crossed his face before his jaw set. "No."

"You won't call me by my name?"

"No," he repeated. "To all of it."

She crushed her disappointment, having foreseen the Duke of Camine's resistance. Nonetheless, this scheme would work if she had to strip naked and prove her lack of dancing skills.

"You insist on using my title?" She returned the handkerchief to her pocket. "I suppose you may call me '*Your* lady' if you prefer?"

"Enough!"

The duke rose and stalked forward, his height and broad shoulders as impressive as they'd been as the first time he'd stood to ring the bell pull. With his dark clothes and dark hair, he blended into this dreary and *male* room with its leather chairs, dark drapes, and nondescript books bound in standard brown bindings. No baubles or treasures displayed from trips abroad, no color save for the crimson-dyed rug underfoot and those eyes, a clear and mesmerizing ice blue. The room, and the man, was in serious need of a woman's influence.

He towered over her, making her tilt back her head to hold his gaze. "Whatever childish fantasy you've conjured up in your mind, thinking you can tame the 'wild' duke into a virtuous husband"—he bared his teeth—"you were misinformed."

He seemed to struggle not to shake her, his hands twitching at his sides.

An unexpected thrill raced through her belly at the prospect of feeling his hands on her. Knowing her brother would have received the duke's note and was expected any minute, she stepped closer. Her heart fell when the duke retreated to lean against the edge of his desk.

He crossed his arms, seeming under the wrong impression that the conversation was over. "You should wait in the drawing room. I'll send Mrs. Forthright to keep you company until your brother arrives."

That would not do at all! Charlotte gritted her teeth, dipping her spectacles to the side for the tenth time that evening. She straightened the frames and looked up at him boldly despite heat pouring into her cheeks.

He really was a big man, as handsome as she remembered. His comment about childish fantasies stung, but he was wrong if he thought changing *him* was her goal. She'd said as much.

She ignored her hammering heart and stepped between his knees, feeling another wave of flushed skin and earning a strangled expression from the duke. She glanced at the mantel clock and swallowed her nerves and guilt. Using the duke in such an undignified way was reproachful, but she was counting on her brother's affection for the duke to keep him from demanding any unsightly violence.

"On the contrary." She slipped her hand over his thigh, earning another sharp inhale from the man. Refusing to humor her curiosity to explore the firm muscles, she leaned forward, reaching on her tiptoes to whisper against his lips, "I want you the way you are."

The duke had grown so still since she had trapped him against the desk, she gave a shrill squeak when he suddenly snatched her by the arms and crushed his mouth to hers.

Wild. It was the first and last thought Charlotte had before her brain zeroed in on the duke. His teeth nipped at her lower lip and an explosive heat flooded her core when his tongue aggressively invaded her mouth.

She grasped his shoulders, her legs uneasy beneath her.

His tongue slid against hers, back and forth as if he had all night to make her see how untamed he could be.

Charlotte's mind switched back on. They did not have all night. They did not have ten minutes! The moment her brother walked through that door, her freedom would be locked up, the key tossed away with the rest of her dreams.

She fumbled with the buttons of his trousers.

The duke's hands were instantly there, trapping her wrists together and pulling her away, breaking their kiss.

A lady would hardly call what they had done kissing. She felt bruised, swollen, and completely alive for the first time in her life. No wonder her brother had locked her away in the country. Now that she knew what pleasures the world held, she refused to go back to her cage, good intentioned and gilded though it may have been.

She stared up into the duke's eyes, pleased to see his gaze unfocused and heavy lidded. Her gaze dropped to his mouth, and she swore he growled.

Through the study window a light bobbed down the street.

Her brother's carriage! Panic flared. Charlotte looked down at herself, still far too respectable-looking to fool her brother. She glanced at the clock again and tugged at her wrists.

The duke held fast, a grin playing about his mouth. "Trying to get away now, little mouse?"

Charlotte stilled, frustrated. In Diana's letter, she'd made a kiss sound like a little flirting and no man would resist. Charlotte changed tactics, falling back on the one thing she knew best: honesty. "I have no idea how to get you to touch me without the use of my hands." She shook her arms, the man's grip unbreakable. "Would you mind releasing me so we may proceed?"

Gaze cooling, the duke grinned in a way that told Charlotte he either found her dangerous or vastly amusing. Maybe both.

He confirmed her suspicions a moment later when he said, "I believe we'll stay this way a bit longer until I feel confident you won't attack me again."

Her cheeks flushed with heat. Had she done something wrong? It had been her first kiss . . . "Why did you kiss me back?"

He shrugged. "Curiosity."

She lit up. He *did* understand. She knew she'd chosen correctly. Her gaze tracked the dark shape lumbering down the street, the unmistakable *click-clack* of her brother's brougham sounding like the countdown to her stifling future. The light swinging from the carriage flared as the carriage stopped outside the window.

"It appears your brother has arrived. At last." He released her wrists and went back to his chair.

She followed, anger rising at the relief in his voice. "We're not done."

His expression was the same as the one her brother gave her when he thought her unreasonable. "I assure you, we are."

No! She cursed, repeating a word she'd heard the stablemaster use when their newest stallion had thrown its rider.

She ignored the duke's cough of surprise and ran her fingers through her hair, ripping the pins out and sending a curtain of blonde hair down her back.

The duke watched her with wide eyes until she started on the buttons at her collar.

"What the devil are you doing?" he demanded.

"Undressing."

He stared at her.

She went for the second button, popping the little bead off in her hurry.

Issuing his own curse, a word Charlotte made sure to memorize for later, he shot out of his chair and trapped her wrists a second time.

"Have you lost your mind?"

She tugged, seeing the door to the carriage open. She was out of time. "Let. Me. Go."

He did no such thing. "Do you have any idea what someone would think if they saw us?"

"That you'd ravaged me?" She blew hair out of her face. "Yes."

Her declaration seemed to startle him.

He let go of her wrists, his face darkening and his voice going cold. "You're attempting to trap me into marriage?"

"Of course not," she said, going for her third button with shaky hands. "I'm trying to *get out of marriage*."

HAMISH STARED.

Lady Charlotte continued to struggle with the buttons of her blouse, revealing a lovely valley of smooth, pale skin. The log in the fireplace dropped, light flaring and sending a wave of heat through the already infernal room.

When he'd said he'd been curious about the kiss, he'd been telling the truth, if by 'curious,' he meant a heavy arousal and the image of her spread on either side of his lap, those tiny wrists behind her back. He had hoped to try just that when the lady had opened her mouth and spouted such an honest and innocently erotic thing that Hamish knew she was far too tempting to remain in the same room.

"I have no idea how to get you to touch me without the use of my hands."

Good God, smiling, moving, *breathing* in his direction, and he was strung like a top. A little instruction and the lady would be a siren on land. Looking at her disheveled hair and full lips pouted in concentration, he had a sneaking suspicion an entire country between them would not be enough.

He frowned, her last statement registering, seeing an uncomfortable encounter with a jilted fiancé in his future. "You're betrothed?"

She stopped unbuttoning long enough to glance at him, her chin stuck out stubbornly. "Not if I can help it."

Giving up on the buttons of her blouse, she worked the clasp of her skirt open.

Worried he would be too distracted to learn why he was about to get into a bloody fistfight with his friend if the lady kept disrobing, he grabbed the ledger from his desk and tossed it. "Lady Charlotte."

She looked up and, with quick reflexes, caught the ledger with two hands. She stared down at the thick volume and then at him. "You threw it."

He did not hide his surprise. "You caught it."

Her mouth made an enticing *O* shape before she pursed her lips again. "You threw it at me!"

He shrugged. "It was the only way to make you desist with undressing."

She scowled. "What was wrong with grabbing me again? That would be less likely to end in bruises."

Not the way he wanted to push her against the wall and hike up her skirts. Gentle wasn't in his nature.

The glint in the lady's eye told him she would not be opposed to the idea.

"I liked it," she said, as if reading his mind. "I liked being restrained."

Cock jerking in approval, Hamish gripped his desk, fingers digging into the oak top to stop from reaching for her and giving her exactly what she'd asked for. Either the lady was a minx who knew what to say to seduce a man, or she had a gift for erotic speech without any idea. If the former, he'd throw her out of his study, leaving Renard to take her away like unnecessary baggage. If the latter . . . the image of her in a pale dress, her hair teased up in a formal coif, startled him into saying, "Tell me why you'd risk your reputation to avoid marriage? Most women live their lives pining for it."

She snorted. "Most women are idiots." She glanced out the window for the fifth time, her gaze darting back to his. "We don't have much time before my brother bursts through your door."

Confident in his housekeeper's inhuman ability to stall his friend, or any man with eyes, Hamish crossed his arms and cocked a brow. "Make time, or I'll retrieve your brother myself."

Seeming to realize he meant it, she blew a strand of hair out of her face with a huff. "Very well."

He nodded. "What offending lad has offered for you?"

Her earlier scowl returned. "Nothing was offered. My brother and the Marquess of Slasbury decided I was little more than a fine heifer to be bought and sold."

Hamish flinched.

Gunther Flarborn, Marquess of Slasbury, was a man of few brain cells and many pleasures. For a woman of any intelligence, he'd be an absolute bore. And demanding in other ways.

Hamish frowned at a stab of anger over the idea. He'd met the man once, but a few months ago at an obligatory function; as the new Duke of Camine and sole contributor to numerous charities now that his father had passed, Hamish couldn't exactly say, "Leave off" to the board.

The marquess was titled and fair-haired, and he had investments as rich as Hamish's—the public ones, anyway. There were worse candidates for an eccentric lady.

"The marquess is a respectable gentleman." The word *respectable* made his stomach churn with renewed anger, but he pushed it aside. "He'll make an adequate husband."

"The man has the personality of a litter runt. Determined to compensate for everything he lacks through overindulgence and drooling."

Hamish choked on his laugh. The lady's tongue was as sharp as a butcher's blade, and just as damaging. Damn it all if he didn't find her company refreshing.

Lady Charlotte Louis was a dangerous woman.

He sobered in time to hear a deep, male voice from the hall. A soft knock rapped at the door.

"Enter," he said.

Lady Charlotte stiffened as the door opened and her brother walked in.

Renard Louis struck an imposing figure in the low firelight, his suit tailored and his expression severe. His gaze went from Hamish to his sister's less-than-respectable appearance and back with falcon-like precision.

"Tell me, Hamish . . ." Renard's voice rang like steel. "Can we laugh about my sister's misguided notion of spoiling a young man's heart over a glass of scotch? Or am I to ruin my best overcoat so early in the morning?"

Hamish glanced at Lady Charlotte, her face falling at her brother's accurate conclusion.

She whirled to him, her eyes pleading.

Hamish saw the words in her gaze.

Help me.

He turned from those piercing eyes, displeased at how the woman had affected him. "She is unspoiled. The lady had a fit of heat and decided her collar was the culprit." He chose the words carefully, knowing they were crude, but a fitting lie for all present.

The sooner the lady realized the futility of her situation, the sooner she'd be safe in marriage, a loveless one. It was best, expected, and it would completely snuff out the brilliant light he'd seen in her eyes.

Hamish clenched his fists, thanking the good Lord when Renard took his sister by the arm and sighed.

"I see." He shot Hamish a grateful look, his faith Hamish wouldn't have taken advantage a mark of their lifelong friendship.

"Sorry for the trouble. I'm afraid the time away from society has left my sister ignorant of decorum . . . and when it is appropriate to let the 'heat get to her.' I hope there's no offense?"

"None taken."

"No!" Lady Charlotte tugged her hand out of her brother's grip. "I refuse to be treated like a child."

"Then stop acting like one!" Renard snapped.

Hamish waited for the lady to crumble in a heap at the chastisement, but she raised that stubborn chin and went up another score in his book when her expression turned downright haughty.

"A gentleman mustn't shout at a lady," she said. "It shows a lack of refinement in his upbringing."

Both men were silent, giving each other a glance equal parts exasperation and shared school memories.

Renard at last chuckled and towed his sister towards the open study door, throwing over his shoulder, "Come by the house this week, Hamish. I'll have that scotch waiting."

Hamish followed, his gaze everywhere but the lady digging her heels in. "Count on it."

Renard paused on the threshold, his unruly, blond hair falling into his eyes without his usual top hat to hold it at bay. "I trust you'll be discreet about my sister's . . . heat stroke?"

Hamish knew his friend did not ask for his benefit. They had been keeping each other's secrets since they were kids, and Hamish would take Renard's to the grave. Renard understood his sister's resolve was not easily broken.

Hamish slipped into a mischievous grin, the one that had won him more than one lady's affections—and twice as many fists to the jaw. "Not ravage a young lady caught in my clutches? My reputation would turn positively decent."

Renard grinned.

Hamish started to shut the door when Lady Charlotte put up a hand to stop him.

"Why?" Her eyes were watery, but the tears did not fall, held back as if by will alone. "Why couldn't you have lied?"

"I'm not a gentleman in the sense of the word," he said. "I have no intention of marriage or children or scandal. And frankly . . ." He had to look away before striking the last blow. "You're too much trouble."

The door snapped shut, and Hamish felt like a true lying ass.

CHAPTER FOUR

CHARLOTTE COUNTED THE seconds after the door of the carriage latched until her brother flew into one of his legendary lectures.

Three.

"Of all the reckless, dangerous, hazardous—"

"Those last two mean the same thing," Charlotte said.

Renard's gaze hardened. "This has to stop. You're not a child anymore. I know you've always been wild—and I'm to blame for not putting a stop to your behavior running off every governess and chaperone in England after Mother and Father passed—but you've gone too far this time."

Charlotte angled her body on the bench to face Renard as fully as possible. As the brougham only had one bench for sitting, she'd used the tight space to her advantage. If Renard thought *he* was mad, he'd regret not bringing one of the bigger carriages when she knocked one of the items off her list as she knocked in his insufferable teeth.

"Do you know how terrifying it is to be woken in the middle of the night to find your sister has vanished?" He rubbed his face, the beginnings of golden stubble on his chin. "And then to find you've come here. I told you of the marquess's intentions only this morning. I shudder to think what insane scheme you would have come up with if given a full day."

Guilt sank its teeth in, but Charlotte wouldn't forget her

brother's plan to sell her off like cattle. "I chose your friend knowing he wouldn't hurt me."

"Then you know nothing. Hamish Hurstfield is a bull-headed scoundrel. Why do you think I like him so much?" Renard leaned back in his seat and hunched his shoulders. "As luck would have it, he *was* the perfect choice, since he's currently seeing a woman considered the most beautiful in England. An innocent lady would hold no interest for him."

Instant jealousy gave Charlotte pause. No, that couldn't be right. She was attracted, yes, determined. But she had no designs on the man. It was simply frustration that Hamish had brushed aside her advances. If he was seeing another woman, no wonder he'd stopped her. She frowned. Except he hadn't kissed like he hadn't been interested. She hadn't known a kiss could be so possessive yet freeing.

Thinking about his teeth nipping at her lips and tongue brought on another rush of heat.

"Seeing a woman considered the most beautiful in England."

She straightened her spectacles, wishing she would have done the proposing without them. But she hadn't memorized her list, and she was hopelessly blind without them. Her hand bunched in her skirt. She'd been so concerned about sneaking out without needing the assistance of a maid to dress, she'd deliberately chosen her most comfortable and modest petticoats. The crinolette and padding she'd done without entirely. And the grey color had been practical. Why wear a cream muslin or flashy hair ornament when one was meant to blend into the night?

"How in the good Lord's name did you think going to a noted rake's home would benefit you in any way?" Renard asked.

Charlotte crossed her arms and slumped back against the wooden bench, her anger somewhat quelled by her lack of planning. "I had a list. Your friend is known as a gentleman who appreciates boldness. I'd hoped he'd be so intrigued, the manner of my marriageability would be overlooked. If he had agreed to help me with some of the . . . more *adventurous* items, then I would reveal my secrets to you, and you would end any agreement with suitors."

"Camine would never say anything to besmirch your reputation or mine. It would remain a secret, and, if it were a secret, why should I call off anything?"

Charlotte blinked. "Because *we* would know. Your principles wouldn't allow you to hand me off as a virtuous bride when you knew better."

Renard glared at her, then glanced at the papers in her hand. "A list of what?"

"Faults. Goals. Dreams."

Renard threw his head back and barked a laugh. "I would have paid to see his face. I bet he was scrambling to get away."

Charlotte's frown deepened. The duke had done far worse than run; he'd seemed genuinely amused. She kept that tidbit to herself. After spending her life tucked away, locked up on the anxious mood shifts of her brother and the staff, she'd become an expert on reading what people wanted, from her and themselves: silence on her part, a rapt audience for the latter.

The Duke of Camine needed a laugh and something she couldn't identify. There had been a light in his eyes when she'd said she'd enjoyed being restrained. He'd been lustful, naturally, but vulnerability had also flashed across his face.

She had no idea if being bound was uncouth. Honestly, she didn't give a fig. After being denied every indulgence since her parents' deaths a decade ago, she wouldn't apologize for her desires. Given the chance, she'd indulge in every single one, no matter what society deemed 'unnecessary,' or more aptly, 'fun.'

A bunch of stiff boards in a broom closet. That was her impression of the *ton*. Seemed to her someone needed to open a window and let the fresh air remove the stale or, in her case, open the door and toss the lot out.

The fashionable homes of the city gave way to the ultra-fashionable and Charlotte scowled at the fenced-off stone houses with their jointures of pillared arches and neoclassical façades:

lovely cages all of them.

"The marquess sent a letter this afternoon requesting a visit next week," Renard said. "Let's thank heaven he's out of town. Any gossip will be conclusively squashed by Hamish's staff by then."

"Your confidence in household loyalty is unfounded." She'd learned more during her time eavesdropping on the servants at Lux Manor than in any proper instruction with her governess.

She massaged the bridge of her nose, her spectacles pinching. "Really, Ren, I'm sure the marquess would make a lovely husband . . . for someone. This is my first season. Shouldn't I be looking forward to whispered affections and stolen kisses? What's the rush?"

"Kisses?" Renard's horror was palatable. "I told the staff to keep nonsense novels out of view. That is not how proper courting is done. Chaperoned visits, chaperoned outings, dances—"

"Chaperoned, I presume?" Charlotte snorted. "How is any woman supposed to get to know a suitor that way?"

"You get to know a man *after* marriage."

"That's nonsense! What if he's a drunk? A philanderer?"

Renard frowned at the unladylike topics. "That's exactly why the male guardian makes the decision. To better discern a gentleman's character."

She'd have better luck befriending a lord's physician. At least then she'd know the likelihood of contagion.

Charlotte shook her head. She loved her brother more than the air in her lungs, but there were times when his naivety surpassed her own. She closed her eyes, the ache in her head reaching horse-galloping level. She was tired and in need of a bath and redressing and far too exhausted to continue this fight.

Not that she was giving up. Far from it. If the notorious 'wild' duke wouldn't help in her endeavors, she'd find another gentleman. She'd walk through the London streets in her nightclothes if it would forestall her being shackled to a man who'd be as stifling as her brother.

As the scandalized pariah or the revolutionary woman, she'd resolved herself before she'd stepped into the duke's study, she'd be free. Free to live and learn as she pleased. Life was anything but certain.

She thought of their parents then, kind and outgoing, shunning society and its rules to live in the country and raise their children instead of relying on a proper nursemaid. They'd been happy. Charlotte fingered the lace at her shoulder, imagining the scar underneath.

It was like a brand that burned, a physical reminder that everything could be lost in smoke at any moment if one didn't fight for life with every breath.

She'd be happy again, no matter what.

Charlotte settled into her seat, preparing to dig in—in many ways. In whispered ballroom conversations or in bold print in the scandal sheets, London society was going to know her name.

And heaven help the man who got in her way.

"SORRY TO BE in the way," Hamish said.

Renard cleared his desk of papers and set out a half-full decanter of amber liquor and two glasses. "You've given me an excuse to enjoy my favorite vice."

"Favorite?"

Renard grinned and poured, his mind never far from the bedroom. "Second favorite." He handed Hamish a glass. "I didn't expect you so soon, to be honest. Shouldn't you be ogling one of Gregori's new contraptions and making another bucket of gold appear out of thin air?" The look he gave Hamish was pointed. "You set a poor example for the rest of us useless gentlemen with all your advances and day-to-day *work*."

Hamish grinned. "Gregori is investigating an innovative

approach in India. He isn't due back until next week. Leaving me a leisurely break to enjoy my own vices."

Renard raised his glass. "Hear, hear."

Hamish raised his glass but didn't drink. Truthfully, he didn't want the break. More specifically, he couldn't *stand* the break. The whispers through the black market over India's breakthrough were too good to pass up. Even a *hint* of the formula would put Hamish ahead of the competitors in London by years, but that didn't mean he bloody well had the patience to wait.

He swirled the amber liquid in his glass. "What of your endeavors, Renard?" He glanced around his friend's study, the floor-to-ceiling walls of books and imposing marble mantel with its lion heads on either side as fierce and eccentric as when the last Duke of Lux had lived in residence.

Renard flinched. "Lady Luck continues to elude me." He knocked back his drink in one gulp. "Good thing Charlotte's trust is set up, or I'd be leaving her destitute."

Hamish scoffed. "Even half as rich as me, you'd never spend all that money in two lifetimes. Three if you lay off the whiskey."

Renard sighed. "If only I'd started sooner."

Low voices in the outside hall had Hamish's ears straining. He cleared his throat. "Speaking of the infamous lady, should I lock the door or hide in the drapery upon her arrival?"

Renard blew out a laugh. "Fear not, my friend. After last night's escapades, my sister promised me a twenty-four-hour window before she tries another reckless stunt bent on giving her old brother a heart condition. If she's to be believed, she's at the modiste, commissioning a dress for the Tailormans' ball."

Hamish couldn't fathom why his chest fell hearing the lady wasn't at home. He wasn't some young, idiot suitor looking to steal a glance at his sweetheart, nor was he a man who troubled himself with the drama of other people's vapid lives. And he most certainly didn't care if a young woman, far too marketable and intelligent for a man with any desire for a peaceful existence, was in residence or not.

Last night, he'd been half-drunk after a lively poker game with his man Percy and two yawns away from bed when she'd stormed into his study. There was no way he'd find a lady so innocent and outspoken attractive in the light of day. Obviously, he was disgruntled to have his efforts thwarted to prove so.

"It's too early for you to be thinking so hard," Renard said.

"It's two in the afternoon." Hamish threw back his glass, the cheap liquor burning his throat. He winced. "What happened to the good stuff?"

Renard shrugged, throwing back his own drink and refilling both glasses. "No point wasting Ballantine when I plan on getting drunk enough to serenade the family portraits on the gallery walls."

Hamish took his glass, watching his friend down and refill his drink a fourth time. "All the more reason. Though the illness to follow will surely keep my mind from recent disturbances."

Renard choked. "Dear God! How much trouble was she?"

Knowing exactly which 'she' his friend meant, Hamish remembered how Lady Charlotte had caught his ledger and grinned. "She's a handful."

Renard saluted him with his glass, sloshing golden liquid down his front. "Hence the forthcoming concert."

"She thinks the marquess is an imbecile."

Renard's eyes widened. "She told you that?" He ran a hand through his hair. "The man is a fool, but he'll treat her right. Provide stability."

"Not up to the task, big brother?"

Renard laughed, but the sound was hollow. "You know me. I like my life like I like my liquor: hazy, golden, and in excess." A shadow passed over his face before clearing. "Charlotte is the only decent thing in my life. I'd see her settled down and cared for before one of the angry suitors gets lucky and hits something vital."

Hamish grinned. "You should steer clear of the married ones for a while. The widows are just as fun, with more experience."

"Showing concern for your dear old friend?"

"I'd hate to find another bloke stupid enough to get caught changing the locks on the dormitory toilets."

Renard sputtered. "Headmaster Smith chewed me out so long, I thought my ears would fall off." He leaned back in his chair, wiping the drink from his chin. "When Charlotte said that line about how a gentleman shouldn't shout, I was right back at school." He smiled. "I had to lock my jaw to keep from apologizing on reflex. Like a born headmistress, she is."

More like a warrior queen. "Would it be the end of the *ton* if she had a choice?"

Renard's gaze narrowed. "You're showing an uncharacteristic amount of interest in someone other than yourself. Didn't go and grow a heart while I was in the country, did you?"

Hamish avoided his friend's gaze by taking a long sip. "Nonsense. We have a common plight now is all." He raised his glass. "To the chaos of women."

Renard clinked his glass and sipped. "How is the lovely Miss Crim?"

It was Hamish's turn to groan. "Expensive."

Once discreet, lovely, and infinitely creative, the singer had grown tedious, falling into fits of tears whenever she felt neglected, leading Hamish to purchase bigger and pricier gifts to gain back her favor. Games and deceit. That was all it was. It had never bothered him before. It was the expense of keeping his freedom without the worry of the marriage noose. It wasn't until recently that Hamish had the inclination to want something different.

Hamish stood, not wishing to chance running into Lady Charlotte on her way home. The room tilted, and he steadied himself against the chair. "I have to go."

Renard glanced up at him, eyes heavy, passed foxed and mumbled, "Club later?"

Hamish waved a noncommittal hand on his way out.

The air outside was uncharacteristically fresh and light—an

unseasonal breeze pushing the putrid fumes from the factories farther east—reminding him of the person he needed to avoid and bringing about a string of curses. It had been less than an hour with the chit and here he was running away like a young lad avoiding his governess's wrath.

As it was too late to go back inside and face the woman like a man, he balled his fists in his pockets and set out towards Camine House on Arlington Street, cutting his way through Green Park as to avoid any of the modiste shops.

His father, the former Duke of Camine, would have turned in his coffin if he'd known his son had let the ancestral home in Piccadilly. Choosing an exclusive neighborhood over the most coveted in London was a slight the old bastard must have felt in the bowels of whatever pit in which the Devil had caged him. Hamish whistled thinking about the man's tortured soul.

The scotch sloshed in his empty stomach and had gone straight to his head, leaving the early budding bushes and trimmed trees off the path in a hazy frame. If he could manage to get back to his bed in one piece, he'd ring for a fresh bottle and finish the job properly.

New purpose in his stride, Hamish grinned and looked up.

His smile slipped.

Lady Charlotte glided down the park's path, a hazy goddess in a blue day dress that left her skin glowing. Sensing his gaze, she looked up, her green eyes flashing in recognition. She glanced in the direction of her brother's townhouse at his back, clearly seeing whence he'd come.

He bit back another curse and tipped his hat. "Lady Charlotte—" He spun around, frowning. "Where are you going?"

She threw him a smile that would've sent a lesser man, a sober man, to his knees and called, "The servants' entrance is around back. Better not dawdle. The housekeeper is a stickler for promptness."

The cheeky, little minx!

He took off after her, bent on teaching the lady a lesson. The 'wild' duke didn't avoid a woman or flee a room like a damned coward. The lady—with her curious eyes and smart mouth—had cast a spell on him that he'd break here and now with the reality of their differences in experience.

He snatched her wrist, a sense of triumph clearing the fog from his mind when she whirled around, her lovely eyes going wide.

"What do you think you're doing?"

Her pulse hammered against his fingers, a perfect staccato of emotion. Fear? Excitement?

What was he doing? Hell if he knew. She was a whirlwind, a tornado of destruction, and he couldn't stop himself from racing into its direct path. Drunken fool as he was, it was a public park. One keen eye, one loose tongue, and the damage would be irreparable.

But that pulse. How fast and hard it beat, like a seductive rhythm drumming the woman's preferences.

Groin pounding to that same relentless beat . . . fast, yes. They'd start in a frenzy of hot kisses and needy touches. But he'd teach her the joy of leisurely too. How delay was a torture of pleasure she'd come to crave.

He flashed a smile and leaned down, an intoxicating blend of rosewater and lemons tickling his nose. "I'm doing exactly as you suggested, my lady." His fingers lifted her chin until their mouths were a breath away. "I'm not wasting any more time."

CHAPTER FIVE

A PROPER LADY would've screamed, would've torn away from the Duke of Camine and not looked back until there was a sturdy oak door between them.

Boots were no proper footwear for running, and she was anything but proper.

He smelled of strong spirits and horses, a combination she'd come to love despite its frequency in the country home where she'd grown up. Her skin tingled and flamed where his fingers gripped her chin. His touch was hot, possessive, and scandalously indecent in the public park.

And her body begged for more.

"Where is your chaperone?" he asked. "Let me guess: Traveling unescorted was also on that fearsome list?"

Charlotte bit her lip. When Harper learned she had left the modiste through the back to avoid a nursemaid, her lady's maid would be livid.

"I've no need to be watched."

Smiling, the duke bent his head lower. "I beg to differ."

She hummed with anticipation. He wouldn't hold back. She could see it in the glazed set of his eyes, the way his hands stroked her jaw, her neck. He'd destroy her reputation here and now.

"You're too much trouble."

His words last night repeated in her head.

She ground her teeth and pushed him away, her stomach

dropping when he stumbled before righting himself. Her gaze darted around the deserted park, grateful for the chilly day keeping away those looking to take in the April air.

"Changed your mind?" He frowned. "How like a woman."

Charlotte sniffed, unwilling to give him the hysterics he no doubt expected. "You made your disinterest clear last night, Duke. Woman or not, I refuse to lower myself to desperation. If you don't want me . . ." *To help me.* She cringed at her mis-speech but continued. "Another man will."

He laughed. "Good luck, *Lady Charlotte.*" He saluted and slurred, "I offer you my best wishes in finding your most incomparable knight."

The man would pull a muscle if he were any more smug. "What are you insinuating?"

"Only that if such a man hungry for roleplaying existed, he'd be more likely to hire a skirt he could pay to keep their mouth shut."

Charlotte's fingers curled into talons. "You didn't seem to mind my mouth earlier, *Lord Camine.*" She stepped close. "You know what I think? I think you're a sad, lonely man, bored with his circumstances and too damn afraid to take hold of anything or anyone who might see through your public façade." Her chin notched up when his expression darkened.

"You can keep your best wishes, Your Grace. I will, however, offer mine in hopes you one day overcome your need to pretend, because while you waste away in that stuffy study, drinking and 'roleplaying' your way through your life, I will take hold of my future with both hands."

The duke growled low in his throat, feral and angry, but when he stared down at her, his eyes were clear, opened. He bowed stiffly. "Good day, Lady Charlotte."

He stalked off, leaving Charlotte looking after him and her chest unusually tight.

HAMISH STUMBLED THROUGH his front door, pleased at how the drawn curtains cut the glare over the polished floors and left the hall in front of him in shadows. After his beastly actions in the park, he had no desire to see himself clearly in the light.

Someone cleared their throat.

Hamish glanced to his right at the flight of stairs leading up to the second-floor bedrooms and sighed. "Greetings, my dear. How was your day?"

His housekeeper eyed him like a worm infesting her favorite house plant. "You look like an ass," Camille said, her nose scrunching. "And smell like one."

Hamish didn't have the energy to lecture her again on proper etiquette, but after the verbal beating he'd taken in the park, he couldn't resist needling, "You're supposed to call me 'Your Grace.'"

She crossed her arms over her chest and popped out a hip, her dark eyes bright. "You look like an ass, *Your Grace*."

He chuckled, his head already pounding, reminding him he had a date with a bottle and was running late. "That's my girl," he said on his way to the study. "Truly, I treasure our time together, Camille."

"You have two letters."

Hamish waved the news away. "Later."

He'd start with the brandy and work his way through his collection by alphabetical order until he couldn't remember what letter came next.

"One is from *her*."

He stopped, a strange thrill going up his spine. "'Her' who?"

Camille produced the letters, her sneer returning. "That half-rate stagehand you call a mistress."

The thrill evaporated, leaving Hamish questioning who else he'd thought 'her' may have been. "She's the first soprano, coveted by every man in London."

"Bragging to impress me, or to remind yourself of her few accolades?" Camille snorted. "All fluff and no substance. I forgot how shallow men are—no conscience, only gratification. You'd do better with someone like Lady Charlotte. She is lovely *and* her head isn't filled with cotton. She might even add some life to this haunted mausoleum you call a home."

Hamish snatched the letters, his mood souring. "You risked her reputation and more letting her in. How would your conscience have felt then?"

The look she gave him was smug. "She would have borne it like a queen."

"How on Earth did Lady Charlotte earn such high praise? I thought there wasn't a person alive you cared for?"

"Just you, dear Hamish." She turned to leave, her words ripe with disdain. "Enjoy your letter. Let me know if you need assistance with all the misspelled words."

"No wonder you like Lady Charlotte," he grumbled. They both wielded sarcasm like a military weapon.

Even now, the sting of the lady's words left him sore. Lady Charlotte thought he didn't want her. The uncomfortable tightness in his trousers would deny that emphatically. He couldn't blame the drink this time. Before he'd grabbed her, he'd felt that stirring. That dress, the way it had come up to her neck and remained tantalizing, Hamish was horrified to realize he wasn't merely intrigued, he was attracted.

Of all the ridiculous notions, a lady of the *ton*. Unmarried, innocent . . .

No! Hamish shook himself. He'd agree with her scathing tirade of his current life; he'd grown bored was all. The lady was amusing, but a few hours more and his interest would wane like always.

With that, he opened his mistress's letter.

Dearest lover,

My bed grows cold. Come to me and bring the warmth of summer to my dreary spring.

Yours,
C

Hamish folded the letter and put it in the vest of his coat, waiting to feel more than vague interest. He had no time for flowery speeches and word games. Better a person spoke outright than resort to poetic nonsense.

His gaze caught on the second letter, the script formal.

He broke the seal, revealing the first of many obligatory invitations. "Lady Tailorman invites you to the first annual gathering of the season." The date was tomorrow evening; the invitation must have been misdirected to his country home to arrive so late.

Remembering Renard's comment about dressmakers and a ball, Hamish felt a kernel of life flare, along with the beginnings of a plan.

Forgoing his response to Miss Crim, Hamish bypassed his study and what would have been a solitary afternoon of drinking until he grew ill, and instead retrieved his hat from the entry table and opened the front door.

Camille poked her head out from an interior room and gave a disgustingly loud shout. "Where are you going?"

Thank God he'd had a mind to thin out the household to the most skeletal of staff.

"I've a date," he said.

A quick evening out and he'd scratch whatever respectable itch was impeding his designed indifference.

The coldness was unmistakable in her voice. "Use protection. Wouldn't want to catch anything sharp from the whooperup."

"Good advice." Hamish grinned, pausing one foot out the door. "My tailor can be quite the prick."

CHARLOTTE TOOK THE letter off the tray, her spirits lifting seeing her friend's tight script. "Thank you, Harper," she said. Her lady's maid curtsied, her bonnet secured around her hair with a no-nonsense knot at the nape of her neck. "Of course, my lady. Would you care to change for dinner?"

"Change?" Remembering another of society's wasteful customs of changing outfits like courses at a wedding, she shook her head and lifted the letter. "Later. I'll finish my correspondence first."

Having realized after a week as her maid that when Charlotte said, "Later," she meant not at all, Harper frowned. A permanent wrinkle had formed between the young woman's brows. An unfortunate crease on an otherwise kind face.

A mar *she'd* left.

Her excitement over her letter lessened. She reached out to Harper, the touch light, knowing a proper lady didn't show affection. "Would you set out my green gown? The one with the rosebuds. I'd like to freshen up before I dress."

Seeming to grasp the effort she'd taken with the concession, Harper didn't admonish the touch.

"I'll take it out promptly, my lady."

"Thank you."

Charlotte watched her maid retrieve the dress from the wardrobe and take pride in smoothing out the fabric on the bed before exiting the room with a soft latch of the door.

Charlotte slumped back in her chair, her reflection in the vanity like staring into the oil painting hanging over the fireplace in the library—her mother's portrait. Delicate and pale, pointed nose and narrow shoulders, both Renard and she took after her features and temperament, the similarities causing more than one uncomfortable mistake by the staff over the years.

She turned away from the mirror and the faces of those she

loved only for her gaze to fall on the dress on her bed, a dress she'd need assistance buttoning and navigating like a ship on the ocean.

Everywhere she went, she was making herself a fool. She didn't understand when to dress for dinner or which gloves were proper for which occasion. Of the hundreds of books in her father's library, not one held the secret, or practical reasons, for the specific time a lady may call on a friend or from which side of a cup a lady may drink her tea.

What did it matter?

If it hadn't been for Diana's letters, she'd surely have never left the country and been forced to learn such nonsense in excess by one of her brother's employed tutors. Perhaps she'd been too hasty running off every day and dismissing all those lessons. She *did* wish to learn the rules of society so she could break every. Single. One.

With that, Charlotte opened her letter, the familiar cramped writing setting her heart at ease.

My Lady,

Charlotte smiled, seeing how her friend had crossed out the formal greeting in lieu of a warmer one.

Charlotte dear,

I know you wished to meet. I've been remiss in calling upon you now that you are so close, but I've come down with a bit of a chill. Nothing to cause concern, but I'm afraid we must postpone our visit. As you know, my apartment is situated above the bakery off Fleet Street. And while the smell on any given day is divine, the baker's wife is far less inviting. Dreadful woman. Most discourteous to any of my guests. I would hate for you to make the trip across town, only to be turned away. Please accept my regrets. When I am feeling myself again, we shall make our mark on London together.

More importantly, how goes the hunt? I trust your visit

with the duke went according to plan? Your brother's incessant desire to play matchmaker could rival the fiercest debutante's mother. Perhaps even now you are free from the marquess's clutches and are preparing your own happily ever after. The Duke of Camine would certainly be an adventure!

If, however, the mission failed, I pray you don't lose heart. If the betrothal isn't solidified, there is time. I pray you find your happiness, dearest friend. You deserve a man who sees you for the crazy, honest, beautiful woman you are.

Your friend and conspirator,
Diana Yamsbee

Charlotte clutched the letter to her chest, tears welling. Her friend's words were straight from her own mind. Freedom, adventure—it was all she wanted. She wouldn't lose heart. How she wished to visit Diana. Fleet Street wasn't so far. But she'd respect her friend's wishes to stay away. If Diana's claims of Charlotte not being permitted were true and any sort of scene took place, someone may take note of a duke's sister visiting—by Diana's own admission—a lady of some scandalous repute. Charlotte scowled, hating society with fresh vehemence. Proper associations, proper manners, proper attire: To be proper all the time, how did the bulk of people not stop in the streets and scream at the voluntary containment? She'd never accomplish anything that way.

She eyed the high-waisted dress on her bed, the modest neckline and dull color of her usual attire the exact opposite of what she needed.

She rang for Harper, scribbling a note to Madame Lane for some last-minute alterations to her gown for the Tailormans' ball.

She sealed the letter and sent it out before her nerves overruled practical decency.

Her friend was right: The hunt would start anew. A ballroom full of gentlemen was the perfect grounds in which to select her prey.

Charlotte looked at her reflection again, her smile turning feral and completely her own.

Every good hunter needed a weapon or, in her case, a *dress* to kill.

CHAPTER SIX

THE DRESS WAS killing her. Thirty-eight hidden buttons down her side dug mercilessly into her skin without a corset. Even if she could survive the hours of back stiffness to wear the garment, her dress's design wouldn't have allowed anything underneath. Fourteen cream pearls pinched her scalp. And these slippers the modiste had raved over as the latest fashion must have been the single worst torture device known to womankind. But the pain was worth it.

Men swarmed around their small party at the entrance to the Tailormans' ballroom: young, old, and somewhere in between. Men of standing—the few she recognized upon introduction through her brother—men of less titled caliber but no less important for her needs. Renard excused himself after making formal introductions, leaving her with her none-too-helpful chaperone, Mrs. Smith—an older friend of her mama's who'd been long in the tooth and mostly deaf ten years ago—and therefore perfect chaperone. Almost at once, Mrs. Smith sat and bade Charlotte to grab her a drink before then promptly falling asleep, so instead of making her way to the punch table, Charlotte surveyed her pool of prey with blurry but exacting eyes.

Now to narrow down the search.

Her man must be a gentleman of decent character, a man who'd keep his word, and hands, to himself past the necessary. A man who didn't thrive on scandal but could weather the gossip as well. A man who could teach her some of the less accessible things on her list wouldn't hurt, either.

Lord Berstein was a self-proclaimed master swordsman, though the lack of calluses said he rarely took up the practice. His companion, a Mr. Remington, claimed no joy of the sport—no joy whatsoever as far as the man's solemn expression and hunched shoulders conveyed—and since she wished to learn fencing and not how to stand erect while looking bored with a sword in hand, the man excluded himself from the list of potentials.

Scrutinizing the other gentlemen a step farther away—and therefore less blurry—that took Mr. Hamshere and Lord Fairborne and their severe frowns out of the running too.

Upon inquiries, the three other men in their group admitted an elementary education in the art, though the tallest of the three—she hadn't caught his name—did say he was an avid huntsman. Number seven was as good as crossed off her list. But the man's merit was quickly stricken from the record when his hand wandered south of the small of her back.

Charlotte found that the torture of her slippers could be shared with a discreet stomping of one's foot on another.

As the tall man winced and found his distance, Charlotte thought of another tall man, dark and mysterious, a man who wouldn't need to touch her to set her blood on fire.

He wouldn't be here. The Duke of Camine's idea of a productive night included heavy drinking and insulting young women too unworldly to tempt his fancy.

And yet she couldn't help but scan for his broad frame amongst the milling numbers of gentlemen in the crowd. She bet he was an expert with the sword, and pistol, and other, more mysterious weapons one used for more sordid hunting.

Charlotte jabbed at her side until the pain of the buttons pushed thoughts of Camine from her mind. Wishing for a man who'd rejected her, twice, wouldn't secure her future. A part of her may have taken extra care with her appearance tonight, imagining the scandalous Duke of Camine struck dumb by her bold transformation. But the end result was for her and her alone.

Number six: Be more complicated. *Be bold.*

Red dresses and low necklines were only the beginning.

"I *am* bold."

"What was that, Lady Charlotte?" one of the men asked.

She glanced over her gathered party. What would these men think of her plans to lure one of them into a sordid position and then disappear into the world a free woman? Most of the men wouldn't mind, it seemed, as they pressed closer, full of inquiries of her person and family.

Others, those genuinely searching for a proper wife, would run for the hills given privy to her inner thoughts. A woman wishing for independence? Disgraceful!

Turning to one of the lords—an older man known for his outspokenness when it came to women's rights—she knew which of those fools she'd cull from the herd first.

"Now, Lord Fairborne . . ." She pulled him aside and spoke softly so only he could hear. "I've always thought a woman should have the choice whether or not to exercise her marital rights, despite her husband's wishes. Any thoughts?"

The man made a most ungracious sound through his nose and continued to fall into a coughing fit before excusing himself from their party.

She watched the man retreat and hid a smile behind her hand, knowing should the others see, they'd witness a feral slash of teeth of a predator out for blood.

HAMISH STOOD INSIDE the Tailormans' ballroom, the years spent avoiding the *ton* rushing back in an unpleasant scene of catch and release as debutantes came in shoals in their elaborate skirts and bustles to snare unsuspecting bachelors into forgoing their freedom, wealth, and ultimately, life as they knew it.

Hamish eyed the most recent barrel of poor bastards too young and skirt-struck to see the hooks digging in.

He'd arrived late, forgetting that on time was early and everything after remained fashionable, leaving him spinning in a whirlpool of introductions from every angle. After a quarter of an hour, he'd escaped to the ballroom.

Hundreds of candles hung above, their light reflected in the polished floor below. Wax dripped precariously off the edge of the chandeliers, catching fortunate men in the thick padding of their evening coats, and not-so-fortunately on the bare shoulders of more than one lady.

His gaze darted around the room, searching for pale hair. One quick conversation and he could return home, before another lady grew bold and cast a line his way.

Imagining idle chatter over weather and which invitation was most coveted this season, Hamish shuddered and doubled his efforts when a hand clapped him on the back.

"The 'wild' duke, unbelievable!"

Hamish flinched at the moniker, returning the man's greeting without any of the warmth. "Mr. Pendor."

"You look fit, my boy. Keeping well in this unseasonable warm spell? It isn't good for the body when the weather takes such a drastic turn."

Hamish gritted his teeth. "Well enough."

The older man was an acquaintance of the late Duke of Camine and a good two heads shorter, leaving Hamish's neck at a harsh angle to look the man in his ruddy-complexioned face. A headache was forming above Hamish's right eye, the first of many if the mundane conversations continued, though the irritant to his head could well have been the clash of the lime-green vest Mr. Pendor wore over a daffodil-yellow shirt. Hamish resorted to counting the hairs on the man's head as a distraction, all ten of them.

The bite in his words went unnoticed by the older man. "Of

course you are. Of course you are." The man clapped him on the back a second time.

The smell of liquor stung Hamish's eyes. He looked towards the library, interested in his own vice to dull what was shaping into an excruciating evening. "If you'll excuse me—"

"Sorry to hear about your father." Mr. Pendor's mouth turned down at the edges. "He was a good man. Now that he's gone you must take his place at the club. A generous line of credit included, of course."

Hamish pulled away from the man's grasp. "I appreciate the offer, but—"

"'Course that scandal put a damper on some of the boys at the table, but that'll blow over soon enough."

Hamish stiffened. Drink forgotten, his words sharpened to razor edges. "Always another scandal on the horizon."

"That's the spirit!" Mr. Pendor laughed, his jowl swinging. "Not to worry. Not to worry. With that creature's circumstances, that bastard will be lying in the gutter before winter." He elbowed Hamish, conspiratorially whispering, "Then it'll be a problem for the coroner."

It was to the man's benefit there was a room full of witnesses or Hamish might've been tempted to inconvenience the coroner yet this evening. Reining his temper, he said, "I have no intention of following in my father's business, private or otherwise."

Mr. Pendor's face fell, seeming to finally notice his companion's lack of humor. "After you've taken some time, I'm sure you'll feel differently. Your father—"

"My *father* was a right bastard," Hamish ground out. "The only thing the man gave society was a love of drink and a weak liver. Good evening, Mr. Pendor."

He left the man slack-jawed and staring.

Hamish's rage hummed in his veins. The previous Duke of Camine had been well thought of in society, charitable and generous. A man for the peerage.

To his son, he'd been as hard and cold as granite, and just as attentive. When it had come out a year ago that the scrupulous duke had been floundering with another woman for two decades and sired a bastard child near the same age as Hamish, his mother, the Duchess of Camine, hadn't survived the shame.

She'd sequestered herself in the country and faded away in a matter of weeks.

If Hamish had gotten half the devotion from his mother as she'd given his father, he might have mourned. As justice had it, his father had succumbed to a long-standing liver complaint less than a fortnight later, subsequently leaving Hamish with five properties and a tarnished title at the age of three and twenty.

A flash of blonde hair had him shuffling through the crowd, a rare sense of excitement pulling the corner of his mouth into a lazy grin and, with it, wiping away the past.

He imagined Lady Charlotte in another high-collared dress, her body hidden and unnoticed by everyone but him. How her eyes would widen at his suit, cut and lined to showcase his tall frame. She'd look up at him, young and innocent, and he'd know immediately how foolish he'd been.

His grin turned into a smile. He might still salvage this evening with Miss Crim and a stiff . . . drink.

The crowd parted, and she was before him.

Hamish misstepped.

Gone was the mousy blonde with her drab dress and pursed lips. Her hair had been teased into a mass of curls on top of her head, the white jewels at her ears giving the impression of a sea of starlight ending in shooting stars. And her dress . . . Whoever had constructed the deep-V back and swooping neckline to reveal expanses of flawless skin against the red silk should be hanged . . . or given a dukedom. What the bloody hell was wrong with Renard, letting her dress like that? Did the man not have eyes?

Lady Charlotte glanced at him, glasses gone and emerald eyes flashing. She turned back to her gentleman companion as if Hamish were nothing of note.

It was then Hamish realized the lady's transformation hadn't gone unnoticed. Half a dozen young men hung on her every word—dandies to damn fortune hunters in their unpolished boots—and had been for some time if the plethora of glares from the other ladies in the room were any indication.

One of the men handed Lady Charlotte a drink, a lad in a well-cut coat in the most grotesque shade of puce—dandy, then—his hand resting on her elbow much longer than necessary, her *bare* elbow. A risqué dress was one thing. For Renard to allow his sister to go without gloves . . . but he wouldn't. Sure enough, as Lady Charlotte turned to accept the drink, something white peeked out of a pocket in her skirts. The lady must have stripped the gloves off the minute Renard's back had been turned. Hamish smirked. Even at a ball, the lady couldn't be bothered with propriety.

She turned a dazzling smile on the dandy before taking a sip, a quick laugh escaping her as the bubbles tickled her nose.

Something dark twisted in Hamish's gut. He was across the space in an instant, displacing the little fish with a superior frame, title, and the air of a man itching for a fight.

He removed the offending, over-ringed hand from her arm and replaced it with his own, the bare flesh of her elbow sizzling through his glove. He pulled her close, smelling her fresh scent, seeing the delicate pearls woven into her hair, until their noses were inches apart and all he saw were those eyes of green fire.

"Dance with me."

Lady Charlotte startled and squinted into his face. "Ham—Duke?" She corrected herself. Was that a note of relief in her voice? She smiled and whispered so only he could hear, "Let me go, or I will dump this drink on your head."

Her gaze locked with his, and Hamish knew a moment of weightlessness. If he'd had a clear head, he would've realized his mistake in approaching her, in laying claim in a room full of the keenest eyes and ears for gossip in the world.

His head wasn't clear, and he did not let go.

One of the braver minnows stepped forward. "Now see here.

The lady promised the next dance to me—"

"Hold this." Hamish plucked the drink from her fingers and shoved it into the man's hands before tugging Lady Charlotte towards the dance floor.

Not risking a scene, the lady allowed herself to be led out of the crowd and out of earshot before she whirled on him. "How dare you?!"

He leaned in, her lovely scent filling him with images of a lazy summer day in bed. "I dare, my lady." He tugged her again. "Come."

They stepped onto the dance floor, the previous song ending.

She ripped her arm away. "I won't be led like some dog. You said you weren't interested, so stop getting in my way."

Hamish glanced over the top of her head at the six outmaneuvered dandies grumbling in the wings. "You said you wished to learn to dance."

That stopped her short. For a second.

"You presume too much. Release me at once."

"Not a chance."

How expressive her face without glasses to hide the murderous look in her eyes. "You are a brute! A bloody, brooding, black-hearted bear."

"Please, you'll make me blush, Lady Charlotte."

Hamish grabbed her about the waist and drew her close before her scathing insults turned him into a burning, big-cocked bear. Poor plan on his part when he felt the delicious muscles in her back without a corset to interfere.

Forgoing undergarments at a formal ball. The lady never failed to scandalize.

Regaining her composure, she jabbed him firmly in the ribs. "Unhand me."

The music began, a lively melody with harmony made for long sweeps and solidifying his win this round.

"Must I?" He grinned down at her as his hand slid down her arm to claim her bare hand. "I do believe it's a waltz."

"WHAT ARE YOU doing?" Charlotte clutched his shoulder, the first sweeping step sending a wave of vertigo over her. "I'll fall. I-I can't see."

Their steps slowed but didn't stop.

"Where are your glasses?" he asked.

She looked away. "In the carriage." She hadn't wanted them on, knowing men preferred a fresh face. Plus, the lack of definition in all those faces had greatly lessened her nerves. She wouldn't have a clue if one of those gentlemen stopped her in the street.

The duke *tsked*. "I'll have someone retrieve them. Where is your chaperone?"

Fighting another dizzy spell, she indicated the corner chair where the blurred image of the ancient woman her brother had engaged snoozed, not caring a fig for the ball or her charge after five minutes of standing.

Snorting, the duke said, "I must have a word with Renard. Clearly, a woman born at the time of Adam isn't up to the task of accompanying a young woman."

Hiding her grin, she said, "How unkind. The dear is younger than Noah at least."

She wished for her glasses then so she could see the expression on his face when his head whipped around.

There was a smile in his voice. "How about a compromise? Methuselah?"

What about that? The brooding bear *did* have a sense of humor. She pursed her lips as if mulling it over. "Agreed."

He swept her around again.

Charlotte's stomach dropped, and she clutched his shoulder tighter. "Please!"

His arms tightened around her. "Lean into me. Yes, like that. Let me show you."

A voice inside rebelled at the call to submit, so like her brother's domineering attitude. She squinted at his face. Even with her fuzzy vision, somehow, his eyes were clear.

He seemed to see her inner conflict because he drew back. "Your decision."

He wasn't pushing, she thought. He offered direction, experience. A chance to learn without fear of shame or ridicule.

His brows rose in challenge. "How about it, mouse?"

A smile spread her mouth, along with a false confidence she grudgingly attributed with the blur of a man before her. She resituated her arms, imitating the other women dancing around them. "Try to keep up."

His chuckle warmed the air between them, the little there was of it.

"Let go," he whispered. "I've got you."

Lulled by his rich voice, she allowed the music, and the man, to sweep her into a series of steps and bobs, the only way she could describe the alternating long and short strides. The other dance partners vanished around them, and they were flying.

A light pressure to her waist and he spun her in a whirlwind of skirts.

Charlotte let out a joyous cry, completely lost in the moment.

She returned to his arms, and his voice was a rough purr in her ear.

"Be careful, my lady. You'll have every gentleman from here to Scotland begging for a dance."

She was breathless when she replied, "I've always wanted to see a man in a kilt." Though the burly, bearded Scotsman fantasy had given way to a tall, dark-haired man with eyes the color of a summer sky.

"Have you?"

Was he smiling again? "Number one hundred and nine," she said.

"You've added to it." *Definitely* a smile. "How many now?"

"Two hundred and three." And counting.

"You've been busy."

His voice was sin, that velvety tone easing the secrets from her like fabric on skin.

"What is the last on the list? Fencing? Polo?"

Heat flamed her cheeks, and the Tailormans' family crest painted on the floor was a boon from the fierceness of his gaze. "Kiss a man."

He snorted. "It wounds my ego to point out, but I *am a man*, Lady Charlotte. You can mark that particular item complete."

"No." She shook her head, the heat reaching the tips of her ears. "*You* kissed *me*." She licked her lips. "*I wish to initiate the kissing.*"

A shock went through his body, radiating across them and through her hands.

Ridiculous and unladylike, but the confession was true and freeing and an apology would be a blatant lie.

He let out a long breath, his body somehow remaining tense. "I see."

One ... two ... "That's all? No speech on impropriety?" Renard would've had her bound and gagged for the convent by now.

He laughed. "I suffer from the Devil's reputation, not hypocrisy."

"Some would say the reputation is a worse offense." Though most people were idiots.

The tension of his arms loosened. When he replied, his voice was too quiet. "I know."

She wanted to ask what he meant, but the music slowed; the dance was ending. She dug her fingers into his shoulder as if she could hold the moment in place. The music swelled, the last note fading.

They pulled apart and applauded the orchestra before Charlotte curtsied. "Thank you for the dance, Your Grace. I'll never forget it."

And she wouldn't. For a moment, she'd felt free. No, *been*

free, sweeping through the bars of her cage as if they were smoke, and the Duke of Camine had danced right alongside her.

"Lord Camine dancing?"

Charlotte whirled around at the disapproving tone of her brother. Even half-blind, she saw the scowl on his face.

"I assure you," Renard said, glancing at the duke. "No one will forget."

CHAPTER SEVEN

HAMISH TURNED TO his friend, pasting a bland expression on his face. His head was whirling, and it had nothing to do with the dance. Lady Charlotte had been a dream in his arms, giving herself completely to him. He'd been content, a sliver of his mind rationalizing that his growing fondness for her was like that of a sibling. They'd be friends.

And then she'd laughed.

Chesty, musical, it wasn't the laugh of a young girl. It was the siren song of a woman.

Hamish had reacted immediately, closing the distance between them to answer that call like a sailor drawn to the inky depths of the sea. At the last minute, he'd caught himself and whispered a warning in her ear.

There would be no friendship. There would be nothing. And as soon as he got the hell away from her, maybe he'd believe it himself.

"Kiss a man."

The woman wanted to experience life with no borders around what a lady should or shouldn't try. Their first kiss had been his brutish way of intimidating her with his expertise, intimidation that hadn't worked. The idea of the lady taking the reins had a delicious appeal all its own.

Renard's disapproval was clear.

Hamish smiled. "Did I embarrass myself terribly?"

Renard returned the smile, all teeth. "Not at all. I'm so thankful you could keep my sister company while I was away."

The anger in his eyes had Hamish smiling for real. They'd have words—more likely fists—and he would welcome the release of agitated energy. "Don't mention it."

It was then, Hamish noticed the other gentleman beside Renard. Young, blond, and clinking the chain of his pocket watch against his vest and fixing his blue eyes on Charlotte. A sinking feeling started in his chest as he recognized Lord Gunther Flarborn.

Renard turned to his sister. "Lord Slasbury, may I present my sister, Lady Charlotte Louis. Charlotte, this is the Marquess of Slasbury."

Hamish watched the introduction as if behind glass.

Charlotte's eyes lit with recognition while the marquess's trailed over her with a boldness that had Hamish grinding his teeth.

Over my corpse.

Hamish jerked away. Where the hell had that thought come from?

The orchestra struck up a spirited polka in opposition to the tension in the air.

The marquess bowed and held out a hand to her. "Would you care to dance, Lady Charlotte? I'm not as skilled as the duke, but I make up for my experience with sheer clumsiness."

Charlotte laughed at the idiot and placed her hand—her still *bare* hand—in his. "I'd be honored."

Hamish saw red. "I need a drink," he blurted.

The trio startled, and Hamish headed towards Lord Tailorman's study without farewell.

He heard Renard behind him. "I'll join you."

THE STUDY DOOR shut, and Hamish thanked God the other

gentlemen hadn't yet found their way to the study for drinking and smoking.

A fresh bin of wood and tinder lay piled up in the hearth as if a maid had built up the logs and forgotten to light it before rushing off to perform other duties. The mantel itself was polish and sturdy, a pillar of manly intent, except for the white doilies blanketing the shelf above like a lacy shawl thrown over a perfectly fertile man.

Women would turn them all into pinned and stuffed cushions if given the chance.

Renard opened and shut the door behind Hamish, quick on his heels. "Care to tell me what the hell you were doing?"

Having a mild case of severance from reality, Hamish thought. Dancing, jealousy—that nasty emotion he'd felt in his gut when the marquess had touched Charlotte—perhaps he suffered from the same liver affliction as his father. He'd make an appointment with his physician tomorrow.

He felt Renard's growing agitation as the silence stretched.

Hamish sighed and fell into his usual easy grin. "Saving the lady from a horde of young men. Something that fossil of a chaperone had no interest in doing."

Renard glanced around as if he expected the woman to protest from the ballroom. He frowned. "Young men?" His eyes bugged. "Charlotte was conversing?"

Hamish selected a cigar from Lord Tailorman's box. "Shocking, isn't it?" The irritation in his voice was genuine. He clipped the end of the cigar and struck a stick match, burning the end before tossing it into the cold hearth. The tinder caught and a healthy red glow grew as flames licked the sides of dry wood. "You're welcome."

Renard ran a hand over his face, bypassing the smoke as usual and going straight for the whiskey.

Hamish cocked a brow. "Rough night already?"

"I need something for my nerves." He stared into the hearth. "Young men?" He turned and leaned against the mantel. "What the hell am I doing? I'm not our father."

Hamish chuckled. "Better yours than mine."

"She used to bring me bugs in a jar, dozens of them every other day. Our housekeeper threatened to walk out after she misplaced a bundle of worms in a dress pocket." He grinned and took a sip, his shoulders slumping. "She's a woman now, willful, stubborn. She doesn't want me messing with her life."

Hamish clapped him on the back. "Buck up, Ren. She'll always need a brother intent on giving unsolicited advice."

Renard snorted. "Be thankful you're an only child."

The instant guilt stung. He'd missed Renard while he'd been away in the country, never staying in the city long enough over the past year to get into any real mischief, or to be better informed by the ever-wagging tongues of the *ton*.

Hamish looked at his friend, his grin crooked. "About that."

Renard glanced at him. "Eh?"

Hamish shrugged. "I have a sister."

THE MARQUESS HADN'T lied when he'd said he was clumsy.

After catching her slipper on a wrong step, and a twirl knocking them into another couple down the line, Charlotte knew the bruises she'd have tomorrow would send her lady's maid into a fit. At least the need to focus on every step kept the spinning at bay.

Despite all that, the marquess was not bad company. The quiet and blank-faced gentleman she'd met last summer at a neighbor's country garden party was nowhere to be found.

Charming, self-deprecating, Lord Gunther Flarborn was anything but a drooling pup. That still didn't mean Charlotte was keen to become his personal property.

"You're looking at me like I have two heads, Lady Charlotte," he said.

Charlotte shook herself. She had been staring. "Forgive me, Lord Slasbury. It's only the second time I've danced, and I find clearing away my thoughts is less likely to cause a collision."

He winced, glancing at the couple next to them and seeing how they eyed their movements, waiting to dive out of the way if she and the marquess made another miscalculated twirl.

"Alas." He sighed. "I've danced the quadrille dozens of times and have no excuse."

She smiled, her misguided assessment of him making her charitable. "As the novice, I take full responsibility for any missteps."

"So kind." He shook his head, his smirk boyish. "But I cannot allow a lady to take the blame. I'm hopeless." He raised his voice for the couples closest to hear. "Hopeless dancing, I admit it."

Charlotte laughed. "At this rate, we'll never decide who's worse. We should call it even and stop tempting fate, else she will intervene, and we take out the orchestra next."

He grinned. "A most practical solution. I submit. We're both hopeless."

His humor was contagious.

Charlotte watched his eyes and mouth, the lines speaking volumes of a man used to laughing and, clearly, making others laugh. "I must apologize to you, my lord."

"What's this?" he asked. "Truly, your trampling of my feet was most endearing."

She smiled and shook her head. "I made a snap judgement of you at a previous engagement. A wrong judgement."

His brows rose. "That I'm a roguishly handsome man with a rapier wit?"

She cringed. "I likened you to a dog with an overactive salivary gland."

A hard look flashed over his face before it smoothed into that eye-crinkling smile, making Charlotte wonder if she'd imagined it.

His hand went to the chain on his vest without him seeming

to realize. "Which engagement?" he asked.

"The Quickners' garden party last summer."

His eyes lit with recognition. "Ah. I'd had a disagreement with a friend early in the morning and was in a frightful mood the rest of the day." He continued quickly. "Of course, that's no excuse." The music came to a merciful end and the marquess bowed low. "It is far too late for any redemption, but my deepest apologies for an inexcusable first impression, Lady Charlotte. I beg your forgiveness."

His sincerity softened the tension in her chest. "I suppose I must," she said. "I'm the last person who should hold a grudge over a poor impression."

"Thank you, my lady." He looked up at her through blond lashes, his gaze flicking to something over her shoulder. His jaw clenched before he came back to her. "Might I correct the impression further with a visit next week? I've a new tea I brought home from my travels."

Confused at his expression change, Charlotte battled a wave of uneasiness and responded on reflex. "That would be lovely."

He took her hand and paused, as if noticing her bare skin. Gaze flicking to her face, his lips stretched to reveal a slash of teeth. He kissed her knuckles without breaking eye contact. "Until next week, my lady."

Her stomach flipped at the hot breath against her skin. How she wished she'd kept her gloves on. Too late to back out now, she confirmed, "Next week."

CHAPTER EIGHT

RENARD STARED AT him. "You have a sister?"

Hamish smiled at his friend's gaping mouth. "You look like a caught trout."

His mouth snapped shut, only to open two seconds later. "Since when?"

Sighing, Hamish prepared for a multitude of questions, and the unpleasant story to follow. "Twenty years or so now. Caught in the act a year ago."

"Twenty years! Not Helen?"

Hamish grinned. In private, Renard had always referred to Hamish's parents by their given names, the same way Hamish had called the Duchess of Lux "Mother" before she'd passed, upon Lady Lux's insistence.

His humor was answer enough for his friend.

"No, I see. The other one, then." Renard sneered, referencing Hamish's father. "Does she have horns and a tail, the Great Devil's mark on her forehead? I may start reading the papers again, if only to see the caricatures."

"Worse," Hamish said. "She's attractive, intelligent, and sarcastic."

"Sisters!" It sounded like a curse. "What happened to her? He must've set up something for the girl if he'd dedicated two decades to her mother."

The anger Hamish had worked to suppress resurfaced, this

time directed at the dead. "None. Once the *ton* shouted her existence from every news's post from here to Bristol, he cut ties, leaving the mistress destitute and the girl to keep the bill collectors at bay alone."

"You intervened, I take it?"

"The best I could." Hamish flinched at the memory of a pair of shoes coming straight at his head. "My efforts weren't appreciated. I tried to set her up in a flat, but she wouldn't hear of it. Refused to be a 'kept woman,' as she put it. She came around eventually to take a job I set up for her, but not before I was clobbered with a lady's boot."

Renard laughed. "Sounds like my kind of woman."

Hamish glared at his friend, only half-joking when he said, "Stay away from my sister, Ren, or I'll have a pair of boots permanently rammed up your arse."

Humor restored, Renard returned the glare with a tight smile. "Same here, Hamish."

Topic back on Charlotte, Hamish scowled and took a pull of his cigar as he bit out, "She seemed taken with the marquess. Looks like your troubles marrying her off are over."

"Your words to His ears." Renard crossed himself. "By this time next year, there'll be a wedding at Lux estate, and we'll be toasting my lack of responsibilities."

This time of year, the white roses and philadelphuses would be near blooming, the perfect color to set off a woman with hair the color of corn silk. She'd wear a simple dress, her hair swept back, and easily prove the most beautiful bride of the decade.

Her children would have pale features, fiery eyes like Charlotte's, and a long nose like their father's.

The marquess was a lucky man.

For some reason, the idea made Hamish want to break bones. No rules, no mercy, the more blood, the better, broken nose required.

"Well?" Renard said. "Aren't you going to congratulate me? We'll be back to our reckless ways in no time."

Drinking, women, gambling their fortunes away or, in Hamish's case, doubling his money drunk or not, a woman on each knee. The idea didn't elicit anything but boredom.

"Congratulations," he grumbled. He glanced at the amber liquid in the decanter, weighing the consequences of a glass on an empty stomach.

The door to the study opened, flooding the dim room with brilliant candlelight from the hall.

Percy, Hamish's personal runner and bruiser, poked his head in, unkempt black curls swinging into his face.

He saw Hamish and the relief on the man's pale face shouted the man's disdain for social gatherings. "Thank the good Lord," he said.

He stepped inside, spotted Renard against the mantel and bowed. "Your Grace, it's been a while."

Renard startled. "Percy? My God, how did you get in here?"

Taking in the man's fine liveries in place of his usual nondescript moleskin, Hamish guessed one of Lord Tailorman's servants was missing a uniform.

"Were you seen?" Hamish asked.

Percy grinned. "I served a lovely young lady refreshments."

Hamish shook his head, his confidence in his man's ability to move freely without detection absolute. "This couldn't wait until I returned home?"

Percy shrugged, a slight, metal sound telling Hamish he hadn't come unarmed. "When have you known me to miss a party?"

Hamish and Renard replied together, "Always."

A letter appeared in Percy's hands as he chuckled.

Hamish took the letter and broke the seal. A heavy piece of cardstock had three words written in a cramped script that Hamish recognized immediately.

I have returned.

G.

At last.

"Any complications?" he asked.

"A bit of a skirmish at the docks," Percy said. "Nothing I couldn't handle."

Sailors were a rowdy and unpredictable bunch at sea and on land. Gregori must've been in his own personal hell.

Renard glanced over his shoulder. "Problems?"

"Not at all." Hamish smiled, mood lifting. Finally, he'd have something worthwhile to occupy his time and distract him from recent revelations.

Noticing his friend's sharp mood change, Renard rolled his eyes and went back to his drink. "Only one person makes you light up like a kid on Yule's Day."

Hamish was halfway out the door with Percy on his heels when Renard called out, "Give my regards to the crackpot, won't you?"

GREGORI'S MIND WORKED on another plane of reasoning. Gears and genius where others saw a young man in need of a shave.

Hamish saw a man part machine, his personality nothing but clinical and cool calculation in juxtaposition to the squirrel-like necessity to pack bits of scrap metal and cogged clock wheels in every corner, cranny, and nook available.

Ramming his toe into an indecipherable lump of metal—beside a second nondescript bit of twisted wire, but across from the vaguely shaped triangle of barbed steel that lined a narrow path of open oak floor—Hamish cursed.

"You're late," Gregori said, not bothering to look up from the contraption in his hands.

Hamish snorted. Gruff greetings were commonplace, and he rarely took the man's shortness in offense. The unshaved face and spattering of oil all over the young man's sleeves, however, were enough to make Hamish smooth his own striped shirt, a newly bought disguise from the readymade shop down the road. "We didn't set a time."

The other man waved his excuse away. "Punctuality is a gentleman's privilege, not mine."

"Then time is irrelevant," Hamish said.

Gregori's head popped up. He watched Hamish for a moment, as if he'd said something infinitely profound. "Just so."

He set down what looked like a box of glass slides on one of the many tables spread throughout the space, his expression changing to business. "I've seen the new formula. The design is flawed but has potential. If left as is, we'd still make a fortune. The 'inhabitants' won't know the difference in quality."

Referring to the multitude of immigrants overcrowding the rookeries, and the people who'd make up most of their clientele, Hamish frowned. "Can you improve the formula?"

Gregori's mouth quirked. "I knew you'd say that. Come."

Hamish followed the smaller man to a far corner, picking his way carefully around piles—some as tall as himself—of bric-a-brac and stopped at what looked like a large machine hidden beneath a grey cover.

For dramatic effect or keeping the space dust-free, Hamish could only guess. Gregori was an unpredictable man, driven by logic, but not without a sense of humor.

Hamish suspected the former reason for the covering when Gregori whipped the fabric away with a flourish.

"Huzzah!"

Stepping close, Hamish recognized little. There was a miniature crucible for a forge and bags of ground substances he knew Gregori would combine to make a flawless product. Everything else looked like tools one would find in a coroner's office.

Impatient, Gregori named the various tools that *sounded* like they belonged in a coroner's office and rushed on. "I'm missing the last ingredient."

He handed Hamish a formula that he couldn't make letters or

numbers of.

"Is it hard to come by?" he asked.

"Not in its raw form. I could make the grit from scratch, but it will take time we don't have. There's a facility in Virginia that has a reputation. Comes over by the barrel."

Hamish's mind whirled, calculating numbers and contracts automatically in preparation for the next phase. Shipments from America took weeks, if not longer, depending on weather and crew. But captains could always be persuaded to look the other way if a crate or two never made it to an original buyer. Speed was of the essence, but if he were to overtake the market, he'd need a product of the purest quality. Good thing he'd memorized the charters of the Atlantic crossing ships.

"There's a ship due to port in the next few days." If the product was as common as Gregori had said, there'd be stock to spare. "How soon until production?"

"Couple of weeks, less if you can find a man with half a brain to get the shipment on time."

Hamish nodded. "I'll have Percy take point. You'll have your grit by week's end." He'd have to pay a small fortune in bribes, but the shipyard master was a widower whose gratitude kept his mouth firmly shut.

Gregori scrunched his nose. "You're more likely to gain a visit from Scotland Yard than the docks with that one."

As if by magic, Percy materialized in the doorway, servant's uniform gone, replaced with a dark coat and a flat cap pulled low to cover a shock of midnight hair. He'd entered silently, the various pockets in his coat no doubt full of any number of weapons.

Hamish was grateful, not for the first time, that the man owed him a debt worth more than his life, and not the other way around.

"Come now, Greg," Percy said, "we all know the 'bobbies' have little interest in East End now their new building is done. Besides, you've never complained about my results before."

Gregori eyed the man, his hands twitching as if to snatch the tools away from thieving hands. "Your *methods* are another story."

Percy cracked his knuckles one by one. "Are you still sore about that bump on your head from that little noise at landing? Truly, friend, I got there as quick as I could."

Gregori's eyes narrowed into slits. "I bet you hired those ruffians as a sick welcome party."

Percy smiled. "That's an idea for next time."

Hamish stepped between the two, his gaze zeroing in on where Gregori fingered the back of his head. "You were harmed?" Had his competitors realized the object of Gregori's visit?

He whirled on Percy. "Were they Hamel's men? Spies tailed from India?"

"Hardly," Percy said, nostrils flaring. "A couple of inexperienced pickpockets in over their heads." He jerked his chin towards Gregori. "When the genius here noticed a thread pulled out of place, the kids freaked and got physical. Of course, compared to our foreign damsel here, I'm sure starving street urchins *are* quite terrifying."

Gregori's color was high, but his expression was smug. "Strange how a couple of 'starving urchins' managed to escape your clutches."

Percy rubbed the stubble on his chin, a challenge in his eye. "Can you even perfect the grade without compromising the application?"

Gregori smiled. "Better than I can load the Enfield strapped to your ankle."

Percy's brow cocked. "Touché."

"If you two are done?" Hamish interjected, relieved. "I've other business to discuss with both of you."

At the prospect of a new project, Gregori brightened. "Another trip?"

Pulling the list from inside his coat, Hamish grinned. "Itching to leave already? I've a list I want finished in two days." He rattled off the first three items, finishing with a more complicated request from a man of exacting taste.

"Those are basic," Gregori complained. "You can find the cheap stuff in an apothecary or hack doctor's office. Why waste my time?"

"I have specifications, and I need a man who can get the batch right the first time. Besides . . ." Hamish's look was hard. "We have an arrangement."

Gregori huffed and took the list, scanning the notes and nodding. "*Three* days. Pick them up here. I'll have a preliminary batch for you to sample by then as well . . . if the cutthroat can do as he's told."

Percy blew the other man a kiss.

Hamish tipped his hat to the inventor, but the other man waved off his show of respect, nothing else mattering with work to be done.

Hamish turned to Percy. "Walk with me."

Percy followed out the door, calling a farewell, "Good day, genius. Don't forget to eat."

The responding call echoed, "Keep both eyes open when you shoot."

Hamish shook his head. He could never tell if the two men hated each other or not.

They reached the nondescript, black carriage around back, his means of transport when dealing with his private investments. "I need you to look into a gentleman for me."

Percy patted his breast pocket, which jangled with a telltale metal sound. "Look into?"

"Information only. Contacts, mistresses, vices, debts."

"Anything in particular I'm looking for?"

"No."

Percy's cool demeanor cracked with surprise. "What's the interest?"

"It's a favor for a lady."

Percy grinned. "What's the name?"

Hamish hesitated, second-guessing his intentions for the twelfth time. It wasn't for the lady's safety alone, he told himself, but also to assuage his friend's anxieties. "His name is Gunther Flarborn, Marquess of Slasbury."

CHAPTER NINE

THE NEXT FEW days went by in an appalling bout of rain. Charlotte sat at her vanity, the simply adorned mirror reflecting the water-streaked windows while she reflected yet again on her conversation with the Marquess of Slasbury.

The minute he'd left her side at the ball, a sense of anxiety had birthed in her gut. With next week looming closer, and with it the marquess's forecasted visit, that feeling grew. There'd been a moment when he'd kissed her hand, when Charlotte could only describe the man's expression and touch as *unsettling* . . . No, the man's reaction to her lack of gloves had been understandable. The gentleman had been well-mannered—amusing, even. Simply amusing wouldn't do. She wanted a man with the devil in his eyes and a touch that set her heart racing.

Tea was a terrible decision. Pretty manners and charming smile aside, marriage to a gentleman came with a shopping list of expectations and limitations too exacting for any woman interested in keeping her identity. Once the vows were spoken, the trap would latch closed.

Marriage didn't sound all bad: children's laughter, the security of her own home. But the husband who came with it needed an adventurous spirit to match her own.

And not be threatened by it.

Ice-blue eyes and a certain gentleman's wicked smile popped into her head. Finding another man to ruin her reputation wasn't the problem. The problem was she liked the one she'd found.

She glanced at the papers on the table, the pages folded and refolded so many times, the ink was faded at the creases. She'd added to her list since that night in the Duke of Camine's study. Goals, dreams, adventures—a list of a life worth living.

If society had their way, she'd never experience anything aside from matrimony.

A light knock predated her maid's voice. "My lady, are you awake?"

"For hours," she wanted to reply. As if only servants and sailors got up at dawn. Her sour mood sweetened with the beginning of an idea. "Come in, Harper."

Her maid opened the door, a tray of tea and a light breakfast in her hands. Harper's sharp gaze landed on the four-poster bed, already made, and then shifted to her mistress, already clothed in a simple grey day dress, disapproval deepening the crease between her brows.

Charlotte cringed. "I know you told me not to. It's just . . ." She waved her hand to encompass the dark floors and pink, floral curtains. "In the country, I took it upon myself to do simple chores to build up my strength. I find it hard breaking the habit."

Mention of her long-standing weak health seemed to soften her maid. "I understand," she said. "If it is that great a comfort, I can ring for several more dresses like that one so you may feel productive. *Only* to wear around the house, of course."

Charlotte's gratitude was genuine. "Thank you, Harper. That would be a great comfort." Dressing without help meant easier escapes in the future. Which brought her to her next question. "Harper, what do you know of sailors?"

"Sailors!" Harper jolted, and the teacup rattled on the saucer she set before Charlotte. She cleared her throat and set the cup to rights. "They are a brutish, dangerous bunch, infesting Dockside with their wildness. Cursing and drinking with a commonality far beneath a well-bred lady." She glanced at her, her reprimanding frown back. "And far too improper for *anyone.*"

Charlotte squashed her inner glee and replied with a bland expression, "I see. That is unfortunate."

Harper looked unconvinced. "Would you care for breakfast, my lady?" She uncovered a plate filled with her favorites. "Eggs, toast, and marmalade."

Charlotte's stomach growled on cue. She accepted the tray, prepared to eat the plate clean. For what she had planned, she didn't know the next time she'd get a warm meal.

CHARLOTTE FOUND HER brother in the library.

His legs swung over the arm of a leather chair in a carefree manner that reminded her of when they'd been children. His usual drink within reach, he sat reading a recent publication titled, *Understanding a Young Lady and the Feminine Mind.*

She glanced over his shoulder, reading a passage.

"A woman's need for constant attention means a man must keep a firm hand, else she fall into a state of depression."

"*What* are you reading?"

"Gah!" Renard startled and flung the book, where it landed in a heap on the plush carpet. He glared up at her. "Don't sneak up on me." He stood and grumbled, "Like a cat."

Charlotte had no sympathy. "Be prepared for claws if you think about using that drivel. 'Firm hand.' What nonsense."

He retrieved the book and snapped the cover shut before replacing it on a nearby shelf. "These are professionals, Lotte."

"Just because it says it's written by a 'doctor' doesn't mean the man has any idea about women."

"And you're an expert?"

Charlotte waved a hand over her person. "Wo-man." She stressed the syllables. "Feeling lost on how to handle your willful charge?"

"Frankly, yes." He ran a hand through his hair. "I'm worried about my *sister*'s happiness."

His honesty stopped her short. The dark circles under his eyes she'd noticed on the way home the other night looked like smudges of charcoal, while his clothes hung on him like a scarecrow, the straw torn out by the birds.

"When was the last time you ate something?" she asked.

"I had a brandy last night."

"Renard Leopold Louis, that is not a proper meal." She stomped to the bell pull and gave two sharp tugs. She whirled on him, hands on her hips. "Toast, eggs, coffee, and whatever else the cook can come up with. The tray better be licked clean, sir."

Renard's somber expression warmed into a smile, matching the tone in his voice. "You sound just like Mama when she used to scold me for skipping meals to go play at the pond."

Heart squeezing, Charlotte was transported back a decade earlier. "You'd come home caked in mud and all she'd say was, 'Did you eat?'"

He chuckled. "I'd ruined three priceless rugs, and she was madder I hadn't packed a sandwich."

"And Papa would appear in the hall, toss you a plum, and all was forgiven."

Renard rubbed his chin. "I'd forgotten about that. Berries, plums—I swear he had a secret stash of fruit hidden somewhere."

They shared a moment of quiet grief, and joy. The memories were a mix of bitter and sweet that no one else understood. They'd both been thrown into roles that weren't meant for them after the fire. Renard had risen to Duke of Lux and guardian at the pivotal age of fourteen, and she'd become an obligation. No longer co-conspirators and friends. With her compromised health and the sudden weight of responsibility, their relationship had come to be one of lord and charge.

Taking in his ragged appearance, she knew this was her chance. If she could make him see reason to go along with her plans, they'd both get what they wanted.

"Ren," she began.

He groaned and sat back in his chair. "That tone always

means you're about to say something I won't like."

She smirked and sat at his feet, looking up. "You've watched over me all this time. Giving up friends, opportunities."

"You forget I went to school—"

"But you came home every holiday break," she said. "And you always made sure I had what I needed: clothes, books, tutors, governesses and chaperones to terrorize."

He laughed.

The sound gave her courage. She could reach him. "I don't wish to marry."

"Lotte—"

"Please." She held up a hand. "I'm not ready. I want to travel, see things before I'm tied to a life of responsibility. You should understand that more than anyone."

His face softened. "I do, Lotte, truly. But I have a responsibility to see you taken care of."

"I've thought of that." She'd thought of it non-stop since he'd brought her to London. "I'll live on my own. Wait until I'm finished." She gave him a hard look when he opened his mouth to interrupt again. "You know I've no interest in society. I've been kept apart too long. Don't you dare apologize!"

Renard's mouth shut, and he waved a hand for her to continue.

"I'd accept a companion, someone appropriate to continue my instruction." She shrugged. "Eventually, I'll figure out where I fit in." She hoped. "I want marriage, children . . . eventually." Maybe.

Renard shook his head. "I overindulged your wild spirit while you recovered. It's my fault you don't know any better. The life of a lady doesn't work that way."

"But it could," she said. "With the trust Father set up for me, I could live a comfortable life. In two years, I can fully support myself—"

"No." Renard's gaze was sad, as if he knew his next words would change their relationship irrefutably. "I reworked your trust into a dowry."

She blinked. "Dowry?" That meant—"I won't have access to it until after I'm married." When it legally became her husband's property, which also would include her. She bolted to her feet. "You can't do that!"

"It's done."

The sinking feeling wouldn't stop. Charlotte reached out to the closest shelf to steady herself against a rush of nausea.

Trapped. She was truly trapped. The scar at her shoulder ached, reminding her of that night, the pain, the fear, the loss.

Her fault.

Tears burned her eyes. Was this punishment? She'd walked away with a nasty burn and weak lungs, but she'd lived when her parents hadn't. Perhaps her suffering thus far wasn't enough to satisfy God.

But she wouldn't believe that. Mercy, love, forgiveness—no father wanted his child caged. This was a human punishment. Her brother's, society's, and right now, she didn't give a fig what either wanted.

She pushed down her tears and stood tall, glaring down at the man who looked and sounded so much like her brother. "I don't know you anymore." She shook her head, a single tear leaking out. "I'll never forgive you."

SHE STOOD IN the hallway adjacent to the foyer, the light from the east-facing windows down the hall erecting harsh shadows around her. She knew her brother wouldn't follow. He believed what he'd done was right.

She'd had a solution. They could've gone back to being siblings. Independent and carefree once again. But he'd dug in his heels, and a mule in mud was easier to move.

Her skirt pocket bulged and crinkled, her list so long now, the six pages barely fit. She'd wanted to show her goals to her brother and laugh at the absurd. She saw now she'd wanted to share her dreams with the brother from her childhood. The brother who'd taught her how to fish in their estate pond and who'd pointed out where to find the best bugs hiding in the roots of the trees.

She entered the foyer, leaving behind her expectations and the hope brought on by memories. The light here was blinding and cold.

Her brother's overcoat and boots lay in the entryway, a rare breach in the servants' normally assiduous efforts.

Her heart gave a twinge. She picked up the coat, a well-worn cap falling from the sleeve. She held it to her and hugged it close.

Their family butler materialized from the drawing room across the way—most likely alerted to his post by her steps—his bald head and black boots reflecting the light from the windows. "My apologies, my lord. I was detained with a matter in the kitchens. Would you care for me to take that—" The man froze, his face turning red. "Apologies, Lady Charlotte. I mistook you for His Grace." He recovered and offered a hand once again. "Shall I take those, my lady?"

Charlotte shook her head. "That won't be necessary, Mr. Peters." She watched him contritely bow out of the foyer, feeling less and less capable of anything resembling civility when compared to the *stranger* down the hall. The mistake was not an uncommon one.

She and her brother had inherited their mother's delicate features and their father's tall frame. When they'd been children, before her brother had grown into the muscles and broadness of manhood, relatives, and even the staff would mix them up.

She glanced down at her small chest. Mind whirling, she held up the coat again, her mouth curling into a grin. With her brother's recent weight loss—the man apparently believing alcohol sustaining enough—the staff wouldn't look twice.

Harper's words echoed through her head. *"Dangerous and highly improper."*

Charlotte rushed up the stairs, her brother's coat and boots in hand. Her rage and disappointment changed into determination.

Improper?

Perfect.

CHAPTER TEN

F OR A WOMAN dressed as a young man, in need of keeping her activities secret from the staff, sneaking out through the kitchen entrance, walking two streets down, hiring a hack with a bit of pin money, and getting to the docks was a surprisingly easy affair.

"You sure you be wantin' me to drop eh off 'ere, lad? 'Tis no spot for a gentleman," her driver said.

Charlotte gazed around at the wooden boardwalk, the few ships bobbing like toy boats in the harbor. Wild profanity sounded in the distance. She smiled at her driver, keeping her hat and voice low. "Here is fine."

She tossed him an extra shilling for his trouble and concern, flicking it up with her thumb like Renard had taught her during the same summer when he'd claimed himself a pirate and the pond to be his territory.

The man's eyes widened at the payment. He pocketed the coin and tipped his hat. "Much obliged, mister. I'll stick 'round if ye need? Give a holla', and I'll come fetch ye."

Charlotte heard the beginnings of an argument in a nearby alley, followed by a muffled sound like a fist hitting something soft. Swallowing, Charlotte nodded, not *entirely* nonsensical. "Much appreciated."

She touched the front pocket of her coat, her brother's coat, feeling the comforting weight of her list and her brother's

Webley. She'd prefer to go straight to the nearest sailor and ask for a lesson, but she suspected the action would end in humor, at her expense. Plus, she was shaking so bad, she was likely to be avoided for ill. If she didn't steel her nerves immediately, she'd miss her opportunity.

She perked, another idea on her list popping into her head. The perfect solution to dull her anxiety and learn what she wanted to know without any awkward conversations. She turned back to her driver, remembering the slang she'd heard from the gentlemen in her brother's poker game she'd just so *happened* to overhear one evening when she'd been meant to retire early. "Know a good place to drink 'round here?"

"I NEED A drink," Hamish grumbled.

He had an appointment to keep and, if the two idiots before him came to blows, he was going to be more than late.

"You scratched it!" Gregori waved the glass slide before Percy's face.

"Get your eyes checked, genius." Percy's hands were in fists at his sides, no doubt itching to take the glass and stick it somewhere personal. "It's a smudge. If you'll stop nagging, I'll clean it off and you can go back to wasting time playing with toys."

"*Toys!*"

Hamish had never seen that shade of red on Gregori's face. If he weren't in such a hurry, he would've propped his feet on the nearest table and watched the two men strangle each other. It would've been the highlight over the past few mind-numbingly boring days. Boring, rainy days.

He hated inactivity. Waiting for Gregori's letter and Percy's report was a test of patience he'd failed miserably. For two days, he'd lumbered around his townhouse, snapped at his staff, and tossed books around the library in hopes of finding a worthwhile distraction. Camille had told him to get some air or risk his new suits.

He would've been thrilled at the notion of a duel of insults had his housekeeper not produced a pair of wickedly sharp-looking shears and a new cravat he'd received that morning from the tailor.

Thankfully, Gregori's note came soon after or he'd have had to attend his standing appointment today in a pile of shredded silk.

"See, you loon? Good as new," Percy said.

Gregori examined the glass, holding it up to the light filtering down from the window overhead. "Hmph. You're lucky. Keep your hands to yourself or lose a finger."

A spark of challenge lit Percy's eyes. "You haven't the stomach for all the blood."

Gregori bared his teeth. "I studied medicine before I decided to pursue engineering. I'd take off both thumbs at the proximal phalangeal. Let's see how cocky you are when you can't undo your trousers to take a piss."

Percy laughed, wiggling his thumbs. "I'd love to see that."

Percy's unhealthy fascination for the macabre aside, Hamish thought the procedure an interesting one as well. Which meant he'd been static for too damned long.

"Gregori." His voice was sharper than he'd meant. "You called. I'm here. I'm not a man to be summoned like some dog for no reason."

"As opposed to a dog called for a good reason?" Percy asked.

Hamish ignored him. "Do you have what I asked for?"

Mention of work pulled Gregori instantly on point. He shuffled around the warehouse, picking up parcels with no seeming pattern. "Organized chaos" was what he called it.

Hamish couldn't complain. Any thief who broke in would have no chance finding anything.

"Lucas, Barnes, Markus." Gregori identified the recipients of each package as he placed them in Hamish's hands.

"And the prototype?"

"Tomorrow," Gregori said.

The two back to their normal curtness, Hamish stuck the packages under one arm. "Noon."

THE AIR OUTSIDE the warehouse was salty and sour, the reek of rotting fish polluting an otherwise pleasant morning. A rare sky of thin clouds and bright sunshine warmed the breeze coming off the sea and made Hamish sweat under his workman's disguise.

He climbed into his carriage, removing his hat and overcoat, but lifting the window screen to let in the light.

Percy hopped in behind him, the heat not seeming to bother him in his many layers.

Cold inside and out, Hamish thought. "What did you find?" he asked.

"The marquess is a proper dandy. Tailor, home, White's, home, bank, home." Percy handed him a list of times and places, always thorough. "Aside from my detour to encourage a certain captain and master to make haste unloading the cargo, I followed him for two days straight. Nothing stood out."

Hamish puzzled over his disappointment. Had he wanted to find something? "Then the marquess is as he seems," he said to himself.

"People are never what they seem," Percy said. "Finding nothing is a concern in and of itself."

Hamish frowned. "You think the marquess is hiding something?"

Percy's hand twitched towards his left pocket as the carriage lurched into motion. He relaxed after a moment and said, "I find when a man smells like roses, it's rarely because he's carrying flowers."

Hamish knew that kind of man, intimately. His father had been a pillar of generosity and honor in society, masking the hard indifference he'd reserved for those too young and trapped to complain. Where the former Duke of Lux had been uncommonly kind and open in both his children's upbringing, Hamish knew his childhood had been the same as that of many in the gentry. In fact, he'd had it easier than some. Many men had personalities more destructive and violent. Maybe if his father had been less of a monster, he could be as improper and charming as Lady Charlotte.

"Dig deeper," he said. "Talk to the staff, tailors, the flower girl down the street if you must."

Percy nodded, as if he'd expected as much. "Give me a week, and I'll have the man's shirt size, his teeth count, and the name of his first dog."

Hamish ignored the ridiculous list. Percy was the best runner in London. If the man said he'd count the hairs on top of the marquess's head, he'd do it. The Devil's own secrets wouldn't be safe if Percy decided to get serious.

"All this for a lady?" Percy mused.

Hamish looked up to find Percy's amused expression. Was it truly for Lady Charlotte's safety? Renard's piece of mind? Renard may as well have already signed the bloody marriage contract and washed his hands of the responsibility for how little he'd cared. The reveal of a simple routine in the marquess's life and any sense of obligation should have been satisfied.

The sudden memory of Charlotte as they'd danced at the Tailormans' ball surfaced. Open, exhilarated, she'd cried out in pure joy. Hamish looked out the carriage window, seeing they'd entered the main square by the docks. The truth was he liked her. After all the trouble she'd caused, the irritation, Hamish had enjoyed the disruption in his life. She'd been forward, witty—two things he avoided in a woman, but he'd secretly thrived on the challenge. She was exciting, unpredictable, and honest to the point of painful. She was also stubborn and amusing as hell.

He shook his head, his answer as honest as he'd allow out loud. "I took a dislike to the man after we met. He didn't appear good enough for the lady."

"Ah," Percy said. "Lady Charlotte is quite the woman."

Hamish frowned at the teasing look in Percy's eye. He blew out his frustration. Of course the man knew which lady he'd meant. He dropped his guard completely. "She's a handful. The marquess has no hope of reeling her in."

No man did.

He shifted his attention back to the docks, his gaze locking on four figures vanishing down an alley. He pressed his face to the window, his breath fogging up the glass. "It can't be."

He tapped the top of the carriage and bolted out the door before it had stopped.

His feet ate up the pavement, and his heart thundered in his chest. He barely heard Percy above the blood rushing through his ears.

"What is it?"

Hamish didn't stop to answer. His gaze fixed on the three men at the mouth of a dark alley. And the young woman in a gentleman's suit being dragged into the shadows.

CHAPTER ELEVEN

CHARLOTTE HELD NO doubt she resembled that which the sailors traded in as she stared open-mouthed at the boisterous bar patrons. If the bar—with its low-lit candles and gleaming, mahogany wood stools and tables—weren't enough, the dozens of dark-blue naval uniforms scattered around the room were like a reflection of the churning sea outside.

A band of shipmates, deep in their cups, sang and cajoled, laughing and spilling alcohol, food, and profanity like it was water.

Finding a booth free in back, Charlotte kept her collar up and her cap low, hiding burning cheeks. She hadn't any idea of half the insults. The other half were truly a magnificent jumble of filth with so many discrepancies in physicality, Charlotte made sure to memorize each one.

She leaned forward in her seat, determined to suss out what a 'vazey ratbag' meant, when a young woman approached her table, her face hard.

"Drink, mister?"

Charlotte straightened, smacking her back on the chair, and fumbled to keep her long hair secured under her cap. Noticing the woman's dark hair and amused gaze, Charlotte cleared her throat. "Whiskey."

"Food?"

"No," Charlotte said, then, "Thank you, miss."

The woman nodded. "I'll be right back."

Charlotte blew out a breath, her heart racing. Who knew ordering a drink in a sailors' bar could be so invigorating—and educational?

"Who you think the buyer is?" one of the sailors asked at the next table over.

"A big fish," another said. "Throwing blunt around all secret."

"Illegal?"

Charlotte's ears perked. Someone was waiting for a shipment. What kind of illegal stuff?

The other sailor shrugged. "Long as I get me money, don't care."

The young barmaid appeared and set a tall glass of liquor on the table, tiny scars on her fingers flashing a filmy white under the lamp light. "Here's your drink, my lord."

Charlotte refused to touch her own scar at her shoulder and took note of the woman's honorific.

The clothes. Of course a seasoned barmaid could tell the difference in clientele. While her brother's broadcloth coat was worn from age, it was still a far superior cut and style than the usual dark-colored wool worn by most townsmen. If Charlotte had taken the time, and risk, she would've borrowed the stableboy's uniform, or an old, rural smock left at the house to rework into a serviceable rug.

Glancing around, she saw others had noticed her attire as well, their gazes shifting away when she turned to look. She took a sip, the sudden burning down her throat like fire.

The barmaid leaned over and whispered in her ear, "Let me know if you need anything else." Her fingers danced suggestively over Charlotte's thigh. "*Anything.*"

Eyes as round as plates, Charlotte looked the woman in the face and wished for her spectacles. With their telltale small frame and short bridge meant for a woman, she couldn't very well wear them without giving herself away.

She really was pretty. Curly hair framed dark-blue eyes, and she stood with a confidence that Charlotte envied.

She removed the woman's hand from her thigh, giving a soft squeeze, and found the truth second nature. "I'm not what you think, but"—she smiled—"I'm flattered."

The woman's brows furrowed, then smoothed. "You're—"

"Wench! I've got a tip for ya. Come get it." The sailor at the next table over rubbed his lap crudely.

The men sharing the table snickered.

The woman's shoulders slumped, as if this were a common occurrence.

Charlotte's heart went out to her. Cages came in all forms, it seemed. To be the object of such vulgar displays was unacceptable.

"Vazey ratbags," Charlotte said.

The woman smirked and suddenly sat in Charlotte's lap, calling to the sailors, "Sorry, boys. I've already got my hands full."

And she kissed her.

Charlotte had only been kissed once, by a man who defied lust itself, but she found the woman's kiss pleasant. Soft lips, sweet scent, and altogether an experience that hadn't been on her list that she'd add and check off at the soonest availability.

The woman pulled away, hopped off Charlotte's lap, and winked. "Thanks, love."

Charlotte blinked. "Of course?"

The barmaid laughed and tended to her other tables, leaving Charlotte to her drink and her improving mood.

Three things off the list and the sun hadn't reached its highest point. Today was a success.

"Bet ya think yur special, eh?" the vulgar sailor said. "What luck to 'ave blunt big enough to get the wenches."

Emboldened by her third sip of whiskey or the disguise, Charlotte couldn't decide, she looked the man in the eye. "Perhaps." She finished her drink, tossing payment on the table as she stood. "Or maybe the woman responded to respect. I find manners are nearly irresistible, especially when you mean them." She looked down her nose, appreciating how she had the man's full attention.

She tipped her hat, their confused expression like icing on fresh cross buns. She felt alive, heard.

For all of three steps.

"Let go, Rufus!"

Charlotte followed the woman's distressed voice, seeing the same barmaid trapped by a burly man with wandering hands.

"Come now, lass. You been flauntin' your wares all mornin'. Give us a kiss."

The woman's smile was forced. "Not interested—ow! Let me go."

"Playing hard to get," the burly man said. "I like a bit o' fight." His grasping hands pinched her backside, eliciting a pained cry from the woman and cheers from his two companions.

Charlotte snatched up the vulgar sailor's drink and marched up to the table. "Excuse me," she said, and then she poured the nearly-full mug over the burly man's head.

The man sputtered and stood, towering over Charlotte so she had to tilt her head back to keep him in sight.

"Son o' a bitch!" He let the woman go to stick a dirty finger in Charlotte's face. "Ya gonna die, Dandy."

"Rufus, please." The barmaid glanced over, fear furrowing her brows. "The boy didn't know yous was playin'." She nuzzled up to the man. "Fancies 'imself a hero."

His hand went to her bum, and the woman's resulting cringe sent Charlotte's temper over the edge.

"Actually . . ." Charlotte ignored the panic on the woman's face, making sure to stare the big man down. "I was thinking this piece of shit needed a good wash. The smell was ruining my drink."

"What?!" Rufus exploded. He grabbed her by the collar and sneered in her face. "Come on, boys. Seems like the lad wants a lesson in manners."

The barmaid clawed at his arm. "He didn' mean it, Rufus.

Please!"

Charlotte struggled to breathe around the man's grip, but she put on her best smile and said, "No worries, miss. Rufus wants to have a friendly chat is all."

Rufus laughed, releasing her collar to drape an arm securely around her shoulders, anything but friendliness in his eyes. "That's right, boy." He nodded to the woman. "Be back in a minute, Scarlet."

Scarlet clutched her chest, her gaze frantic.

Charlotte allowed the big man and his two friends to drag her out of the pub. Her heart pounded and her palms were sweaty, but she couldn't bring herself to give in to the fear. She wasn't naive. As soon as she'd decided to help the barmaid, she'd known the resulting conflict would most likely end in a pistol to the face.

"Down here." Rufus shoved her into a back alley. "Now, boy." He cracked his knuckles. "I'm gonna break that face o' yours. We'll see how big a hero ya be when yo 'ave to drink yo booze through a straw."

Charlotte sighed, the initial rush of panic giving way to annoyance. The reek of urine and rotting food was stronger here. She'd had a perfectly wonderful time in the bar, where it had only vaguely smelled of unwashed bodies. "If you go back and apologize to Miss Scarlet, I'll let you go."

Rufus barked a laugh. "You must be wrong in the head, boy." He stalked closer, fishing out a knife from his vest, the silver glinting in the single bit of light in the dark space. "Yous not leaving this alley alive."

Seeing the blade caused a horrible churning in her stomach. "I see you won't be reasoned with." Charlotte hated how her voice shook. "Very well."

A muffled sound from the mouth of the alley distracted Rufus long enough for Charlotte to pull the pistol from inside her brother's coat. She'd questioned her instinct to delay her departure to grab the revolver from its place in her brother's study drawer. Now she was glad she'd taken the time.

Rufus was grumbling to his companions but swung around when she pulled back the trigger mechanism.

She pointed the barrel at his nose, watching his ruddy face pale. Charlotte heard more of a scuffle in the alley, but she kept her focus on the man in front of her, lest he rush to disarm her.

Without her glasses, she couldn't make out more than a few blurry human shapes.

Battling a wave of adrenaline that threatened to shake the gun out of her hand, she spoke low and slow and bluffed her *vazey ratbag* ass off. "I wanted to avoid any unpleasantness. I've never fired a gun before, you see. I hope the blood won't stain."

Rufus swallowed audibly, raised his hands, and backed away. "All right, boy. I see yo was serious. We was just messin' with ya, right? A friendly chat."

Charlotte advanced, one step forward for one retreated. "This model holds multiple rounds, Mr. Rufus. I'm sure to hit my mark if the first misses."

The big man froze, voice going an octave higher with panic. "I get it. I won' touch the lass again. Didn' knows ya was sweet on 'er. She didn' say she was kept."

"'Kept'?" Temper flaring again, Charlotte waved the gun in the air. "That's the problem with you men. You think women are property. Makes me sick."

She raised her hand back to deliver a stinging slap.

The man's eyes rolled back, and he fell.

Charlotte skidded back, avoiding the man's huge body as he crumpled to the ground.

She didn't have time to think about why he'd fallen, because another man had come into the alley, a man she recognized even half-blind and in the shadows. "Duke?"

The Duke of Camine stepped into the light, his blue eyes hard enough to break bone. "Give me the gun, Charlotte."

CHAPTER TWELVE

CHARLOTTE RUBBED HER eyes, certain she was hallucinating. The gun's trigger caught her finger and she winced.

"Damn it!" Hamish snatched the gun from her, clicking back the hammer and opening the barrel. There was a quick inhale and then, "This isn't loaded." Instead of relief, the knowledge seemed to enrage him. "Reckless, stupid. Your brother is going to kill you!"

Knowing she wasn't imagining that superior tone, she rubbed at her nose, her hand coming away dirty. "How did you know it was me?"

"Anyone with eyes would know you're a woman. As for knowing it was *you*, it didn't take much to deduce which woman would be reckless enough to impersonate a man in broad daylight."

She pointed to the three unconscious men on the ground. "They didn't figure it out."

"What would you have done if they had? Your gun was useless." His voice grew louder with each word. "Do you know what could have happened?"

She shrugged, her body feeling like it weighed two hundred pounds more. "A few bruises. An unbearable lecture from my brother."

"You could have *died!*"

He was in front of her, his hands suddenly on her shoulders, over her neck, touching her face.

Burning up at the feel of his fingers against her skin, she asked breathlessly, "What do you think you're doing?"

His touch hardened. "Stand still," he growled, his voice not sounding quite steady. "I'm checking to see if you've suffered a head injury."

She pulled away. "I'm fine."

"Well, *I'm* not!" He turned to the side, his hand over his face. "You honestly believe men like that would have tattled to your brother? They would've used those knives. Or worse. A young woman, alone in a dark alley. Even *you* can imagine what three drunks are capable of."

His words sank in, along with an image too vulgar and cruel to process, and Charlotte felt the blood drain from her face. She looked with open eyes at the three men. She pressed a hand to her throat, unable to swallow. There'd been three knives and no indication there hadn't been more hidden in pockets. She met the duke's direct gaze for the first time, her words sincere.

"Thank you."

The gratitude or the attention, Charlotte didn't know which, seemed to make him uncomfortable.

He pushed the unloaded gun into the waistband of his trousers and turned around with a grunt. "My carriage is this way. I'll escort you home."

Remembering her nice driver, she said, "I have a hack waiting."

The duke didn't stop walking. "Send him away. I don't need you running headfirst into more trouble when I'm not looking."

The command pricked her temper anew. Moreover, she very much wanted to kick him in the shin like a child. It was then Charlotte realized her legs were lead beneath her. She cleared her throat, praying he didn't hear her embarrassment. "No."

He stopped and turned, a frighteningly intense look in his eyes. "'No'?"

She raised her chin, willing her body to move. "I will not."

He faced her fully, an edge to his voice. "You will come with me. I refuse to leave you here unprotected."

HER SHOULDERS STIFFENED at his command.

He waited for the sharp retort he knew she chewed on, but the tension left her in one long exhale.

"I can't." She stopped his next threat with a raised hand. "I'm not arguing with you. It's just . . ." She looked up at him, her expression uncomfortable. "I can't seem to move my legs."

The offending limbs drew his attention. His mouth went dry seeing how the dark suede clung to her legs. They were long, sculpted as if she made it a point to walk regularly. They were also shaking.

Hamish cursed himself. "Your body is in shock."

"Oh," she said, nodding. "I see. That makes sense."

He heard her embarrassment and a lingering note of fear that made his insides twist. He steeled his mind and, before he could acknowledge the rush of pleasure he experienced from looking into her startled eyes, lifted her into his arms.

Legs numb, her arms seemed unafflicted as she pounded his chest. "Put me down this instant! This isn't done."

Hamish trapped one of her arms against his side, subsequently bringing them chest to chest and setting his body aflame. "How would you know what is or isn't done? I thought you hadn't learned society rules."

"This couldn't possibly be allowed," she said. "It's far too . . ."

"Yes?"

She scrunched her nose in the way she did, the soot now smeared across her cheek. "Exciting. Enjoyable."

"Fun?"

"That too."

He grinned. If she was bantering with him, she must have

been fine. Now that he had her in his arms, the anger leached out. Take away the brutes and the situation was outrageous. A lady dressed as a what, impoverished lord? Bluffing her way out of an altercation with the air of a trained soldier. And she'd called *him* exciting.

The lady couldn't lie to save propriety.

"You're smiling," she said.

His face muscles were aching again. "It seems I am."

She studied him. "You should smile more."

They were back to the point where Hamish knew he shouldn't ask. "Why?"

"You're quite handsome."

The words threw him. No, not the words. He'd been complimented many times, by many women, and in areas that had nothing to do with his face, but none had ever spoken so factually. As if there were no ulterior motive.

"I bet you could convince the Devil to stay for church with that face," she said.

He laughed. "Complimentary now, I see."

"Being rescued does put one in a more generous state of mind."

He looked down into her eyes, the green somehow shining in the dark. Instead of turning away, she met his gaze boldly, curiously, and Hamish was glad the lady hadn't a firm grasp of society manners. Once their gazes met, he couldn't bring himself to look away.

She fit in his arms, soft and curved the way he preferred in the bottom, with long legs perfect for wrapping around a man as he played between them.

As if seeing his thoughts, her own gaze darkened with desire.

She'd been a shockingly quick study when he'd kissed her before. Distractingly, he wondered if she'd be as responsive in other areas of pleasure? His gaze slid to her mouth.

She licked her lips at the attention.

Hamish knew kissing her again was inevitable. He bent forward, loving the hitch in her breathing. "Hold still," he whispered.

"Step away from the boy," someone ordered.

Hamish turned and was displeased to find another gun aimed near his person by a young woman dressed in a wool skirt and filthy apron—no doubt one of the bar wenches that frequently worked the docks. "The boy is unharmed. Lower your weapon."

The woman's wool skirt twisted when she took aim. "I'll see for myself. Put him down."

With no thought of the cap sliding off, Charlotte glanced over his shoulder. "I'm well, Miss Scarlet. It's so kind of you to check on me."

Seeing Charlotte's bright face, the woman's expression changed, the relief so strong, she dropped the gun to her side. "Thank the good Lord. When they dragged you out . . ." She shook her head. "I thought I'd be too late. I'd never have forgiven myself."

Sentiments aligned, Hamish said accusingly, "You're the woman the fight was over."

The woman, Scarlet, nodded, her gaze turning to Charlotte. "You shouldn't have stepped in. Rufus is a rough bastard, but he wouldn't have done anything in the open."

"I'd do it again in a heartbeat," Charlotte said. "You didn't wish to be touched. The man didn't have permission. My one regret is I only grabbed a single glass to dump on that man's head when I had two hands."

A sense of pride filled Hamish. She was fearless. Stupid and reckless, but she stood up for her values without a second's hesitation. His lady was a force, one he couldn't help but admire. Hamish's thoughts sputtered.

His lady? Where the hell had that come from?

"Thank you." That same sense of awe was evident in Scarlet's voice. "No one else would've spoken up."

Hamish shook his head in wonder. Wenches, dukes . . . He may have been able to lure the Devil to church, but Lady

Charlotte would get the bastard to take communion and convert.

"You're welcome," Charlotte said, her lashes fluttering with exhaustion.

A sudden need to see to her care had his arms tightening around her. "We're leaving."

He knew he was right about her state when he garnered no argument. He stepped past the woman and headed towards his carriage still waiting in the street.

"That's quite a woman you have there," Scarlet called.

"I know," he mumbled to himself.

Clearly not as tired as one was led to believe, Charlotte's head popped up. "When did you figure it out?"

The other woman's voice was laced with humor. "Before the kiss."

Chapter Thirteen

Whatever qualms Charlotte had about being carried like a child were forgotten amid the duke's warm embrace. She snuggled deeper, detecting a peculiar smell of ink and horses. It smelled like home.

She sighed.

He made a sound in his throat.

She angled her face to look up at him, a difficult task when he'd plastered them chest to chest. "Did you just growl?"

"No."

"It sounded like a growl."

"You're hearing things," he said. "Must be all the recklessness drowning out your common sense."

He was unbearable!

She huffed and shifted, realizing she had some feeling in her legs. "You needn't carry me now. I can walk."

His arms tightened around her. "If I release you, who knows what other life-threatening position I'll be faced with?"

Whatever warm feelings were growing between them shriveled at the condescending statement. Charlotte stuck out her chin. "I thanked you once. I learned my lesson. Put me down and I'll leave. I know how you detest the trouble."

He winced. "You're not going to forgive me for that, are you?"

"I won't deny the charge. I'm a grown woman with my own

ideas and desires. Both attributes men of all stations detest." She sniffed. "But a lady doesn't wish to hear how little she's wanted."

"I never said I didn't want you."

Her gaze darted to him.

His brows furrowed, as if the statement had come as a shock.

They came to a large, plain carriage. He opened the door and paused, as if surprised to find it empty. He set her on her feet, leaving a warm hand on the small of her back that Charlotte felt to the bone.

"Get in," he said.

The idea of sharing the close, dark space had her stomach fluttering.

"I said, get in," the duke repeated.

Ice replaced the heat. "You can't dictate to me."

He leaned into her face, his teeth bared. "I just did."

The man was insufferable! If he thought he could bully her into following orders, he'd missed the stubborn streak the Louis line was renowned for.

She crossed her arms, prepared for a battle of words.

The duke, however, had other plans.

"Set me down at once!" She flailed, but the hands at her waist were like steel.

He dropped her unceremoniously onto the carriage floor and stuck a finger in her face. "I've had enough confrontation today. If you wish to continue this tantrum on the drive back to Piccadilly, so be it. But I will not be seen yelling at a lady at the bloody docks."

He was right, blast the man. If the adventure in the alley had taught her anything, it was best to keep a low profile. His practicality made her all the irater, especially since a few minutes ago, he'd acted like he was going to kiss her again.

"Fine," she said. "I'll wait until the door closes before I give you the tongue-lashing you deserve."

Instead of expressing annoyance, the duke smiled that Devil-manipulating smile, his words full of amusement that told

Charlotte she'd missed something.

"I look forward to seeing you use your tongue however you choose, my lady."

His words held a note of salaciousness that she couldn't place.

Charlotte scrambled out of the way before he climbed into the seat across from her.

The door snapped shut, and Charlotte squeaked, "Wait! What about my driver?"

"Already taken care of," a man said just outside the door.

She squinted through the open window. The glint in the man's eyes reminded her of the snakes that used to terrorize her father's horses.

"Percy." Hamish pinched the bridge of his nose. "You were there. Did you compensate the driver for his discretion?"

The man, Percy, shook his head. "No need. Man said the lad's kindness was payment enough." He grinned. "Then had the gall to ask if I was planning on making trouble for the boy." The gaze he rested on her was assessing. "What charm you must possess to instill such loyalty in a complete stranger."

Friend of the duke's or not, Charlotte disliked the accusation in his voice. "You sound disapproving."

Percy shrugged. "In my experience, kindness is a sure way to get a blade to the back."

Hamish stiffened, seeming ready to intercede on her behalf.

Charlotte beat him to it. "Less than two minutes in your company, and I understand how *you* may find it necessary to watch your back."

The two men stared at her.

Then Percy threw back his head and let out a guttural sound that might've been laughter. "Your charm *is* quite irresistible, my lady."

Dear God, she was perfect.

In the decade he'd known Percy, Hamish had never seen him laugh like that. The sound was painful and disconcerting, like a predator amused before devouring its prey. The interest in the other man's eyes was unmistakable, and Hamish had a sudden urge to put a fist through the man's teeth.

"I thought my disguise flawless," Charlotte said. "Everyone mistook me for my brother growing up."

There was no question of the Louis family resemblance, but the idea that she'd ever resembled anything less than a warrior queen was unforgivable. He noted her squinting at Percy's face and sighed. "The staff at Lux estate must be as blind as you. Where are your spectacles now?"

She sniffed. "At home. There was no way I could sneak out without someone noticing, and I'd be in dire straits if my spectacles broke during my excursion."

There were so many things to comment on, Hamish chose the most obvious. "If you needed to sneak out, perhaps your excursion was ill-advised."

Her glare was the same she'd given Renard when she'd scolded him for his manners. "Says the man who may go where he likes when he likes."

Percy laughed again, the traitor. "She has a point."

"Don't encourage her."

Percy ignored him. "And a lovely face." He leaned his arm on the open-door window. "Please tell me those lovely curls escaping your cap are your natural color?" He winked. "I've a soft spot for blondes."

Charlotte leaned forward herself. "I doubt anyone can claim the same for you."

The look of shock on the runner's face was priceless.

Hamish nearly applauded until Percy's shock turned into a grin.

"I've found an exception, it seems," he said. "Don't you think insult the precursor to affection?"

The growl that escaped Hamish was becoming a familiar sound. "Don't *you* have a job to do?"

Percy threw the grin his way and, with a dramatic sigh, said, "Alas, I must leave you, Lady . . .?"

"Leave," Hamish ground out.

He did, but not before adding another ridiculous wink in her direction.

"He's colorful," she said.

"Damn fool," he muttered.

"And handsome."

Hamish's gaze shot to her. "*Handsome?*"

She shrugged, as if a lady spouted such compliments flippantly every day. "In a dangerous kind of way."

It was a good thing Percy had vanished into the now-bustling Dockside traffic. Hamish felt his own dangerous nature rising at her easy attention. He rapped the carriage roof twice, leaned his head back, and closed his eyes as he uttered an oath of relief when it lurched into motion.

"I haven't heard that one before. Is it like 'bullocks'?"

Hamish peered at her, wishing he didn't find the quizzical look on her face so charming. "A lady shouldn't ask such things."

"Oh, bullocks."

He smiled, his agitation evaporating with the movement of the ride. "Care to share why you are at the docks so early in the day, dressed as a man?"

"Not really."

He crossed his arms and waited.

"I was having a whiskey."

"You were . . ." He laughed, his side hurting. Renard was going to shoot him between the eyes. "How was it?"

Her scowl told as much of a story as her one-word answer. "Interrupted."

"Hmm." He'd figured as much. "A fight over a lady in a pub. How very male of you."

She took the compliment with a sneer. "They were touching

her without consent. I couldn't just sit there."

"That's exactly what you should've done. Someone else would've stepped in."

"There wasn't anyone else," she said, eyes flashing. "Forgive me if I don't trust a man to protect a woman when she asks."

He heard the words she didn't say: *I would've stood up either way.* She was a damn crusader! Opinionated, scathing, and courageous as hell. He knew men who didn't have half the stones.

I'd protect you.

The thought rattled him.

He was not in the market for protecting anyone, especially a beautiful woman bent on righting every wrong within twenty miles.

"Besides," she said, a mischievous grin tipping her mouth, "it was a most productive morning."

That grin was mesmerizing. He'd give half his fortune to know exactly what the lady had been up to. He was careful to keep the curiosity from his voice. "Aside from crossdressing, drinking, and fighting over a woman?"

She smiled, and it was like the sun had turned on in the carriage. "Don't forget hiring a hack, my first kiss, and learning a dozen more profanities."

Something about the profanities ticked his memory. She'd mentioned 'swearing like a sailor' in that list of hers. Was that why she was here? That damn list! "You risked your life for something as asinine . . ." His brain caught up to her words, touching on the second item on her list. "Your first kiss?"

"Yes," she said. "It was more pleasant than I expected."

Fire scorched his belly. He'd find this *pleasant* kisser and wring his guts into the Thames. He frowned. "What about the kiss in my study?"

"What about it?"

He dared her to lie and say it didn't count. He'd spent every night since then dreaming about her tongue against his lips, her delicate hands digging into his back as if she were a wild animal.

Her cheeks flushed. "Oh, well, yes. That was my *first* kiss."

He liked that blush. Somehow being her first quieted his own animal. He wanted to be her last kiss. His mind blanked. He absently asked while his brain processed that outrageous thought, "There can be more than one?"

"Naturally. I had my first kiss with a woman."

Hamish didn't have to worry any longer about the strange thoughts coursing through his head because, at that precise moment, they went out both ears. The woman from the alley? "You kissed her?" What the hell happened in that pub?

"She kissed me," Charlotte said, her face thoughtful. "Her lips were softer than I expected." She turned those big eyes on him, green and thickly lashed, and entirely too seductive without her spectacles. "Were mine soft?"

Soft? He couldn't think straight. Imagining her kissing that wench, confused at her pleasure of it, was one of the most erotic things he'd heard. The carriage was too small.

She was everywhere. Her knees brushed his leg. Her eyes and smell filled his senses. Every breath was like a caress to his pulsing groin.

Fearing his stays rending any moment, he dug nails into his thighs, praying the drawing of blood would limit the flow to other places. He had to get away. Jump from the damn carriage if necessary.

"Well?" she asked.

He looked over at her, a mistake. She was lovely, delicate, but stronger than iron. The way she looked directly into his gaze, he swore she saw every flaw, scar, sin he'd ever committed, but she didn't look away. "They were perfect."

"Oh." She blinked, that delicious blush returning to her cheeks. "Thank you."

Those two words were the last straw. He crossed to the other seat, pulling her into his arms and knocking that blasted cap off to run his fingers through a wave of silken hair, sending pins scattering across the seat.

He teased her lips, nipping and sucking until they parted. She was a tempest, a dangerous whirlwind of forward and polite manners that ripped every nerve in his body open with yearning.

He wanted to hear those simple words again, for a more intimate compliment. One he delivered with hands and tongue and not a thread of clothing.

CHAPTER FOURTEEN

SHE WAS ON fire. Of all the adventures she'd had that morning, she knew this was the most dangerous. Kissing the Duke of Camine was sinful, thrilling, and she loved it. More than sneaking away in the middle of the day. More than dancing in the finest dress.

Her thoughts should have given her pause. Should have broken her away and had her running from the man as fast as her too-big boots would allow.

He didn't admonish her forwardness or condescend. He did, however, represent everything about society and her situation that made her very thoughts rebel.

Power, arrogance . . . Control over her in a way that was both comforting and so uncomfortable, Charlotte wished she could tear her clothes and then his.

Kissing him felt anything but like control.

"Charlotte."

Her name on his lips was a whisper in the dark that had even her innocent mind drawing up images of bare skin and twisted sheets.

His fingers found the sensitive skin where her shirt and pants met at her waist.

Her own fingers ran over his chest, the silky texture at once grating when she needed to feel his skin smooth to the touch.

He had come to her rescue hatless and coat-less and the flimsy shirt he wore did nothing to pad the hard muscles. His thumb brushed her bare hip.

She gasped. A moment before, the carriage had felt like another cage, stuffed with no room to breathe. Now Charlotte cursed at the vastness between them, tearing at his shirt like a wild cat.

She felt his chuckle through their chests.

"So impatient." He sounded approving.

She would have felt triumphant at making him laugh if her body didn't feel so foreign. "I'm frustrated," she said. "I want . . ."

He stilled, his voice husky against her neck. "What do you want?"

"*You,*" she wanted to scream, but it wasn't so simple. She wanted hands, and lips, and the horrible ache to go away. Even in such a crazed state, Charlotte sought honesty. "I'm burning up. My stomach is fluttering, my chest tingles, and there's a wetness between my legs that feels like the worst and greatest pain I've ever desired." And because deep down, she was still a child, as inexperienced and impatient as he'd implied, she said, "I need you to fix it."

As inarticulate as her impassioned outburst was, he liked it. She saw the battle raging in his eyes. She was a lady, he a gentleman. She was an innocent, and he was best friends with her brother. She pushed, knowing if he rejected her a second time, something in her would break. "Tell me what to do."

She saw the moment he decided. Those devilish eyes darkened until Charlotte saw only night.

His hand threaded into her hair tightly, close to pain and exactly what she wanted.

"Put your hands above your head."

She did so without hesitation, loving his nod of approval.

"Lean back."

She gripped the top of the cushion behind her head and leaned into the plush pillows, her breasts raised high.

His fingers left her hair to cup her breast. He pinched her

nipple through the fabric.

She squirmed. "Hamish!"

His chuckle was sin. "Call me 'my lord.'"

She didn't have time to argue as his mouth replaced his fingers, sucking her through her shirt.

She grabbed for him, but his other hand shot out, pinning her wrists once more above her head. She met his black eyes, seeing more beast than man gazing back. She trembled, accidently knocking something off the seat beside her.

They both looked down at the same time, seeing three small parcels in brown paper.

He released her as if burned, the look on his face still not entirely human. He snatched the parcels, cursing so thoroughly, Charlotte came back to her senses.

She dropped her arms, shoulders aching.

He rapped on the carriage roof a second time and called up a different destination to his driver.

Her voice was hoarse when she asked, "Where are we going?"

"I've an appointment."

She latched on to the anger in his voice, letting it fuel her instead of the disappointment of his release. "Where?"

She wished she'd paid more attention to the small packages.

He hid them from view under his discarded overcoat. "It's private."

The carriage took a sharp turn, and Charlotte tipped forward.

He caught her by the shoulders, their noses a scant inch apart.

He had a beautiful mouth for a man, she thought. Bowed and full on the bottom. She licked her lips, interested in using her teeth on him like he'd done with her.

He frowned and pushed her back. "Hold on to something before you harm yourself."

She had been holding something and enjoying herself immensely. Disappointment flared anew. Being with him was like dressing for early fall: an unpredictable warm afternoon followed by a nasty chill in the evening. And women were said to change as the wind. "Men."

"What was that?"

She looked up, realizing she'd been mumbling. "Your mood swings are rather painful, *my lord*."

Something wild flashed in his eyes. Charlotte swore it was an answering challenge to her sarcasm. Willed his challenge into being. She would've preferred anger, desire—virtually anything in place of the bored mask that muted his expression.

"Fear not, *my lady*. We've arrived."

The carriage was slowing. Charlotte squinted out the window, able to make out row after row of identical dilapidated brick buildings. "Where exactly have we arrived?"

"I've an appointment," he repeated. He grabbed his coat and the parcels, opening the door and descending the steps before his driver hopped from the block.

Charlotte slid her cap back on, tucking in her hair. She moved to the door, but his command stopped her short.

"Stay here," he ordered as he shut the door in her face.

HAMISH COULDN'T STOP seeing the look of rebellion in Charlotte's eyes when he'd slammed the carriage door. Or the feel of silk hair. Or the smell of lemon soap on her skin. Or the taste of sweat and whiskey from her mouth.

Good God, he'd attacked her. He jammed his arm through the too heavy coat, hearing a seam rip.

Somehow, he'd stopped the madness, but not before he'd restrained her.

Shame hit him in the chest. He'd kept his true desires hidden all these years. Taking extra time and energy to be gentle with his lovers. He'd honed sex to an art form, one that left him mildly satisfied and his partners begging for more.

Where the hell had all that control gone? One simple "thank you" and he'd pounced on her like a ravenous dog. More than ever, Hamish knew one thing: Charlotte, *Lady Charlotte*, was not for him. He'd mistaken her reckless and passionate behavior for a decade-long cabin fever. A quick breath of reality and she'd be back to proper lessons and shocking England's fiercest chaperones.

It hadn't been a whim.

She'd blossomed under his orders, opened completely to his desires. So trusting, so innocent.

He steeled his thoughts. She didn't know what he wanted to do to her. She wanted a life without rules or demands; he was everything she hated. What he desired, what he needed, was control. If she truly saw what thoughts lurked deep in his mind, she'd run away screaming.

Wild beast.

His fingers curled into a fist. He wouldn't make the mistake a second time. As soon as his appointment was over, he'd see her straight home and never speak to her again.

He glanced down at his pocket watch, lengthening his strides, and secured the parcels under his arm.

He was late, grievously so. If he missed the window of time altogether, he'd have to wait until next week. He thought of his clients and moved faster.

The only indication he'd reached his destination was a worn sign above a sagging door frame tucked away in a back alley, the occupants too lowly for even this sliver of London gutter to acknowledge.

He rapped on the door twice, the reek of garbage and sickness bringing him back to his task and the importance of punctuality.

The door opened. "You again?" The woman's face had the haunting quality of an apparition in a Gothic novel, without any of the warmth. "The men finished ten minutes ago. Come back next week."

He wedged his boot in the closing door. "Mrs. Banner, a pleasure as always." Damn it! Ten bloody minutes. He thought of the contents of the smallest package. "Is Mr. Laundry still here?"

She let him reopen the door to cross her bony arms. "Maybe he is. Maybe he ain't. These men don't take breaking your word lightly." Her sneer was like sand in his eye. "You're wasting your time here, lordy. Go back to your marble floors and gold ceilings and leave this world before it snaps you up and swallows you whole."

Hamish gritted his teeth. "Is the man here?"

"No."

"You are certain?" It wouldn't surprise him if Markus were on the other side of the door.

She snorted, seeing his suspicion. "Only one door, lordy."

The door snapped shut, and Hamish resisted ripping the rotting thing off the hinges to search the building himself. But he'd sensed the truth in her words. He'd missed his chance. Markus and the others weren't the kind of men to give him a second chance.

"Damn it!" He hefted the packages and turned into a sudden drizzle of rain, determined to find another way into Markus's good favor.

"Mister?"

Hamish glanced over his shoulder at one of the young women from the house sticking her head out the door.

"You 'ere for Mr. Laundry?" she said.

Hope flared. "Is he here?"

She shook her head and stepped into the rain, holding a short cape over her head. "Said 'e was meetin' someone, but the bloke never showed." She eyed his torn overcoat. "You the bloke?"

The rough term was better than he deserved. "Aye."

"Thought so. Was it important?"

"Aye."

She watched him for a moment, her cape now soaked. "All right, mister, come quiet like. Don't want Mrs. Banner to catch me sneakin' you 'round back."

He obliged, not wishing to fool himself into thinking his day's luck had changed.

It had taken months of him coming to this piss-ridden cesspool, months of earning the hard-won trust of men like Markus Laundry, a man with scars and stories too brutal for innocent eyes and ears.

This meeting had been his chance. If he could win over a man like Markus, the rest would welcome him in so he could revitalize his name and estate, no matter the legal ramifications. He could undo everything his father had destroyed.

And he'd been bloody late.

"It's here, mister."

He followed the direction of her nod. They'd stopped at another intersection of darkened alley, this door all but hidden in shadow, though the frame had been replaced sometime in the last century, a minor improvement.

"He's here?"

"They're all 'ere."

"All?" Hamish cursed repeatedly, this time at Mrs. Banner. They'd been this close the whole time? If he could mend the bridge, he'd come straight here next time and avoid the witch.

He pulled a small purse from his pocket and placed it in the girl's hand. "I'm obliged, miss."

She stared at the purse like it was some creature from the deep, then, seeming to realize their seedy location and the more dangerous creatures patrolling here, she tucked the blunt away and looked Hamish in the eye. "Watch 'ur back, mister. They be 'bout in the middle of cards if I got me time right. They get mean when you in'rupt."

He stored that information away and went to tip his hat, remembering he'd left the blasted thing on the carriage seat. He bowed his head instead. "Again, miss, you have my gratitude."

The girl blushed and handed him a towel from her skirt. "'Ere. It's clean. Wipe the wet or you'll get sick."

He opened his mouth to thank her a third time, but she waved him off and left.

He dabbed his face and knocked. The door creaked open on its own accord, and Hamish entered uninvited, aware he was taking his life into his hands.

The hallway was cold. Evidence of bright wallpaper lined the walls, leading to a door at the far end, light flickering under and bringing the sounds of shuffling cards and vicious insults.

Hamish followed the hall and took one last breath to steady his nerves before he opened the door.

A well-attended fire lit the room. Furniture pressed up against the walls to accommodate a large table where six men, and what suspiciously looked like a young woman, sat playing a round.

One of the men threw his hand on the table, a jagged scar on his neck flashing. "Hand it over, Zans. If you can beat me straight, I'll eat me cap."

Hamish stepped over the threshold, his gaze fixing on the scar, his stomach dropping.

"Markus."

The man with the straight glanced over at him, his jovial mood vanishing. "Son o' a bitch." Markus stood and faced him extracting a knife from his pocket, and pointing it at Hamish's heart. "I should kill ye, lying scum."

CHAPTER FIFTEEN

S HE'D KILL HIM!

Charlotte finished stuffing her hair into her cap, imagining all the ways she'd make the Duke of Camine beg for his miserable, domineering life.

"Stay here." Ha!

If he wanted a dog for a companion, he should get a basset.

She descended the carriage and followed him through a maze of alleys, the reek of filth churning her stomach. She padded her inside pocket, looking for the comfortable weight of her brother's pistol. Her fingers dug through empty fabric.

She stopped. "Bullocks!"

The duke hadn't returned her weapon. Loaded or not, it was an easy deterrent without the risk of her accidently shooting off a toe.

She looked up to where the duke had turned out of sight. "In for a penny," she whispered and moved.

Even from a distance, and sans her spectacles, she saw he moved with purpose, navigating the rundown back streets with a familiarity that bordered on criminal. Interest piqued, Charlotte rounded the corner and skidded back to peer at the duke conversing with the palest woman Charlotte had ever seen.

Whatever they were discussing made the duke frown.

Charlotte edged closer to hear.

"You're wasting your time here, lordy. Go back to your marble floors and gold ceilings and leave this world before it snaps you up and swallows you whole."

Charlotte studied her blurry surroundings, not a single marker identifying what world the woman meant. The ground tipped haphazardly underfoot, and a particular smell had Charlotte envisioning burning food and antiseptic.

The duke looked down at the parcels in his arm.

Up close, Charlotte saw how small they were. Each wrapped in unidentifiable brown paper in ordinary shaped boxes.

What could he possibly want with this part of town? And with packages so small, they'd barely fit her wire spectacles?

The woman shut the door with a loud *bang*, and the duke turned in her direction.

Charlotte ducked back around the corner, her mind scrambling for what to do when he inevitably caught her eavesdropping.

"Mister?"

Charlotte paused at the feminine voice. Cautiously, she peeked back at a different woman in the doorway.

She was younger than the last and looked a great deal less like the undead. She was rather handsome for a woman, with real curves and a springy bob that was considered too short to flatter a woman's face.

The woman stepped into the rain, whispering something to the duke that made his face brighten.

For some reason, that made Charlotte's chest tighten. She wished he would turn and see her, but the woman moved in the other direction down the alley, the duke right behind.

Telling herself she was regaining her sense of direction, Charlotte followed.

The streets grew darker and, if possible, closer, until Charlotte felt like a hat in a box, a decidedly small box.

When they stopped this time, Charlotte's eyes widened as the duke handed over a full purse. Suddenly, Charlotte had a rather good idea of what a young, handsome man could want in a dark alley with a beautiful woman.

The woman blushed at something he'd said.

Charlotte felt like the ground had opened beneath her.

A tryst?

This time it was jealousy, hot and cold waves of it fighting back and forth as her thoughts did the same.

He's an unmarried gentleman.

But he kissed you.

He's not yours.

But you were waiting in his carriage.

Charlotte felt justified in her decision to leave the coach. He'd expected her to sit on the street in the middle of Dockside so he could keep his 'appointment'? The man had some nerve and, when she got a hold of him, he'd also have a smarting bruise to the eye.

But the woman didn't bring him into the building. To Charlotte's astonishment and relief, after handing the duke what appeared to be a dish towel, the woman left, leaving him facing the building with a stiff set to his shoulders.

Charlotte pressed into a shadowed doorway, holding her breath as the woman passed.

"Gonna get 'imself killed messin' with those men. Hope 'is product is worth the risk."

She stared after the woman, her rumblings filling Charlotte with dread.

Those men? Product?

She whirled around and watched the duke disappear into the darkness of a hall beyond the door. The lock latched shut, and Charlotte knew the real reason a duke would skulk around the unforgiving gutter in the middle of the day.

Charlotte took off in the opposite direction, praying his appointment would give her enough of a head start to get the bloody hell out of Dockside before it ended.

She wove through the streets, plagued by numerous stops and backtracks from dead ends. By the time she'd found the main street, her stomach was a twisted wreck.

She'd tasted her first whiskey, been kissed by a woman, and nearly made a grown man wet himself with her brother's unloaded pistol, but Charlotte hadn't felt real fear until this moment.

She glanced over her shoulder and broke into a run, putting as much distance between herself and the Duke of Camine as possible.

Whatever the man was dealing, it was far too dark an adventure, even for her.

IT WAS A miracle Markus agreed to give him another chance. A bloody miracle.

Hamish folded the man's new request, along with three of the other five men's, on a square slip of paper and placed it safely in his breast pocket.

Hamish walked back towards the coach with renewed purpose. He'd get Gregori to start work immediately. He'd make sure the product was perfect, the finest crafted in London until all the 'Merry Men' worked with him.

An odd name for the men residing in the guttered streets of Dockside, since they were neither merry, nor all men. They were, however, powerful in their positions and the quickest way to reach his goal.

And when he had London under his empire, he'd expand, and not even the thugs in Dockside would find fault in him.

His steps slowed as he crossed the street in view of his carriage.

Lady Charlotte.

He'd forgotten all about his little troublemaker. Not his, he reminded himself.

He'd need to drop the lady at home before he swung back to

the warehouse, and then he'd wash his hands of her and her incessant mischief.

He squared his shoulders and opened the carriage door, prepared for a lecture of epic length on leaving a lady in a stuffy box.

There was no lecture.

"Where is she?" he barked at his driver.

The aging coachman glanced around, removing his cap to scratch his head. "'She,' Your Grace? I've seen no woman. The young lad with you departed the cab just after you, sir. Did he not come back with you?"

She'd left? Hamish cursed. *Damn the woman!* Had the scene in the alley not been enough for her to realize how dangerous these streets were? Regardless of the increasing number of fools who couldn't tell decidedly that she was. A. Woman.

Had she followed him?

Hamish froze, his veins filling with ice. Had she seen him go into the Merry Men's den? Had she guessed what secrets he hid in those brown packages?

He took off like a shot down the alley, leaving the door to the empty coach wide open.

CHARLOTTE SAT IN the drawing room and stared out the window, watching the afternoon light play across the cobblestone street below.

She'd finally made it back to the Louis family townhouse, hours after sneaking out, to find not one person missing her, everyone believing she'd taken to her room.

Charlotte thought of the ruckus of the Dockside bar, the place warm and full of drunken laughter, and wished she'd never left.

Quiet. That's all she'd heard for the past decade. With her brother's infrequent visits from school full of duty, and her success to rid herself of every governess and chaperone within twenty miles, she'd been left with the proper and silent staff of a duke. A house run as if by ghosts elicited the worst kind of loneliness.

Her chest tensed. She wished someone would cough, slam a door, break a dish—anything to make her feel like she wasn't sentenced to fade into nothingness.

Movement on the street below caught her eye.

She stared down at a man in dust-ridden clothes, his overcoat torn down the back seam.

As if sensing her, the man looked up.

Charlotte gasped as the Duke of Camine mouthed her name, his gaze wild.

He crossed the street and out of view.

Bang! Bang! Bang!

The pounding on the front door echoed through the quiet. Charlotte shot to her feet, whirling around to find a means of escape.

But she was too late.

The drawing room door slammed open, revealing the duke and a servant fidgeting behind him.

"Leave," he snarled.

The servant fled, and the duke slammed the door, his gaze never once leaving her.

"Where the hell have you been?"

Charlotte gripped her skirts and forced herself to calm down. She'd vowed after she'd caught him in the alley that she wouldn't give herself away. The man's business was not her own. The trouble she'd wanted from him initially had been ill-placed. She wouldn't make the mistake a second time.

She smiled and indicated the settee. "Sit, Duke. Would you care for tea?"

"Tea? *Tea!*" He advanced, his anger and tall frame crowding her until the back of her legs struck the window seat.

He didn't stop until he towered over her. "I've been traipsing across all of London looking for you. Why the hell didn't you stay in the coach like I ordered?"

Self-preservation didn't stand a chance with a gentleman's arrogance taking up all available space.

"Ordered, indeed!" she replied. "Call Scotland Yard because I refused to stay in that hatbox when you left me to go who knows where for who knows how long. I returned home, after you said you'd escort me and didn't." She thrust her wrists out between them. "Take me away, constable. Mystery solved."

His words retained their bite, but the anger in his gaze cooled. "You could've been accosted."

She heard the echo of concern from their earlier conversation. No. He was concerned over her brother's ire should he find out his sister had vanished under his care.

She couldn't stop herself from saying, "Rest assured, Your Grace, the only accosting was done in your carriage."

He froze. His voice was decidedly quieter when he said with real contrition, "Forgive me, my lady. I acted deplorably. I swear to you there will be no further incidents."

The apology was like acid down her throat. Incidents? How could he possibly call what they'd done anything less than pure bliss? Had it truly meant nothing to him?

"I refuse your apology."

He startled. "You can't refuse."

"I can. I do." It was her turn to push him back, her arms gesturing wildly in her tempered state. "Of all the insulting, asinine, *male* things you've said, you honestly think you can say you're sorry and everything is forgotten?"

The duke raised his hands in surrender. "I understand the incident—"

"Stop calling it 'an incident'! It was intentional and savage and the best moment of my life!"

She grabbed him by the lapels and kissed him.

Chapter Sixteen

I N ALL OF Hamish's experience, and it was extensive, before Charlotte, he'd never once let a woman take the lead. It was disorienting, chaotic, and yet he didn't stop her. Not when her nails dug into his ruined overcoat and pulled him closer, and certainly not when her tongue ran the seam of his lips like a Goddamn succubus sent to tempt him from his very soul.

He growled in his throat.

The sound seemed to shake her confidence, because her grip loosened, and her tongue retreated.

"No!" He reached for her, refusing to let her get away. He gripped the back of her head and forced her mouth back open with a firm thumb to her chin. His tongue pushed inside, taking, *needing* her passion, her anger, her submission.

Catnip to a cat.

Flesh to a monster.

Hamish broke the kiss and pushed her away, shame and guilt fighting for dominance while something more dangerous rose to the surface.

Longing.

"We have to stop," he said. "If we're caught, you'll be expected to . . ."

"I know, a forced proposal." She rolled her eyes. "Pistols at dawn with my brother." She reached for him again. "I have no intention of trapping you."

He avoided her touch like a goose by the fire, certain one brush of skin on skin and he'd let them roast alive and damn the consequences. He loved roasted fowl. "No, Charlotte. We need to stop. If someone were to see, you'd never have a proposal—ever."

That stopped her, but it wasn't gratitude in her voice. "Stop telling me what I need. What I need is to make my own decisions about my life and body. What I need is for you to kiss me again. What I *need* is for someone to finally see me and not run away!"

Hamish stared at her, for a second unsure if the words had come from her mouth or his soul. When he did speak, he found his fingers brushing her cheek. "Who doesn't see you?"

She shook her head, her gaze dropping away.

He made a point to stay away from people and their ridiculous insecurities, but he couldn't stay away, not when he saw the brave front she offered hid more than a woman brimming with intelligence and fire. He turned her face back. "Tell me."

Her gaze met his.

Hamish saw vulnerability, but, as with every soft side he'd uncovered of hers, it came with a strength of will that humbled him. Strength to reach for what she wanted, to face her darker thoughts and impulses. Strength above all to speak the truth even at the risk of rejection.

"Tell me," he repeated.

A single tear rolled down her cheek. "Anyone."

The one word destroyed him. To think anyone could turn away from her sheer brilliance. She was like a living sun, impossible to ignore.

But hadn't he done the same as a young boy? What an ass he'd been. An oblivious, blind ass.

A loud, masculine voice in the hall broke the spell.

She returned to the present, wiping her face with a sleeve and donning the air of a woman receiving a visitor without a hair out of place.

He hated it.

"He's here? Why wasn't I told immediately?" The door opened, and the Duke of Lux strolled in, the servant from earlier in tow. "I told you to inform me the minute the marquess arrived." His voice cut off as he took in Hamish, overcoat torn and no doubt smelling like rotting fish. "You're not the marquess."

"Must be the lack of drool." Hamish winked at Charlotte, needing to see her smile again. "Hard to differentiate when we both know I don't underindulge in anything."

The tiniest smirk curled her mouth, and the clouds parted to reveal a blazing ray of sunlight.

"Amusing." Renard sounded anything but. "Come for another glass of cheap swill?"

Hamish glanced again at Charlotte to gauge her reaction. "I'm in the mood for something sweeter."

She turned a tantalizing shade of pink.

Oblivious, Renard said, "Sherry? Drinks will need to wait, I'm afraid. I expect the Marquess of Slasbury any minute."

Charlotte stiffened. "He said next week."

Renard waved her statement away. "I've been in contact. We decided to expedite the visit after you expressed your anxiety over the match." He circled her with a critical eye. "Grey washes you out. Don't you have a dress less depressing you could wear?"

"I've worn it all day without you commenting."

Her words were clipped and so full of venom, Hamish worried his friend would walk out of the drawing room with fang marks.

"And I wasn't *anxious*," she said. "I refused the match. I will not marry him."

Renard rubbed his temple, shooting Hamish a regretful expression. "Sorry for all the trouble again. Sisters, right?"

For the first time, Hamish didn't feel the easy comradery or see a man desperate to protect his sister; he saw a man eager to hand off his responsibilities, deaf to the pleas of a woman who needed only the attention of an affectionate brother to be happy.

"Do not be condescending," she said. "I've catered to your selfish and stubborn nature. I've tried outwardly refusing. You still don't hear me." She reached out her hands, pleading. "Please, Ren, hear me."

See me.

Hamish heard the words she didn't say. The beast deep inside of him lifted its head and snarled its acceptance.

Renard's ears were sewn shut. "Go change into something more appropriate. Try something ruffled, feminine. We can discuss this more when the marquess arrives. I'm sure Lord Slasbury can assuage all your concerns over tea."

Her eyes swam with unshed tears.

The sadness was for the breaking relationship between her and her brother, Hamish thought.

Renard only saw the tears. "Now, now, Lotte." He patted her head. "There's no need to fret. The marquess will make a fine husband. Kind and stable. After you've married, he'll bring you back to the country, where you can go back to your quiet life."

Charlotte recoiled. "I don't want stability. I want to *live!*"

The passion in her voice called once again to his beast, and Hamish felt a claiming in the roar that followed.

A bird. That was exactly what he saw when he looked at her. A beautiful songbird, intelligent, inquisitive, and locked in a gilded cage of helplessness.

A bird that wanted to be free.

See me.

And the decision was made.

"It's done," Renard said.

"No," said Hamish.

They both looked at him.

Hamish repeated, "No."

Renard ran a hand through his hair. "Sorry, Ham. I know how much you loathe drama. Go on to the library."

He continued to ramble, but Hamish was looking at Charlotte, who watched him, heard what he was saying.

"I'll join you promptly," Renard continued. "We'll toast to the marquess's good fortune."

Hamish said again, holding her gaze, "No."

I see you.

Her eyes widened.

"You were right, Renard," Hamish said. "It's done."

Renard paused, seeing the look between them for the first time. "Did I miss something?" He stopped, understanding draining the color from his face. "No," he whispered. "Ham?" He looked at Charlotte. "Lotte?"

"It's done," Hamish said again, his eyes all for her. *I see you.* "She's ruined."

"THAT'S NOT FUNNY," Renard said.

Hamish shrugged, landing the final blow. "The freckle behind her left knee was too much to resist."

"What?!" Renard exploded.

Charlotte didn't hear her brother. Didn't see him. Lord Hamish Hurstfield, Duke of Camine, took up her whole view.

I see you.

She heard him and, in that moment, knew she'd care for him the rest of her life. Her life. It was hers now. To share or not. To fill with laughter or quiet. It was her decision.

"I'll kill you!"

Renard's blow landed with a nasty crunch and Lord Camine fell, not seeing the hit coming, not bothering to look away from her, as if she were the only person in the room.

"Get up, you bastard!" Blood ran down Renard's knuckles, but he didn't seem to notice. He stood over Hamish, raising his arm for another blow. "She's my sister. I'll kill you!"

Charlotte socked him in the eye. The thrill was quickly curbed by a stinging pain in her knuckles. "Bullocks!"

She cradled her hand, her thumb aching.

Hamish was up and at her side, not an ounce of pain showing on his face despite a bloody nose. He inspected her hand, his touch gentle, the skin-to-skin contact blazing.

He grinned. "Nice punch."

She grinned back. "Another item off my list."

He prodded a tender spot on her hand.

She winced. "Is it broken?"

He shook his head. "Sprained."

Renard clutched his eye. "Bloody hell, Char. What was that for?"

"For being a ruddy arse." She nodded at Hamish. "At least one of you is civil."

"Civil?" Renard dropped his hand to point at the other man, his eye already swelling. "You've been ruined by my best chap, and *I'm* being uncivil?"

"You needn't shout, Ren," Hamish said. "I'm sure the whole house knows by now without the outburst."

Charlotte shook her head, unable to stop smiling. "You shouldn't bait him. He may still call you out, you know?"

The smile he gave in return was devilish. "A bullet to the chest is worth seeing him planted on his ass."

"Enough!" Renard went to the sidebar and poured himself two fingers. "I'm glad you two can joke. No one will marry you now."

"You *do* care if I remain virtuous, after all?" Charlotte said, recalling her brother's insistence that Hamish would keep any liaisons between them a secret.

"I only said that so you wouldn't think your mad idea worth implementing. Of course I care. What if the servants talk?"

Charlotte didn't regret it. She wouldn't apologize. What she did regret was the look of defeat on her brother's face, defeat that he'd be saddled with supporting her a day more than necessary.

"I'll take the trust like I planned," she said. "I'll leave England." She could visit America and its exotic mixture of wild and industry. She'd try her hand as a seamstress or a governess, after she'd done all the things she'd dreamed up on her list. A life of adventure.

"She will marry," Hamish said.

Charlotte frowned and opened her mouth to ask what she'd missed, but her brother's snort cut her off.

"And who exactly would bear the brunt of this scandal? What man would take her now?"

"Me."

Charlotte swung around, finding his eyes on her, not a trace of humor in them.

Renard voiced her disbelief. "It must be the whiskey in my ears—"

"There won't be a scandal," he said. "She'll marry me."

A knock on the door left them all frozen in place, Hamish's words hanging in the air like theatrical farce.

"Your Grace?" The same servant opened the door. He bowed and looked up. When no response was forthcoming, he cleared his throat. "The Marquess of Slasbury has come to call." His gaze darted to his master and then to her and Hamish. "Shall I tell him you're out?"

No one moved.

They stood like that, no one speaking, all waiting for someone to applaud, to confirm that Hamish's words were as empty as Renard's glass.

But when Hamish turned to address the servant in his master's stead, he confirmed the sneaking suspicion that made Charlotte's heart both skip and drop.

"Send him away." Hamish grabbed her hand and brought her bruised knuckles to his mouth, sliding his lips scandalously over bare skin and capturing her gaze. His words held a note of finality that echoed in her soul. "She's mine."

CHAPTER SEVENTEEN

HAMISH HURSTFIELD, DUKE of Camine, notorious 'wild' rake of London, had just proposed. He was as shocked as the rest of them.

He'd saved her. She'd wanted independence and a chance to choose her own path, and he'd given it to her. They'd walk away from each other, her life changed forever and his filled with yet another bruise from an angry brother, spouse—whatever man decided to play indignant protector for the day.

And then she'd said she'd go away, leave the country.

"Leave England."

The very idea of her gone, out of reach, had left him frenzied. The beast inside had clawed its way to the surface, taken control of his voice while his mind had seized function.

"She's mine."

He thought he'd regret proposing marriage as soon as the words were spoken, but regret never came. There was a truth in claiming her, a truth not just of taking responsibility for his garish actions over the past week, but something internal. Her fire soothed the cold creature lurking in the dark. She'd caught only a glimpse of the monster he was under the tailored suit, but she hadn't run screaming like the others.

She'd begged for more.

Hamish knew then and there he'd do anything to have her, to nurture her darker inhibitions. He'd teach her to like what he offered, and, in return, he'd set her free. An exclusive sexual relationship, he'd demand that. The rest of the time would be hers to do with as she wished.

He kissed her hand again, minding her injury. "Pack a bag. We'll be to Gretna Green by tomorrow."

The glass slipped from Renard's fingers and thumped to the rug. "Really?" he asked at the same time Charlotte said, "No!"

Hamish's stomach dropped.

She tore her hand away, wincing. "That wasn't the agreement."

"I never agreed to your terms," Hamish said, burying the rush of anger at her refusal. "The fact remains you're ruined by my hands."

Renard groaned. "Can we stop saying that?"

Hamish ignored him. "We will marry."

That beautiful, stubborn chin stuck out. "No."

The absolute challenge in her eyes set his body aflame. His hands twitched to take her here, in the middle of the day in the light of the drawing room window, the servants going about their business, ignoring the only thing in this house that had any value.

He knew what she'd do, refuse profusely. But Renard would never hand over her trust, not now, which left one option.

He grabbed that chin and stared down into those eyes, daring her to look away. His voice was a purr and a warning. "I won't let you run."

Her eyes widened, confirming her plan.

He brushed kisses along her jaw, watching her gaze snap to her brother still clutching the bar.

"That's right," he said. There was no place she could go where he wouldn't find her and finish the game they'd started that night in his study. He left a last, lingering kiss on her lips, whispering as he pulled away, "There is no escaping this."

And he left her there, staring after him with one last call to Renard, "Make sure she's ready. Two hours."

He wiped the dried blood from his face and set out into the

warm London air, waving down his coachman, who must have arrived while he was inside. Good thing he'd instructed his driver to make for Louis Townhouse instead of Hamish's residence.

"Home, Mr. Jones, and be quick about it," he said.

His driver bowed and opened the door. "Yes, Your Grace."

"Your Grace?" someone said.

Hamish looked over his shoulder, one foot on the block.

The Marquess of Slasbury stood on the walk, conspicuous with a top hat and a gold-inlaid walking stick, and his usual golden chain. A right dandy, indeed. A dandy who'd lost his lady.

With no small amount of satisfaction, he acknowledged the other gentleman. "Lord Slasbury."

The marquess nodded to the coach. "I thought I recognized your crest." His gaze flicked back to the Lux Townhouse, his brows drawn. "Did you come from seeing the Duke of Lux? I was told he wasn't at home."

The unfailing propriety of English servants, Hamish thought. The papers would hear of it soon enough. "Lady Charlotte, actually."

"The lady?" Slasbury scoffed. "What would someone like you want with a lady of the *ton?*"

"Someone like you."

The words ripped open a long-buried scar from a lifetime ago. When Hamish had found the forbidden side of a woman's attention exciting and new. Only to realize his inclinations would garner nothing but disgust from a proper lady.

Not every lady.

Charlotte was a revelation, untouched by tainted ideals or the prudish tendencies of society.

Mine.

He smiled. "What else would 'someone like me' want with a beautiful lady?" He reveled in the marquess's shocked expression, aware the truth should be far more so.

He climbed into the carriage and told the driver to go, his day brightening with every second. Calling out the open window, he waved farewell to the other man. "The Duchess of Camine has a lovely ring to it, don't you think?"

Hamish faced forward as the vehicle jolted into motion, finding the title did indeed have a nice ring. Sounded like ringing bells instead of what he'd assumed marriage would conquer up in a chained man. In fact, the tinkling of metal restraints sounded like a perfect way to celebrate the end of bachelorhood.

"DID THAT JUST happen?" Renard asked.

Charlotte came back to herself at her brother's quiet disbelief. She was engaged. It had indeed happened. She'd become Lady Hurstfield, the Duchess of Camine.

"There's no escaping me."

The duke didn't come across as a man who broke his word.

"There's no escaping me."

Heaven forgive her, she didn't *want* to escape. The darkness she'd seen in his eyes drew out her body and mind's deepest desires. The harshest, most disciplined governess wouldn't stand a chance at holding back.

He challenged her, encouraged her, and never once expected anything but what she was: raw and honest. His darkness called to her.

But she hadn't liked *all* the darkness.

In the mayhem of him charging through her door, quite literally backing her into a corner, she'd forgotten the alley and the duke's less-than-amiable dealings in Dockside.

A chasm opened in her stomach. She could still run, board a ship to America and plead with God she'd make it to foreign soil before he dragged her back to England. Surely, someone there would help her escape.

I wanted adventure.

Charlotte shook her head. She did want adventure, but not at the cost of her life or someone she . . . cared for. She was grateful to him interceding on her behalf. She liked him, nothing more.

Her friend's words replayed over and over. *"The Duke of Camine would certainly be an adventure."*

Charlotte couldn't help but smile.

He certainly would be.

She'd write a letter to her friend. If the duke was truly coming in two hours' time to whisk her away, she didn't wish Diana distress over her lack of correspondence.

Which was a lie. She didn't want to raise an alarm with her friend, but truthfully, she needed advice.

"I'll be in my room," she said on her way out the door. She paused on the threshold, a last sliver of hope waiting for her brother to rouse from his liquid state and show some semblance of sibling concern.

He retrieved his glass from the rug and nodded.

Charlotte left with her answer.

In her room, she found Harper in a flurry of motion, boxing the contents from her vanity, laying out the dresses from her wardrobe across the bed, gathering odds and ends around the room and placing them meticulously in large trunks.

She's packing, Charlotte thought stupidly.

Whether the walls truly had ears, or the servant who'd gone and fetched Renard had stayed long enough to hear her brother's outburst, the staff knew about her very recent plans for departure.

Charlotte continued to watch the whirlwind that was her maid, finding herself detached, especially when another maid arrived to help without a word.

Was this what her life would be like? Being left in the wake of people going about their days, only acknowledging her when obligated?

Being a duke's sister didn't allow friendliness with the staff, but would being a duchess? Renard hadn't seen fit to discharge his housekeeper of her role of running the household without consultation with the lady of the house. At the estate, too, there'd never been a discussion of Charlotte overseeing the staff, like her mother had.

Charlotte's emotions jumbled together, a laugh tumbling out in the confusion. She was as prepared for being a duchess as she was to take tea with the queen.

Was she accepting the duke's proposal, then? Not that he'd *asked* her.

"*We will marry,*" he'd said. No pretty speech or offering of affection.

The ache in her stomach grew.

Her feet moved on their own, seeking the one person who had never steered her wrong. She sat at the little drawing table she'd begged Renard to put in her chambers and smoothed out a new piece of parchment before inking her quill.

Dear Diana,

I'm at a loss. I wanted to escape impending nuptials with the marquess, but I may have escaped one noose for another, more dangerous one. It seems we must postpone our meeting indefinitely now.

The Duke of Camine explained that we are to marry. Even now my maid continues to pack my every possession away for Gretna Green, as if a life may be picked up and left in two—no, three trunks.

I had no intention of marrying so soon. A man will never allow his wife to explore. But I find myself torn. Should I stay? You yourself said the man would be an adventure, and I must agree.

Then again, my stomach feels quite sick, and I can't shake the feeling that a life, even one destined for the altar, should amount to more than three trunks and a bodily complaint.

I wish you were here. You'd know what to do.

Your friend,
Charlotte

Charlotte instructed the maid to send out the letter and was shocked when a reply came not an hour later.

Dear Charlotte,

The mission was a success? How did he propose? One knee? Flowers? I must assume you have some feelings for the gentleman if you're considering marriage. As for eloping, what's the rush? Were you caught in a compromising position? (Not that I would think less of you if you were.) Does the public know?

If you have a speck of concern, then you must stop and evaluate. From what I've heard of the man, he must care for you as well, or he'd never have offered. Men believe bachelorhood grants some misguided freedom, the silly creatures.

What is it you want, Charlotte? Even when you struggled making decisions before, you knew the right course. A man shouldn't change your mind, perhaps merely your perspective.

Your life, your decision.

A man, marriage, nothing need change that.

Your friend always,
Diana Yamsbee

Charlotte finished the letter, already knowing her decision.

When had she let the Duke of Camine take control of her future? Whatever notion the ladies of the *ton* had, believing a wife submitted to every whim of their husband, was ludicrous.

She prayed that Hamish's feelings were warm towards her and not out of a fleeting sense of obligation. Honor was a beautiful thing—it also led men into loveless marriages.

She refused to be a part of any of it.

If the duke wanted her, he would be reminded she was a woman with her own mind, and unafraid to use it.

"Harper, stop," she said.

Her maid turned with startled eyes, as if she'd forgotten Charlotte were there. "My lady?"

"Stop," Charlotte repeated. She looked to the other maid, who'd stopped as well. "What is your name?"

"Ellen, my lady," she said.

Charlotte smiled. "Ellen, please fetch my brother and bring

him to the study."

The young woman curtsied and left without another word.

For once, Charlotte was grateful for the unquestioning loyalty. She returned to her lady's maid. "Harper, I require a smaller trunk. Pack for warm weather for two weeks' time. Then I need you to gather the rest of the house staff and bring them to the study as well."

Harper's brows furrowed. "All of them, my lady?"

"All."

Harper dragged the smallest of the three trunks over and began repacking. "Are you not going to Gretna—" She cleared her throat. "Not going on an extended trip, my lady?"

Charlotte ignored her maid's horrified squeak and assisted with packing, knowing she'd need every minute of the last hour to set her plan into motion before Hamish returned.

She grabbed two of the gowns Harper had procured for her, the ones that required minimal help to get in and out of on her own.

The ache in her stomach had vanished. Her smile resurfaced. "Not Gretna Green, anyway," she said. She imagined the smell of horses and the feel of warm sunshine on her face. "I have a completely different destination in mind."

CHAPTER EIGHTEEN

AFTER SENDING A quick word to Percy to retrieve the splintered conveyance—once identified as his carriage—from the main thoroughfare, Hamish stepped through his front door, his shin and elbow smarting. Of all the times for his coach wheel to come loose!

He'd been lucky he'd had enough mind to push himself away from the seat when the damn thing had tipped, or he'd be suffering much worse than a few bruises. As it was, he'd pulled something in his arm half-dragging his driver to the nearest clinic. He'd have a word with his soon-to-be-fired coachman about proper maintenance on all his carriages once the man regained consciousness. The bloody accident had set him back a solid half an hour.

He dropped the ruined overcoat on the foyer floor, leaving whatever course of care for the garment, whether mending or burning, to the discretion of his staff.

He needed a bath and a shave. *Two baths*, he thought, getting a whiff of stench he'd acquired stomping through the infested back alleys of Dockside.

His housekeeper materialized in the hall. "You look like right shit. Again."

He laughed, the reaction becoming standard. When had he stopped scowling all the time?

Camille pinched her nose and gave him a wide berth on his

way to the study. "Tell me that's not actual shit on your boots?"

He shrugged. The side street he'd cut through to get home hadn't been exactly pristine. "One never knows."

She followed him down the hall. "What happened? You look beaten, and I've never seen that goofy look on your face." She eyed him suspiciously. "If I didn't know better, I'd say you were . . ."

"Happy?" he supplied.

She looked horrified and peered out the study window. "Has London frozen over, then?"

Hamish set about scribbling two notes and handed them to her. "Have this one sent to Gregori. Use the usual runner. This one goes to the post."

He kicked off his mysterious-substance-coated boots into the fireplace and rang for his valet.

"You're betrothed!"

He whirled at his housekeeper's outburst, not surprised she'd opened his letters. "It's a criminal offense to read a man's private post."

"Poppycock," she said. "Is it Lady Charlotte?"

He frowned at her rush of enthusiasm and took a turn to examine the streets outside. "Must be frozen."

"The lady is a delight and far too good for you."

He had to agree. "A lesser man would call your loyalty into question, dear Camille."

"It *is* her!" She fluttered around the room like a damn sparrow.

"You *are* capable of feeling joy," he said dryly. "Who knew?" Charlotte truly made everyone fall in love with her. Bruisers, wenches, hack drivers, even frigid would-be housekeepers.

"She said 'yes,' right?" Her expression dimmed. "You didn't go and do something garish and tell her it was a man's obligation?"

"I asked." Thinking about it, he realized he hadn't asked at all. His ears went hot.

Missing nothing, Camille smacked herself in the forehead. "Idiot!"

"I never used the term 'obligation.'"

"I'm sure words of poetry and affection poured out of your mouth like too much spit." She snorted. "You'll be lucky if she's still there when you return. If I were her, I'd run as far as possible."

She'd voiced the very fear whispering in his mind. He'd given Charlotte two hours. Now he wished he'd dragged her back here with him to keep her close.

Charlotte wouldn't get away.

He went for the door, wasting no more time. "Get Mr. Bernard to prepare the water for my bath and pack my bag. I want to be ready to leave by the time I've finished bathing."

She didn't acknowledge him.

He stopped. "Camille!"

She sent him a scathing look. "Yes, Your Grace?"

He knew that look and imagined the shredded formal wear at her revenge. "Mr. Bernard," he said.

She curtsied, the gesture freakishly perfect. "Your valet will be informed posthaste. Is there anything else you demand, my lord?"

He flinched at the honorific. His cravats would die a painful death at the bottom of his bin. He wouldn't need cravats in Scotland, he reminded himself.

"Yes." He cleared his throat. "Make sure Bringon looks over all the coaches and carriages, especially the wheels. I want the phaeton examined and pulled up to the front by the time I finish refreshing myself."

Brow quirking, she nodded but didn't press for details.

He turned to leave, and her words followed him out the door and all the way up the stairs.

"Better hurry, Hamish. The longer you wait, the more time the lady has to come to her senses."

"Ha!" he called back.

He hurried.

⟶⟫⟪⟵

HAMISH WASHED AND clothed in record time. Two quarters of an hour later, he was knocking on the Louis family's door, his foot tapping the walk, waiting for a servant to allow him entrance.

One, two, three... After ten taps, he readied to burst through unannounced, as he'd done not three hours previously.

The door opened and the same spindly young servant from before nodded. "Your Grace, welcome."

Hamish paused. The servant's calm demeanor was so different from his last reception. Where was the butler?

His neck prickled. The formal greeting, the delayed answer to the door . . . Something had changed.

He entered, his voice unnaturally loud, "Where is she?"

The boy didn't bat an eyelash at his rudeness. "Lady Charlotte will be down promptly."

He vanished down a bisecting hall, leaving Hamish standing in the empty foyer, not a person in sight.

Panic gripped him. He bound up the steps two at a time, his gaze trained on the top step, willing her to appear.

Then he heard a feminine voice above him.

He froze halfway to the top. The voice grew louder.

For a moment, he thought she wouldn't show, foolishly dismissing his threat and taking off in one last stand of defiance.

A second later she was there, descending the stairs in that same grey dress, her expression serene as she stopped on the stair above him, not a trunk in sight.

"Hello," she said.

His body warmed at the purr in her voice. "Where is your luggage?"

"It's coming," she said.

He didn't like the look of her smirk.

"Good." He offered his hand, needing her secure in his carriage before he'd allow himself to breathe. "Let's go."

At that precise moment, two servants arrived on the stairs, a laughably small trunk between them.

The servants passed, and Hamish's suspicions grew. "Since when does a lady bring less than half the house when traveling?"

"You've never traveled with me, Duke." Her smile was positively feline. "Half the house isn't reasonable where we're going."

"You've been to Scotland before, then?"

"Not once," she said. "But I look forward to seeing it—in the *future*."

Her emphasis on 'future' didn't escape him. He smelled another venture coming, and it had the reek of trouble. "And where, pray tell, are we going?"

She smiled that sun-blazing smile.

Hamish had to grasp the railing to keep upright.

"What every bride does when they find the man they'll marry," she said. "I'm bringing you home."

"'Home'?" Hamish tested the word, feeling like he'd missed the detached emotion that should've been prevalent in her voice. "The country house you hate?"

"'Hate'?" She blinked. "Dear me, I see I've given a most unflattering impression. I don't hate the country. Merely the quiet."

The way she said 'the country' piqued his curiosity. He crossed his arms. "I'll play along. What will we be doing in the country?"

"Courting."

What the hell? "Usually, when a woman agrees to a man's proposal, the courting ceases."

She responded to his dry tone with one of her own. "As you've not asked and I haven't agreed, I don't see your point."

"Ah."

Damn Camille! Where the hell had that insipid advice about flowers and poetry been three and a half hours ago?

"Your point is moot," he said. "The fact is, you're ruined, and any second the post will receive a letter confirming you and I are betrothed."

"'Betrothed'?" That terrifyingly calculated look she got sometimes was back. "Then the *ton* has no reason to demand a quick wedding. Giving us a solid month before anything must be decided."

What a fantasy world the lady lived in. "Hate to ruin your naive dream, my dear, but this isn't a normal betrothal. Your staff has already blabbed to every grocer, stableboy, and runner within a square kilometer. If the *ton* isn't shouting 'scandal' by the end of the day, they will be tomorrow."

"What a horrible pessimist you are," she said. "There's no worry about any such betrayal."

"And how have you come to that unlikely scenario?"

"Simple. The whole staff will be joining us."

It was then Hamish noticed the flurry in the house. Servants hauling livery trunks, cooks bringing a favorite pot or pan in a cacophony of discordant banging.

She wasn't bringing half the house.

He shook his head. "You can't bring the whole staff in one carriage."

"Now who's being naive?" She *tsked* and descended the stairs. "Of course one won't be enough. We'll bring four."

CHAPTER NINETEEN

S HE HONESTLY WAS packing the entire staff!

Hamish's gaze cut from one person to the next. "Where is Renard?"

She shrugged and walked towards the door. "Around."

Drunk, stuffed in a trunk, and strapped to a carriage unwilling to put up a fight, Hamish imagined.

"Come along now. Don't dawdle," she called over her shoulder.

Hamish stormed after her. "Listen here! There is no way I'm participating in whatever spectacle of a parade you've cooked up—"

She thrust a pair of gloves into his hands. "Hold these." She added a second pair. "And these." She waved a hand. "Go on. You were griping about my plan so righteously."

"I . . ." He fumbled as she stacked another three pairs of kid gloves in his filling arms. "How many gloves does a lady need in the country?"

She grinned. "You did seem to think I should pack more."

He dropped the gloves in a heap on the entry table, his voice echoing in the vaulted foyer like a god declaring his absolute power. "Enough of this farce! We are going to Gretna Green. End of discussion."

＊＞＞＞＞Ｘ＜＜＜＜＊

AN HOUR LATER, they were on the road to the Lux country estate, Hamish's legs permanently stuck to his chest so as not to disturb the mountain of trunks placed haphazardly on the seats and floor around him while the lady sat a comfortable three in a carriage at the front of their caravan.

Madness. He'd suffered a fleeting case of madness to agree to Charlotte's ridiculous terms. It was the only explanation he'd accept.

He wouldn't be swayed by the wistfulness in her voice when she'd talked about her childhood home. Nor thinking of how a month of courting the lady would be a heavenly experiment in sweet drinks, lazy days, and stolen kisses.

He wouldn't be thrown off so easily. He'd take advantage of the quiet and lack of distractions to begin her instruction in the darker side of pleasure. A week and he'd have the lady begging to bind herself to him, in more ways than one.

"You're grinning like a snake. I find it disconcerting when there's no one for miles to hear my screams for help." Renard's voice came from a small break in the luggage, no doubt buried under a certain lady's instruction.

"It doesn't appear *my* wrath is what you need worry about."

Renard sighed. "I don't know when my sister became a military general. She had the whole staff jumping at her orders. By the time I'd sobered up enough to object, it was too late." He closed his eyes and leaned his head back against the seat. "The damage is done regardless. My only hope now is she comes to her senses and follows through with a proper marriage."

Served the bastard right. It surprised Hamish how attractive he found Charlotte's strong will and stubborn nature when it wasn't directed at him.

"Speaking of terrifying relations, does the postponement mean I shall have the opportunity to meet this infamous sister of yours?" Renard asked.

Hamish tapped his thigh. He hadn't thought of inviting his sister. Now it looked likely there would be a week at least before he could talk Charlotte into reconsidering her scheme, he could send for her. The pomp, the show, and of course the bride-to-be . . . His sister would shit herself laughing.

"If this farce goes more than a few days, you may get your wish," Hamish said. At least *someone* should enjoy themselves.

Charlotte was sure to enjoy the company, whether a companion be blue blooded or some color more common or, in his sister's case, more colorful than a light prism.

"I don't understand," Renard said. "You swore you'd never marry. Now here you are, trailing after the nonsensical whims of a lady. I say run while you still have the chance."

"Delivering unsolicited advice now?" Hamish scoffed. "Does this make us friends again?"

Renard shrugged. "It would be too much work training a new companion to ignore my dull personality and profuse drinking."

Hamish heard a note of the good-natured banter that had characterized their friendship since childhood. Unlike the irresponsible prick who'd been impersonating the Duke of Lux the past weeks.

Hamish took a good look at his lifelong friend.

Renard had always been a simple boy with simple pleasures. Even after inheriting a dukedom at a terribly early age, he'd taken the bone-crushing responsibility in stride, deferring to experts when he could, delegating when he couldn't, all without losing that simple spirit.

It was the one trait Hamish envied. If only Renard's fastidious nature had been applied to Lady Charlotte's education, they wouldn't be jammed into this carriage like sardines. It was like Renard had stayed as far away from his sister—emotionally and physically—as possible after their parents' deaths. A far cry from the boy always going on about his clever little sister.

The man across from him in no way resembled the friend

he'd always known. Dark circles, clothes hanging off his frame like a poorly dressed scarecrow. Hamish had been so overwhelmed attempting—and failing—to resist the charms of a certain nonsensical lady, he'd missed his friend slowly fading away.

To quote his housekeeper, "You look like shit, Ren."

There was a quick chuckle from under the luggage. "You've looked worse."

"This very afternoon," Hamish agreed.

"The difference is a decent scrub, and I'm back to my rugged good looks."

"I don't think a scrub will do it this time."

"What are you saying?"

"You need a new tailor."

Renard ran a hand through his hair, ramming an elbow into a box at eye level. "Ow! Damn it." He cradled his arm and sighed. "I hadn't realized how little I'd been eating. Cook's been ramming tarts and tea down my throat like I alone will keep the English pastry market in business." His gaze went distant looking out at the fading light.

Their earlier conversation from their scotch drinking came to mind and something clicked. Hamish recoiled. "Good Lord, you're smitten!"

Renard flinched but didn't deny it.

Hamish reeled. The 'wild' duke tamed would set tongues wagging; the 'rogue' duke caught would have the *ton*'s tongues falling off. "Who is she?"

"Doesn't matter." Those two words said everything.

"She won't have you, then?"

His shoulders slumped, looking like an overcoat on a metal wire. "Hates my arrogant, chauvinist arse."

"*Chauvinist* is true enough," Hamish said. "*Arrogant* is a little harsh."

"Her words, not mine."

"I've never known you to give up so easily. A year ago, you'd have slung a woman over your shoulder and carried her off like a true barbarian."

"I'd considered it, believe me. But she disappeared."

"She ran?"

Renard nodded.

If Hamish believed in silly things like lost love, he'd have sworn his friend looked devastated.

"I've searched everywhere, sent out the best," he said. "France, Scotland . . . I've a man stationed at Paddington day and night in case she thinks to use the railway. She's nowhere to be found."

The ugly side of affection, Hamish thought. Obsession, he understood. Was this what would become of him if he lost Charlotte?

Ridiculous. He wasn't a besotted fool. He'd never stoop so low. Besides, the lady wasn't going anywhere.

"You claim you've hired the best." Hamish thought of Percy. "I have someone better. When his business with me concludes, I'll have him find your wench."

A sickening flash of gratitude crossed Renard's face.

Hamish suddenly needed to make sure this horrible spectacle train wasn't a ploy for Charlotte to sneak away in the dark.

The sunset's warm reds and pinks were cooling into the purple and navy of evening. He searched the road for markers. He hadn't been to the Lux estate, or Camine estate, for that matter, in years, but he couldn't remember the trip taking this long.

"How much farther?" he asked.

He looked over to find Renard studying him.

"Not to worry," Renard said, a cryptic look on his face. "We'll be there before you can say, 'I'm an oblivious fool.'"

THE LUX COUNTRY home came into view.

Charlotte's gaze followed the grand entrance and gleaming, marble pillars glowing in the fading light to the two more recently built stables farther back on the grounds, the painted colors in the sky reminding her of the flickering reds and yellows of an altogether less pleasant day years ago.

The scar at her shoulder itched, as if the sight of the grounds were enough to summon the ghosts of memory.

"Shall I ring for a later supper, my lady?"

Charlotte nodded to Harper, conscious of the two other maids in the carriage and knowing how gratitude made the staff uncomfortable. "Did you send word ahead?"

"As you instructed, my lady. The room across from your suite was aired out in preparation."

Charlotte heard the censored disapproval but didn't bother addressing it. If her lady's maid found her demeanor unbefitting a lady in town, she'd be horrified at the familiarity with which the Louis family conducted themselves away from the prying eyes of the *ton*.

The carriage stopped on the drive, the magnitude and majesty of her family's ancestral home inspiring a war of conflicting emotions: joy, sadness, comfort, anxiety.

She was home.

⟫⟪

IF THERE WAS one thing no woman could resist, it was charm, and Hamish had been graced with a king's share. But for some blasted reason, the ladies inhabiting the Lux estate appeared impervious. "Come again?" he asked.

The housekeeper, a middle-aged woman with a tight bun, more skin than hair, repeated, "My lady is not at home."

"Not home?" His carriage had pulled into the drive not five minutes behind the rest. The staff was busy unloading it in the yard's flaring torch light as they spoke. "And where else would a proper lady be after dark, if not at home?" There was nowhere to go.

"Out." The Lux housekeeper could rival Camille in sheer audacity. She looked down her nose as if he were a stableboy daring to enter the house from the front.

Charlotte was gone.

He took back every amiable compliment he'd thought to describe Charlotte's honest nature. She was the most maddening, manipulative creature in a bustle. Was that her game? To *annoy* him into breaking their engagement?

She was here. He knew it as surely as he knew he'd seek her out.

Hamish looked to Renard, waiting for the master of the house to inquire after his sister's whereabouts.

The Duke of Lux simply rubbed the back of his neck and grumbled, "I need a drink."

Hamish gritted his teeth and returned to the housekeeper. "Then perhaps you'd be so kind as to point me in the direction of my room?" He was famished and there was a real possibility his left leg wouldn't straighten after being stuffed in that carriage like a fattened yule goose.

The shrew nodded. "This way, Your Grace." She was deceptively quick for a woman of her age.

Hamish's aching muscles struggled to keep pace up the grand staircase and into the master wing.

She indicated the door to her right. "The green room. Your trunk will be delivered, and a tray will be sent up for you to sup. Good evening, Your Grace."

Hamish retreated to his room, fearing the woman's gait would turn into the stiff march of a toy soldier if he watched her leave. Frigid, mechanical, he wondered if there was a secret course given to those of the status, or if the position attracted the cold-natured creatures. Camille had certainly taken to the role with relish.

The space was grand, as expected of a room in the master

wing, and tidy despite the faint musk smell of a room hastily aired for unannounced company. After discarding his boots, he crossed to the western-facing window and pushed it open.

He breathed in the beginnings of a humid night, his gaze following the dark shapes of rolling hills. He knew from previous visits the hills were lush and would house early morning fog as the air cooled in the wee hours.

A dark shape raced across the farthest hill, coming from the direction of the stable.

Hamish cursed and tugged his boots back on. Whoever was riding horseback was a fool of the greatest proportion. Only an idiot risked throwing in the dark.

The figure raised their arms, long hair streaming behind and a cry of unadulterated joy reaching Hamish, so out of place on the grounds of an esteemed duke's household.

Hamish bolted for the door, knowing who, precisely, would cry out in wild abandon when she should be safe and snug in her expertly turned down bed.

CHAPTER TWENTY

THE WARM BREEZE in her hair, the powerful muscles of her horse beneath her, and the privacy of a half-moon; it was freedom. An illusion of it, anyway. With her brother's threats of dismissal to the staff, she'd never been permitted to ride, but the beast beneath her was not so frightening. Yes, her hands had trouble gripping the mare's mane and the horse's hard back bruised her behind without a saddle, but she could cross another item off her list.

The house was still in sight, though only the dim light of a servant working into the night remained lit.

Charlotte despised the quiet, what it stood for: refinement, order, expectations. *A lady never raises her voice. A lady never speaks out of turn.*

A lady shouldn't speak at all.

Charlotte threw her arms out and cried her refusal to the heavens.

Three weeks ago, she'd never have considered leaving the house and racing across the hills. A week ago, she'd never have thought she could enter an unmarried man's house with a straight back and a clear head. And was it merely that morning she'd impersonated a man, drunk in a sailor bar, and gotten into an altercation with three ruffians over a woman's honor?

Charlotte cried out again, looking forward to what tomorrow would bring.

It had all begun with that first conversation in the duke's study, when she'd shared the very wishes of her soul. It was then the wishes had become tangible and not the fantasies of a shut-in with no knowledge of the world.

A rebirth. Out of the pits of hell and into heaven.

A bit dramatic, but a decade alone felt like purgatory.

A figure stepped into the path, and her horse bucked. Charlotte screamed and fell, right into the arms of a devil.

THE DUKE OF Camine pressed Charlotte against his chest, and she wasn't sure if the pounding against her breast was her heartbeat or not.

She shuddered in his arms, and his fingers immediately searched her for injury.

"Talk to me," he said. "You're safe now. There's no need to fear."

"Fear?!" She pushed away. "I'm not afraid. I'm *livid*! What the hell were you doing?"

His own temper flared. "Stopping you from breaking your neck."

"By scaring my horse? I was perfectly safe until you decided to jump out of the dark like some demon."

A whinny echoed in the distance, and Charlotte sighed. She'd never catch the mare. She'd have to send out the stablemaster in the morning and pray the horse's stomach didn't lead her into the garden for a late-night snack.

Now that the excitement was over, Charlotte realized how tired she was. She turned back to the house, but the duke's snarl stopped her.

"Where do you think you're going?"

He towered above her, nothing but an impressive shadow in the dark.

She sighed again. "Can we save the righteous speech for tomorrow? It's late, and I'm cold, and whatever practiced scowl you'll use to leer at me will be utterly wasted without my spectacles."

Strong hands grabbed her by the shoulders and shook. "I should put you over my knee. Stupid, reckless." He crushed her to him. "You said you couldn't ride. One misstep, a loose shoe, a damn snake, and there would be no stopping a throw."

Charlotte heard something besides anger in his words. The chill growing up her arms vanished at a sudden flood of warmth. "You remembered." There, in his arms, Charlotte felt safe. Strange that it had taken a big man, of no relation, to make her feel the comfort of the shadows.

"This place holds so many memories," she whispered. "Some of the worst of my life. Even the happy ones from being a young girl are tainted." Her fingers buried into his coat, a decade of buried sadness pouring out of her like a recount of the past days' weather. "I wanted to make one entirely new, without the past overhead to ruin it."

She wouldn't let the past diminish her present any longer.

"Damn it, Charlotte." The anger leached from his voice as he smoothed her hair with one hand. "There are other ways to go about it. Safer ways."

"How was I supposed to know it was dangerous?" she snipped. "I've never ridden before."

"Common sense. Being a woman, I suppose that's asking too much?"

Charlotte didn't take the bait. "I know my faults, Duke, without your added insults. Common sense is tenth on my list."

"Again with that bloody list!"

SHE WAS LIKE a hound first on the scent; if she weren't trained properly, there would be worse consequences than a runaway horse.

"Fine," he said, setting her on her feet. "We'll start tomorrow. Ten sharp. Meet me in the library."

The moonlight cast her furrowed expression in white light, her hair falling around her in a halo of starlight. "Start what?"

"Your list."

"My . . ." Her expression morphed into disbelief and something akin to excitement. "You want to help me?"

More like make sure she didn't accidentally shoot off a toe, or fall into quicksand, or summon the Devil with a seance. The last two sounded just absurd enough to be what the lady deemed 'living.'

"This list is important to you?" he said.

No hesitation. "It is."

He sighed and offered his arm. "Then I believe we'd all be safer if you had a chaperone. And there's no one better at navigating the dangers of uncouth diversions than the 'wild' duke."

"Do you enjoy that moniker?"

Hamish shrugged and dropped his arm. "It's what society dubbed me. Who am I to say 'no' to an apt description?"

"You looked ashamed when you said it."

Hamish tensed but managed to keep his tone light. "How would you know? Can you see anything without your spectacles?"

She was too clever to allow the change of subject. She put her hands on her hips. "Do you like the name, yes or no?"

The 'wild' duke moniker had fallen on him as soon as his first exploit had landed him in the papers. A young man unafraid of breaking decency and behaving no better than a wild animal with shocked lady companions. There had been four, after all.

The truth was, he hated the name. Somehow, Charlotte had seen that. Feeling exposed, he shook his head. "No. I don't."

"What would you prefer to be called?"

He chuckled. The lady was easy to confide in. "What's wrong with my given name? You've used it previously."

"That was before."

"Before what?"

"Before you agreed to court me."

"I'm confused." And he was. "You've decided to share your list of mischief with me. Wouldn't a pact such as ours mean we can drop the formality? We are engaged, after all."

"Engaged to be engaged, Lord Camine, and it is quite the opposite. You haven't proven your trustworthiness. I'm not sure you're up to the task."

Hamish was grateful for the shadows, else the lady would see nothing but teeth. He'd never enjoyed an insult more. She didn't trust him. Good. She wasn't a complete imbecile.

It seemed he'd found the perfect solution to keeping the woman out of trouble and easing her into a different kind of partnership.

Who knows, he might enjoy a spot of fun. The woman was certainly fearless. Maybe he'd add a few items to her list, a condition of his participation.

"How about 'Camine'?" he asked. "Surely, no one would admonish that?"

"Camine."

She rolled the name on her tongue, holding the *n*. "Agreed."

"And what name am I allowed? Duchess?" he teased.

"I'm not a duchess."

"But you will be. That is why we're here."

"You may call me 'Lady Charlotte.'"

"Hmm." Hamish led her over the last hill and to the back entrance of the house, where a door stood ajar. He bade her enter first, catching that same lemon soap scent from before. Loath to end their time here, he asked, expecting her to decline, "May I walk you to your door, Lady Charlotte?"

"Thank you, Camine. That would be lovely."

You're lovely.

The clouds passed overhead, blocking the moon and plunging the cold kitchen into shadow with his thought in the forefront of his mind. Everything about her was lovely. The way she frowned when she didn't understand something. Or the way she teased him. Or the little sounds she made when his fingers brushed her bare skin.

He itched to run his fingers through her unkempt hair. It was longer than he'd thought, skimming the swell of her bottom and drawing attention to her legs when she walked.

Hamish's thoughts turned feral. How he'd love to lay her across the cook's table, where he'd use the pot hooks above to secure her bound wrists, spread out like a feast just for him.

Suddenly, the need to build the trust between them came with a plethora of down sides. He wouldn't touch her until she was ready. He'd be patient. If he spooked her, she'd run far and wide, like her horse.

Logical. Calculated.

But every second standing in the deserted kitchen was his personal hell. His words came out roughly. "Lead the way."

She wove through the downstairs. Up the servants' stairs, they ascended to the second level.

Hamish memorized the route for a later occasion. Renard had done more harm than good sheltering his sister. Any proper lady would realize the dangers of a man knowing the location of her bed chamber.

She turned down his hall and stopped in front of his own door.

Not so sheltered, after all.

"It seems you've delivered me instead," he said, feeling rightly outfoxed. "Didn't like the idea of the 'wild'—" He cut himself off, pleased to hear her clear her throat. "Unsure of showing me where you rest your pretty head?"

The window at the end of the hall lit up with moonlight, revealing her smile.

Hamish inhaled at the picture she made.

Ethereal. Beautiful.

"On the contrary." She stepped to the door across the hall and turned the handle. "I made sure to keep you close." She entered her room, glancing back over her shoulder with a smirk. "Wouldn't want you to break anything looking for me in the middle of the night."

Her door latched shut.

Hamish blinked, the dryness in his eyes telling him he'd been staring. She was just across the hall?

The little minx!

He returned to his earlier assessment, wondering who was playing whom? Lady Charlotte, *Lady Charlotte*, was a puzzle he couldn't solve. He'd thought he'd figured out where one piece fit, only to find the piece was a cog in an enormous clock.

She was exciting.

Given a single hour head start and she'd out maneuvered him—twice. He couldn't wait to turn the tables, or more poignantly, wind the lady so tight, she chimed for him every hour on the hour.

Hard to the point of pain, he entered his room, knowing sleep was a long way off.

When he did sleep, he dreamed of a bare-chested beauty on horseback, with hair the color of starlight, and a secret smile just for him.

Chapter Twenty-One

CHARLOTTE PEELED HERSELF out of bed after a fitful night, her body unwilling to settle knowing the duke slept not one hundred feet away. Donning a robe, she grabbed her spectacles and list from the vanity and descended to the library on light feet, an old habit even though the staff had been up for hours.

But when she opened the door, it was to discover she wasn't the only early riser. "Camine?"

He looked up from the chair by the fire, his gaze raking over her. "Good morning."

Charlotte pulled at the collar at her chin.

He rebuffed neither her state of dress nor her greeting. His gaze narrowed in on the stack of papers under her arm and rubbed a hand over his face. "I suppose we should ring for a pot of tea. This is going to take a while."

"Better make it two," she said.

"First things first," he said. "I'd better take a look at this list before I know how many physicians I need on retainer."

THREE-QUARTERS OF AN hour later, their shouting could be heard all the way to the kitchens in the back of the house.

"You can't possibly think you can get away with it?" Hamish addressed her with an incredulous wave of his hand. "You'd be discovered immediately."

"I'd be in disguise."

"No!"

"I'm not asking for permission."

Hamish shook the papers, all eight damn pages. "White's, I can understand but Parliament? Why would you wish to go there?"

"Because it's not allowed."

"There's no reasoning with you!" He sat at the chair behind the desk and did his best to negotiate them out of being hanged by their knickers in front of a firing squad. "I'll give you the club and falconry, but lose Parliament."

Charlotte leaned forward in her chair. "We'd already agreed on falconry. If you're going to take Parliament off the table, I want something else."

She was relentless. If she'd been born a man, she'd have conquered the Americas for England. "Fine. Name your price."

"White's wager ledger."

"How do you know about that?"

Her shrug was anything but innocent. "People talk."

Women talked, but Hamish had seen no evidence of a female acquaintance since their entanglement. "You mean your Miss Yamsbee?"

First thing after securing their engagement was to find the rebellious chit and kindly ask her to refrain from putting such wild ideas into his lady's head.

He didn't have time to wonder about the possessive nature of his thoughts because she grabbed the last page in her list and moved to the next item.

"Number two hundred and thirty: Smoke a cigar."

Hamish sighed. "How many more are there?"

"Five."

Thank God. "Accepted. What else?"

"Learn poker."

"Yes."

"Paint a nude."

Hamish's eyebrows hitched. "Does the model matter?"

"Are you volunteering, Camine?"

He took a flexing position. "If you think you can handle me, Lady Charlotte?"

She flicked his arm and smirked at his twinge. "I'll manage, sir."

He rubbed his smarting muscle. "Next?"

"Learn to bake a pie."

His stomach growled at that. The sooner they came to a decision, the sooner he could break his fast. "Preferably this morning," he grumbled.

"I'll take that as acceptance," she said. "Number two hundred and thirty-four: Sleep under the stars."

"Done." He stood, imagining a pile of eggs the size of his horse.

"There's one more," she said.

He headed for the door. "Out with it, then. The tea is long gone, and I need sustenance to keep up with your madness."

"Fall in love."

Hamish froze, door handle in hand. Of all the impossible things, she'd chosen the most fabricated illusion in history. Amusement, he could do. Pleasure, no worries. Affection was possible. Love . . . He didn't turn around when he said, "I can't promise that."

The quiet was so overwhelming after their shouting, her whispered response was like a gunshot in the room. "I know."

He closed his eyes and pressed his forehead against the wood.

"But there are other intimacies to a marriage."

His eyes opened, but he didn't turn around, didn't want to stop her. "There are," he offered.

"Admiration," she said. "Affection."

His heart rate sped up, hearing her confidence building as she moved closer.

"Companionship."

Yes. Yes. "Yes," he whispered the last. She was right behind him, the brush of her thin robe driving his hunger to those of flesh and sin.

"Trust," she said.

"Yes."

"Sex."

The word unlocked him. He whirled.

She'd already untied the sash at her waist, revealing a virgin-white chemise.

He pushed her robe to the floor, his hands running down her sides and cupping her glorious backside. "Fuck, yes," he said and then he captured her mouth.

He sealed his promise with lips and tongue, vowing to give her what he could, along with pleasure she didn't yet know she wanted.

There wouldn't be love. They'd be tied together with something stronger: Need. He'd teach her to crave him, crave what he could do for her.

"Hamish," she gasped against his lips. She grabbed for him.

He pulled her hands behind her back, breaking the kiss and eliciting a whimper from her.

"Wait." He went to his knees, keeping one hand around her wrists. He ran his cheek against the silky underclothes at her thigh.

She writhed and pushed at him with her hips.

He chuckled. "So wanton."

"I want you!"

He rewarded her honesty with a nip on her hip.

Her arms jerked and pulled him closer.

His grip tightened. His free hand closed around the sash on the floor. He stood, bringing her arms in front of her. Wrapping her wrists, he finished with a silken bow.

All the while she watched him, her eyes growing curious.

Hamish studied her, waiting for the minutest sign of uncertainty or fear. He paused after he finished, waiting for her permission, waiting for condemnation.

There was no hesitation. "Show me," she said.

He lifted her into his arms and carried her to the desk. He laid her out just as he'd fantasized last night, extending her arms over her head and hooking the sash on the handle of the desk drawer. "Don't pull," he ordered.

"Yes, my lord."

He growled at her submission and stood back to admire how her raised arms lifted her breasts, her nipples peaked and pressed against the fabric of her nightgown.

She writhed under his attention, her thighs rubbing together.

He met her gaze and was satisfied at her arousal.

He dragged his fingers down her thigh and gripped the hem at her ankle. "Keep looking at me."

She nodded.

Hamish lifted the hem inch by inch, watching her breath come shallower, hearing her gasps as he left her exposed to the hip.

Her legs were shapely and lean-muscled.

He ached to press his mouth to her skin. He'd start behind the knee, inside her thigh, kissing higher and higher until she learned how good submitting to him would be.

But he wouldn't touch her. Not yet.

There was still one final test to see how far he could push, to see if she would follow where he led.

He stared down at her, the tension in his gut full of past regret and shame and hope. One final command. "Open for me."

She did.

Hamish knew if it were possible for a monster like him to fall in love, it would've been in this moment, when his prey said the one word that changed everything.

"Please."

His fingers wrapped around her ankle.

Charlotte bit her tongue to keep in a scream.

His fingers were like fire along her skin. First at her ankle, then her knee. Branding her, consuming her. His mouth replaced his hand and, this time, she did cry out.

"Hamish!"

She felt his smile against her thigh, and the muscles deep within clenched with an instinct she couldn't comprehend.

"Quiet, dear one. We wouldn't want to arouse curious ears."

She nodded, not trusting herself to speak.

He licked a sensitive spot behind her knee.

"God!"

He lifted his head, his eyes dancing. "While I appreciate the compliment, you must be quiet, Charlotte."

Easy for him to say. She nodded at his throat. "Your cravat."

Amusement plain, he asked, "What about it?"

"Gag me with it."

His humor vanished. He pulled her hem down, untied her wrists, and fetched her discarded robe, his face unreadable.

Charlotte sat on the edge of the desk, watching him in a daze. Disappointment and frustration ate at her. Why had he stopped? Again?

He held out her robe. "Here."

She didn't move. Tears welled. "Did I say something wrong?"

He cursed and crossed the room, wrapping the robe around her shoulders and leaning his forehead down to hers. "You did nothing wrong." The conviction in his voice surprised her. "It's me. I . . . I like certain things. Aggressive things others don't find decent."

"You didn't like what I asked you to do?"

"No!" He cradled her face, his nose brushing hers. "Christ, Charlotte, I liked it too much. A minute more and I wouldn't have stopped."

She huffed, relieved and confused. "I didn't ask you to stop. In fact, you need to stop stopping. It's vexing."

He smiled.

Charlotte felt him pulling away. She gripped his hands on either side of her face. "I don't care what people say. I know what I like, and I won't apologize for it." She waited until he looked up to see her earnestness. "Neither should you."

He exhaled, as if he'd been holding in a lifetime of shame. He stroked her chin, his thumb playing with the seam of her lips. "You can't be real. Ow!" He pulled back. "Why did you bite me?"

"I'm real," she said. "And the next time you stop, you'll see how aggressive I can get."

He grinned. "Yes, my lady."

She liked the way he said that, as if it were true.

"My lady."

Her duke.

And Charlotte remembered where she'd heard that same cherished note; it was what her father had called her mother the last time they'd been together as a family.

It had been unseasonably warm that final summer, and they'd gone to the lake for a picnic. Her father had snuck her a bite of tart while her mother and brother had set up the blanket, but her mother had caught them.

"Malcolm, you'll spoil her lunch."

Her father had held out his hand, the rest of the tart in his palm. "Why, do you want a bite?"

"Of course not!"

"Come on. I won't tell the staff."

Her smile had broken free. "You're a terrible influence." She'd taken a big bite.

Her father had pulled her mother close. "Only for you, my lady."

Hamish stiffened and Charlotte came back to the present, feeling a wetness on her cheeks.

"You're crying," he said.

She wiped her face with her hands. "Women are known to do that."

"You don't."

She laughed. It was good to see the infallible duke flustered with a few drops of salty water. "Yes, Camine, even I cry. Unbelievable though it may be, you are capable as well."

He grinned. "Gentlemen don't cry."

"I bet you would if I kneed you in the personals."

His eyes widened. "Planning ahead?"

She liked this side of him. Easy, fun, wildly inappropriate, and teasing. "Self-defense is on my list."

He threw back his head and barked a laugh. "On that ominous note, I believe I smell fresh rolls."

Charlotte's stomach growled.

They both laughed.

"I should dress," she said. "There's only so much scandal my brother will stand."

His gaze swept down her body, shooting awareness to her core.

"A pity," he said. "Make sure you find a decent shirt and trousers as well." He went to the door and opened it wide, checking to see if the walls had grown ears. At the clear hall, he sent her a wink over his shoulder. "We start tonight."

CHAPTER TWENTY-TWO

HAMISH HAD SAT down to a pile of eggs, ham, rolls, and marmalade one could only describe as gluttonous, when a servant handed him a telegram.

Noticing the code Percy used, he asked, "When did this arrive?"

"Just now, Your Grace."

He tore the postman's seal open.

Unforeseen delay.

P

Hamish cursed and startled the servant when he demanded ink and quill. When the servant returned with the items, Hamish dipped the quill in the ink and wrote a quick line, using the banister as a makeshift desk. He handed it to the horrified servant, but Hamish wouldn't think of the disgusting display or how the staff at the Lux estate would twitter about the unmannered actions of the 'wild' duke.

"Make sure this finds Lady Charlotte at once." He headed to the open door, paused at the threshold, and turned back. He snatched two rolls from his overflowing plate and put a third in his pocket, the ungentlemanly display freeing after a decade of forgoing every impulse.

He wondered what Charlotte would make of the smudges of

marmalade across the paper? Imagining her scrunched nose kept his stride light as he waited for his horse to be saddled. He'd ride hard to make the city within the hour. Then he'd spend the rest of the day planning for that evening.

He grabbed the roll from his pocket and took a big bite, pleased to find it was still warm.

"LOTTE, WAIT!"

Charlotte turned at her brother's voice, feeling like she hadn't heard it in months.

He stopped at her door, pausing as he took in her blue dress. "You look nice."

Charlotte warmed at the compliment. She might've asked her maid to lay out the swoop neck dress, the same color as the ribbon woven through her hair. "Thank you."

He shook himself. "We need to talk."

Charlotte brushed past him. "Camine is waiting in the breakfast room."

He kept pace down the hall. "That's exactly what I want to talk to you about. Charlotte, he's not the right man for you."

She rolled her eyes. "You mean, he wasn't your choice."

"He's not good enough for you."

"He's your best friend."

"Exactly." He stepped in front of her, keeping his voice low. "I know everything there is to know about Camine, and, trust me, you won't suit."

She hated how he crowded her, making her feel ten years old again. She lifted her chin. "I'm done with you telling me what suits and what doesn't. Your interference is too late."

She sidestepped him.

He blocked her a second time.

"What do you want, Ren?"

"I can make it go away."

"What?"

"The scandal." His voice lowered to a whisper. "The marquess is still interested. He understands how things . . . happen."

"Happen?" Charlotte recoiled. "Nothing has happened. Not really."

"You mean he hasn't . . . you haven't been . . . prodded?"

She pushed him. "An apt description, brother. That is all I am, right? A heifer? Tell me, is the marquess interested in me for my producing ability or as a hunk of beef?"

"It's not like that, Lotte. The marquess will treat you right. He won't be rough like Camine."

"He isn't rough. He's barely touched me," she grumbled.

Relief smoothed a solid decade from his face. "He hasn't touched you? Then why the hell are we here? Why is *he* here?"

"Because *he* is my choice." Charlotte froze. She'd meant the situation was her choice, not the man. Nothing but a slip of the tongue.

"Lotte." Renard shook his head, his superior expression making her grind her teeth. "That's what I'm telling you. He's the wrong choice. The things he likes . . ." He ran a hand through his hair, his gaze darting away. "Jesus, Lotte, a gentleman doesn't discuss this with a lady."

Charlotte crossed her arms. Was it possible there was something she didn't know about Hamish? Did this have something to do with his dealings in Dockside? "As you've pointed out multiple times, I don't behave like a lady. There's no use treating me like one now."

"Damn it, Charlotte! He's into weird stuff, dangerous stuff. They call him 'wild' for a reason." He threw his hands up. "You see why I wanted to keep you out of his clutches? He's a monster."

Charlotte stared at her brother. She processed the words slowly, and revulsion sunk deep. Not for Hamish. She'd seen his desires, and she wasn't afraid.

"Monster."

Was this why Hamish had been so ashamed? Was this why he'd turned from her in the library?

Her hand flew on its own.

"Ahh! What the hell?" Renard held his cheek. "What the hell is wrong with you?"

The voice that came out of Charlotte's mouth was her own, but the calmness came from some other place, a dark place that had nothing to do with a monster and his dangerous desires. It was pain for a misunderstood man who'd rather walk away to save her innocence than revel in the beauty of a shared life.

She shook her head, seeing clear for the first time in weeks. "You've known him your entire life, and yet you know nothing about him. He's not a monster, and he deserves your loyalty."

Renard reached out as she walked away. "Blood is stronger than friendship, Char. You will always come first."

The words tore at the piece of her heart that yearned for family. When she looked back, it was to see her big brother from the past, not yet fourteen, his hands reaching to take her away from their parents' cold bodies. Just like that night, her throat was raw with unshed tears. "If that were really true, Ren, you would never ask me to choose between freedom and your affection."

His expression crumbled.

Charlotte turned away, leaving her brother to his own darkness. A darkness he'd carried since that night, a darkness that, no matter how much light she shone, couldn't reach him.

She lumbered to the stairs, her emotions leaving her fatigued. She needed someone she could reach. Someone who'd share the darkness and not balk at her own.

"Lady Charlotte."

Her attention snapped to a young servant. She cleared the emotion from her throat with a quick cough. "What is it, Mr. Peters?"

"The duke bade me give this to you in all haste."

Charlotte took the paper, confused at the opened telegram.

"Is the duke not eating breakfast in the rose room?"

Mr. Peters shook his head. "He was called away. He left in a hurry, but made a point to"—he coughed—"write to you before he left."

Unsure of Mr. Peters's pause, she nodded. "Thank you. I'll read it now."

He bowed and went about his business.

She held up the paper, the two-word telegram indecipherable.

What unforeseen delay would take him away so early? And who was P? Something sticky slid over her forefinger. She rubbed her fingers together, the smell of cook's peach marmalade reminding her she had yet to eat.

She turned the telegram over, discovering a second message in smudged ink.

My Lady,

I've returned to London. Meet me at the location of two hundred and three in my carriage at midnight. My driver will be waiting.

Dress appropriately.
H

Charlotte read and reread the message twice more, her head spinning and her heart flying.

He'd gone back to London.

But he hadn't forgotten her.

He wanted her to meet him at White's, in disguise.

She folded the note, making sure the paper caught and flared in the lit fireplace in the breakfast room before she sat down at the table. The smell of peach hung in the air like a promise of sweet adventure to come.

BY THE TIME the duke's carriage rolled up to the infamous

gentlemen's club, Charlotte's sweet dream had sunk to a sour pit in her stomach.

What if he didn't show? What if someone recognized her?

Unlikely.

Charlotte resituated the garish top hat on her head, the pins holding fabric to hair pinching.

She had no idea of the dress code, though it wouldn't matter. Her non-existent skills had left her cravat more knot than tie, a perfect match to her too-small overcoat and too-loose trousers. Impersonating her brother meant she had to forgo her spectacles once again, but at least the shoes she'd borrowed from her brother were recently polished.

When five minutes had passed and still no duke, she bit her lip and prepared to turn the carriage around.

The door opened and Camine appeared, clean-shaven and looking like a Greek god in all black. He squinted into the dark carriage. "You're early."

She ignored his offered hand, ready to take her gender swap to the finest detail. She misjudged the space between the step and the walk, nearly landing herself on her face.

A strong arm caught her and set her straight before vanishing.

"Thank you," she grumbled.

A choke had her head snapping up to discover the Duke of Camine looking as if in pain.

"Did you raid an actor's costume rack?"

Charlotte blew the cap feather out of her face, his humor now apparent and infectious. "The man's next rendition of Shake-speare will be in the nude, I'm afraid."

His laughter poured out, rich and full.

Charlotte saw stars.

Each time he collected himself, he'd glance at her and fall back into great shakes of humor.

He looked so young laughing.

Men coming and going from the club stared at them as they passed, all impeccably dressed.

The feather fell back into her face, and Charlotte saw the scene through Camine's eyes.

The crisp lines of starched linen, perfectly laid silk cravats, and her, stuffed and feathered like a chicken with a rooster complex.

Her laughter joined the fray, light and high, in perfect harmony to his rumbling bass.

Something clicked into place. Somehow here, in the most discriminating city in England, in front of the most exclusive club in London, impersonating her brother and laughing like a fool, Charlotte felt like herself, more so than she ever had in the extravagant gowns and the one ball she'd attended of the *ton*'s elite.

Their laughter trailed off, leaving them both gasping, but humor intact.

"If marriage to a handsome duke doesn't work out," he said, "you've a future in the big tent as a dapper clown."

She smirked. "Lost confidence in your skills of seduction, Camine?"

"More like trying to regain it after choosing such an inapt partner. Why did you have to murder your cravat?" He poked at the wad of silk. "Positively dreadful."

She huffed. "You're lucky I'm wearing it at all. After fighting with it half the ride, I almost decided to show up neck bare and vest-less."

Taking in the sheerness of the white shirt underneath, Hamish smiled. "A pity for all involved." He navigated the knots with deft fingers, untying and retying before tucking an expertly made cravat into her collar. "Leave off the feather but keep the coat. There's nothing to be done about the fit. You still look like an ad for a readymade shop, but at least that peacock duster won't signal every eye from here to Lux estate."

Charlotte picked out the feather and handed it to him, her nerves taking hold looking at the massive building behind them, the revered patrons striding through the doors with purpose.

"Will I be allowed in?"

"Nervous?"

"Any scene I may cause, I'd prefer to make inside."

He faced the club beside her, mirroring the two ornate lanterns on either side of the low fence. He tipped her hat at an angle to cover more of her face. "Stand straight but shuffle your feet. If we're lucky, the doorman will be half-blind and mistake you for a fairer, soberer version of your brother."

Charlotte's sour stomach flipped anew. She hadn't realized how unrealistic many of the items on her list were without someone to guide her through the world of intrigue and men. She nodded. "I follow where you lead, Camine."

"Be careful," he purred in her ear. "I like the sound of that."

Flustered and not altogether sturdy on her feet, Charlotte followed him up the walk and through the door.

EVEN WITH HER face half-covered and missing her spectacles, Charlotte gaped at the grand atrium, the polished floor, and the blurry room beyond filling the space with deep voices and a thick perfume of cigar smoke and staked entertainment.

"Welcome back, Your Grace."

Charlotte peered at the butler. Not a thread, hair, or manner out of place.

Camine nodded. "Good evening, George. Is the library open tonight? The Duke of Lux and I are looking for a quiet dinner."

The butler bowed. "It is, Your Grace. Follow me, gentlemen."

Charlotte followed, impressed by her partner's adroit greeting, encouraging the butler to both glance over her character and put the older man to task without the need for questions.

Left in an impressive book-lined room, Charlotte didn't pay attention to the men's discussion before the butler departed with another bow.

"I hope you like grouse?" Camine asked.

"Not sure my nerves will allow my stomach anything that isn't amber and liquid."

He chuckled and plopped into a plush, red chair, crossing his ankles and looking every bit the raffish gentleman the clubhouse was renowned to admit. "As much as I'd enjoy watching you drink your dinner, and whatever inebriated antics that followed, if we are to tackle half a dozen or so items on your list, you'll need something in your stomach."

That was logical. She nodded. "Where do we start?"

He produced two cigars from a box on a side table, cutting the ends with a finger-trap blade that looked sharp enough to take the finger.

Stomach heaving again, Charlotte took one and rolled it between her thumb and forefinger. "I'm not to drink on an empty stomach, but I may smoke?"

The duke lit a long match from the roaring fireplace and demonstrated how to ignite the cigar end with a half-turn motion. He handed her a second match and exhaled a puff of tear-jerking smoke. "If your body disagrees, it's better on an empty stomach, trust me."

She lit her cigar, replicating his technique. The smoke burned her throat, but the smell was a comforting reminder of stolen moments with her father after dinner.

Camine studied her. "Not bad."

She smiled at the praise. "Better than my brother?"

"Wouldn't know," he said, leaning back in his chair. "Never seen him touch a smoke."

"Really?"

"You sound disappointed?"

She took the seat opposite and sat forward. "My entire vision of you and him smoking and drinking as young chaps is ruined. Does that mean there was no debauchery, either?"

He laughed, the action seeming to come easier with frequency. "Oh, there was that."

"Here?"

"In this very room."

Charlotte's gaze took in the space, her new experience with Camine in her own library widening her view of where one might experience a tryst without a bed. "But women aren't allowed in."

He cocked a brow. "And yet here you are, my dear."

She pulled another lungful of burning smoke, a calmness settling over.

"You're taking this very well," he said. "Not as I expected."

She snorted. "Because women are vapid creatures incapable of enjoying vice in a quiet room."

"I know of no other women who'd enjoy men's clothing and a smoke."

"Aren't you lucky I'm a proper scandal?"

"I'm beginning to see the appeal."

Charlotte peered at him, unsure if he was mocking her or not.

A knock sounded, followed by a waiter and a cart filled with the most impeccably dressed fowl Charlotte had ever seen.

The waiter placed a plate in front of each of them. "Roasted grouse with apple relish and mint chutney, Your Graces. Would you care for anything else?"

"This will be fine, Charlie," Camine said, not bothering to wait for the man to quit the room before setting his cigar on the tray and indicating Charlotte should do the same.

Charlotte savored the sweet and savory aromas, suspecting she was about to have the best meal of her life. "You're on a first name basis with the staff?"

He didn't look away from his meal when he explained, "'George' and 'Charlie' refer to all the waiting staff here."

"Like a title?" she asked. "Whatever for?"

"A gentleman doesn't like to sound crass and shout, 'You there' to be served."

She rolled her eyes. "We wouldn't want a privileged man to

feel inferior." She cut a sliver of fowl in sweet-smelling sauce and bit into heaven. Forget the drinking and the gambling; the evening was a success by the dinner alone.

"You may take your pick of entertainment after we're finished. Billiards, darts, cards."

Charlotte wiped the corners of her mouth with her napkin. "What would you suggest?"

"It would be prudent to steer clear of the card tables since the men here aren't ones to drink to excess and glance over a lad more dame than dapper."

Charlotte leaned back, having wolfed down half her plate in less than five minutes.

Between the full belly and her early rising that morning, exhaustion weighed her down, despite the initial excitement. "I'm familiar with billiards, and any activity that encourages me to throw sharpened hand spears without my spectacles would be ill-advised," she said, passing her grin to the man across from her. "I would be interested in the legendary betting book."

His eyes narrowed. "How do you know about that? And don't lie again and tell me it was house gossip."

"Do you deny it exists?"

"No."

"I appreciate your candor."

"Hmm." He rubbed his jaw. "Speaking of secrets no one should speak aloud, how do you propose going around without drawing the attention of every man in the vicinity?"

"What do you mean?"

"Hard to believe as it is, your brother is a popular man. He has friends visiting this evening who won't hesitate to approach us."

She picked up her still-smoking cigar from the tray where she'd placed it and shrugged. "I could always introduce myself as 'Lady Charlotte' and give the men a good scare."

Camine ran a tongue over his teeth, his smirk reptilian. "At the risk of missing out on what would, I'm sure, be an uncomfortable and entertaining round of introductions, I'd advise you to imitate your less-desired peers and learn to mislead the peerage."

"You mean lying?" She wrinkled her nose. "I exaggerate from time to time, but that's not the same thing."

"'Exaggerate'? One step from the confessional," he teased.

"I don't *lie*," she said. "Not once in my life."

He stood and poured two glasses of amber liquid and offered it to her. "Then, my dear, let us toast to an evening of firsts."

CHAPTER TWENTY-THREE

HAMISH HAD TO admit, seeing White's through Charlotte's squinting but unbiased eyes was enlightening—and amusing as hell. She wove through the hallowed halls meant for the male gentry's freedom, tainting it with her own.

The truth was, he enjoyed her company. For a man who'd exclusively shared space with the fairer sex for one of two reasons, the second being a combative relationship with his sister, the realization was alarming. A quiet meal, a quick cigar, and not a speck of sexual promise, and still, he was at ease.

Not to say the air between them was platonic. He could slice the tension with the same knife he'd used on the most coveted fowl in England. And the longer they spent in this men's-only club, the more he wanted to steal her away to a private room only for him.

"Is that it?" She pointed to a leather-bound ledger sitting on a gold inlaid table.

He grinned and nudged her finger over . . . over . . . over. "There."

She frowned at the tomb. "It looks like an ordinary book."

"Were you expecting a sign in large, gauche letters?"

"Frankly?" she said. "Yes. There's not even a seedy silhouette anywhere to let people know."

"A glass case laced with virgin's blood?"

"*Something!*"

He chuckled at her profound expectations. "All the seediness is on the inside."

Her face lit up. "Really?" She opened the book to the current page and looked up at him helplessly.

He smiled, his teasing coming from the same unearthly place as his earlier laughter. "Tell me I'm here as more than a substitute for your spectacles?"

"Don't forget getting me past the butler."

"Can't forget that."

"And ordering that splendid bird."

"I'm practically a hero of old."

"But without the pesky weaknesses."

"Weaknesses?"

"Achilles and the heel, Samson and the hair." Her expression mocked seriousness. "Do you have a crippling obsession with nymphs?"

"A beautiful, unattainable woman? Don't all men?"

She put her palms together. "Be my eyes, hero?"

He'd give her the moon if she asked with those sparkling eyes and teasing tongue.

The clock in the hall chimed half past one, and Hamish instinctively checked his pocket watch.

"Am I keeping you from something?" she asked. "Or are you stalling?"

He replaced his watch inside his vest. "Now why would I be against sharing the immorally deplorable gambling of a bored gentry with an innocent lady?" He smirked at her pursed lips. "I've a meeting at two out front."

She looked skeptical. "A meeting? At two in the morning? Why not have it inside? Isn't the club for leisure and business?"

"This particular associate isn't up to the establishment's refined tastes." To think of Percy as anything remotely refined was blasphemous, almost as great a crime as smuggling a fine lady under the guise of her brother's title into White's. He'd wanted to meet earlier, having sent a runner to the usual haunt, note in hand, for Percy to come to the flat, but the reply had come promptly.

Need a few more hours.

Meet at the secondary location. 2 a.m.

P

The coincidental meet-up at White's did not escape Hamish. Knowing Percy, the man had probably surmised his secret rendezvous with Charlotte and worked his schedule to accommodate.

A truly terrifying man.

If Hamish hadn't seen the man's red blood personally, he would have been led to believe the bruiser was, in fact, a demon with eyes and ears running loose all over London like minions of hell.

Charlotte shifted at his side, her normally open expression closed, and her gaze darting towards the exit.

A group of young men spilled out of the gaming room, disquieting the space with light and drunken laughter. Recognizing a few of the men as fellow classmates and acquaintances of Renard, Hamish turned his body to block Charlotte from view.

She looked up at his sudden nearness, eyes startled, and parted her lips.

He stared at those lips, remembering how soft they'd been. "Shall we get on with it?" he asked, his voice low.

"'It'?" she asked, breathless.

He tore his gaze away and flipped the pages in the book with a quick thumb. "Tell me when to stop."

She glanced at the book and back at him. She licked her lips, their mouths close. "Stop."

He let the pages fall and pointed to the first entry. "Lord Brimley bets one hundred pounds Chancy will deliver before Christmas."

"One hundred pounds! That's outrageous." She leaned forward and squinted. "Who's Chancy?"

Hamish grinned. "The man's English Setter."

She blinked. "He bet a fortune on a dog?"

"Bored, entitled men will bet on anything from the day's weather to the ruination of a woman."

"The latter sounds far more diverting."

He smiled. "Shall we try again? It's only a matter of time before we come across a bet befitting a lady's scandalous expectations."

"By all means."

He flipped again.

"Stop," she said.

He read another entry about the winner of an amateur boxing match that had won Lord Mercer twenty-five hundred pounds.

"How savage," she said, clearly enjoying herself.

He turned the page, a name and recent bet catching his eye. He read the bet, his jaw locking.

"What is it?" she asked, desperately trying to read where his finger pointed.

Hamish spoke through his teeth, refusing to deny her, not in this. "Ten thousand pounds the Lady Charlotte will be married by the month's end to . . ."

Charlotte made an unladylike sound in her throat. The "to whom" part didn't matter. "A fortune over matrimony. Who needs a dowry anymore? What poor idiot made that bet?"

Hamish waited for her to look at him. He knew the ramifications better than anyone. "The Marquess of Slasbury."

Charlotte stared at the betting book, the gentleman's title playing over and over in her mind. "The marquess?" She reeled with the reminder of Hamish's meeting and the implications of whatever illegal dealings he ran, but not . . .

"Renard?"

She was a bet. Her brother's name was nowhere to be found, but the marquess? Her nails dug into her palms. It had to be her brother's doing.

"I say, Lux?"

Charlotte turned to discover she wasn't thinking her brother's wretched title. One of the young men from the drunken crowd was near shouting it at her.

The man held himself well in a dark suit, his hair and hat fashionable. He took in her ill-fitting disguise—and what many would deem a pale appearance for a man—and frowned. "It's been an age, Lux, but I can't say the years have been kind."

Hamish stiffened beside her. "Lord Alistair Richmund, it has been a while."

Stomach tightening, Charlotte catalogued the boon of a surname and ignored the warning tone her partner directed at her. She dropped her shoulders like her brother always did and dropped her voice even lower, faking a chuckle and turning it into a cough. "I've a sibling, remember? Chasing after the whims of a troublesome woman leaves little time for things like eating and sleeping. Can't shake this cough, either."

The man smirked. "You mean that little sister of yours? Can't handle one woman? No wonder you're still a bachelor."

Charlotte hated Lord Richmund. His arrogance, his snide comments, the small dig at her brother's expense. Ratbag or not, Renard had raised her, and no one else had the right to put him in his place. That was the sole job of a troublesome sister.

As if sensing her anger, Hamish moved closer, his fingers brushing her palm. Not to stop her, but to let her know he was there.

She glanced at him to see he was already looking at her—no, grinning down at her as if he knew what was coming.

He knew the risk better than anyone if she was found, but still, he didn't take control.

He smiled then, and Charlotte knew what he was saying.

"I trust you."

At that moment, she wanted nothing to do with gentlemen's clubs and irritating patrons. She would have given up that magnificent meal to be in a dark carriage with him again and show him how much that trust went both ways. In fact, she may do just that.

But first, she needed to deal with the dandy standing between them and the exit.

"I say, Richmund, does that mean you're married, then?" She cut him off before he could reply. "You'd have your own problems hiding that righteous self-importance. And here we were only talking about a duke's hardships." She placed a hand on his bony shoulder, infusing her voice and expression with pity. "Forgive my selfishness. You need more support than I." She balled her fingers into a fist and bumped his shoulder, harder than necessary. Men always seemed to strike one another, no matter the emotion. Happy, angry, generally breathing in the same area. She leaned in and offered him some 'brotherly' advice. "Not to worry, old chap. I'm sure the unfortunate lady won't come to her senses before you can mask that annoying tongue-clicking habit of yours."

She walked past, swearing she heard Hamish cough to cover a laugh as he followed. She bit the inside of her cheek to stop from joining him and called over her shoulder, "Congratulations, Richmund, and good luck. I'm sure you won't need it."

Lord Richmund stared after them, the look of panic on his face promptly closed off, as the front door to the club shut behind them with a final farewell from the butler named George.

CHAPTER TWENTY-FOUR

THE LATE-NIGHT AIR was refreshing after the smoky halls. Though that wasn't all that was refreshing.

"Bloody magnificent," Hamish said.

Charlotte preened at his attention.

He shook his head. "You castrated him."

She grimaced and then chuckled. "A heifer taking out the bull. Sounds like justice."

"Sounds like I never want to cross you."

She turned that smile on him. "You're a smart man."

Not smart enough. If he had any semblance of intelligence, he'd have dragged her into another private room and made her wholly his. No more games.

"I told you I look like my brother," she said.

"And I told you, any man who thought so was an imbecile."

She scowled. "He was that. What an odious man."

What a spectacular performance! He'd likened her awful suit to that of a stage actor, but she surpassed all expectations. She'd stuck to her morals, not one lie passing through her lips, while concealing her identity, while also putting down a ratbag without so much as a flinch.

Hamish glanced around, everything seeming bright and bold in detail despite the dark sky and cold light of the streetlamps.

She brought every color and feeling into sharp focus with her tenacity for life, accepting the beautiful and ugly as two sides of one coin.

Hamish feared it was addicting. *She* was addicting. Even now, he loathed the scant inches between them, craving that high. Craving her.

"Good evening, boys," someone said.

The voice grated in Hamish's ears. He turned to his man, the sneaky bastard a quarter of an hour early. "Percy."

"Hope I'm not interrupting?"

"Yes," they answered at the same time.

Hamish grinned.

Percy smirked at Charlotte. "I see."

Hamish would see the other man choking on his own blood for the way he looked at her.

Percy, seeming to notice the murderous intent of his employer, turned to the lady in question with a wink. "A pleasure to see you again, my lord. If possible, you look more beautiful with every hour we're apart."

Unaffected by the demon's charms, Charlotte sneered. "A man doesn't like being referred to as 'beautiful.'"

Good girl.

Percy bowed. "Forgive me. I'll endeavor to choose an appropriate adjective to proclaim your handsomeness in the future."

Her brows rose. "I've a descriptor most apt for you, sir. Would you like to hear it?"

Hamish stepped in, ready to cheer the lady on or pummel the idiot baiting her. He did neither. "Perhaps a change of venue, gentlemen?" He addressed Percy. "Your note sounded urgent."

Percy glanced at Charlotte, who looked uncomfortable with the change of topic.

"Shall I hail a hack?"

"No need." Hamish signaled his driver from across the street, and the man pulled the carriage around. The duke opened the door and offered Charlotte a hand up.

She looked down at his hand but made no move to take it. "I feel properly dismissed."

There was an edge to her voice Hamish didn't understand.

Suddenly, he didn't want her too far, either. He called up his orders to his driver and watched her eyes widen.

"I'm not to go back to the country?" she asked.

"We've other business." He was convincing himself of his actions as he convinced her. "It will be a waste of time to go back and forth every day. Think of the horses."

"But . . ." She composed herself with a pause. "Why there? What's wrong with Lux Townhouse?"

He dropped his hand and knew he'd won. "You mean the one with no staff because someone thought to pack them all up like a caravan of Romani?"

Her mouth made an *O* shape before she nodded and stepped into the carriage with far more grace than she'd exhibited when she'd previously exited. She settled into her seat, her gaze downcast. "I'll send a missive to my brother to keep him from beating down every door in England."

Hamish nodded, his stomach clenching as she pulled away from him, her bright light dulling.

He shut the door, his gaze searching hers. "Good evening, Lady Charlotte."

Her eyes brightened for a second, then flickered out. Her smile was forced, her jaw too tight. "Good *morning*, Camine."

She tapped the carriage top, and it lurched into motion, leaving the two men behind.

Leaving him behind.

The carriage turned off St. James Street and out of sight.

Hamish whirled on Percy, his anger unfathomable. "Your information better be equivalent to the Tower of London aflame, or I'm going to make you bleed."

Percy's smile was crooked. "May I choose where?"

Hamish flexed his fingers, following the man into the quiet street. "By all means. Would you prefer the left side of your head or the right?"

The bastard actually looked like he was considering.

"What happened?" Hamish asked.

Percy extracted a slip of paper from his inside pocket with a tally and handed it to him. "Yesterday, a man approached Brody and offered him a bribe to stall the shipment."

Hamish froze at the amount on the paper. "There's another buyer?"

Only thugs, politicians, and gentlemen were so conniving.

A light rain started. Percy led him to the shelter of a lone tree on the walk. "I confirmed with the merchant we are to be supplied first, but it nearly doubled the original price." His smile was vicious. "Brody took some convincing."

Hamish's brows rose. Seaway robbery, but he only nodded. "Good work. Any word on who approached the captain?"

Percy shook his head. "Didn't get a good look, he said, but the blunt was fresh. I took the extra hours to run down a contact I know at London Trust. Four men withdrew notes in the past few days."

Hamish ignored the fact that Percy's gutter slang had vanished and asked, "Any names?"

"Two days."

They didn't have time for another interested party. He'd finally garnered a deal in good faith with Markus. But losing the supply would ruin the demand before he got his business running. "Night or day, when you get a name, I get it."

"Aye, govena'."

Hamish rolled his eyes at the change in speech. "Did Gregori get the first shipment, then?"

"Aye," Percy repeated. "Ol' crazy is tinkering away as we speak." He took out a second item from his coat. "Asked me to pass this along."

Hamish weighed the small, paper-wrapped package, his mind racing. Gregori had finished already? "How was the cut?"

"Thanks to that new mechanical contraption, flawless, as far as I saw."

Once he'd taken the prototype to Markus, the old man would

take him seriously. He'd go first thing—Hamish checked his watch—in the afternoon.

Which meant he had roughly nine hours to kill, and a woman waiting at his townhouse.

Gleaning the look in his eye, Percy shook his head and strolled into the night, one long whistle followed by a laugh. "Enjoy the rest of your evening, Your Grace. Tell the lady 'sweet dreams' from me."

"In *your* dreams," Hamish grumbled.

Percy's laugh pierced the night.

Hamish shuddered. "Eyes and ears everywhere."

SITTING IN THE duke's study, still dressed as a man, though less blind with her replaced spectacles from her pocket, Charlotte contemplated fleeing. Mrs. Forthright hadn't said a word when Charlotte had shown up unannounced. The young servant had taken one look at the carriage outside, the Camine Crest boldly painted across the wood, and escorted her to the study.

Charlotte removed her hat and roughly pulled the pins holding her hair in place until the mass gave way and fell down her back. She couldn't remember the last time she'd had so much fun. Drinking and laughing, not an embroidery hoop in sight.

But then that man, Percy, had shown up. The same man from Dockside, all angles and dishonest smile, and she'd remembered Lord Hamish Hurstfield, Duke of Camine, was a criminal.

She had no proof, of course, and she hadn't a clue what he smuggled in. She paused and waited for the fear and panic to set in.

Nothing.

Camine had been so attentive, kind. He'd laughed like a little boy for heaven's sake! Could he be so disreputable and monstrous as her brother said? Renard was one to talk. The run in with Richmund had distracted her from that awful bet. But her brother's treachery couldn't hold a candle to Camine's dismissal, a far worse betrayal. The Duke of Camine had secrets. Dangerous ones.

Did it matter?

The question was so simple, the answer more so.

That was when Charlotte realized the truth. She was in love with him.

The weight in her chest took on a name: fear. Not that she'd be harmed, not physically. Fear of rejection, of him not feeling the same way.

She shook her head, taking the list out of her vest pocket and flipping to the last page.

Number two-hundred and thirty-five: Fall in love.

She dipped a quill into the ink pot on the desk and crossed it out with one smooth stroke, but the action felt hollow.

She stared down at the words, the line reminding her of an arrow shot from the cherub's bow. Shouldn't there have been fireworks? A parade? Not this overwhelming pressure.

The last item had been a childish addition in a moment of whimsy. She'd wanted love, wanted what her parents had.

Which meant exactly one thing. She had to make Camine love her back.

New plan set, Charlotte replaced the list and set the quill to a clean sheet of parchment.

Dear Diana,

I was glad to read in your earlier letter that you are on the mend. The timing of your cousin calling you away so that our meeting must be delayed yet again is unfortunate. With your departure to the north and my brother's continued refusals to answer any of my letters, I confess I feel alone in a world unknown.

I need your advice more than ever, dear friend, for I've discovered a most alarming thing. I'm in love

Her quill stopped. She bit her lip as embarrassment flushed her skin. Her first instinct was to tell Diana everything, everything she only recently admitted to herself, but Diana's excuse about visiting her cousin gave her pause. The timing *was* unfortunate and the second such delay to avoid a meeting. Charlotte shook her head to dislodge the beginnings of doubt. No, instead of directing the letter to the bakery, she'd send a servant this time with the explicit orders to hand the missive directly to the recipient, or at least to her landlady. Then there'd be no question of her friend's story.

She looked at the clock, the time now well past three in the morning. She dropped her head to her hands. She needed sleep, needed to sort out the swirling storm of chaos in her mind.

She threw down the quill, the ink leaking onto her unfinished letter. Who was she kidding? She needed him. He'd come to be like air. With him gone, she couldn't breathe or think.

"Where the bloody hell is he?"

The door to the study opened, and Charlotte's heart leapt.

Then fell.

Mrs. Forthright—fully dressed even at this hour—took in her expression and closed the door behind her. "I take it I'm not who you were hoping to see?"

"You recognized me?" *Stupid Hamish was right.* Charlotte shook her head, refusing to spread her sour mood. "It's nice to see you again."

The housekeeper smiled. "I can't tell you how pleased I was to hear you were to marry Hamish."

For some reason, Charlotte found the duke's name on the other woman's lips unpleasant.

I'm jealous.

She slumped in the desk chair, feeling foolish all over again. A smitten fool. How would Hamish ever resist?

Mrs. Forthright came to the desk, her frown severe. "So, the master of the house has lost his mind and idiotically left you here alone?"

Charlotte grinned at her audacity, returning the frankness with her own. "We had a wonderful adventure and then *poof*, I was thrown into a carriage and bid goodnight. Now he's off somewhere, most likely getting into trouble without me." She'd meant the words to sound sarcastic, but her worry was evident even to her ears.

Mrs. Forthright had heard it too. "You care for him, then?" She glanced at the ruined letter on the desk, her eyes brightening. She smiled. "I see. You're in love with him."

Charlotte groaned and covered her face with her hands. "He doesn't believe in love, Mrs. Forthright."

"Oh, bullocks!"

Charlotte peeked between her fingers, watching the other woman sit on the edge of the desk, the exact opposite picture of proper.

"First, call me 'Camille.' 'Mrs. Forthright' sounds like a bad political campaign." She held up one finger and then another. "And second, men are too dense to know *what* they believe. The duke is worse than most."

"You speak so boldly." The fact had nagged at Charlotte since that first night. "Forgive me, but most masters would never tolerate such impudence."

"So why does the duke put up with me?" Camille was quiet a moment. Then she sighed. "The truth is we grew up together, in a way. We both had fathers who were less than desirable." She shook her head, her mouth curling upwards at the corners. "Deep down, I think the duke believes having me around, even as *intolerable* as I am, that I'll stop him from becoming his father."

The pain in the other woman's voice pulled at Charlotte's heart, even as it swelled with further evidence of Hamish's character. She placed a light touch on Camille's hand. "I'm sorry. It's evident you both are good natured."

Camille patted her hand and smirked. "You and I know that, but the duke can't see it." She rolled her eyes. "Dense, as I said." She rapped her knuckles on the desktop. "It'll be our job to make him realize his denseness and come to his senses."

Hope flared. "'Our'?"

"Of course," she said. "I'm going to help you." She clapped her hands and wrinkled her nose. "Starting with burning that outfit."

Charlotte smiled, a sudden thought twisting her insides with anticipation. Stomach aflutter, she said, "I have an idea."

"Oh?"

"I'll need to raid your kitchen."

CHAPTER TWENTY-FIVE

HAMISH RETURNED TO his townhouse, surprised to find it dark. He stepped through the door, expecting to find a lovely woman in men's clothing in the foyer, a scathing lecture about leaving a woman to fend for herself flying from those rosy lips.

There was no lecture, no light, and no woman.

Had she not arrived?

He marched down the hall to his housekeeper's chambers and raised his fist.

The door opened on its own, as if she'd been waiting for him. Camille popped a hip, her nightgown stretching over her legs. "You were actually going to knock?" she asked. "I thought for sure you'd skip the manners and come barging in. Seems I owe Lady Charlotte five pounds."

Her name sent his heart racing. "Where is she?"

Camille yawned and pointed up the stairs. "Fine job leaving her. Women love being thrown into a carriage and ordered away."

Shit. "She's mad?"

"Worse. After raiding the kitchen, she went straight to her room and said not to disturb her, no matter how much screaming I heard."

Hamish flinched.

"So much for winning the lady over. The renowned charms

of the Duke of Camine, flopped at the first chance at courtship." She shook her head. "Pitiful."

"Whose side are you on?" he asked.

"Hers. Now . . ." She turned him around and gave him a shove. "Remember, groveling and apologies, begging if she has a blunt object in hand."

Hamish groaned and took to the stairs, her humor doing nothing to ease his fears. "And if that doesn't work?"

She smiled up at him. "Cover your balls and pray she grows tired of smashing in your teeth."

With Camille's words, and the image of his bloodied face in mind, Hamish knocked softly on the guest quarter's door. No response.

He knocked again.

Silence.

There was no light under the door.

Had she fallen asleep? Hamish checked his watch in the dim light from the window at the end of the hall. Four in the morning.

He blew out his tension and turned to his own door. Maybe the sleep would lessen her anger. Knowing the lady, the extended time would give her ample time to devise an elaborate plan for revenge.

He rubbed his face, prepared to counter in the event the lady really did strike him.

The light under his door shifted, and Hamish vowed to double Camille's pay for lighting a fire for him. Wishing for nothing but his bed, he opened the door and froze.

Charlotte hadn't gone to bed; she had been waiting in his room.

Without a stitch of clothing.

Hamish took in her high breasts, her nipples dark and her skin glowing. Her hair tumbled over her shoulders, the golden hues dancing in the firelight. She lay stretched in front of the fire, her back propped up on a cushion, her shy smile making him instantly hard.

He cleared his throat, his cravat too tight. "You're awake."

"I am."

"You're not mad, then?"

"No."

He swallowed, sure she must have been sleep walking or her clothes had vanished by some unnatural means. "You're undressed."

Her laugh was silk in his ears. "You *did* notice?"

HE CLOSED THE door, sending his face into shadow and yet, Charlotte felt those eyes, burning hotter than the fire behind her. The way he stared at her, both as disciple and master, she felt every nerve come alive under his inspection.

When he didn't come to her, Charlotte self-consciously raised her arms, beckoning him.

His muttered oath sounded like a prayer. He came forward but didn't bend. He stood above her, his hot gaze raking down her body.

Charlotte dropped her arms and resisted covering herself. She wasn't thin, nor curved. She'd forced her body to move every day after the fire, unwilling to let weak lungs be an excuse. She'd grown strong. But the result was more defined limbs than was desirable in a woman.

She'd hoped the firelight would soften her, but the light and shadow played over the muscles with discrimination.

His gaze stopped on her shoulder, where Charlotte knew the skin was stretched and discolored. She grabbed the throw beside her.

"Don't you dare!" His growl stopped her like a physical hand. "I want to look my fill."

She bit her lip, relieved he hadn't asked about her scar. "I know my body isn't the—"

"Perfect."

Her gaze locked on his face. "What?"

"The word," he said, "is *perfect*."

Charlotte's heart ached. "You think I'm beautiful?"

"Perfect," he repeated, his gaze missing nothing. "You don't agree?"

She curled her knees to her chest. "I'm too muscled."

"Put your legs down," he ordered.

Startled, she slid her legs back to the floor, watching his gaze track the movement. She pulled them back up.

His eyes narrowed. He sloughed off his coat with deliberate slowness. "I see I'm going to have to teach you the consequences of disobeying me."

He rolled up his sleeves, revealing sculpted arms.

Charlotte's mouth went dry. How ridiculous to notice a man's arms. They flexed, the skin tan against the stark, white linen. Truly, a man shouldn't have had beautiful arms.

"See something you like?" he asked.

Charlotte's body shuddered at his gravelly voice. "Yes."

"Are you cold?"

She was burning up! She shook her head.

"You mean, 'No, my lord.'"

Charlotte would have scoffed at his arrogance if she hadn't been watching his face.

He'd made the order, and his eyes shifted, as if preparing for her refusal, before his face went blank. It was the same look he'd had in the carriage.

Vulnerable. No. That wasn't quite right. He wanted her submission. Desired it, but it wasn't about dominance. He wanted her trust.

The expression was fear.

He was afraid of his desires, afraid she wouldn't understand.

She offered a smile, letting her legs fall open. "I trust you, my lord."

The shock on his face turned into a rough inhale. And then he was there, touching her, his fingers tracing her secret areas without preamble, a relentless swirling that had Charlotte crawling out of her skin.

"Hamish!"

"You like that?"

She nodded. Her body was so tight. She thought she'd snap.

"Say it."

"I like it."

"Like what, my lady? Be specific."

His fingers brushed harder.

She gasped. "You touching me. There."

He chuckled. "Touching your pussy?"

Her face went hot, but she loved that he didn't hold back. "Yes, my pussy."

He groaned and took her mouth with his, his tongue mimicking his wicked fingers sweeping back and forth over her lips. "Such language," he said. "Sailors beware the blush."

She smiled against his lips, loving the way this 'wild' man teased her, challenged her, didn't coddle her.

Him. She loved him.

"Part for me," he said.

Her lips opened, welcoming his tongue's entrance. The taste of him was ecstasy, cigar and liquor, the taste of their evening together and the scandalous things they'd shared.

And a promise of more to come.

She sucked on his tongue.

He growled low in his throat. His fingers pushed insistently against the throbbing between her legs.

She slid her fingers over his, pushing on his middle finger where it played at the center of that ache.

His finger slipped inside, and she couldn't tell whose moan filled the space.

He pressed his forehead against hers, his voice rough, "So wet, Charlotte. Wet for me." He added a second finger, and

Charlotte bucked against his hand. "And tight."

"For you." She didn't know where the words had come from, but there was no hesitation, no shame. "I want you here, pushing, pulling, filling me."

His eyes went dark, and his growl Charlotte could only describe as 'wild.'

He retreated.

Charlotte gasped at his fingers pulling out.

He untied his cravat, holding the length in his hands. "Lean back."

She did. Her heart raced as he removed her spectacles and placed the silk against her eyes, tying a quick knot. Her other senses raced to make up for the lack of sight. Every flare of the fire sent a flush of heat across her shoulders. Every brush of silk on her skin was a smooth torture of sensation.

His breath came harsh and fast in her ear, the sound curling her toes. His pleasure was like sunshine, and Charlotte turned into it, soaking it in.

Next came her hands, placed behind her head and secured with the end length of the cravat.

A single finger traced her cheek, down her neck, over her collarbone and across the underside of her breast.

She jolted.

The sound of porcelain clanking drew the finger away. The clanking came again, followed by the sweet smell of peaches.

He sounded baffled. "Is this marmalade?"

She blushed. "I remembered your note and how my fingers smelled sweet after. I thought . . ."

His inhale was sharp. "You thought . . .?"

The blindfold made her brave. "I thought we didn't need rolls to enjoy the taste."

"Fuck."

Charlotte gasped as something warm and sticky was poured on her chest.

With her hands pulled back, her body arched, the marmalade

dripped maddeningly over her nipple.

"My God," he whispered. "Suddenly, I'm famished."

His tongue licked at the peach, circling her nipple and sucking as if he hadn't eaten in days.

She moaned, her other nipple puckering and at a loss.

As if hearing the complaint, he obliged, dripping sticky peach on the other side and scraping it off with teeth, all while the remaining marmalade dripped lower . . . lower.

She squirmed.

His mouth left her breast, trailing after the renegade condiment, the scrape of his day-old whiskers so masculine, her body coiled in on itself.

The pressure in her built until Charlotte wanted to scream. Close. She was close to something.

He pulled away.

"No!" Charlotte gasped.

Warm hands pulled the silk from her eyes, leaving her wrists restrained. She blinked in the sudden light.

Hamish gently set her spectacles back on her nose.

She scowled as his beautiful face came back into focus. "You stopped."

He chuckled. "Not for long." He picked up the porcelain and swirled a finger in the pot, releasing another burst of peach into the air.

Charlotte watched his finger into marmalade, mesmerized by the motion. Around and around, deeper. He added another finger, and Charlotte would have given up half the things on her list to put those fingers elsewhere. "You stopped," she said again. "You promised you wouldn't stop."

He set down the pot, his fingers wet and glowing in the light. His gaze locked on her. "I want you to see what I'm going to do to you."

The promise made something low spasm in anticipation. She swallowed and stuck out her chin, refusing to look away. "Then do it."

He smiled, full and wild, and Charlotte knew no other man could take her breath away like the Duke of Camine.

"Aye, my lady."

Then his fingers were on her, in her, everywhere pushing and teasing, all the while filling her nose with that unbelievable smell.

She arched, wanting him closer. "Kiss me," she said.

His smile turned wolfish. "That's the plan, sweetling."

And gracious heaven, he did. His tongue slipped past his fingers, kissing her where she ached. Wonderful, scandalous, the most erotic thing she'd ever seen. He sucked at her, and Charlotte screamed his name.

She was falling, turning, spinning out of control. She fell into waves, the pleasure crashing over her again and again. She gasped, panting, not wanting air, wanting this, him, forever.

She wouldn't come back to the surface. Nothing was worth leaving this feeling.

That was until he uttered two small words that had the air rushing back.

"Marry me."

CHAPTER TWENTY-SIX

H E WATCHED HER fall apart, her muscles clenching around his tongue. If he hadn't already been on the floor, the sight would have sent him to his knees in worship. In that moment, Hamish realized he'd do anything to keep her, even sell his soul to the Devil.

"Marry me." His words electrified the air.

She stiffened, the pleasure disappearing into a frown he was coming to realize was the face she made when preparing for a fight.

"Untie me," she said.

"No."

Her eyes narrowed. "You're out of your head, sir, if you believe I will respond to being restrained and dictated to. I won't be intimidated or bullied into anything I don't choose."

Hamish chuckled at that and sat back. "I know that. You should know me well enough to realize I'd stoop to underhanded tactics to merely even the playing field."

The words pleased her; he saw it in the softening of her clenched jaw. He pressed on. "I've a proposition."

The echo of her own words made her mouth twitch. She inclined her head, knowing now how in control she was despite the restraints. "I'm listening."

His stomach flipped. He had one chance to convince her. He took a lesson from her and was honest. "We're a good match. I do not mean for wealth or status." He searched for the right words, not entirely understanding why he was trying so hard to tie himself to her, or anyone. "You make me . . ." *Happy*. Hamish pushed that word away, knowing it gave her a level of power over him he wouldn't tolerate. "Comfortable," he said at last. "I would not hide you away in one of my houses. You would be free to come and go as you pleased. We'd continue your excursions together. A partnership."

Her shyness resurfaced and charmed him anew.

"You've mentioned how the arrangement may benefit me," she said. "What of you?"

He grinned and ran a finger over her thigh, watching her gaze track the movement. Yes, they would suit. "I ask one thing. You are to share my bed and no one else's. To be available to me and me alone."

Her gaze shot to him. "Fidelity must be two-sided if there is to be trust. If it is for your pleasure alone, I refuse. I want passion. I want . . ." She nodded her head at the space between them. "I want what we just did. More."

"Greedy little minx." He pecked her on the lips, his blood pumping hot. Had she not realized how rare their coupling was? Not even coupling. The passion between them could have started the house aflame, and he hadn't even penetrated. The vision of it, anticipation alone, would satisfy him for days. "Together," he vowed. "Mutual pleasure, to explore our passion. You'd be available to me, but I would also be for you."

Her eyes lit up. "I like that," she purred, licking his bottom lip before pulling back. "I won't hold you to it forever. But I will not be discarded mercilessly. If we tire of our arrangement, we speak at once."

His cock jumped at the feel of her tongue, light and unsure. He wouldn't imagine her with another man. The idea was deplorable, but since he had no intention of leaving her long enough for her to seek other pleasure, the point was moot.

The stipulation, if anything, proved she was perfect, knowing and practical.

"Agreed," he whispered against her cheek, needing to hear the affirmation. "Marry me, Charlotte?"

"What of my brother? Without his consent—"

"The marriage contract was delivered by messenger this afternoon."

Her eyes widened. "Renard signed it?"

He nodded.

She went quiet, her eyes downcast in thought.

Hamish held his breath.

Too long. She was thinking too much.

Hamish grasped for another perk, a bribe, anything to make her agree. He opened his mouth to offer her the sun, when she looked up and said the one word that would set them on their course.

"Yes."

Hamish took her mouth, pushing his tongue inside and branding her. Finding the rhythm she liked, up and down, up, teeth against her lip. He broke the kiss, loving her frustrated sigh.

He gripped her chin and waited for her to come back from her passion. "Today," he said.

"Today," she agreed.

"Good." He growled and sealed the deal with a dizzying kiss that left him light-headed and eager for the sun to rise.

"You're too good for him," Camille said. She turned in her seat beside Charlotte, giving Hamish a cocked brow across the carriage. "She's too good for you."

Hamish grumbled something about etiquette lessons. "I brought you along as a companion for the duchess, at *your* insistence. Not as a vessel to state the offensive."

The former housekeeper looked anything but grateful for

Hamish going against propriety to appoint Camille to a position usually held by a lady from a genteel family. A person's background hardly mattered if they were capable. One more way the duke's outlook aligned with Charlotte's.

"At least *Her Grace* is better company," said Camille.

Charlotte shared a quick smile with her new friend at Camille's continued efforts to rile Hamish, but the honorific hit Charlotte a second later. Lady Charlotte Hurstfield, Duchess of Camine.

The vicar had said her new name, and she'd felt a different kind of cage slam shut, but instead of her behind bars, it was as if she'd done the slamming; her past locked away where she could no longer be trapped.

The world around her stretched far and unfamiliar, but somehow, it didn't frighten her. It thrilled her, and she suspected it had a great deal to do with the man sitting across from her, his all-black attire making him look like a villain, the wickedly handsome kind.

Husband.

His eyes found her, a slow smile setting her cheeks on fire. "Wife?"

Charlotte's eyes widened, realizing she'd spoken out loud. She looked away quickly, the cloudy city skies giving way to bright country sunshine. "Will we be stopping at Lux estate on the way, or will we go straight to Camine Manor?"

"Straight there," he said. "I'll send a missive to Renard and ask him to visit. He, no doubt, has received the happy news by now."

She nodded, her hands wringing in her lap.

"No need to be nervous." Camille set her hand atop Charlotte's, the woman's voice unexpectedly gentle. "The staff will love you."

Hamish grinned. "They'll respect you, anyway."

The words sent a pang through Charlotte's chest, an echo of their conversation.

"Fall in love."

"I can't promise that."

Respect, privilege, reputation—the virtues of the *ton*. Seemed the aristocracy thrived under the stability of affectionless unions. Was she the only person in England who dared for more?

"Ignore him," Camille said, earning a scowl from the duke. "Respect is fleeting and changes with the loss of payment." She squeezed Charlotte's hand. "You will win their hearts."

Hamish grumbled.

Charlotte's gaze darted to him.

Camille stared down her nose at him. "What was that, Your Grace?"

Hamish gave a mocking smile. "Admiring your complete personality change. You almost sound like a decent human being."

"Ha!"

Charlotte smiled at their familiar banter, hope filling the hole in her chest, certain she hadn't misheard her husband's low voice when he'd said she could win anyone's heart.

She hoped the words were true.

THEY ARRIVED AT Camine Manor, the staff out in formal rows, the gardens flourishing under the expert gardener's ministrations, but Hamish saw only Charlotte.

How her fingers fidgeted nervously with her bonnet ribbons, the blue a match to the borrowed dress that was too big in the chest and too small in the hips, but somehow perfect for showing off her fair features and delicate frame. How her gaze flitted from the servants to the maze of hedges to the towering monstrosity of grey stone and baroque architecture that had served as his childhood home.

Truthfully, Hamish preferred any of the other four estates, but, if the proximity to Lux Manor would provide a minuscule amount of comfort for his new bride, he'd suffer through his memories. For her.

His bride.

The title brought a wealth of visions, primarily images of consummating their partnership in the basest of ways with skin and teeth and lovely blue ribbons around her wrists.

Suddenly, the pomp and circumstance grew tedious in its opposition to his true desires to show Charlotte more important things pertaining to their future together. He would've bypassed the entire spectacle if Camille hadn't taken that uncharacteristic moment to follow propriety and usher Charlotte to the front line to introduce the staff one by one with painstaking detail, at the murderous glare of the manor's housekeeper, Mrs. Lodeless.

"Mr. Frendstone is the butler and the meanest man in England," Camille said. "He once threw a man out on his rump for not removing his gloves."

Hamish groaned. Two days. He bet it would be two days—less—before the country staff revolted over Camille's baseless insults.

Charlotte turned the full force of her sunny personality on the ancient man, her smile brilliant. "Nonsense. This young man must be the fiercest butler, I'd say. The other man surely had it coming?"

She leaned in conspiratorially, and Hamish found himself drawn to her mischievous grin and staged whisper like a moth to a lit candle.

"I'm glad you're on our side, Mr. Frendstone."

The hunched man puffed out his chest, instant loyalty smoothing ten years from his face. "Likewise, Your Grace."

And down the line they went, Camille making critiques and Charlotte appeasing egos with enough charm and innocent flattery that Hamish was inclined to believe it was genuine.

At last, they reached the end of the line, Camille introducing Miss Sanders, the head cook, in a fresh apron, her mass of red curls thrown up in a messy bun.

"A pleasure, Miss Sanders," Charlotte said.

Miss Sanders curtsied, her freckled nose scrunching. "I've prepared a light lunch in the parlor, Your Grace. I thought you might be hungry after your journey with these two eating up all the politeness in decent company."

At the familiar tone, Charlotte seemed to sag with relief, showing she'd been holding on to the polite air for the staff's sake. "I'm famished," she said, her gaze flicking to the house beyond. "Please, tell me there are rolls?"

Miss Sanders broke out in a toothy smile. "Fresh rolls and marmalade, Your Grace."

At the mention of marmalade, Charlotte's cheeks flushed.

Desire plowed through him. Those innocent eyes were piercing, replaying their last experience with the condiment. He'd give anything to have the marmalade be peach. In fact, it needed to be on every menu, in every meal, a part of every floral arrangement.

If the staff couldn't procure a supplier, he'd have them grown on site. A massive grove to take his wife where the air would be filled with citrus and sex.

"Back to your duties." The housekeeper clapped her hands and gave Camille a scathing glare before nodding to Charlotte. "I'll escort you to the parlor, Your Grace. Afterwards, we can go over the menus and discuss invitations."

"Invitations?"

Mrs. Lodeless blinked. "In honor of your marriage to His Grace. A ball is expected. The staff are preparing as we speak."

Charlotte's milky complexion soured. "I see."

"The duchess will be quite busy the rest of the day, Mrs. Lodeless." Hamish lifted Charlotte's hand to his mouth for a quick kiss, her grateful expression spurring a chuckle from him. "Until my bride is more comfortable with the manor, I'll oversee the final decisions, if that won't be getting in the way?"

Mrs. Lodeless pursed her lips, looking like she was swallowing a prickly pear. "Whatever you believe is best, Your Grace."

She turned to the main house and waved a hand for the doors

to open.

With a grin, Camille followed, leaving Charlotte and Hamish alone, her hand still in his.

"Thank you," she said.

He smiled and leaned down to whisper in her ear, "My fearless duchess, afraid of an old housekeeper? The woman is terrifying, to be sure, but the way you handled Mr. Frendstone, I have no doubts the woman will come around smiling like a fresh maid."

Charlotte shivered at his nearness.

He had the sudden urge to show her the hedge maze, where they could get lost for the rest of the afternoon, with little hope of being found.

"The woman doesn't scare me," she said. "Running a household, accepting visitors, and balls are another story."

"Ah. I assume the radial education you spoke of didn't include how to be the perfect hostess?"

Her tone was dry. "As I had no aspiration to marry, the knowledge seemed like a waste of time."

Raised voices echoed from inside the manor. He sighed. "You may be free of the obligations soon enough. Come along, wife." He tucked her hand in the crook of his arm, the simple touch bringing an unexpected sense of peace. "We'll start with how to keep the staff from walking out when a guest is particularly dreadful."

Charlotte smiled. "I'm surprised Camille memorized the names of the staff. She need not have gone to the trouble for my sake."

Hamish shook his head as the voices grew louder. "You'll find the saying, 'a woman's memory is long' quite apt with your new companion."

Charlotte cocked her head. "She doesn't forget anything?"

"Permanent pictures in her head is how she puts it."

"Extraordinary."

He patted her hand and led her inside towards the aroma of

fresh bread and increasingly angry shouts. "A blessing to some," he said quietly, regretting handing over the list of his household staff to Camille beforehand. "A curse to another."

CHAPTER TWENTY-SEVEN

TRUTH BE TOLD, Charlotte was too nervous to eat the ornate plating of meats and fruits, too nervous to listen while Camille and Hamish squabbled like children, too nervous to think. Instead, she stared at the colorful trays set before her, her mind eerily empty.

Until it wasn't.

Running a household, she knew once a woman married, the responsibilities of the husband's house fell to her. Knew still, she should've been running her brother's household since the passing of their mother. She knew it and, yet she felt like she'd walked into a blooming rose bush—lured in by the sweet smell and lovely sight—forgetting the less desirable thorns underneath.

She'd never planned anything beyond a midnight rendezvous and a thrilling Dockside whiskey. Surely, Hamish would have told her if he expected such a conventional division of work. Knowing her very unconventional personality, he must have been aware she'd be miserably suited to run anything, least of all what wine went with fish and which went with beef.

She glanced at him to see he was studying her in the sudden silence. Charlotte cleared her throat, her cheeks hot.

Had he asked her something? Was she being unsociable? Would her companions tire of her just like her brother and the Lux staff?

Hamish stood abruptly, the legs of his chair screaming against the oak floor. He came around the table and offered his hand. "Come."

He pocketed a roll and tugged her from the room, leaving Camille alone at the table and grinning like a cat.

Charlotte stumbled along, unable to match his determined pace. "Duke, if I've offended you with my silence, I do apologize—"

"Hamish." He glanced at her. "I think we can dispense with the formalities, dear wife."

She nodded. "You're right, H-Hamish."

They stopped in the foyer, Mr. Frendstone appearing as if by magic.

"Bring my Weston to the far field," Hamish said. "And find my lady's bonnet."

The butler didn't bat an eyelash. "Would you care for pigeons as well?"

Hamish grinned. "You know me well."

Mr. Frendstone bowed. "Yes, Your Grace."

⟫⟩✳⟨⟪

BACK TO THE ankle-twisting pace, Charlotte thought of two more items to add to her shopping list as her husband escorted her across the lawn: trousers and boots.

"Who's Weston?"

"A long-standing companion of mine."

"A dog?"

"In a way," he said. "You'll like him." He released her and turned to walk backwards. "First, we're going to go over the rules."

His certainty didn't set her at ease. She worried her bottom lip with her teeth. She'd never been permitted a pet. Aside from a pony she hadn't been allowed to brush, let alone ride.

"You're nervous," he said.

She nodded. "I know we're married and that there is"—she cleared her throat again—"more to coupling than what we've done." She shook her head. "I'm unclear how to proceed or what the rules are."

His chuckle was low, soothing her nerves as much as his next words. "When the time comes, I will instruct you so there is little doubt. But that's not what we're doing."

Her head snapped up. "We're not?" She couldn't hide her disappointment.

He squeezed her hand. "Trust me, I have every intention of whisking you into the nearest unoccupied space and making you scream my name as I teach you every angle a man and woman may couple."

"Oh." Her skin flushed with a different heat, excitement and desire chasing away the fear. "Why aren't we doing that?"

"Because you looked ready to bolt for the door."

They stopped in an open clearing, majestic green hills rolling in front of them. He raised her hand to his mouth and kissed her wrist, his eyes dark. "When you are overwhelmed, you need only tell me. I never want to see uncertainty in your eyes, not for me, at a ball, or in our home." His teeth scraped her palm, and Charlotte's knees went weak. "In our bed. Do I make myself clear?"

She certainly wanted to go to bed now.

"Charlotte?"

"Yes?"

"I'm giving you an order." He ducked his head, his tone teasing. "This is where you bite my head off and assure your husband you are as hotheaded as ever so as not to make him worry."

She smiled, her love for him growing with every word. "I'm sorry to worry you. I do understand, and I'll prepare several scathing retorts later for your annoyance."

He kissed her forehead, a quick peck that had Charlotte's heart melting.

"Much obliged, my dear."

"You mentioned rules?"

"I did." He waved his hand, spotting Mr. Frendstone and two servants carrying an assortment of wrapped bundles.

Charlotte's eyes widened. "Are those rifles?"

He winked. "That they are."

She gasped as two polished rifles with barrels as long as her arm were uncovered, along with a contraption that looked like a medieval slingshot. "You're showing me how to shoot?"

He took the rifles in hand, his eyes bright, as if pleased by her enthusiasm. "It was on your list, was it not?" He handed her a gun, his expression growing serious. "Now: rules."

⇒⇒⇒≫⫷⇐⇐⇐

HAMISH WATCHED HIS wife load her rifle with a steady hand that spoke more of a year's practice than that of twenty minutes. After a thorough schooling of safety measures and practice fires unloaded, Hamish felt himself relaxing, or even more unimaginable, happy.

His laughter came easier and with more frequency. Every little remark she made, the endearing frown she got when concentrating. He'd smiled more in the past week than he had his whole adult life.

He cared for her.

At first a marriage of mutual passion now seemed subpar. Easy company, shared interests. Hamish smiled again.

How the tongues would wag when the *ton* learned the Duke of Camine had gone and grown fond of his wife.

He watched her snap the barrel into place, the flare of triumph on her face seeding something warm in his chest.

She pointed to the clay disks at their feet. "Now we throw the sparrows?"

He picked up one of the terra-cotta disks and fitted it into the sling apparatus. "Pigeon. Once I release the sling, track the disk, keeping your eyes aligned with the barrel like I showed you. When the pigeon falls into your eyeline, squeeze the trigger. But be ready for kickback."

Charlotte pushed her spectacles high on her nose and nodded, that amusing frown back on her face. The gun fit into her armpit, the weight not seeming to bother her.

Well-defined muscles, he remembered. The image of her naked before his fire was erotic and telling. She'd complained then about her body, but there was nothing masculine or unattractive about the sight of her standing in front of him, the gun held tightly to her chest, her bonnet ribbons blowing in the breeze.

A huntress. A siren. A goddess. The woman could be anything she wanted.

Hamish found himself in the unfamiliar position of *wanting* to give her everything and more.

She lifted the gun, her mouth skimming the metal as she found her balance and giving Hamish countless ideas of putting her mouth to another ridged barrel.

"I'm ready," she said.

So was he.

She glanced at him. "Did you say something?"

Glad the servants had returned to the manor so no one would witness his straining erection, Hamish positioned the sling. "On three. One . . . two . . . three."

He released the pigeon, and the gun went off.

The gun's power sent Charlotte to the ground with a squeal and a grunt.

He crouched down, his hands worrying over her. "Are you all right?"

Bonnet flung off, she looked up at him, her smile glorious and her hair a mess around her face.

And then she laughed. Wonderful, full laughs that shirked convention and filled the air around them with unbridled joy.

The warmth swelling in his chest grew unbearable. She was

sunshine itself, bringing light into every dark space. And he needed to be a part of that light, right now.

He scooped her and her bonnet into his arms, ignoring her startled yelp, and took off towards the manor.

"What are you doing?" She squirmed. "I wasn't done."

He gave her backside a swat, wondering if she'd enjoy the action without the wealth and cushion of skirts. His strides quickened. "I'm going to take you to bed."

She stopped struggling and collapsed into his embrace with a sigh. "Finally."

CHAPTER TWENTY-EIGHT

B Y THE TIME the duke and his wife had reached the manor, the staff had made themselves scarce despite the afternoon bustle of evening chores.

In a grand spectacle, Hamish carried his new bride over the threshold and up the stairs.

Charlotte hid her face in his chest. "Put me down," she whispered. "What if someone sees?"

"What if they do?" he challenged. With the ruckus they were about to make, he'd doubt if the next estate over would be far enough to muffle their cries of pleasure. It was a challenge a man of title must endeavor to strive for, all night if need be.

They reached the landing, Hamish nowhere near winded. In fact, Charlotte felt too light. Remembering she hadn't eaten anything, he took the roll from his pocket. "Open your mouth."

Charlotte shook her head. "I'm not hungry."

Hamish nibbled her ear, earning a squeal. "You'll learn soon enough, wife, that I don't enjoy repeating myself." He put the roll to her lips. "Take a bite."

"My stomach." She pushed the bread away. "I don't think I could eat a bite until . . . after."

Her cheeks flushed on the last word and comprehension softened his will. She was nervous. She'd said as much when she'd confessed earlier in the yard.

"As you wish," he said. "A compromise, then." He pocketed

the roll and nuzzled the soft bend of her neck. "You'll eat *during*."

The reference to their first relations seemed to quiet her. His kisses lowered to her collarbone and her fingers threaded through his hair without hesitation.

His tongue followed the top swell of her breast. Her nails dug into his scalp, and he groaned. Head lifting, heart pounding, he captured her gaze. "I need you. Now."

She pressed against him, her eyes glazed. "Then get on with it."

And she kissed him.

Lips sucking, tongue licking, she kissed like sin, hurried from inexperience and rough, impassioned. They clawed at each other in a frenzy still in the open hall.

With that sliver of rational thought, Hamish set her down to extract a key from his trousers, loath to leave her kisses for even a second. He placed the key in the lock.

"Hamish."

Lips swollen, hair tumbling down her shoulders, she grabbed at her skirts, her fingers rubbing the space between her legs.

He growled, pushed her against the door, and secured her hands on either side of her head.

"Do you wish to touch yourself, mouse?"

She strained against his hold, her body molding to his. "I want *you* to touch me."

The heat of her soft curves against his iron was torture. He rewarded her bold words with another quick kiss. "Have you before?" he asked. The thought of her sitting alone in the dark, her fingers finding that ache . . . He could go mad imagining.

He let go of her wrists to slide a hand up her leg, pushing the volume of skirts up around them and hissing at the exposed skin.

"You're not wearing stockings."

She watched him play with the smooth skin of her thigh, her breath coming in pants. "Or a corset."

"Of course not," he groaned. His wife was temptation itself. Sensual, bold, and all his. "Have you ever touched yourself,

Charlotte?"

Her gaze jumped to his. She bit her lip and nodded.

"Say it," he ordered.

"Yes."

The word unlocked him. Hamish turned the key and pushed the door open.

He kissed Charlotte again, shutting the door behind them, and said against her mouth, "Turn around."

She turned instantly, and the beast inside him roared at her submission. He unhooked the buttons of her dress one at a time, working his way down the deep curve of her back, the reveal of peachy skin inch by inch an exercise in will.

He peeled the dress away and his mouth went dry.

He drew the first sleeve down one shoulder and then the other, the latter revealing a striking scar.

He kissed the taut skin, enjoying her shiver of awareness. "Was this from the fire?" he asked gently, remembering how she'd shied away the first time he'd seen the burn.

She nodded.

His fingers traced the length from the edge of her shoulder down to the underside of her arm. Years had faded the red to white and pulled the skin in places where a girl had become a woman.

"I was ten," she said.

He remembered.

It had been a rare weekend spent in the country with both his parents in attendance. One of the servants had seen the smoke from the grounds, the black haze thick and towering in the afternoon sky.

Fourteen at the time, he and his father, and a service of staff, had scrambled to the Lux estate, but it had been too late. The Duke and Duchess of Lux had perished in a stable fire attempting to save their daughter.

A maelstrom of servants carrying buckets of water had pushed Hamish farther from the fire where he'd found a girl in the grass, too beautiful to be real and too pale to be alive.

She'd lain on the ground, blonde hair golden in the flame's light. Even unconscious, Hamish had thought sorrow etched the lines of the angel's face.

He looked at the same face, older and more beautiful than before. He hadn't remembered the little girl until this moment.

"They saved you," he said.

Sorrow once again traced her faint smile. Her hand came up to cover her shoulder.

"Whenever I wanted a quiet place to read, I went to the hayloft. I fell asleep that day, lulled to sleep by the smell of horses and fresh hay." A shadow of the past darkened her face. "I woke up to the horses' screams and my parents calling my name. Everything was on fire, but my parents stood in the middle of the stable, holding out their arms for me, acting like we were running late for dinner and Renard was waiting."

Her eyes glistened with unshed tears. Tears for her lost childhood, tears for the parents she'd never known as an adult, but more so, tears of pride for the unconditional love that had driven a duke and duchess to lay down their lives to save their cherished child.

Hamish took her hand from her shoulder and kissed her fingertips one by one. "I envy you."

Her gaze shot to him.

"Your memories," he clarified. "Even in death, your parents' love for you was never questioned." A yawning chasm opened in his chest, a hole supposed to be filled with the knowledge you mattered to someone more than their own life. Knowledge denied him by an indifferent father and a duty-bound mother.

Charlotte's soft voice echoed inside that space, filling the dark with light, "Tell me."

"I was a byproduct of my father's ambitions. Produced and set aside to be used when it suited his desires for power and image." Hamish curled his fingers into fists and then let them go slack. "I never felt so helpless as I did when I found out he'd sired a child with another woman," he whispered. A sibling, someone to share ideas, adventures with. Someone to ebb the loneliness that had accompanied cold parents.

That too had been kept from him. His hands clenched into fists again, tight enough to cut off blood flow. When he'd finally found his sister, months later, she'd been everything he'd hoped for, funny and lively. Poor but proud and intelligent. For one second, he'd thought the lifelong separation wouldn't have mattered. They'd start a family together without their father getting in the way.

But a monster's memory hung above one's head long after a flesh-and-blood man died.

When she'd found out who he was, the anger and hurt had cut him deeper than any sharp words his father had deigned to throw his way.

"She hates me," he said. How could she not? "I bear a disgusting resemblance to the late duke." Down to the exact eye shade, ice and sin.

How he wished to tell Charlotte the truth, but he'd been sworn to secrecy. It was his sister's one stipulation in agreeing to let him help her situation.

"Speak of our relationship to anyone and I will vanish without a word." He'd believed her. His sister didn't make idle threats.

Warm hands turned his face. "You are nothing like your father," Charlotte said.

His chuckle wasn't from humor. No, he was much worse. Needing to bend a woman's will to gain pleasure. Needing the control over another person to feel safe.

Coward. Pathetic.

Beast.

Lips skimmed his jaw, their silken texture a balm to his harsh thoughts.

He'd been a fool to marry her. A man like him had no right to taint someone so pure.

"Beast," he said.

"No!" She wound her fingers into his hair to keep him in place. "Don't pull away. Stay with me."

He wanted to. He wanted to lock the door and never let her leave his side, but he wouldn't. She'd risked everything for freedom, and he wouldn't cage her to sate his own selfish needs.

Not unless it was her choice.

"Tell me you want me," he said, bringing their foreheads together. "Tell me you want this." His words rang with desperation, but he wouldn't relent in this. If the answer was no, he'd let her go. She'd have her freedom. He swore it.

Even if her refusal meant something vital in him died.

"Choose me," he whispered.

She bumped his nose with her own, the action playful and subtly asking him to tip his head to look up at her.

"Silly man," she said. "I already have."

SHE LOVED HIM.

She'd heard about the previous duke's indiscretions in one of the gossip columns. A gentleman, pillar of the community, had slighted his wife and son.

Hamish.

His wounds ran far deeper than an unsightly shoulder scar.

She ached to heal them away. His self-loathing broke her. He couldn't see how anyone would choose him.

But she would. She had.

And she'd show him the only way he'd accept.

She let her dress slip around her waist, took his hand, and guided it to her bare breast. "I choose you, husband."

He came alive, the melancholy evaporating with rational thought. He took her nipple into his mouth, sucking deep and flicking the sensitive bud with his tongue.

"Hamish!"

Fire flared wherever he touched.

His suck turned rough and the valley between her legs went wet. She rubbed against his hard thigh and begged him to remove her skirts, pleaded for him to find that ache and kiss it away, but nothing would dissuade him from his worship of her breasts.

He moved to the other breast, leaving his fingers to pinch and roll her throbbing nipple.

Her pants grew shallow. That fire was spreading. Soon she'd be nothing but a pile of ash.

She clawed at his shoulders, earning a chuckle that went straight to her core.

"Patience, my love." He licked the underside of her breast, back and forth, and teased her nipple before repeating the motion.

She threw her head back, the heat rolling over her skin like rain down her back. Slow, maddening, tortured pleasure.

"I don't want to be patient." She gasped.

He pulled back and the absence of touch was worse. His eyes were hooded, but his voice was clear. "I'm going to tease you until you're too far in your pleasure to feel the pain," he said. "You will be patient." He left a lingering kiss on her lips that softened his edict. "Now, step out of your dress."

Charlotte let her garment fall to the floor and pool at her feet.

His gaze raked over her naked body before locking back on her face. "Perfect."

Charlotte preened at the compliment. She wanted to be perfect for him, anything and everything he needed. The way his eyes watched her, she could almost imagine she was. She reached up to remove her glasses.

"Don't," he commanded. "Leave them."

He held out his hand to assist her out of the fabric and turned her towards the corner, where a four-poster bed sat, a sheer, white canopy blocking off silk sheets.

"Walk to the bed," he said. "Slowly."

She walked, the fire from the hearth scorching her already

flushed skin. She reached the bed.

"Stop," he said. "Turn around."

She did.

"Sit."

Finding a slit in the canopy, Charlotte parted the fabric and sat on the edge of what had to be the softest mattress in existence.

"Lean against the pillar," he said.

She angled her hips on the mattress for support and rested her back on one of the bed's dark, wooden pillars, each expertly carved to look like heavy coiled ropes woven into a complicated plait.

His voice went low. "Reach up."

Charlotte found his gaze, seeing his desire. Pride filled her, knowing she was the cause. Holding his gaze, she reached behind her to grab the wood above her head.

The position arched her back and lifted her breasts.

"Dear God," he whispered and then he came for her.

CHAPTER TWENTY-NINE

WHATEVER DEMON HE'D sold his soul to, the sight of Charlotte on his bed following his every command with that insatiable mixture of curiosity and interest would be worth every second of hell.

Hamish held out her bonnet, the blue ribbons dangling.

He placed her cupped hands into the bonnet itself and wrapped the length of ribbon once, twice, around her wrists, his blood growing hotter with every slide of silk.

He'd make her his. She'd chosen him. She wouldn't regret it.

They'd start slow. He'd show her the torture of stalling one's own gratification and the ultimate climax of restraint.

He wound the ribbons a third time, watching her face for any signs of discomfort or hesitation.

Her nose scrunched. Her body squirmed.

A sinking feeling slowed his movements.

She watched him wrap a fourth time, her mouth tense.

"No, wait!"

He released her instantly.

Her hands tore out of the restraints.

Hamish backed away, his stomach heaving. He prepared himself for his damnation and her disgust, both deserved.

Beast. Indecent.

He'd leave. She'd chosen wrong. It was his own selfishness that had made him hope she'd see his needs, and sheer arrogance to think he could teach her to need it too.

She scratched her nose, a sigh of relief bursting out.

He turned to leave when she put her wrists back together. "All right. I'm ready."

He stared at her wrists and then her relaxed expression. "What?"

"I said, I'm ready."

He watched her stick her hands through the loose ribbon, his chest tight. "Ready? You want to continue?"

"Of course. Why wouldn't—" Her eyes widened, then softened. She leaned forward, her eyes narrowing. "Hamish Hurstfield, you are going to secure my wrists and ravish me until I forget your name and mine. Failure to do so will result in the dissolvement of our partnership and there will be consequences."

At once, the darkness of uncertainty faded, and Hamish marveled at his fearless wife and her instinctive knowledge of how to make him feel a fool and amused at the same time.

"Consequences, you say?" He edged closer and slid the dangling ribbons between his fingers, catching them up so they tightened around her wrists. "There was nothing in our agreement about ravishing."

Her gaze darkened at his deft fingers tying the ribbon ends in a perfect silk bow. "You're mistaken," she said, her purr undoing him. "We had a verbal agreement that you are now in serious risk of breaching."

Dear Lord, he'd never thought a conversation over a contract could sound so dirty. He pulled her arms over her head with one hand and leaned down over her upturned face. "A man has been called out for less of an insult." He cupped a breast, no longer able to resist her naked skin. "What point is being contended?"

"Hamish!" She pressed into his hand, her arms straining to keep them raised above her head. "Keep going."

He shook his head and teased her nipple until she cried out again. "This is an area of honor, Charlotte. A man is nothing without his word." He loved teasing her, loved how she rose to every challenge, verbal or physical, and the winner never mattered. "What am I doing that offends you so?"

She huffed. "Stopping."

He forced his face to remain blank. "I see. My apologies, my lady. It seems I was mistaken. However, can I make it up to you?"

"Damn your apology!" She was panting, her legs rubbing. She was on the edge. One finger stroke over her and she'd fall apart.

Hamish knew then there would never be another woman alive for him.

He hooked her binds on a hidden ledge near the top of the pillar, leaving her stretched before him in a position that seemed slightly uncomfortable, but with an ease of access he expected to use momentarily.

He stood beside her, looking down into her lust-filled gaze, and ran a thumb over her bottom lip. "If you wish to stop, Charlotte, tell me so now. Once I begin . . ." His jaw set. "I won't be able to tell your pleasure from your screams."

He didn't know why he'd said it. He'd always bring her pleasure, he knew with certainty, but even now he gave her a pass to find a gentler man, a more suitable man.

"You can't scare me away." She nipped at his thumb with perfect, little teeth. "But I'm beginning to think you're scared of yourself."

Hamish froze.

She saw him. She always had.

"Tell me now," he said, his fingernails piercing his palms. "Do you want me to stop?"

Her gaze pierced him, through him, through the twisted muscle one called a heart. That same cage that had slammed shut that first night in his study opened wide, freeing them both with one infinitely beautiful word.

"Never."

HAMISH KNELT BEFORE her, wrinkling his immaculate suit.

His grin left Charlotte thinking about everything but clothes. His first kiss to her calf had her knees squeezing and her core clenching. She was mortified to realize she was impossibly wet.

His second kiss tickled the sensitive skin behind her knee.

She went rigid to stop a flood of sensation deep inside.

His hand hooked around her ankle to ease her legs open.

Charlotte panicked. "No, wait. I can't stop it."

Those eyes, piercing and all seeing, met hers. "I know, my dear. Let go."

His fingers brushed the folds of her opening.

Charlotte fell. The waves were merciless, beating at her with bone-crushing force. Before the second wave broke, his mouth clamped down on her clit, and she screamed.

His tongue pushed inside, lapping at her like a cat to cream.

She cried at every lash of tongue, every brush of linen, every scrape of his unshaven cheeks on her most sensitive lips.

Ecstasy, torture, pleasure, pain—they blended in a jumble of sensations, solidifying into a memory of touch Charlotte would spend the rest of her life remembering.

A third orgasm struck, and Charlotte's hips came off the bed to meet his mouth's worship.

Tears charted down her cheeks. She squeezed her eyes shut and rolled her head side to side. "It's too much." She couldn't breathe. Any more pleasure and she may perish.

"Look at me, my love."

That deep voice was like an anchor. She latched on to the weight and pulled herself back to the surface. She opened her eyes and found the sea reflected in the eyes of her husband.

"My love."

It was the second time he'd called her that. Words a man whispered in the dark without real feeling, but Charlotte would treasure the softness in his voice, in those ever-changing eyes.

His fingers swirled her clit before sliding deep.

Air hissed between her teeth as a second finger joined the

first.

"So tight." He groaned.

She bucked against his hand.

Then the fingers withdrew, but Charlotte didn't complain this time. She trusted him to finish her pleasure.

She collapsed back against the pillar, her leg muscles shaking.

But they weren't done.

He stood on the bed and towered over her, his expression serious. Or was that the light from the fire playing over his face?

She felt his emotional withdrawal like a physical distance. "Hamish?"

He ran a hand through his hair, his eyes tormented. "I'm not a gentle man. I'll do my best to make this good for you, but I can't promise it won't hurt."

His worry banished any apprehension the mention of pain had sparked.

She smiled up at her husband, seeing the kindness inside he hid from the rest of the world, himself more than anyone. "Take off your clothes, husband."

His gaze flicked to her.

She fought her blush. He'd told her never to be ashamed. "I want to see you."

I see you.

His mouth twisted into a wolfish grin. He shrugged out of his coat and vest and threw them across a highbacked chair, his shirt and cravat following, leaving him bare from the waist up.

Charlotte's mouth hung open.

"Like what you see, mouse?" he said.

"You're beautiful."

He gave her a quizzical look. "I'm sure you meant rakishly handsome."

"And big," she said. "Your torso is as wide as a Clydesdale. Shoulders like an ox."

"Truly, my dear, so many lovely comparisons with beasts will go straight to my head."

Her gaze trailed down to where his trousers did little to hide his erection. "Is that big as well?"

"I've had little in the way of complaints."

'Little' would never be a word to describe him. Left with *little* question where pain entered in coupling, she lifted her chin and crossed her ankles, unwilling to let her nerves show. "Proceed."

His lips twitched. "As my lady commands."

With her new appreciation for the simplicity of men's clothing, Charlotte was still impressed. A flick of his wrist and his trousers fell open as if no clothing, male or female, could deny the charms of the Duke of Camine.

Her amusement at the thought was cut short when his pants hit the floor, revealing him in full glory, and Charlotte decided big wasn't a *big* enough word.

"Like a Grecian God," she said.

"That," he said, chuckling, "will *definitely* go to my head."

She licked her lips, intrigued by the look of soft, tight skin across his length. "Will you fit?"

His eyes darkened. "Deliciously."

The word floated across the space, a promise of opened doors and opened minds in the silken tone.

Charlotte shivered at the conjured image of where he fit, and her core clenched in anticipation.

His fingers trailed down her arm, down her belly, and into the soft curls covering her sex. "Are you thinking about it?" His lips skimmed her jaw as his fingers pressed into her wet folds. "Are you thinking about me here?"

"Yes."

His fingers worked her, bringing the waves closer and closer to that edge once again, rubbing and rolling, plunging inside to retreat in a maddening rhythm.

"Are you scared?" he asked.

Of him? "No." Of losing her heart?

Too late.

"Hamish, please."

He lifted her by the waist and hooked her wrists on the top of the pillar so her feet would dangle without his support.

Her back pressed into the pillar hard enough to leave rope impressions from the wood.

She savored the hardness at her back, nothing compared to the steel of him against her stomach.

The texture was exquisite, like velvet or satin. That soft steel slid lower, finding her opening with urgent pressure.

Her stomach fluttered. Here, now, she'd become his wife in truth. There was no going back.

She pushed against him, the head of him stretching her opening with a telling ache.

"Relax, my love." His fingers left so both hands held her hips steady, pushing her open without losing his hold. "I'll make it good for you after," he whispered.

And he buried himself to the hilt.

Charlotte screamed. The pillar's wood bit into her back. An overwhelming fullness consumed her mind as he filled her body. Burning, stretching: she swore she'd rend apart.

This was the consummation of a holy pact. She finally understood why marriage was blessed by the heavens. For there were no other ways mere mortals might touch paradise.

Her legs came around him, clutching him to her.

"Charlotte." A warm hand cupped her cheek. "Don't fight the pain."

She gazed into his concerned face, shifting her body to get a better angle, sliding him a fraction deeper. She gasped at the shock of pleasure—pain too, the burn of their bodies becoming one.

"Stop," he hissed. "Let your body relax."

She repeated the little buck of her hips, pushing him away an inch before drawing him back in.

Every movement of his steel inside her drew her closer and closer to that ocean. She bucked again, drawing him farther out before her legs tightened and brought him colliding against her.

He secured her hips with an iron grip. "Damn it, Charlotte, stop! Let your body get used to me, or you won't be able to walk tomorrow."

Her gaze was losing focus. His hands on her hips were erotic, the way his fingers dug into her flesh only furthering her pleasure. "I've no need for walking when I'm flying."

His grip loosened. "It doesn't hurt?"

She bucked again and threw back her head. If her hands weren't bound, she'd have ripped out her hair from the madness of fullness. "Hamish," she moaned.

He pulled out farther and surged back in.

"Yes. God, Hamish, don't stop!"

He repeated the action, grinding his hips against hers when he pushed fully inside.

She felt the difference in pressure as he hit a spot that had lights dancing before her eyes. "There! Again, Hamish. More!"

He growled, cursed, and slammed into her faster, harder, until the rhythm alone made Charlotte come.

She ripped over the edge, her fourth orgasm swift and violent compared to the first three. Her womb contracted, bringing him into her soul.

"Charlotte!" His cry of pleasure was more growl than speech. He cupped her to him and thrust one final time, pouring himself into her and sealing their partnership until death took them.

CHAPTER THIRTY

HAMISH UNHOOKED HER wrists from the pillar and gently placed her arms around his neck, her body pliant against him.

He eased them to the mattress, where her bottom woke his spent body into a half-mast.

His forehead rested against hers, his mind in awe. "I want you again." He'd come like an erupted geyser, and his body demanded more? "Amazing."

She rolled her head to give him a lazy smile. "Be careful, husband. Your praise will go to my head."

He chuckled and kissed her nose, the easy gesture of intimacy surprising him.

"You didn't stop," she said.

"Hmm." He rested against linen-cased pillows, bringing her with him where she splayed over him like a cat. "Where did you learn contract negotiations?"

"My father."

"The Duke of Lux, a revolutionary?" A dangerous man to be sure. He rubbed her bare bottom with long strokes.

She groaned and pushed into his touch, and his half-mast rose to full with patriotic pride.

"Dangerous indeed," he grumbled, carefully setting her to her own side of the bed.

She *hmphed*. "I was enjoying that."

"I too," he said, untying the ribbon and releasing her arms, every brush of skin on skin a shock of electricity. "But too much and you'll be bedridden for days."

"Isn't that the idea of a honeymoon?"

He smirked. Clearly, Renard's threats to the staff hadn't stopped her from learning the essentials. "First, you bathe, and then we'll talk about furthering your education."

She settled into the pillows, looking far too perfect reclined in his bed. "You're the first domineering teacher I haven't wanted to scare off with a jar of beetles in your bed."

"A rave review." He stood and held out a hand. "Or do I need to carry you?"

She eyed his hand. "Carry me where?"

"To the bath." He pushed a panel in the wall by the fire where a hidden latch opened.

"A secret door?" Aches clearly forgotten, Charlotte scrambled out of bed, snatching up a sheet to wrap around her, and joined him at the panel door. "You have a tub in your secret water closet."

He smiled. "Indoor plumbing. You'll like it."

She shuffled into the room as Hamish lit candles and scrunched her nose at the web of pipes around the claw-footed tub. "Hot water without lugging buckets two flights of stairs? The servants must adore you."

"They find me rather eccentric. The piping started off as an experiment for a friend of mine to see if he could renovate such a large house." He leaned against the tub, enjoying her curious inspection. "It went so well, I plan to install electricity next year."

"The new contraptions from Paddington Station?" Charlotte's brows rose. "Is it safe?"

"I know a man whose work I can guarantee."

"Soon you won't need any attendants. Camine estate will run on its own accord."

"I find I like doing for myself."

She smiled at him, her understanding expression doing something strange to his stomach.

"I do too."

She ran her fingers over the rim of the tub and skimmed the pipes up and down in a motion that left Hamish envious of the plumbing.

"Would you like to learn how it works?" He shifted her to the side and pointed as he talked. "Place the plug in the tub. Now turn this knob. Check the water."

Charlotte snatched her hand back. "It's hot!"

He smiled at her wonder. "Use the other knob to regulate the temperature to your liking."

She fiddled with the balance of hot and cold, her concentration charming him. Unable to resist, he kissed her neck where the sheet had slid down.

She batted him away. "I'm going to get water everywhere if you do that."

He captured her wrist and nuzzled her. "There's a drain in the floor. Splash away." He moved to her ear to nibble the lobe.

She moaned and turned in his arms. "You make an excellent argument." She ran her lips over his before pulling back with a grin. "But I have a counterproposal."

"Oh?"

"Join me."

He shook his head. "Not today." He turned off the water, deserving a fucking metal. She was temptation itself. He'd call a maid to attend to her and arrange for a real meal. He should've hired a lady's maid the second she'd agreed to the marriage, an oversight he was in no hurry to correct. He liked the idea of her calling on him to dress and bathe. They'd start again tomorrow. Slow, easy—she'd resist at first, but it was for the best.

A sound like soft fabric hitting wood had Hamish freezing. He hung his head at the unmistakable sound of a sheet sliding to the floor.

He glanced over his shoulder, already knowing what he'd find.

She stood in the candlelight, her naked skin gleaming and lips swollen from their earlier kisses. Those lips curled into a smile.

He cursed.

Innocent, goddess, seductress, maid.

He crushed her to him, the citrus of her scent mingling with the sweet lavender salts he'd scattered into the water.

He tried for one last rational thought. "You'll be too sore."

Her fingers curled around his erection, and she ground her hips against his. "Practice makes perfect. Any good teacher knows that."

"Fuck." He gripped her hips, nearly exploding when she threw back her head and cried his name.

He ground his teeth and lifted them both into the tub, cataloguing the positions they'd try.

She leaned against the lip of the tub, lifting her bottom in invitation, reading his mind.

"Hold the edge," he growled.

He parted her cheeks and slammed inside her, bringing her to climax in seconds.

He wound his hand into her long hair and pulled hard enough to make her look at him as he began a harsh rhythm in and out.

"More!" she cried.

He howled his consent.

His own climax came with her name on his lips.

Good intentions be damned. He was only a beast, after all, and she was the moon.

He was defenseless against her.

His wife was insatiable. Over the course of the evening, they'd made love once more in the tub, before he'd deemed them clean, and twice more upon returning to bed. A less secure man would take offense if the activity weren't so intoxicating.

After a record six orgasms during their last lesson, Charlotte lay asleep in his arms, exhaustion finally taking her.

He watched her sleep, her fingers curled into loose fists. A warm sensation flooded his chest.

He never wanted to leave this bed. No, beds were interchangeable. He never wanted to leave *her*.

He jolted and slipped out of bed, yanking his shirt and trousers on.

What had she done to him? He was reacting like a besotted fool.

She sighed his name in her sleep.

He relaxed. It wasn't foolish to desire a beautiful woman, not one as passionate and curious as his wife.

His gaze drifted to the roll on the floor, the hard biscuit forgotten in their passion.

She hadn't eaten dinner, either.

Hamish ignored the flare of pleasure as he brushed a kiss on her brow before going in search of a feast to break their fast. Knowing his little mouse, she'd want to begin where they'd left off, him teaching her how to ride without a horse in sight.

His thighs ached where she'd been none-too-gentle holding her seat. She was a quick study.

He left the chambers and headed downstairs to call for breakfast, not wishing to wake his bride. She'd need her sleep for what came next.

The foyer clock tolled five. With the pride of masters and servants alike in a duke's home, he was unsurprised when his butler greeted him in full uniform, looking fresh and forbidding as usual.

"The post, Your Grace."

Hamish took the paper, his eyes catching on the bold print headline.

Duke of Camine married!

"We said our vows yesterday," he grumbled. Certain one of the maids had ordered the insipid roll, he scanned the paragraph, impressed and disgusted by London's gossip network and its efficiency.

Witnessed by members of the Honorable Duke of Camine's staff, His Grace, Hamish Hurstfield, married Lady Charlotte Louis in an intimate ceremony. Too bad, ladies. Lady Charlotte captured more than hearts at the Tailorman ball, or should we write, the Duchess of Camine? Her Grace's hidden talents will be a secret every lady will clamor for at the next society function.

Hamish read his wife's new title, feeling a smug satisfaction. No one else would give her that title. He had, and she'd taken it, and everything else he'd given. 'Hidden talents' was an understatement.

He dropped the rag on the entry table and nodded to his butler. "Something else, Mr. Frendstone?"

"Two letters, Your Grace." He handed them over and bowed. "And a messenger outside to await your answer."

Hamish shot his butler a glance. "Answer?" He opened the first letter, his gaze zeroing in on Gregori's handwriting.

Preparations ready.

G

"Excellent." Hamish's mind flipped to business as he broke the seal on the second letter. Gregori had finished the prototype. He'd go out at once to test the product. If it met satisfaction, he'd set a meeting with Markus. If all went to plan, he'd have Dockside under his domain by the end of next month.

He unfolded the second letter, and a familiar, heavy perfume tore his attention back to the present.

Dearest,

I hear through the wagging tongues of the ton *congratulations
are in order. Nothing needs to change. When you tire of your
little toy, come find me.*

Yours,

C

"Son of a bitch." He crumpled the letter in his hand. In all the
rush with the wedding, he'd forgotten Dahlia completely. At least
Renard would know by now his sister was married and the
matter settled. The invitation to attend their nuptials he'd sent to
the Lux estate had been returned unopened, with a short note
from Renard:

Take care of her.

They'd have words soon—hard ones. There was no excuse
for Renard's behavior towards Charlotte. Perhaps she hadn't
married the man of his choosing. Perhaps she'd been reckless in
her pursuit of ending any agreement between him and the
marquess. But the end result spoke volumes. Charlotte was now
a duchess. Renard needed to learn to respect his sister and her
choices.

Mr. Frendstone coughed expertly, bringing attention without
interrupting.

Hamish gritted his teeth, knowing which employer's messenger would be brazen enough to wait, and the complication now
standing in the way.

He retrieved his hat from the rack by the door, not wishing to
go upstairs for a proper vest and coat and risk waking Charlotte.

"I'm going out for a bit, Mr. Frendstone. I've business in
London that will take most of the morning."

"Indeed, my lord. What shall I tell Her Grace when she asks
where you've gone?"

Hamish paused, door handle in his grasp. "Tell her I'm sorry." He turned the handle and stepped into the early morning air. The door shut with a firm tug.

The messenger stepped out of the walk-up's shadows. "I take this as your answer?" he asked.

Hamish nodded to Percy, his head having a confusing round with his heart while Dahlia's message was a guilty weight in his trouser pocket. "I have a stop to make first."

CHAPTER THIRTY-ONE

THE MAID WHO answered the door didn't bother with introductions.

She dipped her head and said, "Follow me, sir."

Both knew the honorific was false. There were many *sirs* over the years for Miss Crim, if rumors were to be believed, and not all gentlemen. A staggering number for a woman of only two and twenty, and a fact that had suited Hamish's needs and experience fine. Along with the tidy, if not gaudy, townhouse his mistress maintained without the funds of a titled man.

Former mistress.

As her past suggested, the lady's relentless change of mind would lend to a new lover in less than a fortnight, Hamish thought, if it hadn't already.

The maid left him at the chamber door, the light flickering from underneath expected from a woman who lived for long nights and late mornings.

He opened the door to find Dahlia at her vanity, brushing out long, auburn hair.

Her gaze found him in the mirror. "You kept me waiting."

Her singsong voice that had once sparked his lustful pursuit now sounded whiny and childlike.

He crossed his arms and leaned in the doorway. "I've been busy."

Her mouth turned down at the corners. "I heard. An innocent, no less." Her eyes flashed, a calculated look meant to lure her audience in. "I hope you weren't too hard on the girl? Although you *are* here on your honeymoon. I suppose that is answer enough."

Hamish's jaw clenched. "My *wife* is fine."

Surprise flared before her actress's mask fell into place. "Of course. No need to discuss unpleasant matters. You're here now."

She stood from the vanity, and her sheer robe moved to reveal long legs Hamish had once taken immense joy wrapping around himself.

He looked at her anew, finding her features all a bit too much. Too long, too thin, too painted, too composed. A picture of beauty to observe, but who found warmth touching a painting?

She held out her arms like a master to a dog, expecting the bitch to come when called.

"We need to talk," he said.

Her arms dropped. "I'm thirsty." She turned and poured red liquid into a fluted glass. "Care for sherry?" She chuckled, fully aware of his disdain for the too-sweet drink. "No? Something stronger, then." She moved to a side table where a variety of bottles housed liquids of amber and sherry—for entertaining any number of guests in one's sleeping chamber.

"No," he said.

She paused a moment before filling a glass and holding it out to him. "Come now. You wouldn't let a woman drink alone? I'd feel positively lonely."

He moved to take the drink, seeing the trap coming. His hand wrapped around the glass, and her body molded to his.

Her perfume, a heady fragrance of musk and vanilla, clung to her skin as she leaned into his ear. "I have missed you, lover."

He reveled in his body's lack of response, in how finding an amicable woman showed the pettiness in others.

"I find that hard to believe when you've been with recent company," he said.

She fluttered her lashes. "Whatever do you mean?"

Hamish cocked a brow and glanced at the unmade bed, where a man's cravat was lost in the sheets.

Her gaze followed his line of sight, and she shrugged. "The gentleman was quite persistent and charming. Wouldn't take no for an answer."

Hamish knew not to worry about forced affections with the woman's taste for masochism.

"I was hurt you weren't returning my letters." She placed a hand on his chest. "Forgive me, darling. You know it's only ever been you." She played with the simple band on his ring finger. "We've both been naughty."

Hamish pulled away under the guise of taking a drink. They were similar creatures, passionate and fleeting and insincere. In truth, she was everything a man wanted with her lusty looks and no attachments, but there was a fog over the whole room Hamish hadn't noticed before, hadn't wanted to notice. Like every stage the woman stepped upon. It was artifice wrapped in rouge and costume, all to set the scene in a play that all parties agreed to participate in for the joy of escape.

This room was just another stage, and Hamish felt his role poignantly. Once believing he'd been the dashing hero, now he knew the humiliation of the fool.

Disgust was a humbling emotion.

What Miss Crim offered was intangible proof he was a man. A man who wanted heroism.

"You're smiling," she said.

He glanced at her, seeing her normal pout pinched into pursed lips. Where the singer was all coy and glamour, Charlotte was soft and honest. His smile turned sardonic. He'd never compare them again.

There was no comparison.

And like that, he was done with the games and the pleasantries. He had a lovely woman at home, in his bed, waiting for him. Wasting another second in this false dream was intolerable.

"I've come to tell you we're done." He pulled out a jeweler's box that held a necklace of emeralds and diamonds, a flashy piece like the ones she favored. "For your time."

She looked down at the blue-velvet-covered box and laughed. She crossed to the bed and sat on the edge, showing an immodest amount of skin. "Very kind, my darling, but there's no need to play the faithful husband. As I said, our arrangement need not change because you went and got caught by a grasping debutante."

Fire raged in his gut. "I told you not to speak of my wife."

She laughed again and drained her sherry before placing the empty glass on the nightstand. "I see you've gone and fallen for the girl." She shook her head. "You'll tire of her soon enough. And when you do . . ." She raised her chin in silent indication of herself.

"We're done," Hamish said through gritted teeth. He threw the box on the bed and went for the door.

"You can't be serious?" A shrill edge cracked her practiced calm. "There's no way an innocent could satisfy you. Not like I can."

He glanced back to see her standing at the foot of the bed.

Seeing his attention, her mouth curled upwards. "You'll be back."

He hesitated. He hated himself for hesitating. He was a man of decision. Playing fickle was a trait of a woman.

Yet he'd enjoyed his time with Crim. Crim, never Dahlia. Impersonal was the woman's second talent, the trait that had first caught his interest, along with the legs.

A week had passed and he found the arrangement shallow and unfulfilling?

He wouldn't have believed it, either, except the rage humming through his veins felt very real. Rage at being summoned away from a woman who was anything but impersonal.

Would he truly tire of Charlotte's warmth? Her passion?

His legs ate up the floor. He caught Crim to him and kissed her, pouring frustration and effort into the way his lips and hands demanded her reciprocation, demanded a reaction from *her* and from himself.

She complied, her arms snaking around his neck with a moan.

He deepened the kiss, forcing his hands to explore and caress. His body responded—as instinctual as any man's—with no excitement of what was to come.

He broke the kiss, satisfied with the outcome.

She gazed up at him, eyes heavy-lidded and full of triumph.

"As I expected," he said, smiling as a new feeling of peace settled over him. "There is no comparison."

He turned on his heel, his steps light and his former mistress's sputters of indignation following him out the door.

CHARLOTTE WOKE TO a sore body and a growling stomach. She stretched across linen sheets, images of last night's lessons making her smile in contentment. She remembered a particularly astounding position that had had her riding astride her husband as if he'd been a horse, only backwards.

She flushed as the place between her legs grew wet, eager for another ride.

She rolled over to ask her husband for some morning exercise, but the mattress beside her was empty and had been for some time, judging by the cold sheets. Her stomach growled and then so did she.

He better be on his way with a tray of eggs stacked higher than my head.

There wasn't another acceptable reason for his absence.

She retrieved her spectacles from the side table and sat up. "Hamish?"

Wrapping the sheet around herself, she padded to the water closet and poked her head inside.

Empty.

She huffed. "Available for mutual pleasure, my foot."

She sat in the chaise and leaned back, her cheek resting against the soft lining of her husband's discarded vest.

She pulled it down and breathed in his smell of horses and cigars. She smiled.

Maybe she'd forgive him this once.

It was his first night as a married man, after all. One couldn't expect a proven rake to appreciate the need of a woman to wake up in her husband's arms.

Not when she'd just realized herself.

She dropped the sheet and stuck her arms through the vest, the fabric hanging off her. She flapped her arms, feeling very much like a bird with wings, and laughed.

Something fell from the pocket.

She picked up a crumpled piece of paper and smoothed out what appeared to be a letter.

Dearest Lover,

Charlotte froze, dread pooling in her stomach.

My bed grows cold.

"'Come to me,'" she read out loud. "'And bring the warmth of summer to my dreary spring.'"

Yours,

C

It was a note from his mistress!

She clutched the letter to where a wrenching feeling twisted the heart in her chest.

Was that where he'd gone? There was no date on the paper. Had a servant dropped it off while she'd slept?

She shot to her feet. She tucked the sheet around her waist, not bothering to remove the vest. She made it down the stairs with little tripping and spied the hour on the clock in the foyer before she caught sight of a grey servant's uniform.

"Mr. Frendstone."

He turned at his name and blinked at her state of undress with only the slightest pinking of cheeks. "Your Grace?"

"Where is the duke?"

"Out," he said. "He left early this morning after receiving a letter."

"Did he say where he was going?"

"No, Your Grace. He said to express his apologies to you."

She nodded, not trusting her voice. Left this morning after receiving a note from his mistress. She plopped down on the stairs, where her heart lay broken.

"Shall I ring for a maid, Your Grace?" Mr. Frendstone asked.

She stared at her bare feet poking out from under the sheet. It was scandalous. A lady didn't walk around barefooted. Not even in one's own home.

Was that why he'd left? Was Miss C beautiful as well as refined?

"Your Grace?"

She startled and looked up at Mr. Frendstone's concerned face.

"Is there anything I can do?" he asked.

He knew, she thought. All the staff must have known where the duke had gone. Left early? He hadn't even stayed for their entire wedding night.

Her throat tightened. She knew the look in Mr. Frendstone's eyes. She'd grown up with servants and their quiet pity.

Poor Charlotte. She'd lost her parents. Her lungs were weak. Her husband didn't want her.

"I wish to be alone," she whispered.

He bowed. "Yes, Your Grace."

She didn't wait for him to leave before she opened the letter and read it again, over and over until the words lost meaning. There was only the feeling of loss.

She knew loss intimately. When her parents had died, her loss had been confused, a sense something in her had been removed and nothing would fit the hole left in her chest.

This was different. This was a weight that wouldn't abate to let air into her lungs.

He'd said he couldn't love her. She'd known and yet he'd given his word he'd be faithful.

Anger bubbled up, snapping her out of her ridiculousness. Self-pity didn't help anyone.

"Here I was coming to cheer you up," someone said above her.

Charlotte looked up the stairs to see Camille with her hands on her hips.

"By the look on your face, you've no need." She sat on the step beside her, making a comment about a new fashion in sheet wear before dipping her head and flashing a grin. "Tell me. What idiot thing has the duke done now?"

CHAPTER THIRTY-TWO

CHARLOTTE HID HER bare feet beneath the sheet. "You must find my manners abhorrent?"

"Because you're wearing bed coverings? Not at all." She poked at her side. "Anything is an improvement from these layers of undergarments in this heat."

"I rarely wear them. I've never even worn a corset," Charlotte admitted. "My brother was concerned the tight clothing would restrict air to my weak lungs. I could wear them now, but the fabric feels so foreign."

"Revolutionary." Camille clapped her hands. "Bravo! Burn them all and be done with it. Doctors say they're to prevent ligament strain, yet the Greeks had no issues whatsoever. They're nothing but devices for vanity."

Charlotte grinned at that. "You sound like a friend of mine." Thoughts of Diana had Charlotte's brightening mood dimming. There was no use lying to herself any longer. "Someone I *thought* was a friend."

Camille ducked her head until Charlotte looked her way. "Tell me?"

Charlotte bit her lip, the taste of her naivety bitter. "I've been writing to someone for months. Everything she said, all the advice she gave—her friendship meant the world to me. We've talked endlessly about how we would meet if I ever escaped the country, but once I arrived in London, there was one excuse after another to keep me away. First, it was a chill. Then, the woman claimed to be out of town visiting her cousin in her confinement. When I finally had a mind to research the address she gave me, it was to find the bakery she claimed she lived above had been out of business for years and the mail was being forwarded to a tavern off the docks that doesn't accommodate any kind of residences." The same tavern Charlotte had gone to for her first whiskey, a place Diana had recommended early on in their correspondence. Charlotte lowered her head and squeezed her eyes shut. "I feel like the greatest fool. What if there never was a Diana Yamsbee? What if I was some target for ridicule?" Another bet and source of amusement from someone else she'd deemed precious.

"You are *not* a fool." Camille's fierce assertion had Charlotte raising her gaze. Camille shook her head. "You shouldn't discount your first impressions. I've never met someone who saw the heart of a person like you. If you believe this woman your friend, then have faith."

"But what could the woman hope to gain by lying?"

She shrugged. "Your good opinion, her anonymity for whatever reason, fear of reprisals from your brother if he found out."

"That's ridiculous! I would never cut someone from my life because of circumstance."

Camille fidgeted and looked away. "Fear is rarely logical."

Camille was right. Of course she was. Charlotte released her anger, along with the doubt she'd been holding. She'd write to Diana again. Giving up wasn't who she was. "Thank you. I can't believe I let one misstep destroy the trust I have in myself."

Camille chuckled. "You *are* human." Her expression turned serious. "Speaking of destroying trust, what did *he* do? I'd like to find a fitting punishment for when the duke arrives home. I'm thinking I'll cut holes in the toes of every pair of his stockings."

Charlotte hid the letter in the sheet. Gentlemen were unfaithful all the time. A loveless marriage was expected. "He did nothing, really."

"Try again." She leaned forward and whispered, "And don't

look away when you lie. It gives you away."

Charlotte laughed. How nice to talk with someone who didn't mince words. If more people used honesty and kindness rather than lies and greed, the place might be bearable.

"I like you, Mrs.—*Miss* Forthright."

"It's 'Camille,' please. No more formalities. Tell Hamish to do the same."

Charlotte frowned. Camille had always shown a lack of propriety, a sense of commonality around everyone. As a companion, she was even allowed to dine at the table instead of in the kitchen with the rest of the servants, as if Hamish wished to keep her close. Camille had said their familiarity was for Hamish's peace of mind, but there was another reason a duke may tolerate a servant with a bold tongue. Charlotte froze. "You're his mistress?"

"*What?*"

Charlotte folded in on herself. Camille was Miss C? If she was his mistress, did that mean Hamish hadn't left? Was he waiting in Camille's room right now?

"Lady Charlotte?"

She wasn't listening. Was her companion her husband's mistress?

Her stomach roiled, and she thought she might very well be sick here on the stairs.

"Charlotte!"

She startled at the force of her name. Camille had her by the shoulders, Charlotte realized, and was staring with a concerned furrow of brows.

Charlotte deflated. Camille was quite lovely with long, dark curls and eyes like the autumn sky.

"Charlotte." Camille shook her. "Whose mistress?"

She should have been outraged. Should have feigned a faint or screamed or slapped the woman for her betrayal, but her scathing accusation was little more than a broken whisper, "You're my husband's mistress."

The other woman recoiled. "I am no such thing!"

"There's no need to deny it." If she'd used half a brain, she'd have realized Hamish wouldn't employ an outspoken woman for the sake of his wife's appreciation for directness. He'd done it for access. She choked and grabbed her stomach.

"Charlotte," Camille said. "Listen to me. I am not the duke's mistress."

Charlotte squeezed her eyes shut. Men kept mistresses all the time and their wives survived. She would too, even if it felt like the broken pieces of her heart that had fallen out earlier had been ground to dust.

"Stop." Camille grabbed her again. "I'm not. Charlotte, I'm *not!*"

"It's fine," she managed. "I was surprised is all."

Camille cursed. "I'm not his bloody mistress."

"Truly, it'll be all right—"

"I'm his sister."

Charlotte's thoughts stuttered. "But you were a housekeeper."

Camille winced. "Quite an elevated position for a bastard."

Charlotte gasped. "Your father?"

She nodded, her gaze darting away as if waiting for damnation.

"That monster!" Charlotte stood, the sheet wrapping around her legs. "Where is he buried?"

Camille stared up at her with wide eyes. "Why?"

"Because I've a mind where to throw my next full chamber pot."

"Won't find many of those around here with the plumbing." Camille's face broke into a grin. "Why not hike up your skirts and piss directly?"

There was an idea.

"I'm jesting." Camille shook her head and took Charlotte's hand as she pulled her back to the stairs. "Thank you. No one else would see me as the victim. Or if they do, it's somehow my fault."

"For being born?" She seriously hated society. To think a young woman was considered worthless because a husband had been unfaithful. "Horseshit."

Camille barked a laugh but sobered quickly. "It's not only the circumstances of my birth. I've . . . done things to stay alive, had things done to me. Things a proper lady would find, what did you say? Abhorrent. The duke should never have allowed me to stay as your companion."

Charlotte shook her head. What was with the world taking good people and making them think any action not perfect by society's standards required a lifetime of shame?

"I've kissed a woman, pointed an unloaded pistol at a drunkard, and dressed as a man to mock sacred male traditions." Charlotte fired off the items on her list like a grocer's tally. "I'm not one to judge." Her mind worked through what the other woman had said, and her voice went deadly quiet. "Did you say, 'things done' to you?"

Camille's grin was dark, but she patted Charlotte's hand reassuringly. "I got away in the end. That's all that matters."

Charlotte's rage simmered low but didn't disappear. She'd ask her friend one day for names, and then she'd hunt the monsters down.

Her mind worked backwards, and the aching pressure in her chest doubled until it felt like a carriage was rolling over her. "If you aren't Miss C . . ." She held up the letter, rereading the contents for any clues. "Who is?"

"Where did you find that?"

Charlotte rubbed her face, surprised to find her cheeks tear-stained. "In his vest. I woke up and he was gone. When I found the letter, I came downstairs, where Mr. Frendstone informed me Hamish had left after receiving a letter."

Camille swore. "Crim."

Charlotte frowned, the name sounding familiar. "The stage singer? What about her?"

Camille pointed to the letter.

Her eyes widened. "Crim is his mistress?"

"*Was*," Camille stressed. "Listen, the duke is a fool and has an unfashionable attachment to the color black, but he has a sense of stubborn honor that I'm loath to admit I admire. He hated our father and everything he did to our mothers. He married *you*, Charlotte. I'm sure he forgot that shallow creature the moment he met you. He probably went to tell the wench to leave him alone."

The tears came harder, and Charlotte had to remove her glasses before they were swept away. "Miss Crim is beautiful, right?"

"The most beautiful woman in England."

"How can I compete?"

"Compete?" Camille's sneer softened. "There is no competition. Even if there were, he chose you. For all the asinine choices he's made, being with you isn't one of them. He needed the adventure as much as you. Someone with whom to share all the scary things inside and be loved all the better for them."

Charlotte's tears dried in the creases of a smile. Whatever happened between her and Hamish going forward, she'd never regret the woman's company beside her. "I found my adventure *and* got a nosy big sister as an added bonus."

Camille grimaced. "The *ton* will never accept me. No one can know of my relation to the duke."

"Fiddle-faddle," Charlotte said, falling back on her childhood curse. Whatever questions she had over her relationship with Hamish, she couldn't fathom, duke or not, he'd deny his sister. "He made you his housekeeper! I'll set him on fire alone for such an injustice."

"It wasn't his decision," Camille said, the idea of Charlotte's ideal arson seeming to bring a spark back to her expression. "He wanted to spit in society's face and introduce me with my own season."

"Yes," Charlotte said. "Let's do that."

"No. Society already decided I was a blanch on their perfect aristocracy. I won't give them the satisfaction of a commoner on show like an insect under glass. I accepted the position in the house merely to keep the duke from continuing to send every dressmaker, grocer, and maid to my door in hopes of changing my mind."

Charlotte heard pride in the other woman's voice. Pride for a brother who had a conscience, and pride in oneself to say "no" to hypocrisy despite the glitter of jewels and false comfort.

"You want to make your own way," she said.

"Yes." Camille cocked her head. "You understand I can't stay your companion for long?"

Because a companion wasn't paid for their work. There was an allowance, but Camille didn't seem like the type of woman satisfied with favors from anything that might be interpreted as nepotism.

"I understand."

Faith restored, Charlotte knew if she hadn't already been smitten with the duke, after hearing Camille's jaded account of his actions, she'd have fallen all over again.

Charlotte crumpled the letter in her hand, determined to make the best of her situation. Her husband dallying with his mistress didn't mean her life was over. She tucked the broken pieces of her heart away.

Her friend's revelations had taught her something important; she was not useless. She'd taken great strides to overcome her weak lungs and tragic past. She'd raised herself up to work for what she wanted against society rules, her brother's wishes, and that grueling voice of doubt in her head always whispering she wasn't enough.

She had done that. Not some man, not even the fierce friend next to her.

Charlotte stood in one motion and dropped the ruined letter at her feet to be tossed in the bin with the rest of the garbage. She was already working the logistics of the next item on her list when she declared, "I need another blanket and a canister to hold water."

She secured the blanket and started in the direction of the kitchens, knowing exactly who would have what she needed. If her husband was too busy to show her this crazy, beautiful world, she'd do it herself.

Camille was hot on her heels, brows pinched. "What are you planning?"

Charlotte threw her a smirk. "I'm going to make my own way."

"Ha!" she said. "Is that all?"

Charlotte stopped. "No." She whirled around, having a suspicion her friend would have exactly what she needed in another way. "I need trousers and some boots."

CHAPTER THIRTY-THREE

HAMISH HELD GREGORI'S prototype in his hands and thought it was the second-most beautiful thing he'd ever seen.

"Send a note to Markus," he told Percy.

This would work. Once the old man saw what he could provide, the quality, he'd be quick to partner and Dockside would change, with Hamish in charge.

"What's the rush?" Gregori asked.

"He's itching to get back to his girl," Percy said.

Gregori turned from his tinkering, shocked indeed. "That empty shell of an actress? Darla? Dahlia?"

"A lady," Percy smiled. "With a sharp tongue. I'm not sure I've ever enjoyed an insult before, but she cuts you to the quick."

"She insulted you?" Gregori nodded approvingly to Hamish.

Hamish gritted his teeth. "A note. Now!"

"He seems rather vexed." Gregori fixed him with a calculating look, ever the scientist. "Do you think she took a go at him?"

"If not yet," Percy said, "she will when she wakes up to find him gone."

"Send the damn note!" Hamish said. "If you two would stop your infernal questions, I could get back to my lovely wife."

Neither man flinched at his rage.

"She's 'lovely' now?" Gregori said.

Percy glanced his way and shook his head. "I've never seen a man so deep."

"And oblivious," Gregori added.

"I'm leaving." Hamish tucked the prototype away in a small box, not wishing to risk its damage when he decided to pummel his companions. "Forget the blasted note." He'd go now. Markus could be one of two places—the clinic or his home—and, thanks to the young maid, he knew where the man hung his boots.

"I'll have four more done by tomorrow," Gregori said.

Yes, production. Hamish arched a brow at his runner. "If you're done with your childish taunts—"

"Never."

Hamish ignored him. "I want eyes on this place day and night."

"My guys?"

"The best," Hamish acknowledged.

"You expecting trouble?"

He hated the idea, but something in his gut wasn't sitting right. "Whoever was at the docks may be displeased at being out maneuvered. There's no guarantee they won't come for us directly in retaliation. Have you found a name yet?"

"Nothing," Percy said. "The man is careful."

"You think he gave up?"

Percy looked around, his mouth in a frown. "Nah. Too much blunt to be made round here."

Hamish had suspected as much. Any number of cutthroats and dealers would find his presence threatening, as well as some of the legit businessmen. "Did you look into the shipment we borrowed? Where was it expected?"

"Harbormaster had no idea." Percy's hand snaked inside his coat, fiddling with a blade.

The man was more concerned than he was letting on.

"You know the competition?" Hamish asked.

Percy dropped his hand and shook his head. "No. Just the antics remind me o' somebody."

Hamish nodded. Percy was a cautious man and would tell him if something was amiss. "Armed men," he ordered.

Percy saluted. "I shan't leave the genius's side for a moment."

"I feel the knife in my back already," Gregori muttered.

"Fear not," Percy said. "I won't let you die until you show me how to remove a man's thumbs."

Gregori picked up a pair of pliers. "Shall we begin now?"

Hamish rolled his eyes and headed for the door. "Play nice, you two."

The dual response echoed through the warehouse. "Not a chance!"

⟫⟫⟫✦⟪⟪⟪

"WHAT DO YOU mean, 'He's not in'?" Hamish asked.

The other man rubbed at the stubble on his chin, his nails caked with dirt from the yard. "As in, he ain't here."

Hamish regarded the man, and the dark hall beyond, suspiciously. He'd checked with that monster of a woman first, and she'd said the same thing. Either Markus had a woman on the side, or he'd changed his mind on their deal.

Hamish had never thought he'd pray the old man was a lecherous skirt chaser.

"You the business gentleman?" the man asked.

"You might say that."

"Hmph." The man crossed beefy arms and tilted back his head to lean against the door's frame. "Lots o' business going 'round 'ere. What you pushin'?"

Ignoring the question, Hamish's hands tightened around the box in his hand. "When will Markus be back?"

"Hard to say." The man held out a hand. "Leave it with me, and I'll see he gets it."

Hamish held back his sneer at such an easy lie. He'd seen enough men like this. Once-honorable men thrown down to the gutter, where desperation drove them to violence and petty theft to keep from starving. He'd found his sister in a comparable situation.

A wave of shame crashed his ego to the shore. People's true nature rarely was so obvious. Appearances could be as misleading as rumor, and he knew firsthand the pain of conjecture.

He looked back at the man with untainted ideals. Rough muscles and straight posture for a man of his age meant the man knew discipline. Dirt under his nails could just as easily have meant the man knew arduous work and had yet to wash. Aside from the man's clear evasion to reveal his boss's whereabouts—which spoke of loyalty and cleverness—the only true fault Hamish saw was one of his making; the man sidestepped his efforts.

Which was Hamish's problem.

Hamish held out the box, baffled as to where this sense of hope and trust had come from. He, who trusted no one. "Here."

The man lost his balance coming off the door frame. "You're actually givin' it to me?"

"I told Markus I'd deliver this today, and I'm a man of my word." He placed the box in the man's hand and looked him in the eyes, his voice serious. "Your boss obviously appreciates men with similar honor."

The man's chest puffed. "Aye, sir."

Hamish smiled and pointed to the box. "It's fragile."

He walked off, glancing back only once at the corner of the alley where he saw the man cradling the box like the most precious thing, all traces of the hulking lackey gone, and Hamish knew his trust hadn't been misplaced.

A strange feeling rose in his chest, one of reward and reaffirmation. People were awful, greedy creatures, but with a capacity for kindness that bordered on miraculous. If he'd have assumed the man had been a thug and a liar, that was exactly what he'd have gotten.

Hamish climbed into his carriage at the end of the row and tapped the roof, eager to be off and home.

For some reason, he couldn't wait to tell Charlotte how

much of a fool he'd been to doubt a man's character.

THE LONG HORSE ride to London that morning was nothing compared to the laborious journey back. He hadn't expected to be gone so long, stopping at the local jeweler's, dealing with Crim, and then the two bickering children in Dockside, had eaten up more time than expected.

He patted his coat pocket where the expensive gift was nestled in a velvet box. At least he'd have no fear of fickle emotions from Charlotte.

THE WILDERNESS WAS, quite frankly, overrated. Not that Charlotte could aptly call the well-maintained Camine estate grounds 'wilderness.' Far from the rugged landscape she read about in novels, it did have the two things that mattered most, a view of the sky and bugs.

It was too early in the day to set up her makeshift camp—more bedroll and lantern, if one were to be honest—which left her hours before she may check number two hundred and thirty-four off her list.

She forged around the clearing she'd chosen. Close enough to the manor in case of real emergency, but far enough one felt the embrace of fresh air.

Even before her parents' passing, she'd spent much of her childhood exploring the grounds at Lux estate, outmaneuvering her nursemaid while the lady had taken her afternoon nap. Something she had also been expected to do, but what active seven-year-old ignored the call of adventure?

Charlotte wiggled her fingers under a particularly gnarled tree root and pulled out a moving lump with a loud, "Aha!"

She let the bug crawl over her wrist and admired the large, orange spot on its back. *"Pentatoma rufipes,"* she said, proud of her Latin. She hadn't seen one since she'd been incredibly young, and the little spiked shoulders and antenna gave way to nostalgic memories.

"See the little bundle of eggs?" Renard pointed out, very worldly and wise at the age of eleven.

Charlotte, age seven, laughed. "They look like little faces."

He took her hand and showed her another tree. "And here." He crouched down, bringing her with him. "Look near the roots. Do you see it?"

Charlotte bent close, seeing the strangest shape sticking out of the tree. "Is that a bug?"

Renard carefully pulled the shape free. "It's a cicada husk. They attach themselves to trees and shed their skin when they grow wings. This is what's left behind."

Charlotte's young mind boggled. "Really?"

He dropped the husk into her open palm.

She examined the little feet and the shell face, complete with eyes and cheeks, and looked at her brother with a wide grin. "You know everything."

He puffed out his chest. "I'm your older brother. I study hard."

She set the husk at her feet and hugged her knees. "You're so lucky. You get to learn Latin and bugs. I get dancing and how to sit straight. I only want to study the things I like."

"Then do it. Tell Mama you don't want learn that silly stuff."

She blinked up at him. "I can do that?"

He nodded and winked. "I'll help."

Charlotte set the forest bug back on the tree, the memory bringing tears. After their parents' deaths, Renard had never forced her to take on any of the roles she'd been meant to fill. Her governesses and chaperones had griped and lectured, but her brother had brushed off her antics. A part of her thought he'd remembered that conversation in the woods, that he'd been helping her find happiness while giving the appearance of propriety. But the marriage to the marquess, the bet, his refusal to respond to any of her letters—it was clear now at some point, he'd stopped caring about what she did. He had only taken an interest when it had come to her marriageability.

Renard had gotten his wish. In a way, they both had.

Standing, she wiped her wet cheeks.

Snap!

Charlotte startled, realizing how quiet the forest had grown. She laughed. She'd gotten herself all worked up. "Now I'm jumping at rabbits." And scaring everything else away.

She threw back her shoulders and headed towards a telling buzzing sound. Standing still was no way to get out of one's own mind. She knew better. And hadn't she already decided she'd stop with the self-pity?

She reached the source of the buzzing sound, a large creek, raised high and running fast due to recent rains. Camille, her friend, her sister—the idea was still new and wonderful—had offered to come along, but Charlotte had declined. She was out here, alone, for herself.

Her boots sank into muck and grass, making a most satisfying squashy sound and caking the black rubber.

She had no idea where Camille had procured the boots or the trousers. The boots were a good two sizes too big and the pants two sizes too small, but the freedom of movement was like heaven. It seemed a man's tailor had cut the seams at a most impossible measurement for a woman. A fact that needed immediate rectification. She'd make that number two hundred and thirty-six.

Her foot slipped in a thick mud puddle, the muck coming dangerously close to the top of the boot. She suspected she'd owe the gardener a good thanks by tomorrow morning.

Footing stable at the moment, she crouched by the water and stuck her hand in the rushing stream.

Movement on the opposite bank froze her in place. A doe, big and brown and beautiful, trotted to the water's edge, not four feet away.

Her gasp of awe was swallowed up by the water.

The doe traversed the muddy bank with surefooted grace and drank, her ears twitching.

Charlotte quelled the urge to reach out and touch her, but that didn't stop her thrill at having the animal so close. One needed only to look in the creature's eyes to see the beauty of life. Brown and black, so big, they looked artificial.

A hand ripped her back.

She tumbled backwards, only for her head to slam forward, smacking the water and burning her skin. She thrashed, but her fingers slipped in mud. Her body slid farther. Panic clutched her chest. Her lungs burned.

Nails dug into her scalp.

She screamed, and icy water filled her nose and throat. She coughed. More water rushed in. The cold spread through her chest like creeping frost.

A sense of calm suddenly took hold.

She stopped flailing, her arms and legs too heavy to lift.

Her eyelids fell. She couldn't feel the ice anymore, couldn't remember why she'd been so afraid.

I hope the deer wasn't too frightened.

She was drifting away with the stream.

Thump.

A sharp pressure pushed on her chest.

Thump. Thump.

What an irritating pressure. She heard her name as if from a distance. Her ears strained.

Thump. Thump. THUMP.

Her eyes snapped open. Water shot up her throat and out of her mouth. She lurched over and coughed, retching water and spit and anything else her lungs had the misfortune to swallow.

Hands held her, pressing her against something hard and hot. Burning.

She pushed away, ready to fight off her attacker.

"Charlotte, stop!"

She froze.

Hamish grabbed for her, his fingers running over her face, head, neck.

The warmth of his skin against hers was scalding. She pushed him away again and croaked, "Too hot."

His wild gaze sharpened. He scooped her into his arms. "We're going home."

Home? Weren't they already at home, in bed, doing wicked things with ribbons? Charlotte's head swam. The sound of water registered first, then the trees. She was outside? Yes, she was going to lie beneath the stars because Hamish had run off to . . .

Disoriented and unsure why her dress clung to her so heavily, she pushed away from his chest, her body tired. "I'm busy. I don't want to go back."

"Too bloody bad!"

Charlotte stiffened at the rage in his voice.

His eyes were hard.

Charlotte stared at him. "You're mad?" She hugged herself, her shivers registering. *He* was mad? "Good."

He looked down at her sharply, his jaw working. Something haunted crept into his gaze. "How . . . Why?"

She heard his teeth grinding.

He recovered. "What the hell are you doing out here?"

She tried for aloof, as much as possible when her teeth chattered together hard enough to break the enamel. "Sleeping beneath the stars."

Hamish studied her face. "It's hours before dark."

"Yes, well." The shivers got worse, and she reluctantly snuggled closer. "I had preparations to do first. Make camp. Forage for a fire."

He looked around, his gaze growing colder, if that were possible. "What camp?"

"I don't like your tone. It's . . ." She stopped and really looked at his expression. "You don't believe me?"

"How could I?"

"What?" She gaped. "I came out here to sleep under the stars. Like. I. Said."

"As you say."

She struggled against him, the action clearing more of the water from her mind. "Put me down. I came out here for a reason, and I'm not leaving until I do what I set out to do."

"No!"

She frowned up at him. "I won't be bullied."

"You won't be going anywhere for a long time," he said. "I forbid you to leave my side."

"*Forbid* me?" She twisted the skin on his arm, a trick she'd learned as a child to get her brother to release her from whatever wrestling they'd been doing. The trick worked.

He dropped her with a howl.

She landed on her rump in the dirt, but however undignified her position was, the foul curses pouring from her husband's mouth were worth the forthcoming bruise.

"Damn it, woman." He reached for her.

She stuck out her arm. "Don't touch me."

He stopped, but his hands shook at his sides. He took a deep breath and straightened, seeming to reach for calm. "We will discuss this more inside."

"No." She raised her chin. "I am seeing the stars. My list is—"

"That bloody list!" Calm lost, his face contorted into pure exasperation. "I'll be damned if I let my wife continue to conduct herself in such a dangerous manner."

"Your *wife*," she seethed. "How good of you to remember. I thought I'd simply been dismissed like the rest of the staff. Seems I was merely misplaced. What a comfort."

He reared back, his expression changing to one of . . . disappointment? His voice held a note of the same. "I see."

He took a small box from his pocket, his decidedly wet pocket, where her drenched clothes had seeped over.

Charlotte didn't hide her smugness.

He shoved the box into her hands. "Here."

Momentarily distracted from her anger, she examined the box. Curiosity really was her one flaw. She opened the lid to find a sparkling, purple pendant brooch.

"It's lovely."

He nodded and closed the lid. "Now we will return to the manor."

He started towards the house, seeming to think something had been decided.

She crossed her arms and watched him walk ten paces before he noticed her lack of movement and came back, brows drawn.

"I gave you jewelry," he said.

"And?"

He blinked. "And now we'll return to the house."

They stared at each other, Charlotte's freezing brain working up a sweat. "Did you think you could give me some colored rock and I'd fall into line?"

Hamish's sudden loss of gaze was that of a boy caught feeding his vegetables to the master's hound. "It's amethyst," he said stupidly.

He was actually bribing her to obey, like some shallow . . . mistress. Something in her snapped. "I don't want jewelry, you sodding idiot. I want *you!*"

CHAPTER THIRTY-FOUR

THE SILENCE RANG out after her scream, bringing her words into sharp focus.

Hamish stared down at her flushed cheeks and labored chest. She was alive.

He kept reminding himself. When he'd arrived at the main house, only for Camille to turn him towards the woods with an ominous "Find her," he'd been confused and a bit put-out. But when he'd seen her in the stream, her body frigid and limp, he'd forgotten how to breathe. How to think.

He'd jumped into the current and pulled her out, every second like a knife to the gut. He hadn't taken a breath again until she'd lurched back to life.

"I want you!"

She'd said it with conviction. She'd sneered at his gift and said she wanted him, as if nothing was more precious.

"If that is the case, my lady," he said, his voice rough and strained with cold rage, "then how could you? Why would you try to kill yourself?"

Her shivering paused. "I wasn't trying to kill myself."

"Whatever I did, whatever notion you have that I've mistreated you, it's not worth dying over." He shook his head, the helpless feeling not abating for a second. It was a year ago all over again. His parents. His mother. A gentleman bearing the name Hurstfield, and a lady bearing the same name who felt the need to end it all because of him.

She stood and planted her feet, body and words firm. "I didn't try to kill myself."

"I know you're upset. Camille said as much." He ran a hand through his hair. Was this how it would be from now on? Had he been mistaken about her? To find her in such a state after one night together? Leave for a morning and she would fly off the handle. He'd show her, help her.

"I. DIDN'T. TRY. TO. KILL. MYSELF."

"You didn't?"

"Of course not!" She crossed her arms, her clothes dripping a circle of water around her. "I wouldn't give you the satisfaction."

He didn't dare to hope, but the spark of feeling flared anyway. "Then why were you in the water?"

She stopped and turned to him with wide eyes, her arms falling to her sides. "Someone pushed me." She gripped his shirt in her fists. "They held me under. They were . . ." She let go, her voice going hollow. "Someone tried to kill me."

"What?!" Hamish pivoted around, eyes scanning the area. Someone had snuck onto his property. Someone had tried to kill the duchess. Had nearly succeeded. If he'd been a moment later . . .

He pulled Charlotte into his arms, needing to feel her against him.

She buried her face in his chest, obviously too frightened to remember she didn't wish for his touch. She looked up suddenly. "A doe."

"What?"

"He snuck up on a doe," she said. "I didn't think that was possible. Even with the water so loud, I didn't dare breathe, else I frighten her away."

"How do you know it was a man?"

"His hand." Charlotte shuddered. "It was so big and strong."

Hamish tucked her under his chin. His mind was a whirling top. Charlotte couldn't have been the target. She was too good and innocent to be a threat to anyone. Out here, alone, she was an easy mark, too easy to pass up, but for what?

Had she stumbled upon a poacher? It had been known to happen. Disreputable lunks looking for easy game. But this didn't feel like a hunter. Surely, someone discovered would use the weapon on hand. A quick shot would alert any passing keeper, but the grounds were extensive. It would take a small army to suss out the source, and whatever hunter had been here would be long gone by then. This was a trained killer, after something or someone specifically. Who?

Me, Hamish thought. The killer had to have been after him. He'd made a name for himself in the business world, earning the hushed disapproval of the *ton*, but no puffed-up dandy would take distaste of him to homicide.

Which left his other business pursuits.

He didn't need to worry for Gregori. No man alive could take on Percy. Of that, he had no doubt.

An assassin knew when to change tactics. Percy had claimed such himself dozens of times in their acquaintance. It took intelligence, patience.

The killer could still be out here, watching.

Hamish kept an arm around his wife and tipped back her head. "Charlotte, please. We need to return to the house. Whoever tried to hurt you may still be out here."

She jolted but held his gaze. Jeweler's box still clutched to her chest, she bit her lip and nodded once.

They followed an old hunting trail through the forest, stumbling in and through a small clearing with supplies Hamish took as his wife's camp. He kept her as close as possible without stepping on top of her, but in his haste, he heard her cry out once or twice.

He felt the many eyes of the forest watching them from the shadows.

He didn't slow.

HE HELD HER so tight, she felt his heartbeat hammering against her chest. Or was that her own racing pulse?

Why had she been attacked?

Had the burly cretin—one could hardly call the grasping drunkard a man—who'd fought with her over Scarlet returned to seek revenge?

But he'd have no idea who she was, or that she was a *she* for that matter. Despite her husband's exclamation otherwise, those men knew her only as a nameless gentleman.

Hamish burst through the back kitchen entrance, startling Miss Sanders into dropping a steaming pot of water across the floor.

"Of all the boisterous nonsense, slamming open doors like a boy. I've a mind to take you over my knee." She took one look at them and bustled forward, her expression changing with concern. "What happened? You're soaked to the bone. Come closer to the fire."

She herded them towards the hearth, her constant, fluttering energy reminding Charlotte of her mother when she'd come home with scraped knees or soggy boots as a girl.

The older woman extracted her from Hamish's arms when he told her to shut the door and lock it.

Miss Sanders successfully peeled off Charlotte's coat, taking the box from her hands, and started on a muddy boot.

"Pricilla!"

The woman leveled a haunting glare up at him, an expression no ordinary servant would give the master of the house and keep their position. "Watch your tone, Lord Hamish. Your Grace," she amended.

Charlotte watched his ears turn bright red.

"Apologies, Miss Sanders." Hamish said. "Please. Someone snuck onto the property and assaulted the duchess at the creek."

"Great heavens!" She left at once, bolted the door, and called for the maids in the next room to do the same throughout the house.

She returned and pointed to the pantry. "Take off your clothes. I'll have hot water drawn up for a bath."

Hamish shook his head. "My room's water closet is fully equipped. No intruder would know the room is there."

Cook looked like she wanted to argue, but she took in Charlotte's sudden fit of shivers and shooed them out of the kitchen.

Hamish paused in the doorway. "Pricilla—"

"I know what to do," she said, and some silent message passed between them.

"Thank you."

He practically ran up the stairs, Charlotte back in his arms, a boot on one foot and feeling the chills as water dripped down her back. The tension had returned to his jaw, turning his profile into a flesh statue. That was when she noticed her glasses were still firmly on her face. Near death drowning and the wire rims hadn't budged. She'd grown so accustomed to going without them, the droplet-filled lenses hadn't registered.

She giggled and covered her mouth in alarm.

He cocked a brow. "Something amusing?"

Another bout of laughter escaped. "I don't know what's wrong with me." More laughter bubbled up. "I can't seem to stop. Do you think it's a fever?"

His arms tightened around her, but his voice was firm. "You won't get sick."

The will in his voice was convincing enough that Charlotte believed him.

"It's shock."

"Because someone tried to kill me?"

He kicked open the door to his chambers, the wood groaning, and carried her into the water closet. He set her down to light the lanterns, trailing water all over the wood floor.

One would think the water would have dried by now after

walking so far, but it appeared neither of them could escape what had happened, and what was to come.

His silence was awful.

If emotions gave off colors, Charlotte imagined sparks of red and orange exploding out of his ears and setting everything directly in his path on fire. She stood awkwardly to the side, watching him fill the tub and throw a handful of salts across the top.

He walked stiffly, like his wet clothes chafed.

She knew the feeling. Her underarms and thighs burned with every brush of movement as inescapable as her chattering teeth.

He turned on her, words and gaze hard. "Take off your clothes."

"Hamish—"

"I said, take them off!" He tore at her shirt.

She pushed at his hands, hating the dead look in his eyes. "Hamish, I can do it."

Fabric ripped and air kissed her skin. She crossed her arms over her chest but flew to her trousers when he set to ripping those from her body as well.

"Hamish, stop!"

He batted her hands away. "Hold still." He tore at the lacing of the trousers and ripped them down her hips. They caught on her one boot, and he cursed.

She was prepared to knee him in his arrogant, demanding mouth when she caught something glistening on his cheek. Anger melting, she cupped his jaw and lifted his face. "Let me," she said gently.

He stared at her, the distance in his eyes changing to something haunted. He nodded.

She discarded the boot and pants and touched his arm. "You should undress as well."

He didn't acknowledge her words except to stand and discard his clothes in a heap by the tub.

Charlotte hated her body for its response. His broad shoulders, the hard tilt to his pelvis, his butt. Goodness, a man shouldn't have such a perfect backside.

He turned off the water and pointed. "Get in."

The ice in his command left Charlotte colder than the draft from the open panel door. She studied his face, not recognizing the man she thought she knew.

This man was emotional, strung taut. She held no fear he'd hurt her—she knew better—but this stranger had rage, and it was directed at her.

Chest tight, she whispered, "No."

His word was equally soft. "What?"

She shook her head. "I won't bathe with you."

"You will get in this tub at once, or I will drag you over and throw you in." He spoke in that same terrible voice.

They both knew what would happen if she did as he'd said. He'd climb in behind her and touch her, and she'd lose. If she allowed him to lay with her now, she'd have no grounds to insist they sleep separately later, when he vanished to seek another woman's arms. He'd made his choice. Now it was her turn.

"Charlotte, what will it be?"

She bit back tears, the sight of his face so cruel and so broken tugging on the last fragment of her heart she'd vowed he wouldn't claim. One tear escaped down her cheek. Her two words were the hardest she'd ever uttered, "I can't."

Silence stretched. The last drops of water in the pipes hit the water with a deafening echo.

"Very well," he said, turning to leave and slamming the door behind him.

Charlotte crawled into the tub and cried until the bathwater turned salty.

CHAPTER THIRTY-FIVE

"WHERE'S GREGORI?" HAMISH asked.

Percy didn't move from his position at the study window. The fire burned low, casting his profile in shadow against the dusk-painted panes.

"Safe," he said. "Wouldn't stop grumbling about the delicacy of his work, but the boys are moving the supplies to the secondary location via alternate routes. I advised the men to shake all tails by any means."

One thing taken care of, at least, Hamish thought. *If only women were as easy to move as cargo.*

He had no idea what had happened between them. Leaving her without a word had been a mistake on his part, but his actions hardly deserved the reception he'd received. Last night, he would have boasted to any sod willing to listen how perfect his life was.

"I can't."

Those two words had felt like goodbye. Standing in his water closet, if he hadn't been holding on to his anger like a lifeline, he'd have shattered to pieces at her feet.

Eight hours. Somehow, in that time everything had fallen apart.

"How is Her Grace?" Percy asked.

Hamish fell back into his leather chair, the lack of two nights' sleep adding another layer of black to his mood. "Miss Forthright is with her. She'll be fine."

The way Charlotte had torn away from his touch, he may not be.

"Did she get a look at him?"

"Doesn't seem so."

"Was it a hit?"

Hamish nodded. "She made it clear the wildlife didn't even take note."

"Damn," Percy said. "Not many of us can do that."

The reminder of 'us' and where Percy's true talents lay was a comfort like nothing else.

"How many?" he asked.

"Handful in London," Percy said. "Half a dozen across England."

"That you know of." Hamish knew he was being confrontational, but he needed something else to focus his rage on.

"I make it my business to know the few out there capable of killing me."

"You've been out of the game for eight years now. Things change."

That got Percy to turn from the window, his expression thinly veiled hostility. "You're never out."

Hamish looked away. Percy's past was ugly and using it to needle him into a fight was too low, even for him. "You know the assassin?"

Percy shrugged. "The backer is who we need to worry about. A true mercenary isn't a problem if you can find the owner of the leash."

"A paid killer," Hamish said.

"Is a reasonable killer," Percy finished. "Any idea who'd want you dead?"

Percy agreed Charlotte wasn't the intended, then. "None that come to mind." He'd been careful to keep a low profile. It was true there could be any score of men aiming for his head, but they'd have to uncover his title and fortune first—and then decide if they wanted to take on a well-connected gentleman of the *ton*.

"What about Markus?" Percy asked.

"What about him?"

Percy shuffled to the chair opposite but didn't sit. "Perhaps the old man didn't like you poking your nose in his territory. Men like that settle scores the permanent way."

Hamish had no doubt Markus knew his way around a knife in the dark, but he couldn't bring himself to accuse the man of anything but a loud temper and a cautious disposition.

"It's possible," Hamish allowed. "But the man isn't one to hire a professional. If he wanted me dead, he'd stick the knife in himself."

Percy snorted. "An honest man, how terrifying. Which leaves our friend from the borrowed cargo."

"Did you get a name?"

"Dr. Deinolf."

"An alias?"

"Clearly."

"Damn." Where did that leave them? "What's next? I can't keep my staff on lockdown indefinitely." With Camille at the estate, it was only a matter of time until sarcastic manners turned to altercations involving slippers to the head.

"It'll take me time to track down our dog owner. Any chance Her Grace would agree to an extended trip to the continent?"

"She'd be overjoyed." The thought of Charlotte more than a floor away made his insides flip and churn. "She stays."

Percy cocked a brow but didn't comment. "Then I suggest you find a safe place to tuck her away. Someplace our new friend won't be inclined to show himself."

A killer brazen enough to assault his wife on his property didn't seem a man to forgo risks. "Is there a place?" Should he put himself in the open and draw the killer to him?

"Hmm," Percy said. "What do you think?"

"I've a place," someone said.

Hamish whirled to the woman in the doorway and came out of his chair. "Where's Charlotte?"

Camille leaned against the doorframe. "Sleeping. And unless you expect me to watch the lady snore, I can be of more use here."

Hamish settled into his chair, hating the idea of Charlotte alone.

"Oh, stop with the look," she said. "I left your nosy butler and cook to stand vigil. It's a wonder she fell asleep with those two hovering over her."

"Good." He grunted. There weren't two people more suited to keeping away unwanted guests. He expected he would have a time proving his identity before they allowed him entrance to the room.

Percy shifted across from him, his gaze on Camille.

"Forgive me," Hamish said, using the first lie he could think of. "Percy, this is Miss Forthright. Miss Forthright, this is Percy, my associate."

"I remember." Her lip curled. "You're the overbearing chum who came to fetch me after the scandal hit."

Percy stilled. "You must be mistaken, miss."

"Don't bother. I never forget a face," she said.

The alarm in the bruiser's face calmed to a slick smile. "I'm surprised you recognized me. I was in disguise."

"No one can hide who they really are. Body language, tone of voice—you gave yourself away. Next time, you should walk with a limp."

He smiled, all teeth. "Thanks for the advice."

"This place you spoke of," Hamish said. "Where is it?"

Camille crossed her arms and leveled a hard gaze on him. "You're not going to like it."

She told him.

"Absolutely not!" Hamish shouted.

Camille rolled her eyes. "You're being unreasonable."

"I think it's a splendid idea."

"Shut it, Percy." Hamish shook his head. "The answer is no."

"No one will look for her there," Camille said.

Hamish didn't know when he'd started pacing, but the indentations in the carpet bore remarkable similarities to the size and shape of his booted feet. "I need her hidden, not thrown into more danger."

Camille snorted. "The establishment has more security than the Crown."

"It's true," Percy piped in, his unfettered glee taunting Hamish into putting a fist in his face.

"You've been there?" Hamish scowled. "Then she certainly can't go. The clientele is too questionable."

"Oh, please," Camille said. "The place is a maze. There's a room that holds enough locks and chains; it would take an earthquake to crack it open."

Hamish's blood heated at the mention of chains. Getting Charlotte into a small room where neither of them could escape had its appeal. "And you can get us inside?"

Camille grinned. "The owner owes me a favor."

"Three," Percy said. At her sharp look, he shrugged. "Yes, I'm overbearing, inquisitive—"

"Conniving," she added.

"I like to keep informed on my targets."

"You're not very good at your job, then." Her grin curled. "She owes me four."

Hamish had no idea if Camille was telling the truth. Between her and Percy, he'd never met two people better at deception. If they ever decided to conspire, England was doomed.

"Perhaps someone should ask Charlotte what she wants to do," Camille said.

Hamish didn't miss the pointed look in his direction.

"I volunteer," Percy said.

Hamish stood and buttoned his coat. "How many days do you need?"

Crestfallen, Percy sighed. "Two. Three at most."

"You have one. I want this bastard's guts in the pig pen." For touching Charlotte, he'd deliver the chum to the swine himself.

He strode to the door and stopped at Camille's side. "Contact your friend. I want Charlotte in a locked room by tonight."

"Typical man," she said. She added, "I already did. You're expected for dinner." Her eyes danced with cunning, always two steps ahead of him. "Don't be late."

Hamish huffed; the whole situation was absurd. "Wouldn't want to miss our appointment."

"Money on the hour," she said, her former life flashing in her eyes. She let him pass and laughed to herself. "Don't worry. She'll go without a fuss."

⇥⇥⇤⇤

HAMISH WOULD HAVE preferred fuss. He'd have preferred screaming and kicking and colorful profanity over the lingering silence in the carriage. No good came when a woman went silent.

He shifted in his seat. The carriage wheels' rhythmic clicking over level cobblestones was indication they'd entered a maintained section of the city.

He'd elected to go through the finer parts instead of a straighter shot through the gutters, insisting efficiency over happenstance of the fastest route.

His gaze darted through the window, unable to relax until Charlotte was tucked away. Not that three hours of strung silence helped his anxiety. He'd suffocate from the tension.

And not all from a killer out for blood.

However Camille had convinced Charlotte out of her room and into the carriage—after ignoring all efforts on his part to coax her out—there were apparently no words on his behalf. His wife had walked down the stairs and out the back of the house without a glance in his direction and little more than a sentence from her companion.

"*Make your own way,*" Camille had said.

Hamish couldn't fathom the meaning. The sense of joy he felt at the two women becoming instant friends didn't dull the dread the women wouldn't hesitate to strike down any perceived threat in their path, including him.

What a comfort to know his lovely wife would have help moving his corpse when the women deigned him no longer necessary.

Charlotte rested her head back on the seat cushion and sighed.

Hamish berated himself for latching on to the sound. "We're almost there," he said.

She didn't acknowledge him.

"You'll be safe," he tried again. He waited. "I promise."

She looked out the window, her voice quiet. "Promises are nothing but sincere wishes."

Hamish hesitated. Now she'd started talking, he didn't want her to stop. He hadn't realized how much he'd missed her voice, her thoughts. How he hated her bright spirit dimming since that afternoon. He craved the sun, the essence of her. Whatever had happened, whatever he'd done, he'd fix it.

"What do you wish for?" he asked.

She looked at him for the first time since the bath and what he saw in her eyes was devastating.

"I wish to go back to yesterday."

Yes. "Yes," he said out loud. He leaned forward, holding her gaze. What had gone wrong? He almost asked but didn't. When he'd gotten back to the manor and found her gone, he'd thought she'd left him. He'd felt a hole open in his chest that he'd sworn had filled with the rubbles of his failed relationship with his father. He let that go, focusing on her. "What happened, Charlotte?"

She turned away. "Reality. I found I didn't like it."

He wanted to press, but she'd closed off again. He scrambled to open her back up the only way he knew how.

He leaned back and forced a flippant tone. "So naturally, you ran away."

His provocation worked.

She turned back sharply, her words doubly so. "As I told you before, I was continuing the activities we'd agreed on as a partnership. I wasn't about to wait until you decided to return from your errands."

He let her cold tone wash over him. A twinge of guilt caught him remembering why he'd left. At least her anger was better than that damned silence.

"Am I to assume you will endeavor to perform whatever unruly escapades you fancy whenever I'm called away?"

"It's the best time. More enjoyable when there isn't some man hovering over." She grinned, a small tug of her mouth.

Hamish felt like he'd scaled a mountain.

He latched on to the single ray of emotion shining through. He would fix whatever had broken. And he had no qualms resorting to underhanded bribes or trickery.

"Good." He crossed his legs, letting the barest hint of mystery into his voice. "Since this next adventure was nowhere on your list. My company won't be an issue."

She scowled, seeming to realize his game. But, like she'd admitted, her curiosity wasn't easily ignored. "Adventure, you say?"

"Scandalous, really. No place any decent lady should go."

He knew he'd hooked her when she leaned forward.

"What place?"

Hamish's heart soared at the rekindled spark in her eyes and he grudgingly thanked his sister's less-than-desirable past employment.

He leaned forward as well. He wiggled his finger for her to come closer and kept his gaze locked on her face when he said, "A brothel."

CHAPTER THIRTY-SIX

A BROTHEL. A den of ill repute. Charlotte had heard many terms, mostly by listening at her brother's door when she was supposed to be in some mind-numbing lesson on embroidery.

A bordello. A disorderly house. It sounded like the precise place to organize her own disorder.

She may have been angry with her husband, and the life-threatening situations his illicit activities had brought—lost in lust for a time, she'd almost forgotten his shady dealings in the back alley of Dockside. Sitting in the tub at Camine Manor, doing her best to ward off the worst of her shivers, she'd remembered a different chill and the knowledge there was a side to Hamish he kept hidden.

But she wouldn't miss this opportunity. Brothels had been illegal in England since the Disorderly Houses Act more than a century before, but of course desire didn't listen to royal decrees. A pleasure house. Was there anything more delightful-sounding? A place where one explored their deepest desires. She was aghast at her lapse in memory.

A night house. Prostitutes. Wagtails.

"Painted ladies."

"Come again?" he asked.

She turned, realizing she'd spoken aloud.

Her traitorous body shuddered at the timbre of his voice. She hated how her chest tightened and her core clenched.

It seemed heartbreak had no effect on a body's lust-filled memories. Despite his betrayal, this adventure felt like all the others. Truthfully, there was no other person she'd want to share this with.

Exciting, scandalous—as if it were more so because he was here.

She wished she could say sharing her list with anyone would have been enough, but she was never one for denial.

He encouraged her. When he wasn't lecturing her on recklessness, he was teasing and open to her questions, and direct with his answers.

How a man could treat her as an equal without any real feelings must have been a credit to the drastic differences in their sex.

She'd thought herself protected after her conversation with Camille, but having him in front of her was painful. Setting aside her feelings for him to be present in this moment—what would have to extend into a lifetime for any measure of happiness—was like cauterizing an open wound before she bled out completely.

But she knew how emotional pain worked. It killed one's spirit but left the body alive when it shouldn't.

She wouldn't die. She had too much life to live. It would take a trained killer to stop her from having the freedom she craved.

She was stronger than any infidelity, she told herself.

And so, Charlotte set her feelings aside in a little box in her heart, snapped the lid shut, and looked up at her husband, distancing herself from how his eyes tracked her movement and his stubbled chin made him look even more dashing. She smiled. "Do you think the ladies will be out front?"

He frowned but sat back in his seat. "It's early. Most of the ladies will be getting ready, I imagine."

"Have you been there?" Charlotte scolded herself. She didn't want to know.

He studied her face and nodded. "When I was younger. Recently, once."

The box in her heart cracked open, and she stopped breathing. Was this where he'd gone earlier? Was it more than a mistress she must contend with? She whispered, "Did you enjoy it?"

His sudden bark of laughter took her by surprise.

"No," he said, a knowing smile on his face. "My last experience at the Prodding Pony was not one I'd ever care to repeat."

Eyebrow quirked, she couldn't resist asking, "Did you do the prodding? Or were you the pony?"

He laughed again.

Warmth grew in her stomach like blooming petals.

"Neither," he said. "I had a rather unpleasant exchange with one of the madam's bruisers when I tried to retrieve someone inside who had no desire to go."

"Who?"

"My sister."

"Camille worked here?"

Hamish smacked his elbow shifting too quick. "Son of a bitch." He rubbed the offending limb. "She told you?"

He mumbled something about sailors and wenches that didn't sound complimentary.

"What was that?"

"You're a blasted siren," he said. "There isn't a person alive you couldn't charm."

Charlotte blinked, stunned into honesty. "That's a lovely thing to say."

Recovered, he ran a hand through his hair as if worried. "You-You aren't disgusted, then? That I brought her into my life?"

Charlotte's anger was immediate, at last not directed at him. For society to shame a man for acting honorably and selflessly to aid his family, she reconsidered her list and thought to add 'the downfall of the aristocracy and its idiotic ideals' at the bottom in bold cursive.

She shook her head, her voice rough with emotion. "No matter what happens between us, you must know you are a good man." Her nails dug painfully into her palms. "What you did for your sister was heroic. Anyone suggesting otherwise is a vazey ratbag and can go straight to hell."

His expression subsided and softened. "Thank you."

The crack in her heart gaped.

The carriage stopped in front of a dark doorway with a small sign hanging above with a painting of a horse. He opened the door and jumped down. Turning, he plucked her out without preamble.

A woman met them at the door, her hair and face expertly pinned and powdered, so Charlotte had no way of guessing her age. She was, however, beautiful. Whoever she was, if this standard of creature gave any indication of popularity, Charlotte didn't doubt business was good.

The woman nodded. "Welcome, Your Grace." She glanced over Charlotte's shoulder and smiled. "And to you as well, Your Grace."

Hamish, having regained his composure, bowed over the woman's hand. "We're looking for your mistress, my lady. Would you be a doll and fetch her?"

The woman threw back her head and cackled. "Charming. I'm glad to see my woman didn't leave any scars on that handsome face. I'll warn my girls to be gentle."

Not feeling the least bit charming suddenly, Charlotte said, "You're the madam, then?"

"Madam Clarice." She gave Charlotte a onceover, her eyes flicking back to the duke. "I see you'll have no use for our services with such a feisty duchess." She turned into the hall and beckoned them to follow.

Mollified, Charlotte followed down a long hall and into an end chamber where two simply gowned women waited with black, silk scarfs across their palms like bastardized statues of virgin saints.

Madam Clarice nodded to the girls and turned back. "You'll be blindfolded before you're allowed inside."

Charlotte glanced at the sparse place, brick and stone white-washed and grey in the low candlelight. A thrill of excitement shot up her spine, imagining what she'd see on the other side of the swaths of black fabric covering doors on either side. "We're not already inside?"

"Our patrons appreciate our discretion. No one is allowed to see; therefore, no one can wander where they shouldn't. You will be escorted to your room, where an attendant will wait outside. When you are prepared to leave, you will be brought out the same way."

Charlotte's excitement bubbled over. "Mysterious."

Hamish scowled. "Convenient."

The Madam held up her hand and the two women stepped back as if pulled by strings. "Angel told me you'd agreed to the rules of the house."

"'Angel'?" Charlotte asked.

Hamish snorted. "One name I'd never use to describe Camille."

Madam Clarice clicked her tongue. "I will not permit entrance without acceptance. Everyone here chooses it, with consent."

"You'd make an enemy of a duke?" Hamish asked.

"I protect my girls."

Charlotte had heard enough. She stepped up to one of the women and turned around for her blindfold, placing her spectacles in her dress pocket. "I'm in."

The Madam smiled. "And you, Your Grace?"

Hamish watched Charlotte closely, his eyes darkening. He nodded and turned without another word.

"DOES YOUR ESTABLISHMENT service only men?" Charlotte asked, itching to peek under her blindfold.

Madam Clarice stroked Charlotte's hand in the crook of her arm, the woman escorting her personally. "We've opened our doors on occasion for special requests. A duchess, for instance, would be welcome in one of our luxury chambers."

Hamish growled somewhere to Charlotte's left. "She'll have no need for your offer."

"Every man believes so." Madam leaned in close, her perfume heady and exotic. "The offer stands, Your Grace."

The thought of another touching her made Charlotte's insides turn over.

"Thank you, Madam, but that won't be necessary."

She felt the Madam pull back. "Angel was right, then."

Charlotte wished to ask exactly what Camille had said, but the sound of a key turning in a lock stopped her short.

Madam Clarice pulled her forward and left her side. Shuffling feet behind her told Charlotte it was to bring Hamish inside as well.

"You may remove your blindfolds now." The Madam's voice was fading back down the hall. "Knock if you need anything."

A door shut and locked, and Charlotte felt Hamish beside her, his presence like a pull her body unconsciously knew even blind. She heard him fumble with his blindfold and curse at their surroundings, obviously successful in navigating the woman's knot.

He came up behind her, his heat burning into her back. "Would you like me to remove your scarf?"

His voice was husky.

Charlotte's core clenched. For a moment, she was transported back to that night in his chambers. She'd been blindfolded then too.

"Charlotte."

She shivered at the brush of breath on her neck. "Do I want to see?"

"The room is"—he paused—"well equipped." He chuckled. "I've no doubt you'll see a challenge where other ladies would run shrieking for the exit."

Humor tugged the corner of her mouth. "How fearless I am."

"I've always thought so."

The admiration in his voice hurt. His hands rested intimately on her shoulders and turned her around, so gently.

Suddenly, the emotional distance was too much. She knew him. Poor vision had plagued her since childhood, but she'd always seen him. She'd been a fool to think she could tuck her heart away. And she was tired of resisting the truth.

"Charlotte—"

"I love you." Charlotte stuck out her chin.

He choked on his breath. "You—"

"Love you, yes." She waited, refusing to feel shame.

She heard him move.

He was behind her again, his hands pulling at her blindfold.

Her words crowded the silence. "You laughed about childish fantasies and you were right. Fanciful, childish, irrational—I'm all those things."

He grunted, his fingers pulling at her scarf.

"Hamish?" She reached behind to assist, but he pushed her hands away. Her chest fell. "We need not discuss it if you wish."

"We will talk," he said, his pulling turning rough. "I refuse to continue until I can look at you."

After the frantic tension of pulling the blindfold down, when it fell at her feet in a black snake of fabric, neither seemed rushed to face the other.

Charlotte stared at the silk against dark wood, her heart pulsing in her ears.

The room was well lit. The wood grain stared back at her, stark and blurry. She fumbled to replace her spectacles and wished she could sink into the natural swirls when they came into focus.

How much harder it was to converse when one could see, as if her bravery had sloughed off with the scarf.

Charlotte whirled around and stuck out her chin, ready for

his confusion, revulsion, indifference.

"Charlotte." The softness in his voice transcended into his touch. His fingers skimmed her cheek, his gaze soul searing.

Charlotte remembered the first time she'd seen those eyes. She'd been hiding in the hedge maze at Lux Manor to escape her governess, when she'd spied a boy sharpening a stick by the pond.

"You came to visit my brother over the summer one year," she said, the memory still fresh twelve years later. "You'd decided you would catch dinner one night. Rabbit and venison."

"And pork," he said, his mouth twitching. "I believed a diet of meat would make me grow half a foot before Renard and I returned to school." His smile grew with the memory. "We only managed two measly fish."

"A carp and a pike."

Hamish laughed. "You remembered the fish?"

"I remember everything you did." Charlotte's cheeks heated, but the words felt right. A truth she'd kept locked away since that summer. "You crafted a spear by the lake. You said it was for the great boar you'd stumble across on your hunt."

His grin turned boyish, the same grin that had pulled her quiet self out of that maze all those years ago.

"Optimistic of me," he said.

"And pragmatic. One never wants to stumble upon a tusked beast unprepared." She smiled up at him. "I knew then. A boy courageous enough—"

"Stupid enough."

"And adventurous enough," she continued, "to take on a boar with nothing but a knife and a branch." She shrugged, the easy action encompassing a decade of idolizing and infatuation.

"You were smitten?" he prodded.

Her smile was self-deprecating. "Childish fantasies."

Hamish cursed and ran a hand through his hair. "I said that out of stupidity and arrogance."

"Anger. Don't forget that."

"I was angry," he admitted.

"You thought I was trying to trap you into marriage. Your anger was justified."

"Charlotte . . ." He said her name again, this time with regret. He took her hand and rubbed his cheeks against her bare knuckles. "I'm sorry for leaving the way I did. Tell me we can move past it. I won't deny I'm still given to stupidity and arrogance—"

"And anger."

He brushed his smiling lips across her skin and gazed at her. "And more egregious sins. Forgive me?"

Charlotte made to look away, to pick out those pieces of her heart like a mirror, so smashed and scratched to be unrecognizable, and find if she could still see herself in the frame. She needed space to feel, to think, but then he said the one word that seemed to patch even the largest cracks.

"Please." He pressed her hand to his chest, his skin scorching hers through layers of linen. "Please let me make this right."

Everything inside screamed her acquiescence. Mistakes would be made on both sides, expected with any relationship. She loved him, every part. Arrogance, anger, pride, childish naivety. And she loved the man, secretive and caring and far more tender and honest than he realized.

The question wasn't: Could she live with only a piece of him? The question was: Could she live without any of him?

"No."

He made a strangled noise, heart breaking enough Charlotte realized he'd mistook her inner battle as an answer to his plea.

She grabbed his hand as he pulled away, the despair in his face edged with a ray of hope so dim and fleeting, Charlotte knew one word could snuff out every speck of light for good.

And she loved his insecurities. That a man as strong and intimidating cared, even a little, what she thought.

"I'm also arrogant," she said. "And reckless and unrefined and brash."

His expression tipped to one side with the list of her flaws, along with a hint of humor. "Would you go so far as to say, 'angry'?"

"Meters of temper," she allowed. "Leagues."

"Oceans?"

"It spans the world map." Charlotte forced her thoughts to clarity, knowing the words she chose next were crucial. "There is nothing to make right. I—" Her voice cracked with emotion, but the words had to be said. "I love you. I said I wouldn't trap you, and yet I let my anger trap you in expectations that weren't of your making. I cannot expect you to make me happy." She smiled into his confused face, finally understanding what it was to let go of childhood and find one's truth. "I must make myself happy."

CHAPTER THIRTY-SEVEN

S HE LOVED HIM.

He was flying. She loved him. If heaven were a place in the clouds, an angel had been misplaced in humanity's common throngs. And she stood before him.

Her comment about happiness was the truest statement he'd heard. He wanted to deny it, scream from the rafters he would make her happy in their marriage.

A carriage wreck he'd made of it so far.

She loved him, but she was still angry.

"Was me leaving without you such a grave sin?" he asked. "Please, tell me. We're partners."

She frowned, then scowled. "When did you go to her?"

"Her?"

"Crim."

He stiffened. "How did you know?" He shook his head. "It isn't what you think—"

"Don't bother denying it. Was it before or after we'd fucked?"

Her curse rang between them. Charlotte didn't blink or blush, telling Hamish she was past angry.

"You're upset?" he asked dumbly.

"No."

Hamish stopped her with a light touch. He sucked in a breath at the tears in her eyes. "You *are* upset."

"Of course I am!" she shouted.

Hamish's jaw worked, the lack of contact with her ravaging the muscle in his chest.

"I am strong, determined to be happy," she said. "But I'm not frigid. You think I like sharing you with someone else? I promised myself I wouldn't cage you, and I meant it. That doesn't mean I want to be humiliated."

"What do you mean 'share'?" Hamish's eyes widened. "You think she and I are—" His heart gave a painful thump. "Charlotte, I broke things off with Crim after our night together."

She glanced at him but said nothing.

He reached for her gently, something in his gut easing when she came willingly into his arms. It was all a mistake. He couldn't believe she'd thought he'd still kept a mistress. Even if he'd had the inclination, one night with her and every other woman had been ruined. She didn't want to trap him. He understood her words and actions after the river with perfect clarity now.

"Charlotte." He willed the jumble of emotions wreaking havoc on his insides to show in his eyes. Words were not his forte, but for her, he'd try; for her, he'd draft an entire book of poems to express his sorry state since she'd stormed into his life.

"All this time, I thought I needed someone control to feel safe, to be happy. I bound and dominated you, and you took it like a saint. But it was me being bound by my own darkness all along. Truly, I'd forgotten Crim existed after the very first time seeing your light." He tilted her face to look at him. "When I found you unconscious in the river, I thought I'd never be free of the dark. I knew then I would put you first at any cost."

She huffed a laugh. "You mean *after* I'd nearly been killed by an unknown murderer? Men are such ridiculous creatures."

He loved her teasing tone. He loved how she mentioned such peril with a smile. With her askew spectacles and unending courage, he loved her.

Good God, he *loved* her.

She cleared her throat.

He startled, realizing she'd said something. "Yes?"

"This would be an excellent time to kiss me."

He leaned over her, heart and life painfully full, but he hesitated.

She was everything, an angel and salvation.

He was a mere mortal and if he wished to skim the clouds, he would need to let go of the weight he carried in his heart.

"My father was not a kind man," he said.

If she was confused at the change of subject, she didn't show it. She watched him and waited, as if sensing how hard it was for him to speak of his past.

"Society saw the previous Duke of Camine as a gentleman who bled gold. Everything he touched flourished: charities, speculations."

"A trait you inherited."

"The only thing worth inheriting, trust me," he said. "Society praises a gentleman for gaining on property and titles already prospering. I've always thought a man of business who makes himself from nothing garners more respect than a titled man handed everything. A sharp mind knows no title."

"Or sex."

He smiled at his wife's inability to hold her tongue. "I'm attempting intimacy, woman."

"And I keep interrupting."

He cocked a brow in a silent, *"You said it, not me."*

She smiled and bit her lip.

Hamish waited until she promised no further comments. "After I found out about his mistress, I broke ties. I would have shunned the title, fortune, my entire inheritance, if only to watch the bastard witness the end of his 'golden' line." He stared at a section of stone wall over her shoulder. "But the bastard died before I finalized my trip abroad. And then there was Camille.

"I'd sent someone to investigate. Had he returned and reported my sister well and settled, I'd never have interfered. My father had left her nothing. I would have used all my father's assets in lodging and connections for her to have a comfortable life. When she refused, I put it all in a dowry for her to use for her and any future family." He ran a hand through his hair, unsure how to express everything so she'd understand.

"Nothing I own now is paid for by my father's estate. Every last farthing I borrowed to start out I've replaced with money I've made through my own affairs." He paused, stomach pitching. His voice echoed around the faux dungeon, but he refused to be a prisoner to his secrets any longer. "I want to run my own business." He rushed on before his nerves overtook him. "There's an untapped market where people need cheap but quality goods. If I can impress the right people, I'll have exclusive rights to sell. Quality of life will rise; people will have more opportunities to work."

He glanced at Charlotte.

She stood with her arms crossed and her brows drawn.

His chest tensed. "I know it's considered uncouth for a gentleman to work in trade."

She looked up at that. "What? Oh, I don't care about that." She scratched her head. "Does your business require illegal shipments?"

He blew out a breath. "I won't lie. Some of my dealings bend the rules at times."

"Dockside?"

"Yes." The word grated against his throat, but he wouldn't subject her to more ridicule. "If you can't bear the secrecy, I'll understand if you wish to take up residence in separate homes. It's just . . ." He opened his hands, exposing his palms. "I can't stop. I need to do this. I'm not like my father. I want—*need*—to help these people."

"You're nothing like your father." She grew animated with sudden passion. "Hamish Hurstfield, you listen to me. Your father was an ass with two amazing children he couldn't match in integrity or honor if he'd had five lifetimes."

His mouth twitched. There had been plenty of family dinners he and his parents had attended in the country with the former

Duke of Lux, seeing as his father and the duke had been neighbors in both land and rank, but Hamish never remembered a little girl with hair like the sun at any of them. "Did you ever meet him?"

She sniffed. "No need. Any father who makes his son question if helping people in need is the right decision is two parts fiend and one part cad." She took his hand. "Your father cared about his name for his vanity. You'll keep your name secret out of honor, but . . ." She bit her lip. "Wouldn't smuggled contraband be worse for Dockside in the long run?"

"Contraband?" His brows furrowed. He hadn't heard of any new laws passed in Parliament. "Despite borrowing supplies from other merchants, which I always pay back, we don't participate in anything illegal."

"Then what would you call the drugs you delivered?"

"What drugs?" Where the hell had that idea come from? He'd never touched drugs, physically or business wise. If drugs flooded the streets of Dockside, everything he was working for would be for naught.

Charlotte shrugged. "Drugs, alcohol, whatever it is in those little, brown packages. Besides increasing jobs, how will that increase quality of life?"

Good lord! "Is that what you thought I was carrying in the carriage?" No wonder she'd run like the very Devil had been after her that day after the alley brawl.

He took an identical package from his coat, a backup prototype Gregori had offered for his personal inspection he hadn't yet opened.

He handed it to Charlotte. "Here."

She stared down at the box, but her well-known curiosity had her ripping the paper and opening the lid. Taking the small, metal frames from its container, she held them up and then looked at him with a blank expression. "These are spectacles."

He smiled. "Yes."

She weighed them in her hand, clearly familiar with the quality of upper-class frames. "These are so light." She opened the arms and gazed through the lenses. "Is this real glass? They're so clear."

Hamish plucked the pair from her hands and admired Gregori's craftsmanship. The man was a no-nonsense pragmatist, but brilliant with his hands. "I met a young man on one of my travels east. He was rotting away in a clockmaker's backroom in Germany, making the most intricate engraving work I'd ever seen."

Hamish smiled, remembering how he'd offered Gregori a job and how the man hadn't asked about money or status. Gregori had asked only one question before he'd hopped on the next train and uprooted his life to come to England. "He'd asked me if the work would be challenging." He handed the spectacles back to Charlotte. "I'd had this idea to bring specialized spectacles to those of the lower class, men and women who could advance if only they were given a clear image, just like any person of privilege. So many of the apothecaries and doctors only offer the most basic lenses with no understanding or care for how a person's eyes differ."

He felt his body warming with that same call to action he'd felt after his father's scandal. "I want to offer affordable and specialized eyewear to the people who have no other opportunities to help themselves. Once I get the men running the underground market on board, I'll be able to open a clinic especially for those people. *Ton* society spouts nonsense of encouraging idleness when they've never gone a day hungry or desperate. But I'll offer payment plans or have clients work off their debt with good, honest labor."

He'd use Markus's connections to keep the business quiet. Since the former army captain had taken it upon himself to play police and defender in a place where no official officer of intelligence would make their rounds, he'd become the perfect face for Hamish's endeavors. Any whisper of the lower class receiving what the *ton* considered unfair handouts would bring down all kinds of scrutiny on the lives of good people who deserved a fair shot, just like any gently bred aristocrat.

Charlotte held the spectacles in her hands. When she looked up at him, her eyes were wet.

Hamish balked at her tears. "Why are you crying? I meant what I said. No one will know, and I wouldn't dream of forcing you to participate in my activities—"

"Shut up." Tears streamed down her face, but she smiled. "You are amazing." She offered him back the spectacles and wiped at her face. "Helping people is a noble trade, no matter how a stupid society may react. I'm not ashamed, Hamish. Great Lord above, I'm proud of you."

It was as if the chains binding him inside had snapped. One more moment not touching her would kill him. He pulled her to him and kissed her fiercely.

He spread kisses along her jaw and down the column of her neck. He growled against her throat, "You're perfect, wife. Sublime, without flaw."

She shuddered in his arms. "Those mean the same thing."

He cupped her bottom, bringing them breathlessly nose to nose. "It bears repeating," he said.

She giggled. "Whatever you say, *my lord.*"

This time, his growl was primal, leaving his words gruff, his hands more so gripping her against his pulsing erection. "I want to chain your legs open to that table and feast on you until you learn to properly respect your husband."

Her breathing hitched. Her gaze flicked around the room, obviously taking in the chains and leather straps for the first time when her fingers skimmed her nipple without thought. She swallowed audibly and turned back to him, a coy tip to her lips. "You'd be waiting years, sir."

He smiled. "We have forever."

He led her to the table in the corner, losing articles of clothing with every gasp and moan that passed between their lips.

"Is there a place for a reckless, troublesome lady in your business?" Charlotte asked.

Hamish grinned as Charlotte's mass of curls spilled across his chest and said to the back of her head, "Any particular lady you have in mind?"

She propped her chin on his stomach, brows raised. "You'd agree?"

"Reckless *and* troublesome?" He kissed the tip of her nose. "What man could resist?"

"Don't tease. I want to be useful."

"Hmm." He flipped her onto her back, the chains clinking seductively, still loosely twined around her ankles. He flicked her nipple with his tongue and tugged on the peak until she arched off the table.

Her voice was breathless, but her grip firm as she grabbed his face with both hands. "You're trying to distract me."

He rolled her other nipple between his fingers. "It's working, too."

"Hamish."

He sighed and released her.

She lifted onto her elbows. "If a gentleman can be forgiven for having a profession, why can't a lady?"

"As I said before, my title is the only reason I won't be thrown out of every ballroom if my identity gets out."

"I am a duchess, you know." She huffed. "I bet the blasted *ton* will secretly be tickled over a duke working with his own two hands. The ladies will swoon. Hypocrites."

He smiled. "Shall we run away to the country, then? We can pick up where we so sadly left off and work until our very tenants are scandalized."

"And what of my attacker?"

Mention of the invasion of home and privacy set his body on

edge. He intertwined their fingers and rested his forehead against hers. "No one will touch you," he vowed. "We'll go to Scotland, North America if we must. You will be safe."

"We mustn't run away."

"Charlotte—"

"When I do finally get to see the forests and strange peoples, I want to do so without looking over my shoulder."

"You don't understand." His throat strained with the crushing guilt. "You were targeted because of me. You can't stay in England until he's caught."

"It's not your fault." Her expression clouded, then cleared. "The killer is connected to your business."

Hamish's guilt was momentarily overshadowed by his wife's sharp mind. "It's what we suspect."

"'We'?" She frowned. "You and that snake man, you mean?" She sighed. "I guess a man that shady must be good at his job or you wouldn't employ him."

He laughed. Percy could charm the queen when it suited him, but all his efforts appeared in vain when it came to charming his wife, who seemed to see through people's façades like an image through gossamer.

"Your perception is astute. But he will find the man, of that I have no doubt."

"Perhaps."

Her sudden silence paired with a twist of her mouth gave Hamish the dreaded suspicion that marvelous mind was devising a plan he wasn't going to like.

"There's a ball tomorrow," she said.

He glanced at their current surroundings of solid stone and assorted restraints. "I believe we'll be otherwise engaged."

"But we need not be." Charlotte grew animated. "I can write to Lady Leishire. Everyone would know by mid-morning, the Duke and Duchess of Camine are to attend."

He didn't hide his confusion. "Because a duke is noteworthy?"

Her smile was blinding. "He is, in fact."

His face froze. Forget dislike. He *hated* her plan. "I will not let you be bait." Of all the asinine ideas. "A carriage is the easiest thing to run off the road or hijack or . . ." His voice trailed off in anger. He collected himself and finished lamely, "Or any other violent outcomes unacceptable to your person."

Even if they could fortify the coach wheels and use decoys to arrive at the ball, a parked carriage was easy to sabotage. He could leave Percy to lay in wait, but if by some miracle, the assassin got the jump on the bruiser, there would be no one to protect Charlotte in the privacy of a dark drive.

"Transport isn't an issue," Charlotte said, as if reading his mind. She sounded confident. "The carriage won't be targeted."

"You see the future now?" he said, only half in jest. "And you know this how?"

"Because the assassin will be at the ball."

Hamish thought of how easily Percy had blended in at the Tailormans' ball. The overabundance of staff and musicians all in matching liveries were impossible odds. He shook his head, knowing he should've thought of it. "We'd never uncover the imposter in time. Any servant could be the killer in disguise."

"It won't be a servant," she said, her confidence unwavering. "He'll be one of the guests."

Hamish laughed, nearly dismissing her revelation with an arrogant wave of his hand, but a nagging feeling in his gut wouldn't abate.

Hired killers were cold, calculating. A targeted man would find himself alone in a dark alley; no one would find him for days because a detached killer was careful, clean.

But this man had gone after Charlotte, even though Hamish was a few hours' ride in London. No, Charlotte's attack had been personal and sloppy, as if the killer himself had lost his patience and lashed out at the first opportunity to punish his real target.

The sudden implication shook Hamish to his very foundation. He stared at his wife, so brilliant, so perceptive, and realized there was a calculating mind sharper than the one bent on his destruction. He whispered the truth, his mind finally catching up. "The assassin in a member of the gentry."

CHAPTER THIRTY-EIGHT

A NOBLEMAN WAS the assassin. It made no sense. With all the comfortable living and frivolous entertainments available to his peers, what gentleman took such risks?

There were always underhanded dealings. Dandies who owed money to dangerous men or men hired for the underhanded schemes of a gentleman.

One and the same was unfounded. Any bloodthirsty tendencies were easily remedied through sport, of which a nobleman's access was near endless: shooting, boxing, fencing. There were always the less desirable pastimes of drugs and alcohol to excess. He'd never have imagined a peer stooping to hunting people.

But Charlotte had. For the third time in as many minutes, Hamish marveled at his wife. Her mind was a clockwork of logic and connectivity that rivaled his professors at Cambridge. He'd always found the stigma that a woman's mind inferior misogynistic horseshit, but he was humbled to realize he'd never considered a particular woman's mind might be *superior* to his own.

"So?" Charlotte asked. "What do you think?"

"I think I'm an ass."

She blinked, her expression and words honest as always. "Sometimes."

He grinned and nuzzled into her neck. "You're supposed to say I'm perfection itself, my dear."

She drummed her fingers on his cheek. "I wouldn't want to lie."

"Unforgivable!" He kissed her jaw and tickled her side.

She squealed but wouldn't be dissuaded. "What of the ball?"

"No." He placed a finger on her lips. "I won't deny the brilliance of your plan, but I won't put you in harm's way until we've exhausted every other option first. Send the confirmation for tomorrow night," he said. No doubt the assassin would show, having outwitted them all, except Charlotte. "I'll send Percy. We'll force our own trap, suggesting you've had a fit of vapors and sought a quiet room."

Charlotte scrunched her nose, clearly unhappy with the prospect that even fictitiously, she'd succumb to anything resembling weakness. "But instead of finding me in a vulnerable position—"

"He'll find my man," Hamish finished.

She didn't like it, he knew, but her insatiable desire for adventure wasn't impartial to negotiation. "I'll give you Parliament," he said.

Without question, Charlotte nodded. "I'll write to Lady Leishire."

"I'll send for Percy."

But the second letter proved unnecessary. Not ten minutes after the letters were sent, the bruiser materialized outside their door, his taunting voice alerting both Hamish and Charlotte they had a visitor.

"Oh, Your Graces? Are you decent?" he called.

Hamish threw a blanket over Charlotte's naked body and walked to the door. He opened it and Hamish stared at his man, standing solo and un-blindfolded in the hall. "How did you get in here?" The security had been formidable.

Percy shrugged. "It seemed I had information the Madam wanted. She showed appreciation with full access?"

"'Full'?"

Dear God, the man had the Devil's own favor. Only one other establishment had a more discerning client list, and White's had none of the security.

"I just sent you our plan to trap the man responsible." Hamish glanced at Charlotte, pride filling his voice. "My wife surmised the man was a nobleman."

"Really?" Percy eyed her with appreciation. "And how did you come to such an accurate conclusion?"

Charlotte rose from the table, the blanket bunching around her shoulders, the chains around her ankles snaking across the floor. "You found proof, then?"

Percy's grin was smug. "Better." He turned to Hamish. "Get dressed, Your Grace. I have a name."

CHARLOTTE STARED THE two men down, vowing the next one to repeat she shouldn't be along she'd throw from the moving carriage.

"Charlotte—"

"I have as much right as you two," she said.

Hamish turned to the other man.

Percy must have valued his un-flattened body because he admitted, "She was almost drowned by the bastard." He winced. "Apologies, Your Grace."

She nodded. "Your language isn't strong *enough*. A reprehensible offense."

Percy smiled. "A black-hearted devil, maybe?"

"Don't backtrack now, sir. A right ass, at the very least."

A vein ticked in Hamish's temple. "You've both lost your minds. This is too dangerous."

Charlotte turned her best governess impression on him. "We have a plan. What safer place is there than at your side?"

"Walking through the front door isn't a plan," he said.

"It is bold," Percy said.

"And it has the element of surprise," Charlotte added.

Hamish grumbled, "Terrible plan."

"It was *your* plan."

"I wasn't thinking!" Hamish leaned forward in his seat. "You'd be safer at Lux Townhouse until this is over."

She rolled her eyes. "Because an empty house isn't the perfect place for an assassin to hide."

"Damn it, Charlotte." He ran a hand through his hair. "Who knows what the maniac has planned? This could all be some ploy to lure us right to him."

Percy sniffed. "I'm offended at your lack of trust in my skills."

Charlotte pointed in Percy's direction. "You said he was the best."

Percy sniffed again. "I'm flattered."

"He duped us all," she continued. "The man's arrogance and ego are his blind spots, and we're exploiting them. It's a good plan, and I will be part of it."

"No!"

"Hate to interrupt," Percy said, "but unless you plan to tie the lady up and leave her in an undefended carriage . . ." He tapped the glass window. "We're here."

Charlotte raised her hands. "What will it be?"

She watched his internal turmoil manifest in the way his hands and gaze twitched back and forth. He cared for her. The absolute certainty warmed her chest and eased some of the anxiety swirling through her veins since Percy had named her attacker.

Hamish's fists clenched in his lap. He released his breath in a hiss of clear displeasure, but they both knew what he'd decided before he said, "You'll come, but you'll stay behind me." He pointed at Percy. "You won't leave her side for anything."

The other man saluted.

"I'll go in first." Hamish's expression was fire and violence. "The Marquess of Slasbury is mine."

⟫⟩⟩⟩⟨⟨⟨⟪

"Who the bloody hell are you?"

Hamish eyed the room, with its obnoxious display of trophies and gilded fringes on the divan, and marched towards the marquess's middle-aged butler and his round belly. "Looking for your master. Give him up or you'll drink your meals out of a straw for the next year."

The man squinted and fumbled with the monocle from his coat.

Hamish frowned. Upon closer inspection, the man's attire was too starched and silken for that of a servant. A relative, then?

Having secured his eyepiece, the man balked. "You're the Duke of Camine!"

"Aye." Hamish's voice went cold. "And every terrible thing whispered about my ruthless reputation is true. Now, where is the marquess?"

He felt Percy stiffen behind him. He glanced back to make sure Charlotte was secure.

"I beg your pardon?" The man puffed up like the stuffed peacock he and his green-and-blue vest resembled. "Leave immediately before I send for the authorities."

Percy shifted. "Your Grace—"

Hamish took the man by the jowls and slammed him against the adjacent wall. "Where is the marquess?!"

The older man clawed at the hand around his neck and gasped. "I *am* the marquess, you lunatic!"

Hamish smiled, all teeth. "That won't work now. Whatever trick you and that bastard have planned, we've seen through the charade."

"*Your Grace.*" Percy's voice held an alarming note, the only reason Hamish didn't crack the gluttonous pretender open at the head.

"What?"

Percy's wide eyes had Hamish's firing rage smoking with a sudden, cold shock.

"This is the Marquess of Slasbury."

Hamish's grip didn't falter. "No, he's not."

Percy shook his head. "This is Gunther Flarborn, only son of the previous marquess. My government contacts confirmed it when I began surveillance."

The dread in Hamish's system pooled in his gut. He released the man, ignoring his gasps. "Are you sure?"

Percy's serious expression only solidified his unfailing information. "His favorite color is green."

Hamish's mind whirled, twisted, backtracked. "This can't be him. The marquess is a young man. I met him. Renard met him. He danced with Charlotte at the Tailormans' ball."

"No." Percy pointed to the bulbous dandy rubbing his neck. "This is the man I followed. This is Lord Slasbury."

Impossible. He'd met the marquess on previous occasions. Charlotte had too.

"Last year's garden party in the country." He turned to Charlotte and took in her wide eyes. "You met him?"

The peacock coughed. "All this trouble. When will it end?"

Hamish whirled on the man, not entirely convinced the blond-haired fiend wasn't hiding in the overly floral curtains on either side of the fireplace. "What end?"

The man eyed Hamish. "May I take your questions as confirmation you won't attack me again?"

Hamish crossed his arms. "For now."

The man grunted, crossed to the large settee, and poured himself two fingers of scotch. He fell back into the cushions, drink in hand, and with an exasperated expression to match his tone, spoke. "For bloody sake. How much more must I endure?"

Patience thinning, Hamish crossed to the chair opposite and sat, less than an arm's length from the iron fire poker he'd use as 'incentive' if the man kept from making sense.

But the drink was more than enough to loosen the man's

tongue. "I've only arrived back in the country and this"—he waved his hand to encompass the room and its occupants—"lunacy refuses to cease. Debt collectors demanding preposterous sums, strangers claiming themselves mutual acquaintances—the list of visitors has been endless. My staff was dismissed and a new one hired. The butler wouldn't let me in when I arrived, claiming the previous marquess had succumbed in America from a hereditary defect. Of all the unforgivable slander." He thumped his chest with a fist. "As if I would be from such flimsy stock."

Hamish felt his insides turn to lead. The longer the pompous peacock rambled on about lively seed and superior bloodlines, the more certain he became the man was whom he claimed.

"I'm not sure whom the duchess met last year," the real marquess said, "but I wouldn't make the month-long sail for less than a king's fortune, and never at the expense of my family's name."

Charlotte moved to Hamish's side. She broke her silence to voice what the rest of them suspected. "He's telling the truth."

Hamish took her hands in his, his worst fears realized. "I was outwitted soundly."

Charlotte ignored decorum and sat in his lap—to the averted gazes of the other men in the room—and ran a light touch down his cheek. "Whoever he is, he outfoxed us all."

He laughed, though no humor was present. "A striking set of blond curls is distracting for men and ladies, it appears."

She smirked. "We should've known he was a devil, then. No mere man would wear his hair so shamelessly curled."

"What did you say?"

They both turned at Percy's overly loud voice.

"The pretender," Hamish said, a touch of real humor creeping into the chaos. "Blond hair, curled quite ridiculously."

"I think it was natural," Charlotte said.

Hamish chuckled. "Inhuman, indeed."

"The man," Percy said, his voice urgent and his face pale. "The man posing as the marquess had blond curls? What of his eyes?"

"Brown, I think," said Hamish.

"They were dark blue," Charlotte said, a shudder shaking her in his arms. "Like a moonless dusk."

Percy's curse and slumped shoulders had panic scratching up the walls of Hamish's mind. He came out of his seat, bringing Charlotte with him. "You know him." It wasn't a question.

The bruiser's sudden laughter edged towards madness. "I know him, and I know what he wants."

The man had posed as the marquess and secured an engagement with the Duke of Lux's sister. Hamish's arms tightened around his wife. "Charlotte." She had been the target.

He ran his palm around her back in small circles. "He won't have you." Whatever the demon's plans, he'd die before the other man touched her.

"Not the duchess," Percy said.

Hamish shook his head. There wasn't another connection. "Then whom?"

"Camille."

That stopped him short. "My sister?" The bruiser had finally cracked. "Percy, he attacked *Charlotte*." Aside from tall and lithe frames, the two women were coloring opposites.

The condescending tone seemed to snap the other man out of his haze. Percy smirked in a pale version of his normal self. "I'm aware ladies are not interchangeable. Your sister's past"—his mouth worked to find the right word—"*profession* attracts my kind. Easy lust, little complaints. Not to mention your sister's incomparable ability to remember the smallest details. She'd be a prize among trophies."

Hamish kept his arms around his wife to keep from unleashing on the other man and his too-casual assessment of his flesh and blood. The man was grasping at smoke. "But Charlotte—"

"Is your wife," Percy said, interrupting. "You took Camille away. You hid her where no one would find her."

Hamish forced himself to consider. The trail his man had laid out so shrewdly had merit, though there were holes.

His business had been targeted before his scandal with Charlotte. Charlotte had been attacked only after forming an alliance with him. The man's initial interest in Charlotte may have been sheer coincidence, a way to mask his presence and give his story credibility. His connection to Renard was well known. Any scandalous circumstance that befell his lifelong friend and his sister would have Hamish butting in at the first opportunity to assist.

Whatever Renard's virtues, he was an easy mark for a man of charm and an offer to rid him of responsibilities. There was no doubt the bet at White's had been Renard's doing, at the behest of the pretender, probably with a pretense of adding extra dowry to secure Charlotte's marital happiness from third-party participants. Hamish cut a look at Percy. There was something he was withholding. Hamish knew it in his gut. And, knowing the man as he did, Percy had a reason for not sharing.

His gaze cut over to the marquess, who nursed his scotch like a man parched. There was a time and a place for telling secrets. Now was not that time.

"She said she escaped someone," Charlotte whispered.

Hamish turned her in his arms to see her face, hating the note of anguish in her voice. "What is it, my love?"

She faced him, her voice growing stronger with thoughtful reflection. "Camille told me she'd 'gotten away' from a dire situation, but I got the impression she was referring to a specific man." Her fingers dug into his shirt. "It must have been him."

The need to break something was reflex. To hurt a woman was criminal. To lay hands on Hamish's own was to call down divine punishment. As the vessel, he wouldn't be responsible for the carnage that followed. "I'll tear him apart with my hands."

Charlotte's gentle touch eased his fingers from the white-knuckled fists at his sides. "Get in line."

He kissed the top of her head. Only his wife could put a smile on his face when he was devising the best way to disembowel a man.

"We haven't lost yet," she said. "There's still the original plan. Lure him in and set a trap."

"Cheap tricks won't work," Percy said, sounding truly regretful. "Whatever you have planned, he'll see through it."

Hamish wouldn't question. Hearing how they'd been outmaneuvered at every turn showed how hollowed-headed puppets they'd all been. While they'd been skirting the betting book for easy tricks, this killer had been closing the very pages around them until they'd almost been crushed under the cover.

There couldn't be any illusions. No tricks. To end this, they'd have to put everything at risk.

"Better steal a pair of gentleman's clothes this time, Percy." Hamish pulled Charlotte closer, feeling his heart break at the knowledge he'd have to put her in harm's way.

He loved her.

Charlotte met his gaze, her silent understanding and agreement of his decision another weight on his conscience.

"I still don't know the polka," she made light.

"I'll teach you," he vowed, brushing his lips across hers in a whisper of a kiss. He'd tell her when this was all over. He'd show her a world worth living, with him. "After tomorrow, I'll deny you nothing."

She pulled back, her smirk reassuring and precious. "That's quite the statement, my lord."

"Yours." He lifted her chin with two fingers and sealed his silent promise with a kiss. "My lady's duke."

CHAPTER THIRTY-NINE

CHARLOTTE FLINCHED WITH every brush of fabric, every too-loud laugh, every offer of congratulations on their marriage, every flicker of candlelight in the too-crowded ballroom.

Lord and Lady Leishire had spared no expense, settling what had to be a fortune on shipping fees to transport ferns and trees of non-native species to transform the gold-trimmed parapets into a canopy of jungle.

Hamish cursed at her side as a couple nudged them passing by. "Of all the evenings the entirety of the *ton* had to attend, this was the one."

Charlotte picked at her gloves. Not for the first time, one of the delicate, pearl buttons popped off and was flung into a nearby vase. "Are you sure Camille received your letter? The killer may still go after her and skip the trouble."

Hamish's hand was a comforting weight at the small of her back. "If only men were as sensical as we wish those of the fairer sex to believe."

"You think he'll come anyway?" Her gaze darted around, every dapper dandy and lavished lady looking suspect.

Jaw set, his voice was hard. "He's here."

A prickle of unease trailed up her neck. "I swear there are eyes on us."

"All for the beautiful lady next to me."

She smirked. "Your efforts to distract me are noble." She

sighed. "At least we know whom we're looking for. No man can keep a low profile with that shade of hair."

"If the man has any sense, which he's proven, he'll wear a disguise."

Charlotte's scrutiny of the crowd redoubled. "At least Lady Leishire forwent the fashion of a masquerade."

"Small mercies," Hamish agreed.

Another pearl button flew across the room with a sharp *ping* in the vase.

Hamish discarded her glove in one motion, which was followed by the second, and tucked her bare hand in the crook of his arm. "I believe the garment is too innocent to undergo such violence."

Charlotte watched the silk vanish into his coat pocket, but her anxiety was too immense to care that any society crone watching would scream 'improper' up at the vaulted ceilings.

"This wait is maddening," she said. "I'm going to rip my hair from the roots. One look our way and the man will know we mean to play him for a fool."

The orchestra trilled a discordant note in the far corner of the ballroom, punctuating the already tense atmosphere.

Hamish smiled suddenly and held out his hand. "Well, then, my dear, let us blend in and merry make."

She stared at him. The crowd must have gotten to him. "You want to dance?"

"How can we resist? It's a waltz." He leaned in and left a scandalous kiss on her neck. "Imagine how scandalized the *ton* will be if you dance with your husband."

IF ONLY THE dance wouldn't end.

Charlotte twirled again and returned to the safety of her husband's arms. Here, in this small moment of time, there were no assassins or society. She closed her eyes, and the rest of the room faded away.

She loved him; she'd found her happiness.

The orchestra hit the final refrain in a swell of cords, and Charlotte held on to the last notes and blazed this moment into her memory.

No matter the future, her joy was her own. Fought for and found by herself, and hers to release or not.

The dance concluded and they turned first to the orchestra with applause and then to each other with expected bow and curtsy. They moved together with the shifting couples towards the refreshments, her hand tucked into his arm.

All was as it should have been, until he leaned down and whispered in her ear, "It is reasonable a lady may be overwhelmed by heat after such a long dance."

She glanced up into his eyes, hating the fear swelling in her chest.

His hand pressed the top of hers in his arm, his eyes whispering the courage she needed.

I see you, they said.

Charlotte took a deep breath and lifted her chin. "Together," she said.

His fingers squeezed hers. "Together."

And then she fainted.

It wasn't the most graceful fall. Not fitting for any stage anywhere, but her legs gave out, her head pushed back, and the result was the same. She was on the floor, her hand thrown over her eyes—to keep from seeing dozens of faces staring down at her—and the exclamation from a nearby couple meant the whole ballroom would know in a matter of minutes that the Duchess of Camine had fainted.

Charlotte counted to ten. Ten seconds seemed a good amount of time for a lady to be overcome and still rally to her senses with moderate respect.

Hamish crouched next to her. His cool hand felt good on her

flushed forehead.

"My lady? Oh dear. My lady?"

Neither of them would win any awards for their acting.

Charlotte dropped her hand and fluttered her lashes to appear startled and hazy. "My lord?" She grabbed for his extended hand. "What happened?"

His mockingly concerned face gave way to a passing relieved one. "You fainted, my dear. Are you all right?"

"I think so." She sat up slowly, making sure to hold her head and look around as if confused. "It must have been the dance. How silly of me."

"It wasn't silly at all." A lady in a lovely navy gown crouched on her other side, her genuine smile and disregard for her wrinkled dress making Charlotte instantly like her.

"This room is ridiculously crowded and warm." The woman threw a scowl at the man next to her. "Go tell Lady Leishire to open the balcony doors before someone else falls ill."

"Right." The man scampered off like a dog on command.

The lady stood and reached down for Charlotte's elbow. "Let me help you up."

Hamish was right there on her other side, taking most of her weight. He nodded to the other woman. "Lady Daniella, yes? Thank you for your kindness."

Lady Daniella waved his words away, her voice edged, "It seems I'm the only person capable of basic human decency. Odd in a room with two hundred people packed like cattle."

Charlotte smiled. The woman was young, nineteen at most, but she did little to quiet her voice. Charlotte took both the woman's hands in hers, feeling, for the first time, society may have some happy surprises for her still. "Truly, Lady Daniella, thank you. I'm the Duchess of Camine."

Lady Daniella returned the smile, her eyes sparkling. "An honor."

"My lady?" Hamish was beside her, his tone pulling her back to the mission at hand, and the gravity of their ruse's success.

Charlotte swayed back and forth, hoping for a look of blankness over her face. "Oh, I do feel a bit lightheaded still."

The gentleman from earlier returned, done with Lady Daniella's errand. "The balconies are open, if the lady is in need of fresh air."

Silent alarm filled Charlotte's chest. It would make more sense for a lady to seek fresh air after a heat spell. She bit her lip, and her mind whirled for an excuse to bypass the air and opt for a quieter room.

"No." It was Lady Daniella who spoke, her gaze hawk-like on Charlotte's face. Her mouth tugged with a knowing smirk. She sobered and turned to the crowd clustered around them. "No, Her Grace must find a place to rest her head for a moment. There is no place on the balcony befitting the nature of her convalescence."

Charlotte swore Lady Daniella winked at her as she turned to Hamish.

"Your Grace, you must find an unoccupied room for Her Grace to lie down. If I'm not mistaken, every good Englishman has a library on the main floor and should have just what you need."

And just like that, their obstacles turned into a perfect excuse for Charlotte and Hamish to sneak away. Hamish tucked her hand in his arm, donning the right amount of contemplation and concern for his wife's physical state. "Come, my dear. We'll do just that."

Charlotte stopped for a moment, trusting her instincts and turned back to Lady Daniella with a low voice. "Thank you, Lady Daniella. I'd be honored to call on you soon and repay your kindness."

Lady Daniella smiled, too big and genuine to be considered demure. "I'd like that, Your Grace."

Hamish tugged her along and they wove through the easily parted crowd, the gentlemen and ladies already knowing their destination from the lightning-speed gossip only accomplished in a tight space with so many eager mouths and ears.

After a fluttering of concern from Lady Leishire and a well-directed nod from Lord Leishire, Hamish escorted Charlotte into the lord's library and shut the door to a firelit room and a table full of cigars and alcohol.

"We'll have a solid hour before any of the gentlemen need to escape the festivities and come looking for a quieter vice," Hamish said.

Charlotte nodded and held her arms to warm the sudden chill reality wove around them. This was where they'd confront the killer. "Is Percy here?"

Hamish shook his head. "Not in this room, but nearby. We don't want to spook the man."

"What of Renard? Is he here?"

"No. I sent a missive and found out he'd declined his invitation to the ball. He's sulking, but it won't last." At her questioning look, he added, "I didn't go into much detail, but I told him about the threats to your person and that it was imperative he meet us at Camine Manor when this was all over."

If this was ever over. Charlotte shivered.

Hamish crossed the room to her and wrapped his arms around her. "You're shaking."

She laughed. At this point, she didn't know if the nerves were from the prospect of coming face to face with her attacker, or from having to pretend in front of hundreds of people. "Lady Daniella was amazing. Did you see how she manipulated everyone into accepting that we find a room?"

"Another formidable lady." Hamish smiled into her hair. "I assume you'll be fast friends. Between you and Camille, it will be a group no man would cross."

She smiled. "Safety in numbers." Charlotte pulled back with a sudden thought. "Hamish, what if he doesn't show?"

"What do you mean?"

"There are two of us."

"And?"

She huffed and blew a strand of hair out of her eyes. "And an opportunist killer would wait for better odds."

"He's not an opportunist. He knows exactly who he wants . . ." He trailed off, his expression smoothing with understanding. "And he isn't stupid. He won't believe a husband would stay with his sick wife when there's a ball and entertainment a door away." His mouth straightened into a tight line. "I don't like leaving you."

She cupped his cheek in her hand. "Percy is close by, and you will be too. We agreed to do this together. Trust me."

His eyes grew haunted. He grabbed her and pressed her close. "If anything happens, if something goes wrong—"

"We'll adapt," she said, locking gazes with him. "No man is infallible. He's shown he can make mistakes. We'll make it through this. Remember you made me a promise."

He studied her face, his grip softening. "Yes, I did."

"Then don't deny me now." She knew her words were harsh, but he wouldn't leave her without total confidence in their plan and her resolve. He genuinely cared for her, and the knowledge made the danger of failing too awful to consider. When this was all over, she'd make him fall in love with her for good.

"Go, Hamish. And keep your promise to me."

He glanced back at her when he reached the door, showing the same amount of trust and resolve in the firm set of his jaw as she felt herself. Charlotte steeled her nerves and nodded in silent encouragement.

Their plan was solid. Once she was alone, any person wishing them harm wouldn't be able to resist.

Hamish opened the door and reeled back at the man in the doorway.

"Greetings, Your Grace," the imposter said. His blond hair was dulled with powder, but his stormy eyes danced red in the firelight. He stepped fully into the light, closing the door behind him with an eerily quiet latch.

The familiar face of the marquess—*not* marquess—standing

so close to the man she loved filled Charlotte with the instinctual need to fight and win.

Or die trying.

CHAPTER FORTY

SOMETHING WAS WRONG. Percy wasn't supposed to have let the man through the door.

Hamish walked backwards towards Charlotte with slow, cautious steps, risking everything to glance around for a weapon, anything to stave off an attack until Percy could get out of whatever trap he'd no doubt found himself in.

"It's no use." The man's voice stopped him cold. "No one is coming to save you. It'll be best for your lovely bride if you hold still and let me kill you quickly."

Charlotte gasped.

Hamish drew her tightly to his side. "I can't allow that." He took a slow step back, pushing Charlotte behind him towards the window and away from the homicidal lunatic. "See, I promised my love the second set waltz, and it would be unseemly for a gentleman to go back on his word."

"A civil marriage, then." The man sneered. "How delightful. Here I thought you'd spoiled her and that idiot brother of hers had called you out."

Charlotte quivered behind him, but her voice was clear and full when she said, "He's nothing if not a gentleman."

The man paused at the steel mixed in with the humor. He cocked a brow and scowled at Hamish. "Do you need your wife to protect you as well as speak for you?"

He felt Charlotte stiffen behind him at the intended insult, and Hamish squeezed her hand. "My lady is more than capable." He glanced back at her, conveying his support with a grin. "But I'd prefer to 'administer the blow,' if she'll permit me?"

Recognizing her own words, her eyes lit up, understanding him instantly. She nodded once.

Good.

Hamish didn't doubt she'd get away when the time came. She was brave and courageous and had a knack for exceeding his expectations, but she wouldn't hesitate this time. There was an unbreakable rope tying their desires and actions together that hadn't been there before.

Hamish knew it was trust, now two-sided and reciprocated by them both. They were partners. If he'd been a romantic man, he may have thought them soul mates—maybe he already did. His darkness, her light... They were one in the way the world existed with night and day.

He loved her. If the flowery nonsense weren't proof enough, he'd know it by the way his heart lurched thinking of her harmed.

She bit her lip, her eyes soft, as if her thoughts and his had become one. "I love you, Hamish."

"And I'm going to regurgitate my dinner," the other man said. He shook his head. "There's no need for this drama. I've no interest in the lady, Duke. It's you I want."

Hamish turned his focus back to the man between them and the door. "Then let her go."

"Ah, that's the rub." He almost sounded regretful. "If I let her run now, there's no motivation for you to tell me what I want."

Charlotte scowled. "What *do* you want? It isn't just Camille."

He waved a hand dismissively. "Of course not. Your dear husband and I have a score to settle on two ladies' accounts *and* a missing shipment of cargo."

He was connected to the barrels they'd 'borrowed' from the ship from Virginia, after all.

"What does a few buckets of sand have to do with anything?" Hamish asked.

He shrugged. "A man must make a living." His eyes darkened. "A living you've made impossible, sticking your nose into my business." He shook his head. "You'd have been better off breaking your neck driving away from your intended."

Hamish froze. The carriage wheel. "You?"

He smiled. "That was a just a bit of fun, to be honest. If I had known you'd taken yet another pawn from my board moments before, I'd have gutted you in the street." He shrugged. "Hindsight."

The man had targeted them over sand and a woman's rejection.

Goddamn madman!

Half a step towards the door, Hamish kept Charlotte squarely behind him, not forgetting the man's former reason. "You said you didn't want her."

"This has nothing to do with *want*." The false marquess sniffed, and Hamish saw the barely reined mania behind the action. "This is about what a gentleman *should* do." His eyes flashed. "And the price when he doesn't."

Hamish took a step farther from the door and closer to safety. He wasn't going to get out of this, but Charlotte would be safe. She was clever and strong. He may have had no hope of beating the man in a fight, but Hamish could damn well hold his own until she got away. If she cooperated.

"Honor?" Charlotte echoed.

The scoffed tone of her voice told Hamish cooperation was far from her mind.

"You're telling me a killer is holding a grudge because another man—"

"Stole you," the man said. "Among other things—things your puny brains would have no hope of comprehending—yes. But don't sneer down your entitled nose, my lady. You were never of any importance. His Grace here outmaneuvered me one too many times; you were the final straw. Finding you in the clearing outside the estate was a stroke of luck, one I accepted too anxiously. When I heard your dear husband stomping through the woods to look for you, I considered having him find your corpse in my arms." His grin was feral. "But this will be so much better, grander. Think of the horror of all those guests out there when your bodies are found mangled not twenty feet from the festivities. And the tainting of reputation to that confounded brother of yours."

Did he mean Renard? The man was mad. They'd been nothing but toys, played and discarded on the whims of a sadistic monster.

Charlotte shuddered, reaching for any thread of reason to pull. "You weren't really going to marry me, anyway." Her jaw clenched. "I was a bet."

His smile was reptilian. "Your brother assured me your acceptance was a sure thing. You seemed a sharp woman, a weakness of mine, and I would've enjoyed bedding you before I knew how common you truly are." Face contorting into a twisted mask of loathing, he spat, "But you couldn't even do that right. I needed that revenue. The people I work with grew tired of my broken promises of payment. Hounding me, hunting me." He ran a hand through his hair, his fingers curled like talons. "I've had to sneak around like a common roach to avoid their retribution, my own plans ruined." He sneered at Charlotte.

"Not to worry." He took a threatening step forward and gave Hamish a nod. "Once you and your paramour are sliced to grisly pieces, I'll make beneficial use of your funds and title. Pay off those vultures and all will be forgiven." Laughing, he smoothed the front of his coat. "The long-lost heir of Camine has a fine ring to it; charming, young, stricken with grief over the family I never knew. The idiot *ton* will eat it up."

Charlotte recoiled. "No one will believe you. People have seen your face."

"Stupid girl, I have many faces. No one will question my disguise; no one will care. One more dead aristocrat to entertain the masses and then you'll be forgotten like every other unimportant corpse."

"So much for your charm," she said.

He laughed again. "Our dance was good fun. You actually thought I was a self-deprecating man, gold-hearted and accommodating?"

"Exactly as you wished to seem," she said, but she wasn't done. "But a snake is still a snake. I knew something was off about you as soon as you looked away."

"Ah." His lip curled with remembered irritation. "I hadn't counted on that half-rate rat chaser playing dress-up at the Tailormans' ball."

Percy, Hamish thought. They did know each other.

Which meant, this was an extremely dangerous man. He had to get Charlotte out of here now.

He squeezed her hand once more and charged the other man. At the last second, he veered to the side.

The killer followed his movements, only for Charlotte to jump in from his blind spot.

She socked the charlatan in the eye. She was petite, but her anger was strong. Her blow landed with a *pop* and the killer fell into a nearby bookcase.

She whirled, holding her hand close, and dashed for the exit.

Hamish charged again to stop the man from getting to his feet, but the man was already up and letting fly a knife that whizzed past Hamish's ear.

Charlotte cried out.

Heart lurching, he twisted to see Charlotte at the door, where the knife had stuck into the oak wood inches from her arm. Her dress was torn, and her shoulder was cut where the blade had scratched her.

Hamish turned with a bellow, ready to tear the other man open with his bare hands. He froze when he saw a second knife.

"Next one goes in her head." The man motioned for her to move away from the door.

She took a step. Hamish's chest tightened. He needed to stop this. If the man could be reasoned with . . .

She took another step.

"No. Stay there." Hamish turned to the other man.

He shrugged. "Have it your way." He threw the knife.

"No!" Hamish whirled.

But the knife didn't find purchase.

Suddenly, Percy was in the open door, his own blade up and blocking Charlotte from being skewered like a Spanish bull.

The blade fell to the floor with a *thud*.

Knife still up, Percy gave Hamish a grin. "Looks like I didn't miss the fun after all."

The killer straightened. "You made it, P."

Percy set Charlotte aside and faced him. "Hello, Nic." He moved farther into the room so Hamish could take his spot beside Charlotte. "Or would you prefer your new moniker?"

"Which one? I have so many."

"Dr. Deinolf." Percy eyed the man as he shifted, his expression weary. "A rather bland alias for you, isn't it?"

"I thought you'd enjoy the irony." Nic pressed a hand to his chest. "Me, a healer. I came up with it especially for you."

Charlotte, ever the wordsmith, got the connection before the rest of them. "Old friend," she said. "It's an anagram."

Nic shot her an appreciative nod that had Hamish wishing for a blanket to throw over her person to hide her from view.

"Not so dull after all, then?" Nic said. "Once I've disposed of these two vermin, perhaps you and I will have a long *chat*."

Hamish stepped forward, hearing the underlying threat. "Over my dead body."

Nic's smirk was dark. "That's the idea."

"Not today, old friend." Percy moved. A flutter of activity, and Hamish saw the unmistakable glint of more blades.

Two blades. Three. The men were suddenly nose to nose.

"You've lost your touch," Nic said.

Percy gritted his teeth, his feet slipping underneath him. He tore back as a blade missed him by a hair's breadth. His own knife lashed out.

And that was when Hamish saw the horrible truth.

Percy was going to lose.

CHAPTER FORTY-ONE

NIC TWIRLED, LASHED, blocked, and lashed again, his smile never slipping. He pushed Percy back to the far wall. "There's no way you can beat me, P. You don't have enough hands." Something metal flashed. "Or knives."

Percy blocked a knife to his gut.

The other knife sunk into his shoulder.

Charlotte cried out.

Hamish stopped her from rushing over.

Nic leaned close, his hand pushing the blade into the hilt.

Percy gritted his teeth but didn't make a sound.

"You never could beat me with a blade," Nic said. "A pity. I'd hoped for more sport."

Charlotte whimpered at Hamish's side.

Nic stepped back, ripping his knife free with a sick, squelching sound, and watched Percy slide to the ground, face pale.

"Now, then." Nic spun his blood-coated knife in his palm before replacing the blade inside his coat. Turning that sadistic smile once again on Hamish, he removed the golden chain from his pocket that he always wore and twisted the ends around each hand to make a truly horrifying garrot. "Since that interruption is taken care of, let's get back to your slow and painful deaths, shall we?"

Hamish tensed. He pushed up on the balls of his feet, ready to spring.

Something metal slashed through the air.

Nic was knocked back. He cursed and held his face, and blood dripped beneath his hand.

Everyone whirled to the big man in the doorway, his dusty clothes and rough shave out of place everywhere but a warehouse or a dark alley.

He tipped his hat to Hamish, the action familiar somehow. "Apologies for me tardiness." He extracted another knife from his vest and turned back to Nic, though he continued to address Hamish. "The ol' man would 'ave me hide if I let somefin' bad 'appen' to you now you's partners and all."

Nic let his hand drop. A nasty cut across his cheek bled down his neck and stained his collar. He scowled at Percy. "You have a new partner. Are you going to betray this one too?"

Percy, though pale and in obvious pain, ignored the question and eyed the newcomer with confusion. "You're one of Markus's men."

Hamish's mind clicked. He was the man from Markus's place. The man he'd given the prototype to for safekeeping.

"Aye. Me name's Zans." The man smiled but didn't take his eyes off Nic. "Would you like me to take care of this one for ye, sir?"

Nic laughed. "As if one big oaf is any hindrance."

Zans shrugged. "Probably true. That's why I brought me mates."

Four more men came through the door in a parade of unshaven faces and sloppy dress that couldn't have gone unnoticed by the Leishires' butler.

For the first time, Nic's confidence slipped. He placed his chain back in his pocket and extracted the same bloody knife he'd used to stab Percy from inside his coat. His sneer was full of venom as he spat, "This isn't over."

Zans smiled. "Aye, friend, it is."

Nic's gaze flicked from one man to another, his body turning squarely to face each threat in turn, before he clenched his knife between his teeth and dove out the library window.

Hamish watched the four big men fly across the room, dive out the window, and expertly avoid Lady Leishire's renowned rosebush and its grasping thorns like some surreal circus performance.

There was a scuffle outside and a whistle that had Zans relaxing against the nearest bookcase. "There's that, then. Won' be botherin' yous no more now."

Hamish fought the urge to cross to the window for proof. After all the trouble and machinations, a man like Nic couldn't possibly be so easy to take down. "Is he dead?"

Zans gave him a long look before he shook his head. "Nah. We Merrys ain't killers, unless provoked. Boys be taken 'im to the Yard and then he'll be a problem for the bobbies."

Immediate danger gone, Charlotte flew across the room to Percy's side.

"How bad is it?" she asked.

Percy gave a pained grin. Sweat dotted his brow. "'Tis but a flesh wound." He took a handkerchief from his vest and tried, but failed, to lift his arm to stanch the not-so-flesh-wound bleeding.

Charlotte scooped up the handkerchief and pulled his shirt aside.

Percy winced. "Be gentle. It's my first time with a stab wound."

Charlotte snorted. "Why don't I believe that?" She pressed the handkerchief to the jagged cut at his shoulder.

"Bullocks! Gen-tle," he stressed.

Adrenaline finally easing back to normal, Hamish shook his head and crossed the room to help. "You complain more when being tended to than in a fight."

"A life-or-death situation has that effect." Percy shot him a weak smile. "Did I ever mention the party responsible for my bodily state when we first met?"

"You mean when I found you battered and bleeding out in the gutter?" Hamish's gaze shot to the window, his revelation a mix with criticism. "That was your partner?"

Percy leaned against the sill, pale and breathing hard. "The very one."

Charlotte replaced the soaked handkerchief on his shoulder with a new one from Hamish's breast pocket. "What is it, exactly, you do again?"

He grimaced at the pressure. "Don't ask, don't tell, my lady."

"I'm not your lady." Her tone was harsh.

Hamish heard concern underneath too. In fact, her hands were shaking so bad, he was surprised she could keep the handkerchief tight.

As if noticing the same, Percy pressed a hand over hers. "I'm fine, my lady," he repeated. "You wound me."

She batted him away. "That's already been done. Stay still, or I'll let you die here and have to pay Lady Leishire for a new rug."

Percy shot Hamish a pained grin. "And a terrible bedside manner. Ow!"

"I told you to hold still."

"Impossible," Percy said. "A beautiful woman nursing me back to health." He sighed. "I may swoon."

Charlotte cast Hamish an exasperated look. "How much does a rug cost?"

Hamish shrugged. "We're rich as a king."

Percy huffed. "I'm getting the distinct feeling my heroism isn't appreciated. Ow! I wasn't moving!"

"That," Charlotte said, "was for being late."

An odd expression crossed Percy's face.

If Hamish didn't know better, he'd have thought the immoral bruiser felt guilty.

"My apologies, Your Grace," Percy said. "I was distracted by . . . something." His expression grew dark. "I wasn't much help as it was."

"He was skilled," Hamish said. More skilled than he'd realized.

Watching Percy, the greatest bruiser to ever come out of

Dockside, lose footing with each swipe, had made Hamish uncomfortably aware Charlotte's survival in the forest had been more than miraculous, it had been a calculated shot at a more gruesome end for the both of them. And that if it hadn't been for the Merry Men's assistance now, they'd all have been permanent stains on Lord Leishire's Turkish rug.

Hamish turned to Zans and stuck out a hand. "Thank you."

Zans looked uncomfortable with the gratitude, but he shook with a firm hand. "As I said, didn' want none o' the ol' man's ire."

"How long have you been following me?"

"Soon as Markus got you's package."

A flutter of hope turned some of the ugly feelings in Hamish's gut to rights. "He liked the prototype, then?"

Zans shook his head. "Nah. He don' know 'bout those things. His girl was the one says you were worth the risk."

"Girl?"

"Scarlet," Zans said. "Said your lady love done her a service, and if yous was good enough for her, yous was good enough for her pops. Ol' man Markus got a soft spot for 'is little girl." He threw a smile Charlotte's way. "Seems everythin' she said 'bout you was true. I never seen a fine woman throw a punch like that."

Charlotte's smile was brilliant as she rubbed her sore knuckles. "Scarlet was pretty impressive herself with a shotgun in her hands."

The barmaid from the alley.

"*She* is Markus's daughter?" Hamish was stupefied. Markus had come to their rescue, offered partnership and protection to him at the behest of his daughter.

No. Hamish looked down at his wife. Charlotte was a siren in her lovely gown of French silk that had cost a small fortune, a gown she hadn't hesitated to wrinkle and stain to help a man she didn't think well of. The assistance, their survival, had all been because of her and her absolute power to make everyone fall in love with her and her light.

That light had a rather murderous look on her face at the moment. "That awful Rufus isn't giving Scarlet trouble, right?"

Zans lifted his cap and rocked back on his scuffed boots. "'E won' be botherin' no one till 'is hands heal, which could be a while." His smile was vicious. "I may 'ave had the surgeon set 'im a little crooked."

Hamish watched his lovely, bloodthirsty crusader nod.

"Good," she said.

A sharp whistle came from outside the window.

Zans cracked his knuckles. "That's me cue." He touched his cap. "Missus." He nodded to Hamish. "Be seeing you, sir."

The biggest man of the five by far, he jumped through the window with the gracefulness of a cat and was lost in the dark garden beyond.

"That was weird." Percy put a hand to his head. "Or am I feverish already?"

Charlotte checked Percy's wound, her face softening with relief. "The bleeding is slowing. Can you move?"

"Of course."

She turned to Hamish. "He needs a doctor and stitches."

Remembering her boast that first night about 'medical procedures,' he asked, "Can't you do it here?"

She shook her head. "I studied in theory, not practice. Besides, I'd need water and bandages; there would be too much blood to explain later."

"Really, my lady, I'm fine." Percy's words lost all credibility when he tried to rise and failed. He fell back against the wall with a groan. "On second thought, I'll stay here a while." He leaned his head against the wall and chuckled to himself. "I'd hate to miss a party."

"Liar." Hamish knew the other man was in terrible pain, but it wouldn't do to have any number of Lord Leishire's esteemed guests stumbling across their ragged party on their way to cards and cigars.

He reached down and shouldered Percy across his back,

mindful of the handkerchief packed against his chest.

Percy grimaced, then sighed. "My hero. Shall we make spectacles of ourselves and escape through yonder window and let our love guide us safely home?"

"I will drop you," Hamish said, not meaning a word. "But you have a point." The rosebush wasn't so easily managed, especially with the dead weight on his back. But they couldn't waltz out the front door, either.

"I have an idea," Charlotte said.

Hamish looked over to see her fingering a lace doily from a misplaced basket of embroidery in the corner. She caught his gaze, hers filled with mischief and adventure.

"You aren't going to like it," she said.

Imagining horrible disguises and a race for the exit, Hamish groaned. "Where have I heard that before?"

CHAPTER FORTY-TWO

CHARLOTTE SCOWLED INTO the night air. "He still won't look me in the eye."

Hamish laughed and turned so they were both looking out at the garden from their chamber balcony. "Can you blame him? You dressed him up as a grandmother and kept calling him 'deary.'"

"I got us out of there, didn't I? Besides, he didn't have to play along and kiss those two lords on the way out when they offered to 'assist the lady dowager to her carriage.'" Charlotte frowned. "You don't think anyone will catch on to the fact that both our grandmothers are deceased?"

Hamish choked on a laugh. Percy had made a rather enchanting old woman. "If anyone asks, she passed away that very night." Those two young men would be devastated when they heard.

Charlotte's conspiratorial smile slipped. "Should we be worried?"

Hamish rested a reassuring hand on her arm, knowing she wasn't talking about the scandal of bringing grandmothers back from the dead. "Markus's men will keep an eye on the Yard. It is over." Hamish ignored his own anxiety twisting his gut and offered, for both of them, "There's no way Nic can hurt us now that he's behind bars."

She nodded, but the fear was still there.

He leaned down and kissed her exposed shoulder where her

nightdress had fallen. "I think a distraction will help." He took a long box from his pocket. "I have a present for you."

She took the present, her grin back. "More jewelry?"

He held out a hand. "Better."

Her fingers lifted the latch, and her face lit up. "Oh, Hamish!"

He took the delicate spectacles from their velvet bed and held them out to her. "I had Gregori examine your current pair and rework the hinges on a new frame to suit your face."

She scrambled to take her old pair from her face, one side already falling off. "I was wondering what happened to my spectacles the other day." Setting the old pair on the balcony ledge, she slid the new pair on. "They're perfect."

Her face brightened the dusk sky.

He wrapped her in his arms. "You're perfect."

"Thank you—"

"I love you, Charlotte."

Her quick inhale made him smile. "I've loved you since you barged into my study and rattled off that ridiculous list." He cupped her cheek. "I've loved you since you told me you'd stand up for my honor." He smiled down into her face, so precious and familiar, he knew it better than his own. "I've loved you since you caught my damn ledger."

Her lips turned up with exasperated humor and a hint of awe. "You've known you loved me since the beginning?"

It was his turn for humor. "Of course not. I'm a man. I didn't realize anything until a few days ago. I'm so bloody blessed, I should be thanking you, my dearest wife. You've given me the world, and all I can give you are a pair of spectacles that fit."

She sniffed and rubbed at the corner of her eye where moisture fell. "You shouldn't say such things when I'm not prepared. Here you gave me this wonderful present and I can't see a thing."

He offered her his handkerchief and waited, his cheeks aching from the smile that refused to fade.

Wiping her eyes, Charlotte laughed to herself.

"Something amusing?" he asked.

"Only your assertion that all you have to offer me is a pair of frames."

"There is of course wealth, security, a surprisingly willing partner in your scandalous antics—"

"Incredible sex." Charlotte smiled at his huff of surprise. "I love you too, Hamish."

"For the sex?" He laughed at her shrug, feeling his heart swell in his chest. "I must strive to keep things interesting for you, then."

The sudden image of her on a horse came to mind. He whispered an idea in her ear.

She pulled back, her cheeks pink. "Oh, my. Is that possible?"

"I've dreamed of nothing else since witnessing your midnight ride."

She shook her head. "You can't be serious?"

"And those boots!"

Charlotte giggled, her fear long gone. "You're being ridiculous. No man dreams of *boots*."

"On the contrary. A very ravishing dream of you in those boots, and nothing else."

"Oh!" She bit her lip and smiled. "Might I make an addition to this dream?"

"Does it involve you naked?"

"Yes."

"Then ask anything."

The deepening blush on her cheeks had his groin pounding. "Marmalade."

He groaned. "Peach?"

"What else?"

He scooped her into his arms and headed in the direction of the kitchens. "My favorite."

They never made it to the kitchens. Drawn by the angry raised voices coming from the foyer, Hamish and Charlotte prepared for the worst.

But it wasn't a killer shouting murder.

It was the Duke of Lux.

"You'd vanished. Of course I came looking!" he shouted.

Charlotte rushed forward. "What's the matter, brother?"

Hamish caught sight of Camille, her arms crossed and warrior face on, and knew this would end in tears, probably a man's.

"Matter? *Matter!*" Renard whirled on Hamish. "Is this what all those letters were about? The summons to visit so late? You wrote of a threat to Charlotte, but I should have known that was just a ruse to get me to come . . . You should've told me sooner that you'd found her!"

Hamish frowned, not remembering his old friend violent when deep in his cups. He'd play along until a servant could be called to fetch tea. "Exactly whom was I keeping from you?"

Renard looked between him and Camille, his expression irritated. "Her."

Perhaps tea wasn't strong enough. A shot of laudanum, perhaps.

"I didn't realize you'd met Miss Forthright before." Hamish glanced at Camille and prayed they'd moved passed her threats of leaving. "My sister."

Renard's anger froze into a moment of baffled expression. "Sister?" He pointed to Camille, who looked pointedly away. "No, *her*. The woman I told you I had to find. I never met your sister." He whirled on Camille, his expression haunted. "Why did you run? Why did you leave, Milly?"

Charlotte stumbled back a step. "Milly?"

A very particular brand of shock and awe battled for dominance in Hamish's gut. The woman Renard had been seeking . . . the woman he was so madly in love with he'd thrown away his health and reputation . . . was Camille? In the end, he turned to his sister, awe winning out. "Well played, my dear."

Plot uncovered, Camille shot him a sad smirk. "If I had known you'd sent for the duke, you'd never have known."

"The first time you didn't get a hold of the post before it went out. Rotten luck." She'd have vanished without a word, he was sure, only to miraculously reappear when Renard had left for home. "And here I thought you were doing me the favor when you agreed to come live with me."

"Live with you?" Renard looked ready to charge, horns up. *"What do you mean, she's living with you?"*

Good-humored despite being soundly strung along by his calculating, yet brilliant, sister, Hamish turned to his oldest friend and watched his red face turn ashen at the truth.

"Forgive me, Ren. Allow me to make the formal introductions. Renard Louis, Duke of Lux, this is Camille Forthright, my sister."

EPILOGUE

"A FEW MONTHS ago, could you have imagined my brother courting your sister?" Charlotte said. "I hope he'll be all right?"

Hamish looked up from the list in front of him and followed his wife's gaze towards the window and Lux estate in the far distance. He grinned, imagining Renard and Camille breaking every bust and vase in their impassioned bouts. "If overcoming society, Mrs. Norris—and her sniveling son—a notorious rookery gang, and a homicidal maniac hasn't broken Renard's resolve yet, I believe the threat is of little consequence."

Charlotte smiled and nodded towards the list on the desk. "How does it look?"

Hamish struck a line through the final item on his wife's outrageously lengthy list—all twelve pages worth—and leaned back in his study chair. "Finished."

Charlotte's smile grew. With her dress disheveled and a missed blotch of green paint smeared across the side of her neck, she was the loveliest woman he'd ever seen.

"How many laws do you think we broke?" she asked.

"On this last one?" He looked heavenward. "Half a dozen at least. Though I've never been fonder of Parliament."

"Nor so active, I imagine?"

He sprung from his chair and dragged her to him. "Minx! I'll never be able to look Lord Bromley in the eye again."

Charlotte's cheeks flushed. She'd recently made good friends with the man's daughter, Lady Daniella, which made an unpleasant situation more complicated. "Think he'll say anything?"

"Dear God, no. I may suffer his glancing attention on *you* for the next year, or ten."

"I was perfectly covered," she said.

Hamish huffed. "I, however, was not."

Her lips curled up at the corners. "I remember. The painting ended up quite extraordinary because of it."

He glanced at said painting in the corner, his face looking regal and confident in brushed oils despite his manhood standing front and center, and erect. For a nude, it was sublime.

He kissed the top of her head, once again astounded at her unending talents. "You are far better than a master's apprentice, my dear."

She beamed at the praise and wrapped her arms around his neck. "It helps that my subject matter is *perfection itself.*"

He lifted them both to their feet and kissed her jaw. "What happens when the painting surpasses the real thing?"

Her hands, already wandering, found his jutting erection and held him through his trousers. "Not in your case, husband."

"Really?" He ran a hand down her back and cupped her bottom, ready to prove his standing. "Shall I take you upstairs and show you how much better the real thing can be?"

Her breath was quick and heavy. "Why suffer all those steps when we have a perfectly good table here?"

He smiled against her lips and pressed her back against the oak, his hands already finding the slits in her skirts. "So true."

She leaned back and crinkled the stack of papers that had become *their* list. Smiling, she pushed the papers towards the open drawer for safekeeping when she suddenly froze.

He pulled back. "What is it?"

Her brows pinched. She turned the pages so they were right-side up. "We missed one."

"What?" Hamish peeked over her shoulder. "Impossible. It's been non-stop since the Leishires' ball."

The past months had been a whirlwind of pioneering in the established American colonies and suffering ungodly heat in the more exotic. Even with Renard and Camille's recent encounter with the homicidal but illusive Nic, Hamish's prospering business and partnership with Markus and his band of 'Merry Men'—a kind nickname, Hamish had learned later, for a group of ex-soldiers too bloodthirsty for the army, and too skilled to be ignored—the continuous protective detail had afforded him and Charlotte free rein to experience everything a person could do while in the confines of the law, and some that weren't.

He grabbed the papers from her hands and scanned through the hundreds of crossed-out lines. Getting to the end of the stack, he pointed to the last item. "Seven hundred and nine, right?"

Charlotte shook her head. "Seven hundred and eight. We skipped one," she said, her mouth tipping up to one side in a way that both thrilled and terrified him.

Afraid to ask, but knowing he must, he sighed. "What did we miss?"

Charlotte ran a finger down his chest, her smile contagious. "I still haven't sung to the queen."

Hamish looked heavenward and prayed they'd be forgiven. He looked back towards Earth and rested a protective hand on her growing belly. "For our child's sake, I hope you sing as well as you paint?"

She bit her lip and shook her head. "Completely tone deaf, I'm afraid."

Somehow, the innocent admission made her even more charming. He leaned forward and rubbed their noses. "You are full of surprises."

She laughed and tapped the first of the list's pages. "I was told a man likes a woman with a bit of mystery."

"That we do, little mouse." He pulled her wrists behind her lightly and captured her mouth with his.

But after a moment, pressed heart to heart with the woman he loved, the tables turned, and he became the one well and truly caught.

The End

About the Author

An educated artist, J. M. Diedrich previously worked as a freelance columnist for the Independent Observer. When she's not writing steamy kissing scenes or driving her characters into life-threatening situations, she's binge-watching anime. She lives in Minnesota with her husband and two boys.